THE ABSENCE OF GOODNESS

THE ABSENCE OF GOODNESS

ISAAC MORRIS

iUniverse, Inc.
New York Bloomington

The Absence of Goodness

Copyright © 2009 Isaac Morris

All rights reserved. No part of this book may be used or reproduced by any means, graphic, electronic, or mechanical, including photocopying, recording, taping or by any information storage retrieval system without the written permission of the publisher except in the case of brief quotations embodied in critical articles and reviews.

This is a work of fiction. All of the characters, names, incidents, organizations, and dialogue in this novel are either the products of the author's imagination or are used fictitiously.

iUniverse books may be ordered through booksellers or by contacting:

iUniverse
1663 Liberty Drive
Bloomington, IN 47403
www.iuniverse.com
1-800-Authors (1-800-288-4677)

Because of the dynamic nature of the Internet, any Web addresses or links contained in this book may have changed since publication and may no longer be valid. The views expressed in this work are solely those of the author and do not necessarily reflect the views of the publisher, and the publisher hereby disclaims any responsibility for them.

ISBN: 978-0-595-53493-7 (sc)
ISBN: 978-1-4401-1670-4 (dj)
ISBN: 978-0-595-63550-4 (ebk)

Printed in the United States of America

iUniverse rev. date: 01/22/2009

Dedication

In memory of *Doug Pokorski* (1951–2004), a reporter for the Springfield *State Journal-Register*. He wrote masterfully about the best and the seamiest sides of Abe Lincoln's hometown. I've missed reading him.

And for *Mary Jane Hanselman*. She might have been a grandmother today.

Acknowledgments

There are many people who helped with this project, and I would be remiss not to acknowledge their participation.

Thanks to my wife, Carol, who spent hours editing and who inspired me in this endeavor as in life, and to my kids, Kristen, Jenny, Marty, and Ashley, who give my life its deepest meaning.

Special thanks to: Kim Thomas, who read the novel through the first time and convinced me it was worth pursuing; my daughter, Jennifer Pacha; Nancy Richter and Nancy McKinney; Sheriff Neil Williamson and Lt. Dennis Karhliker of the Sangamon County Sheriff's Office; Gene Costa, STL; and Susan Soler, MD.

I must give a special nod to Dave Bakke, a writer for the *State Journal-Register*, for his thorough investigative reporting which inspired certain portions of this narrative.

Finally, thank you to Sister Philip Neri (Crawford), OP, for her support on this project and for teaching me in eighth grade to have the courage of my convictions.

IMM

CHAPTER 1 - PROLOGUE

1997

Margaret Donovan screamed.

She couldn't help herself as pleasure suffused her being, setting off shock waves in the center of the brain where it all coalesced. The French had a phrase for it—La petite mort, *the little death, or beautiful agony*—and even though she didn't lose consciousness the experience took her to another place.

"Oh ... my ... God," she said as she collapsed on to him. They were both breathing heavily and were soaked with perspiration.

"You okay?" he asked, running his hand through her now badly mussed up hair.

"Mmmm hmmm," she said with an exhalation. "How are my tonsils, Doc?"

"You certainly know how to boost a man's self esteem," he said.

They lay without speaking, naked atop the sheets on her bed, awash in the smell of sex and in the afterglow of pleasure. Bertie Higgins was on the radio singing "Key Largo," and Margaret was beginning to drift off into a blissful sleep.

"Oh shit!" she screamed, jumping out of bed.

"Something I said?"

"No! I have a meeting in half an hour! I completely forgot!" She kissed him on the forehead before rushing into the bathroom and shutting the door.

"Guess that's my cue," he said to himself, reaching over to pick up his underwear from the floor.

———

Eric Thompson was hot.

That was the verdict of the female deputies in the county sheriff's office. He did something to Margaret's insides the first time he walked into her cubicle to bring her a report on a break-in. He had short hair, like a jarhead, and blue eyes that were clear and reflective like the waters in a Caribbean cove. But it was the feeling of calm and well being that he brought with him when he walked into a room that was remarkable; her father had projected that type of rock-solid strength of presence. In a word, Margaret found Eric irresistible.

There was, however, one small problem. Eric was very, very married.

She wasn't the only female in the department to drool whenever he walked by, but she was the only one he seemed to notice. There were definite sparks that neither of them could ignore. It didn't take much to fan them into flame.

She knew it was ill advised, but somehow the pattern that eventually established itself—after they'd spent two hours one night sweating up the back seat of his cruiser—fit her lifestyle just fine. They had Tuesday mornings together at her place, and it was quality time. Then he went home to get ready for his shift, to kiss his wife good-bye and hug his kids. She knew it would never be more than that, but for now it was enough.

He was sitting at the counter drinking coffee when she came down dressed in her dark brown uniform. He shoved a full cup in her direction.

"Thanks," she said. She swallowed some as she reached down to grab her briefcase. "Hargrove's going to be in a mood today," she said.

"How come you're going in early?"

"A string of meth labs is under investigation near Illiopolis, and we're meeting with the Illiopolis chief. Look, I am so sorry. God, I wanted more," she said, reaching over to brush her lips against his ear.

He started to reach around to grab her but she pulled away playfully. "Ah ah! Makeup. Don't want to be all smeared for the sheriff!" Then she pecked him lightly but lovingly on the cheek. "Next week?" she asked.

"Wouldn't miss it for the world," he said as he watched her walk out the door to the garage, pulling it closed behind her.

"I'll lock up," he said quietly to himself.

Suddenly, the door opened again. "Eric?"

He smiled, flashing those beautiful baby blues. "What?"

I love you. The words found their way to her tongue, and her mouth opened to speak them. What came out, however, was different.

"Take care." She flashed a smile and then shut the door behind her, leaving him for the last time.

―――――

It was almost five in the afternoon as Terry Strother drove east on Clear Lake Avenue. He took a drag on a joint as he headed out of town, bouncing his head up and down to Marilyn Manson. His fifteen-year-old Horizon had rust spots around the wheels, but the radio speakers worked well judging by the unforgiving looks of drivers he pulled up next to. He had been shopping for cold remedies at a dozen or more places on the west side of Springfield. At the Wal-Mart he'd irritated a line of shoppers by standing over the checkout counter carefully reading the ingredients on each label to make sure it had what he needed. He had never focused as much intellect on anything during his years in school. This was important.

Between stores, he downed bottles of Budweiser he kept on the floor of the back seat. By the time he left the stoplight at Dirksen Parkway, he was in fine fettle.

He sang at the top of his lungs with the song playing from his cassette deck. "Get Your Gunn," from Manson's *Portrait of an American Family.* A sudden lurch caused him to look down at the gas gauge. The needle was *hovering near empty. He swung into the left-turn lane and turned into an Amoco station.*

He was high, dizzy and very nervous as he pumped gas into the crackerbox car, looking around as though he expected to be jumped at any minute. He had always been high-strung. Better-heeled families might have sought treatment for attention deficit disorder, but his mother thought of him as a low-maintenance kid. She didn't have time for any other kind.

Once when he was twelve he'd lost it and taken a baseball bat to the television, the lamps, the furniture, the louvered windows, and the walls in his mother's trailer. His mother's boyfriend—was he the fourth or fifth one that year? Terry couldn't remember—had stood outside, fearful and helpless, until Terry had worn himself out.

His Jekyll-Hyde personality contributed to his failures at school, to a string of minor arrests plus one more serious for assault. At age twenty-four, his future didn't look any more promising than it had when he was expelled from Illiopolis High School. He couldn't hold a job for long because of his temper, and now he existed by selling weed and making meth in the empty building behind his mom's trailer. Tomorrow was not big on his list of things to think about.

He finished pumping gas, replaced the hose, and reached for his wallet. Then he stopped and laughed out loud. He was feeling not only good, but also powerful. "Fuck it!" he said aloud, and then got in the car and just drove away. He reached down and felt the cold steel of his .357 under the seat to make sure it was still there. It was.

As he watched Terry pull out onto I-72 heading east, the gas station attendant picked up the telephone.

Eric Thompson had been parked on an overpass near Riverton for about fifteen minutes with his radar gun when the call came in about a blue Plymouth Horizon or Dodge Omni that had left the Amoco without paying. Eric took a drag off his cigarette and waited. In a few minutes he spotted the car coming down the road. Once the car drove under the overpass, he swung the cruiser around and took the eastbound entrance to I-72.

The curving, tree-lined interstate proceeding from the Sangamon River soon gave way to broad vistas of wide-open farm fields on either side of the highway. Eric followed the car from a distance for a few miles. The driver wasn't speeding and didn't appear to be driving erratically. But as he drew closer he could see the driver pounding his hands on the steering wheel. He was obviously bopping to something on the radio. About a mile from the Buffalo exit, Eric turned on his lights.

"Fuck!" Terry saw the lights behind him. "Fuck! Fuck! Fuck!" He didn't slow down, nor did he speed up. After about thirty seconds the cop behind him gave him a short blast of the siren. Terry was perspiring, his pulse pounding. There was enough shit in the back to send him up for a long, long time. When he reached the Buffalo exit, he pulled off and over to the right side of the road as the cruiser pulled up behind him.

Eric called in the license and confirmed that it was registered to a Mildred Maxwell at an Illiopolis address. No warrants and it wasn't reported stolen. But he had suspected that.

Terry Strother. Eric remembered busting the kid for a fight in a bar in Dawson and pulling him in on a couple of stupid-ass warrants. He suspected Terry was into meth, because the kid's face looked like a minefield. The kid had no home life to speak of, unless you counted a mother who was continually the subject of domestic disputes that normally featured a different guy each time.

What struck Eric about Terry Strother was that the kid was always polite. "I'm not disrespecting you, man." That was how he remembered Strother putting it on one or two occasions when Eric had pulled him over. That politeness bought him some points. But, unless Strother had a good explanation, he was going to add a misdemeanor to his sheet.

Eric stepped out of his car and approached the Horizon with caution. Whether he knew the kid or not, he had learned there was no such thing as a "routine" stop and, as his lieutenant was quick to remind him, the excrement could hit the oscillating blade in no time at all.

Strother sat motionless as Eric walked toward the driver side window. Eric stopped outside the window and then leaned down. "Well, Terry, we have a little prob—"

The explosion was deafening and the flame from the blast was searing but at first he barely felt the bullet tear through his left shoulder, an inch *from where his Kevlar vest wrapped under his arm. Eric was thrown backward and rolled about seven feet from the car. When he tried to sit up, he saw the door of the car open and saw the skinny kid in blue jeans and T-shirt get out with a gun in his hand. The look on the kid's pockmarked face did not bode well for Eric. Frantically, he reached down for his service weapon but by the time he had his hand on it Strother was standing over him aiming the pistol at his face.*

"Oh, Jesus! No! Please!" Eric cried, forgetting his pistol and putting his arm up to screen himself from what was coming.

"Fucking bastard!" Strother said. Then he fired three shots into the horrified deputy's head and arm point blank.

For a moment, Strother thought he was dreaming. Then he saw brain matter and blood and the horror of it all threw him into a panic.

"Oh, sweet Jesus!" he said, turning toward the car. He opened the door but then just stood there and shut it again. Cars were slowing in both lanes of I-72, and one had come almost to a complete stop about fifty feet from the fallen deputy.

"Go to hell!" He said, raising the pistol and firing a shot in the direction of the car. Fortunately, the shot went wild and the car took off.

Then he heard sirens.

He began shaking. A long-repressed memory flashed and he was being beaten all over again by one of his mother's boyfriends, the taste of blood in his mouth as his arms tried to fend off the blows. Just like the cop he had just shot. Terry started crying and dropped to his haunches. He fell backward until he was sitting in the roadway next to the car with his head in his hands, the .357 pointed upward.

As the lights from a cruiser a mile or so down the road became visible, Terry shoved the barrel of the gun into his mouth.

The short, miserable life of Terry Strother ended, perhaps mercifully, when his last bullet blew a hole out the top of his head.

———

Margaret had just returned to the car after talking with a witness to a service station holdup in Sherman when she got the call on her radio.

She clicked off the microphone without responding and sat staring at the cornfield across the road. She turned on the siren and drove to St. John's, brushing tears from her face and trying to breathe deeply. At one point she was afraid she would pass out.

She parked in the circle drive and ran into the waiting room at the hospital to see the sheriff and a dozen or more deputies standing around. No one knew anything. No one knew what to say. Eric was one of the more popular deputies. Sheriff Hargrove was brushing back tears.

She saw Eric's wife, Mary, sitting stoically on a sofa, her face blanched and her luxurious red hair uncombed. Mary slipped the cocoa beads of a rosary methodically between her thumb and forefinger, praying desperately for a miracle. She had two children and a vital part of her—their—existence lay on a stretcher behind a closed door in the ER.

Margaret was overcome with a sense of fellow feeling. She sat down and took the woman in her arms, giving comfort to the one person who had what she never could from the man they both loved. She and Mary Thompson were bonded in a way only she could understand and in some bizarre fashion it felt right.

She was still holding Mary when the surgeon, her mask loose around her chin and her surgical gown saturated with blood—Eric's blood—came out to tell them the awful truth. That there had been a heartbeat at all after what Eric had suffered was a minor miracle. Major miracles were not in the cards today.

Now she was alone. Sheriff Hargrove took Mary in his arms and the deputies crowded around them. Margaret's pain was unfathomable, but she had no standing here and no one to comfort her. As far as they knew she was just one of the guys, one of Eric's comrades. If she was going to die inside, she had to do it somewhere else.

After Margaret got home she barely made it to the bathroom before she threw up. After she stopped dry heaving, she undressed and sat in the corner of her shower with water as hot as she could stand pouring down on her. The towel Eric had used earlier still hung from the bar outside the glass door. His smell was still on it.

Three days later, she stood in her dress uniform with her peers as the priest spoke prayers over the flag-draped coffin. Eric had served in Desert Storm. She was startled by the rifle shots fired in salute, and could only later recall taps being played by one of the honor guard members. She remembered watching the priest hug Mary, and then shake hands with Eric's ten-year-old son, Josh, and his seven-year-old daughter, Ashley.

But the one memory that stayed with her was odd beyond her wildest comprehension. She remembered looking down at her shoes. On her right dress shoe there was a spot. The shoes had been polished with military precision, but nonetheless there was a spot she had somehow missed.

She just didn't understand how that spot could have marred the otherwise perfect sheen of her dress shoes. On something so perfect, how could there be a blemish?

Part One

Ex Tenebris

Busy old fool, unruly Sun,
Why dost thou thus,
Through windows, and through curtains, call on us?
Must to thy motions lovers' seasons run?
—John Donne

Chapter 2

2007

"Sister Margaret?"

"Yes, Shawna?"

"Okay, so if God is all good and all that, how come we have death and like all that?"

Margaret smiled. She wanted to strangle the first valley girl who started punctuating her sentences with "like."

"That is a very good question, Shawna. What you are really asking, I think, is if God is good why does he permit evil?"

Shawna thought and then her eyes opened wider. "Yeah. That's exactly what I am saying."

"A Greek philosopher named Epicurus posed the problem. He pointed out that the presence of evil presents a real problem to those who believe in God. He said that if God is willing to do away with evil in the world, but not able to, then he is impotent."

A chuckle came from the back of the room.

"Not that kind of impotent!" The entire class laughed. "He meant powerless. He then said that if God is able, but not willing, then he must be malevolent."

"What's that?" asked Ashton Koch, a big kid who sat in the front of the class.

"It means that he is mean spirited. Then he said that if God is both able and willing to eradicate evil, then why do we have evil?"

"Good question, Sister," said Koch.

Margaret walked over to the side of the classroom and leaned against the window. "God is good and his goodness shines down on all of us, like the sun if you will, but sometimes we choose to sit in the shade."

The eyes of the kids in class were blank as they attempted to reconcile this metaphor. She kept going, hoping to score a direct hit. "Saint Augustine … do you remember Saint Augustine?" A hand shot up. It was Larry Meyer, a football player and a decent student. "Larry?"

"He was the guy who said 'God make me pure, but not just yet.'"

"Naturally you would remember something like that!" Teresa Hollings, who sat next to him, couldn't resist the opportunity to get a laugh. She got one from Margaret too.

"Very good, Larry. Saint Augustine taught that evil isn't a thing that exists. It has no substance; it isn't something solid or real, like the boogey man. It is the absence of something."

Eyes still fogged over.

"Okay, think about this. All of us in this room have our eyesight, and we can see the beautiful day we have outside. Blindness is what? The absence of sight. Wealth is considered to be good, and the lack of it we call, what?"

"Poverty!" yelled Bobby Erickson from the back of the room.

"Precisely. Poverty isn't something; it's the lack of something."

"So, Sister," said Alison Corcoran who was quietly and seriously taking in the discussion, "Saint Augustine was saying that evil is the lack of goodness?"

"That is exactly what he is saying, Alison."

"But if it has no reality how can it hurt us?" Koch again. This football player's physique belied a pretty good brain.

"Evil can hurt us because when people lack goodness those people can hurt us very much. And often do. How many of you watch crime dramas on television?"

The hands of more than half the class went up.

"Then you have probably heard of a very dangerous man named Ted Bundy."

Several heads nodded. Serial killers were the rage in novels and on television, and Bundy was the granddaddy of them all.

"Well, Bundy was described as a sociopath, and one of the ways that people sometimes characterize a sociopath is in terms of a lack. In his case, what he lacked was what we commonly call conscience. This is close to what Augustine was talking about."

"Okay, Sister, but didn't God make Ted Bundy? And, if so, didn't God make him that way?" The bell interrupted the question. The last bell of the day. Alison Corcoran's question wouldn't be addressed today. Margaret would need time to deal with that one, so she felt somewhat relieved.

What kind of God would "make" a Ted Bundy?

"That is another excellent question. But it will have to wait. Papers due tomorrow." Her voice was almost drowned out by the scooting chairs and noise from the hallway as the classroom door opened.

"Goodnight, Sister," several of the students said on their way out. Others just charged out to their lockers, their cars, and their evening plans, whatever those might be.

Margaret placed her papers in her book bag, and then turned to the door and switched off the light. She watched the passing parade of students. She noticed the girls with their navy skirts and white blouses tied in knots in the front to allow a little belly to show. Thank you, Britney Spears. This was clearly against the rules, but she seldom gave those detentions, especially at the end of the day. If that was the worst thing these wonderful kids did, surely God would forgive them.

These children had no concept of evil. Margaret knew evil in ways she hoped they never would.

She walked down a hallway streaked with afternoon sun from a skylight and down the stairs to the office to check her mailbox. Nothing.

Then she walked toward the exit nearest St. Brigit's Hall, the building she called home.

As she walked out, a policeman held the door for her. Roy Walker was the school's safety officer. The Springfield Police Department and the city schools had implemented a program in the 1980s that placed a policeman on the school campuses for at least part of each day. Saint Dominic's hadn't participated early on because of the cost, since participating schools paid three quarters of the salaries for the officers. That was before Columbine. With nearly a thousand kids, Saint D's was almost as large as City High. Many of Saint D's students came from privilege, but incidents like Columbine had shown that madness does not discriminate. The school arranged to share one of the officers part-time with City High and, for two years now, that officer had been Roy Walker. Walker was a familiar figure in the atrium when kids arrived in the mornings, and he would occasionally drop by at other hours of the day. He didn't smile much, but he was always polite.

"Thank you, Roy. Good night."

Margaret's habit was similar to the uniforms worn by the female students. The order allowed women to choose between the traditional head covering and white tunic, and a more modern style. Margaret wore a navy skirt, dark blue nylons and a white, short-sleeved blouse. When warmer clothing was needed, she wore a white sweater or a blazer. Her dark brown hair was bobbed to shoulder length, and her well-toned body cut a figure distinct from many of the other nuns, one that frequently caused the boys to nudge one another as she passed. The only item that set her apart from the girls in school, uniform-wise, was the large, silver pectoral cross she wore.

She was planning to run after school, before evening prayer and dinner. But on her way to her room she saw Sister Theodora walking on the grounds. Theodora waved at her, and she smiled and waved back. Theodora was her Rock of Gibraltar, her mentor, and her confidant.

Margaret entered the two-story stone structure she called home, ran upstairs, divested herself of her book bag, and then ran back downstairs to join Theodora to walk and talk about nothing, anything and everything.

CHAPTER 3

"No man is an island, entire of himself..."

John Donne's meditation had always been one of Margaret's favorites, and in the weeks following Eric's death the poet's phrase proved prophetic. In those weeks, her life hadn't just been diminished; it had been devastated, shipwrecked. No one knew or even suspected—as far as she knew—that she and Eric were lovers, so there was no one to turn to. She was an island, and the isolation was as horrifying as any fear she had ever experienced.

Her work had turned into a form of process addiction. She gave everything to every case that came her way, no matter how routine or repetitious and seldom quit when her shift ended. At times, she behaved recklessly, blindly charging into situations that other officers might have thought twice about, not because of a death wish but more out of a sense of emptiness that the activity somehow helped fill.

One evening, a year or so after Eric's shooting, she responded to a rollover on I-55. A boat trailer had come unhinged from a pickup and careened into the path of a Ford Explorer driven by a woman who had a baby in a car seat in the back. The woman swerved to avoid hitting the boat and overcorrected, sending the SUV rolling across the median. Eventually it came to rest on its side.

Two cruisers had arrived before Margaret's, but when she pulled up she saw smoke coming from under the hood. Deputy John Rogers had rushed over, shut off the ignition and pulled the bleeding driver out of the vehicle. When he turned back, he saw flames starting to lick at the wheels.

"Oh, my God! Alexis!" The mother screamed and started to run back to the car, but the deputy held her back. She hit at him with her hand, entreating him. "Help her, for God's sake!" Rogers, a young man, froze. Margaret didn't give it a second thought.

Before Rogers or the child's mother realized what was happening, Margaret was on top of the car breaking the glass with her baton. Flames were nearly to the height of the left front tire. She reached in and cut the restraints from the car seat with her knife, and after what must have seemed an eternity from the perspective of the deputies and the horrified mother, emerged with a squealing infant in her arms. She jumped off and ran to the mother who was waiting with open arms, handed her the child, and then quickly moved with everyone to the other side of the cruisers as the SUV exploded.

"What the hell were you thinking?" Sheriff Hargrove screamed at her the next morning in his office.

She couldn't really say what she'd been thinking. "I was just doing what you pay me for, Jim. There was a child in that car, and I was not about to let that mother lose her."

She began to tear up and the sheriff backed off. She was right, of course, and his reaction was inappropriate. Still, he suspected that there was something going on here that he didn't understand.

Jim Hargrove was in his third term as Sangamon County Sheriff. His abundant red hair and distinctive mustache were familiar to drivers all over Illinois. Because he was president of the Illinois Sheriff's Association, his picture was on every gas pump alongside a notice reminding people of the penalties for driving off without paying.

A consummate politician, Hargrove had begun his public career as an intern in the Illinois House after graduating from Sangamon State University. He'd later done a stint in the navy where he worked with NCIS. When he returned to Springfield, joining the police department seemed only natural. There he distinguished himself in a variety of administrative activities and was popular with his peers. He also worked many hours for the local Republicans. In time, the party rewarded him with a golden opportunity when the sheriff's position was vacated. A generation had grown up with him in that job and the role fit him like a glove.

Normally a quiet, even-tempered man, Hargrove got emotional when one of his deputies was harmed or, God forbid, killed in the line of duty. His solicitousness toward his people was one reason he commanded such respect. They knew they were valued. They didn't mind being reprimanded for messing up, because it was like getting a lecture from Dad.

In fact, the younger deputies referred to him as "the old man," even though Hargrove was only on the far side of forty.

With Margaret, he was more solicitous than with most. He had known her father.

Pat Donovan had been a legend as the sheriff in neighboring Morgan County. Margaret had a lot of the same qualities as her dad.

After Hargrove settled down, he put Margaret in for a commendation.

———

In the next few years, she continued to distinguish herself. She spent three years on the sheriff's drug task force. Most of that time was spent tracking down and taking out meth labs.

Three years was the maximum time an officer was permitted to serve because of the possible long-term effects of the chemicals associated with cooking meth. Some left well before their time was up. They—or their spouses—couldn't live with the risks. Even short-term exposure to the anhydrous and other chemicals and paraphernalia used to make meth was a health hazard. Studies showed that long-term exposure could lead to cancer.

The assignment took an emotional toll as well. Even if the threat of contamination and the fear of confrontation with crazed users didn't do it, seeing infants and small children playing on filthy linoleum floors in kitchens and bathrooms where the stuff was being cooked was enough to make tough men cry. It frequently did.

Margaret stuck it out without complaint. Some of the others called her the "ice queen" behind her back because she seldom showed any emotion in the face of frightful circumstances. She didn't think about it. She just did what needed to be done.

They called her the "ice queen" for another reason. Dozens of guys, good looking and available, had hit on her over the years. She'd shown no interest. Speculation abounded as to whether she was batting for the other team, but one or two female deputies who approached her found nothing there either.

She had become an island, entire of herself. Her career flourished, but her life had been irrevocably diminished. The self-imposed isolation was gnawing on her from the inside out, and she was on the verge of self-destructing.

One August night, Margaret was on her way into the office to fill out a report at the end of her shift.

As she was turning off of Adams Street into the parking lot, a call came in for backup at the White Hen Pantry on South Grand Avenue. A gunman robbing the place had been interrupted when two city cops pulled up. One cop was shot. The gunman was holding a gun to a clerk's head and the other cop was trying to talk the guy down.

A cop had been shot.

She put her hand to her mouth for a moment, and then turned the car around.

When she arrived, red and blue lights from at least seven city cars were lighting up the night sky, and several sheriffs' cars were also on the scene. An EMT was tending to the cop. Margaret stopped and watched the cop, sensing the pain in his eyes. She briefly thought about the difference an inch or two one way or another can make with a gunshot wound.

She was seeing Eric.

"He's going to be okay," said a city cop who had come up behind her. He was a captain. His name badge read Tolliver. "There's a hostage negotiator on his way."

The gunman was a large, black kid with a nylon skully on his head, wearing low-slung prison-style pants and a black T-shirt. He was broad-shouldered and muscular, in his early twenties, and most likely high on something. Margaret let out a gasp.

"God, that's Rashad James."

"You know him?"

"Picked him up twice last month for fighting. He lives on King Drive. Didn't give me any trouble."

"Any sort of rapport?"

"He would remember me. But I'm not on his Christmas list."

"Excuse me," the officer said, walking over to the ambulance.

Before he could return, Margaret unholstered her Smith and Wesson, handed it to another officer, and walked up to the door.

"Hey!" Captain Tolliver turned back and saw her walking toward the front door. "What the hell are you doing? Get back here!"

"Rashad?" She spoke loudly through the double glass doors.

The cop and the hostage taker both looked suspiciously at this newcomer. James had his arm around the girl's neck and the girl was terrified. Margaret could see a dark spot spreading in the middle of her jeans.

"What the fuck you want? I'll blow this bitch away!"

"Rashad. It's Deputy Donovan, sheriff's office? Remember me?"

"What you want, bitch?"

"To talk."

"You all back off my fucking face, that's all we got to talk about."

The cop looked scared, not knowing what to expect as Margaret opened the door. The situation had been volatile all along and could spin out of control any minute. It wouldn't take much.

"Rashad, you shoot that girl, you go down for life, or one of us shoots you," Margaret said. She eyed the pistol in his hand, an old .22-caliber double-action revolver. The hammer was not pulled back.

"Shut up, bitch!"

"No!" Margaret screamed so loudly that both James and the cop visibly jumped. The cops outside heard it as well, and the parking lot suddenly became very quiet.

"And I'm not your bitch. It's deputy to you, you little shit."

Her voice was still raised. Anyone walking by, not knowing what was going on, would have suspected a domestic disturbance. She was letting out all of the stops, not knowing for sure why, or what would come of it.

"You can't tell the world to shut up, and you can't go around doing whatever the fuck you want just because you need some extra cash. You can't threaten people's lives. You want attention, you son of a bitch? Well you got attention. A dozen cop cars outside, two cops here watching you scare the piss out of some helpless girl. That what gets you off, Rashad? That how you get your little thrills?"

The cop's eyes were wide and his face blanched. "We're going to die," he whispered. Margaret heard it.

"We're all going to die, officer. It's just a matter of time. Are you going to do it today, Rashad? Are you so fucked up in the head that you're going to take a life and lose yours just to … to what? What the fuck are you trying to do here?"

James opened his mouth, but nothing came out. He looked outside, silently and desperately hoping someone would come in and shut this crazy bitch up. But as he glanced through the doorway his hand lowered, just a bit, enough so that the barrel of the gun moved an inch away from the terrified clerk's head. That was all it took.

Margaret grabbed his hand and wrenched it back, pulling him out enough to send a groin-busting knee right into his balls. The gun dropped and slid across the floor. Then she rammed her fist into his neck, sending him into a choking fit. He went down in a heap after she spun around and delivered a hit to the solar plexus with her elbow.

Images of Eric bleeding on the highway blended with the image of the young city cop bleeding on the gurney and she kept hitting at James's head with her fists. He was crying, rolled into a fetal position, trying to protect his face from the onslaught with his arms. She kept hitting and hitting and hitting.

"*Enough, Deputy!*" *The captain pulled her off. "Enough. You did great. You don't have to kill him."*

But that was exactly what she wanted to do.

Chapter 4

"Oh God, make speed to save me," the ancient nun in one of the front prayer stalls intoned the invitatory.

"Oh Lord, make haste to help me," came the response from the assembled. "Glory be to the Father, and to the Son, and to the Holy Spirit. As it was in the beginning, is now, and ever shall be, Alleluia."

Margaret and Sister Theodora stood toward the back, having come into the chapel only minutes before the service. Theodora wore the traditional white dress that stopped just below her knees with a black belt and a white scapular. A white band that trailed a black veil—a mere vestige of the head covering and heart-shaped habit that she had worn for decades—held back hair that was turning white but was still peppered with ample strands of black. She was nearing seventy, but it was obvious that in her youth, she had been attractive. A stranger who saw them together, not understanding the restrictions of religious life, might have mistaken them for mother and daughter.

"As it was in the beginning, is now, and ever shall be. Alleluia."

———

The lights dimmed in the auditorium, and when the stage lights came up Russian peasants were milling about on the stage near a makeshift shack with a thatched roof. The orchestra began to play and a beautiful young woman walked to center stage and began singing *Matchmaker, Matchmaker*.

Alison Corcoran was a senior whose overriding goal in life was to be on Broadway. She had always taken piano and voice; she sang in the church choir, and had performed at the Muni Opera a dozen times—twice in the lead role. Now she stood in full dress rehearsal, singing with a voice that had recently won her a scholarship to Julliard.

She had the looks of a star. Slender and tall—she was slightly more than six feet in height—she had jet-black hair, normally worn in a ponytail. Tonight it hung around her shoulders, partly covered with a headscarf. Without doubt, it was her eyes that commanded attention. They were the color of olives and with their dark pupils they were almost feline. Boys found them mesmerizing, mysterious and completely arresting.

Her voice was unorthodox, but pleasing, and certainly had the dozen or so teachers and parents who had assembled to watch the dress rehearsal swaying, humming along, and smiling. To top it all off, she was a nice kid, a good student, and a decent human being. She had been born to spread joy, and it was abundant this evening, one night before the spring musical's opening

In the very back of the auditorium, under the overhang that accommodated the light and sound equipment, there was one person who watched more intently than any of the others. His fingers moved up and down on his knees to the rhythm of the song, and he was whispering the lyrics to himself. Alison was beautiful, talented, and filled with such potential. She was truly special.

He intended to make this the most special night of her life.

Cars pulled out of the parking lot behind the auditorium. Voices of the cast members were carried across the campus by intermittent gusts of April wind as the last of the sunlight disappeared. The evening was warm and unseasonably humid.

"I'm on my way home now," Alison said on her cell phone just before clicking it off. "Janet!" she hollered at one of the girls walking by. "I got to study for that history test when I get home. Call me later and help me!"

"The blind leading the blind!" Janet said, reaching for her own cell phone as she ducked into her Chrysler convertible. "Later!"

Alison got into her VW bug, started up the car and pulled out onto Monroe Street, turning west toward home.

Alison's parents, Doctor Peter Corcoran and his wife Shelley, lived in a new subdivision about two miles west of town, about three miles north of Old Jacksonville Road, or "Old Jack," as residents called it. Old Jack was sparsely traveled of an evening once you got past Veteran's Parkway, and the three-mile stretch of blacktop between Old Jack and Alison's subdivision was even less traveled.

He was waiting about a mile down the road, having pulled up after what he estimated to be sufficient time for Alison to drive from the school. He was taking a chance that someone heading south might see, but the car was pulled far enough off the road so that trees, tall grass, cattails and wildflowers obscured it. Someone coming off Old Jack probably wouldn't notice except through the passenger side rear view mirror, and the darkness would make identification impossible.

He drummed his fingers on the steering wheel, looking nervously at his wristwatch several times, before deciding now was the time. He popped the hood and then got out and raised it. He stood by the side of the car and watched the road through the trees. He was praying that the car whose headlights he could see about a half-mile down the road was Alison's, but he was prepared to duck back behind the trees if it wasn't.

Good fortune was his. He recognized the Volkswagen's lights. It was her car. He stepped out in the road, and waved.

When the headlights illuminated him, Alison recognized him immediately. She wondered what he was doing way out here at this time of the evening, but she slowed, stopped and rolled down the passenger window.

"Hey!" She said, smiling. He had always been nice to her, and she greeted him warmly. "What's up?"

"I don't know. I was on my way to see some friends and my car started making a pounding noise." He pointed to the car parked off the road. "I pulled up there and it just died."

"Want to use my phone to call someone?"

"I have to get me one of those things," he said with a chuckle. "No, that's not necessary. Since you're heading in that direction, can you just give me a lift? My friend can bring me back and he even knows something about cars."

"Sure thing," she said, hitting the electric lock button. He opened the door and got into the air-conditioned car.

"Who you going to visit?"

He didn't answer. He just turned and looked at her. She felt strange all of a sudden. There was something wrong, but she didn't know what it was.

And why was he wearing gloves?

It was over in five seconds. He shoved the gearshift into park, grabbed her hair with his left hand and her jaw with his right and snapped her neck. Her olive green eyes now stared blankly at him. Whatever joy she might have brought to the world, the world would never know.

It was unusually humid for April and he was perspiring heavily after loading the body into the trunk of his car. The girl's olive-now-blank eyes were still staring at him. He picked up a rag from the trunk and threw it over her face. Those eyes made him shiver.

He shut the trunk and walked around and dropped the hood. He looked down the road and saw lights coming from the direction of Old Jack. They were about a half a mile away. He ducked behind the trees and waited. It seemed an eternity and he prayed that it wasn't someone who would recognize the VW that was sitting on the side of the road. Finally, the car lights got brighter and then it was dark again. The car hadn't even slowed down.

Looking quickly down the road, he ran around to the VW, jumped in and started it up. He did not turn on the lights, but turned it toward the trees and then drove it down a gravel access road that ran between two newly plowed fields for about a quarter mile. It wouldn't be noticeable at night, but it would be clearly visible in the daylight. But that didn't matter. He shut the engine off and walked down the road to his car.

He sat in the front seat, still sweating profusely, and breathed deeply. "One, two, three," he counted to himself, trying to slow his heart rate. It wouldn't do for him to pass out now. Then he started the car, pulled out onto the road and turned back toward Old Jack.

He still had work to do.

Chapter 5

Margaret slept fitfully during the night. A front had passed through which set off thunder boomers and a light show with a terrific downpour before subsiding to a soaking drizzle. At least it would be cooler today. She was late for Morning Prayer. After Mass she went to the dining room and just grabbed a cup of coffee, which she took back to her room.

At eight, she walked across the campus and into the back door. As she walked toward the office to check her mailbox, she noticed several groups of students talking quietly. One or two of them looked at her, but none spoke. She sensed something was wrong.

"Good morning, Sister." Roy Walker had walked up behind her.

"Morning, Roy. How you doing?"

"Fine, thanks."

When they walked into the office, Angie Whitaker, the principal's secretary, stood up.

"Sister Margaret? Sister Kathleen is looking for you. She's in her office. You too, Roy."

"Are we in trouble?" Margaret asked. Angie didn't smile. Not a good sign.

Margaret walked over and knocked on the principal's office door. Inside were Sister Kathleen Martin, a tall, muscular woman with brown hair and dark framed glasses, and Brother Ronald Swartz.

Kathleen set down her coffee cup. "Please come in, and shut the door."

Margaret did so, and then walked over and nodded to Brother Ronald. He was a stout, balding man in his forties. His white Dominican cassock reminded her of something Brother Tom Brightman had said once to her jokingly about Brother Ronald. Something about the white elephant in the room. Not charitable, but then Brother Tom was not always charitable—just very entertaining.

"Sit down, please." Margaret took the chair next to Brother Ronald. Roy sat in the chair next to Kathleen's desk.

"We have a problem," Margaret began. "The sheriff's office called this morning. Alison Corcoran didn't make it home last night."

"Alison?" Margaret's face registered surprise. "That is not like her at all."

"No. It isn't. What's worse, a sheriff's deputy found her car this morning about half a mile off the road that goes to her subdivision. Alison wasn't anywhere to be found."

"We're not talking about a wild kid here," Swartz ventured.

"Certainly not," said Margaret. "Have you talked with her parents?"

"Not yet," said Kathleen. "I am dreading that, and am wondering about going out there. In the meantime, there's a full-scale search on. We will be expected to cooperate as well, and I expect we are going to be doing some comforting around here until we know where she is."

"What do you want me to do?" asked Margaret.

"I want you to speak to faculty members and explain what is going on. I have posted a sign and Angie is announcing it now. Meet in the gym. Just brief them and tell them what to expect."

"Certainly." She got up to leave. Roy stood as well.

"Roy, if you can find out anything more … I'd appreciate it," Kathleen said.

"Of course."

The reaction among the faculty members was predictable: disbelief. Alison was on everyone's "A list" of students. Several of them were fighting back tears.

"We will have a Mass this morning," Margaret said. Kathleen had said nothing about this, but Margaret felt it was a safe bet. "Comfort your kids, because they know and they are worried and frightened. And … I expect some of them may be asked to talk with investigators."

"Do the police think she has been harmed? Or worse?" asked Mike Brady, a slight, balding man with sparkling blue eyes who had taught history at St. Dominic's for more than two decades.

"We don't know anything," Roy said. "It was mentioned in morning report, but the sheriff's office is handling it."

"Joe?" Margaret addressed Joseph Santini. Santini was in charge of student counseling. He was a good-looking, broad-shouldered man with thick brown hair, blue eyes and a slight moustache. He looked up at her.

"You need to have your people at the ready. We are going to have a lot of very upset kids. Do what you do best." Santini nodded. No one could calm the hysterical or smooth over the pain the way Santini could. The only problem was getting the kids to go to someone other than him. He was very popular.

"What are we going to do about the spring musical, Sister?" The questioner was Mrs. Miles, who was directing the musical. Margaret had not even thought of that. "I mean, Alison has an understudy and the show could go on, but do you think it should?"

Good question. "You know, Alice, we don't know anything. As far-fetched as it seems, Alison could be safe and well somewhere; we don't know what was going on at home. I will talk with Kathleen, but if the kids are up to it perhaps it would be best to keep things as … normal as possible."

"The show must go on?" Miles said with a touch of sadness in her voice.

"Yeah. Something like that," Margaret replied. "Any other questions?"

No one said anything. "Thanks, everybody. And if any of you hears anything, please let me or Kathleen know." One by one, they got up and left the gymnasium.

Margaret walked over to Roy. "Thanks, Roy."

"No problem. I'll keep my ear to the ground when I'm here. Kids sometimes tell me stuff."

"I noticed them talking up a storm when I came in. Maybe you're right."

Brother Tom Brightman walked up and gave Walker a high five. Like Brother Swartz, Brightman wore the white cassock of a Dominican, but on him it looked a whole lot better. He was in his mid-forties, but in good physical shape. He had blonde, almost white hair that he wore in a crew cut, blue eyes and looks that caused more than one woman and girl to wonder about his choice in life. He had, as well, a personality that drew others to him, one that people in need sought out.

"What are you thinking?" he asked.

"Nothing good, Tom. I hope I am wrong. We can pray."

He smiled, patted her reassuringly on the arm, and walked out of the gymnasium.

Margaret's next stop was the office. Angie Whitaker was poring over the morning absentee list.

"Angie, can I use Kathleen's office?"

"Sure. She's with Marty. They are on their way out to the Corcorans'." Marty Jeffers was the assistant principal and football coach.

Margaret went in and closed the door. Kathleen's office was larger than most of the others in the office complex, as befitted a principal. Two large windows overlooked the tree-lined circle drive in front of the school; the day was still grey and depressing. There was a vase of fresh flowers on the principal's desk. Angie was such a sweetheart. On the walls were various diplomas and achievement awards in testimony of Sister Kathleen's distinguished career as a teacher and administrator.

As she sat down, Margaret saw a figure pass by the window that faced the outer office. It was Bill Pickering, the day janitor. He was thin, almost wasted in appearance, and his blue shirt and dark blue pants hung on his frame. Thin as he was, his arms were muscular. His blue-veined hands with large knuckles now gripped two long fluorescent light bulbs and suggested that anything he gripped would stay gripped. His head was missing a lot of hair, his eyebrows were dark and thick, and if eyes are the windows to the soul, the lights weren't on behind his. He glanced in, noticed Margaret sitting at the desk, and did a double take. Margaret nodded in his direction, but he did not respond in kind. He merely walked away. She always tried to be kind to him, but there was something about the man that spooked her.

Picking up the phone, she dialed a number she still knew by heart. She was going to call in a favor from her old friend Jim Hargrove.

Chapter 6

The sheriff walked into his office the morning after the White Hen Pantry incident wearing a deep-blue Brooks Brothers suit, an off-white shirt with thin, navy pinstripes and what appeared to be a spanking-new tie. He had an interview scheduled later with Marsha Klinger, the blonde anchor from WICS. She was running a story on a series of anhydrous ammonia thefts near New Berlin.

Margaret was sitting across from his desk, waiting. She was in her uniform, her hair tied back. She looked tired.

"Margaret, I want you to take a two-week vacation."

"What?" She sat up straight, uncrossing her legs.

"Let me rephrase it. You are going to take two weeks off. No discussion."

She sat back. At least he wasn't suspending her.

"I was advised by our counsel to suspend you. But I decided you were going to take a vacation."

Margaret put her hand over her mouth. She couldn't think of anything to say. Hargrove, however, had no such problem.

"I don't suppose I need to tell you that I had quite a morning. The chief of police is after your ass for endangering the life of one of his cops, and I spent an hour earlier today with the local members of the NAACP. The miscreant you beat up last night has his family all worked up and they're

talking lawsuit. Frankly, I wouldn't be surprised to see Jesse fucking Jackson strolling in with a dozen TV crews in tow."

"Sheriff, I ... "

"Don't say anything yet." His eyes were intense, and she had learned that when he was on a roll you just shut up and let him finish. "Of course, they find themselves in a strange situation. A bitch took out the big gangbanger, and lucky for us I don't think he wants to have this information broadcast any more than it has been. His buddies in the slammer would have a lot of fun over that one. And, of course, there are other mitigating factors that counsel is spinning."

"Such as?"

"There was an officer down. It was an emotional response, one that was shared by most of your peers, incidentally. Except that poor cop, who almost crapped his pants when you went off on the guy holding a gun on him and that clerk. But Captain Tolliver said he wished he had a half dozen like you on his crew." He stopped and swallowed some coffee. "And, even though this won't be part of anyone's deliberations, there's also the thing with Eric."

Margaret could feel her face turning bright red. She almost broke into a sweat. "What does Eric have to do with this?"

"You know damned well what he has to do with this, Margaret. You are still grieving, and you've got no place to take it but to work."

She thought they had been so careful. "You know?"

He smiled. "You know, for someone as savvy as you are you can be so naïve at times. You think you guys were under the radar, but you weren't. It's just that your fellow officers are closed-mouthed. Yeah. I knew."

A tear formed in her right eye and slid down her cheek. The last thing she wanted to do was burst into tears in Hargrove's office and she fought it hard.

"Margaret, you know how I feel about you. I have known you since you were in high school. Your dad was like a dad to me. Did I ever tell you how I met him?"

About one hundred and fifty times, but she knew she was going to hear the story again.

"I was a rookie in the association who didn't know my ass from a hole in the ground. Your old man walked over the first day of the first conference I attended and sat at my table. I was by myself, and here comes Pat Donovan, the President of the Sheriffs' Association, and sits at my table. I miss him, and I know you must too. He was special to me, and so are you. I know you are hurting, but if I don't intervene somehow, you or someone else is going to get hurt—or even killed—and then it will be my responsibility."

"We didn't mean for it to happen," she said suddenly, seeing an opening that she had been desperately seeking. Someone who cared; someone she could unload on. She wiped her face with her hand. "He loved his wife and kids. That was the strange part. He loved them, and we never once entertained any notion of making us permanent and disrupting what he had. Actually, it was my greatest fear that she would find out and throw him out. He couldn't have handled that. He needed them. What he and I had was special, and I loved him. But what we had was all I needed."

Hargrove didn't say anything for a few seconds, and then took another sip of coffee.

"Margaret, you're a young, beautiful woman who could have any man she crooked her finger at. If I were you, during your time off, I would ask myself why what you had with Eric was 'all you needed.'"

Chapter 7

"Sangamon County Sheriff's Office."

"Tracy?"

"Margaret! My God—oh, sorry! How are you?"

Margaret smiled at the voice she had come to know so well during her years as a deputy. Tracy Polanski was the office blonde—a title she'd bestowed upon herself. She had endeared herself to the sheriff and to everyone around her because of her penchant for saying exactly what came into her head regardless of the consequences. She had been Hargrove's administrative assistant ("I am not a secretary, thank you very much!") for all but two years of his tenure.

"I'm great, Tracy. It's good to hear your voice again."

"Talk to my husband. He's tired of hearing it. So are my kids for that matter. I sure miss you around this place. Here I am, surrounded by stud muffins without any moral support. Guess you don't have that problem any more, huh?"

Margaret had to laugh out loud. "Wish I could help you out, Trace, but I need to speak to the old man. Is he there?"

"Oh, he's here all right. Grouchy as a raccoon in a trap. Didn't sleep much last night. You want to try and talk with him?"

"If you don't mind."

"For you, honey, anything. Maybe you will put him in a better mood. Love you!"

"You too, Trace."

She was on hold for about twenty seconds before the phone picked up again.

"Good morning, Sister Margaret. I can bet I know why you are calling."

"How are you, Jim?"

"Been better. Good to hear from you though."

"Jim, is there anything you can tell me about Alison Corcoran?"

"Not much to tell. And that's the truth. Her dad called me at home last night around eleven and said she hadn't come home from play practice at school. That wasn't like her. She had spoken with her mother around eight thirty after it was over."

Shelley Corcoran was on the County Board and she and Peter were friends with Hargrove and his wife Teresa. Hargrove would, naturally, be the first person they would call.

"They talked to several of her friends, and no one saw her after she left the school. This morning, Pete said he talked with a lady who lives a couple of houses down from them and she saw a VW on the side of the road between Old Jack and the subdivision last evening on her way home."

"What time?"

"She says it was around nine fifteen or so, which would be about right—assuming Alison really did head straight home. And I have no reason to believe she didn't. She isn't a problem kid."

"No, she isn't."

"I drove out there and Pete and I drove up and down those roads and never saw any cars parked alongside the road or anywhere. It was pitch dark so we couldn't see much anywhere else. Then, this morning, I sent a deputy out to scout around and he spotted a car sitting down an access road about a hundred yards from the blacktop. It was her VW."

"Anything interesting in the car?"

"Nada. I am having the lab guys go over it pretty thoroughly. Got some prints, but won't know anything for a while. Thing is, the passenger window was down and that downpour we had last night did a number on the interior. On everything, for that matter. Any tracks or prints that might have been around there aren't there anymore."

"The passenger window was down? Not the driver's side window?"

"Yeah."

"It was very warm last evening. Assuming she didn't put the car in the field, why would whoever did it put the passenger window down? I'm betting Alison put it down to talk with someone alongside the road."

"Is she the kind of kid who would pick someone up?"

"If she knew him and he was in need of help."

"But who, and what did he do with her?"

Margaret was terrified of what the answer to the last question was going to be.

The show had gone on. Whether due to or in spite of the sadness of the community over the unknown fate of Alison Corcoran, the opening night was a huge success. Marian Teeters, a sophomore with a beautiful voice, filled Alison's role nicely. Margaret stayed after for a while, visiting with parents and congratulating the cast. An unmistakable pall hung over the entire evening in spite of its successful outcome.

Margaret left at about ten thirty and walked across the campus. No rain tonight, only stars and clear spring air. It was cooler; in fact it was getting almost chilly now. She wished she had brought her sweater.

Before going to her room, she walked across the campus to the church. The gothic structure was slated for demolition in a year, and Margaret couldn't imagine the property without it. Since coming to the convent, she had made a habit of visiting the chapel before retiring, usually between nine and ten of an evening. As she walked through the oak doors into the darkened sanctuary, she blessed herself with water from the marble font and moved to the front, genuflecting before the altar before kneeling at one of the *prie-dieux* in front. The pinpoint of light from the sanctuary lamp bespoke the presence of God in the otherwise dark space.

There she prayed for Eric. She prayed for the souls of her father and her mother, and wondered if they could see her now. What would they think? She prayed for Sister Theodora and all of her sisters at Saint Dominic's.

She prayed for Alison Corcoran. And she prayed for the poor misguided soul who had taken her.

She prayed that God would help her overcome her feelings of doubt. Was she running from life after Eric's death? Or was her sojourn here meant to be, and her love affair with Eric just a milestone in her journey to this place? Immanuel Kant had said that motive is everything, that something good done for the wrong reasons lacks moral worth. However good her life may have turned out, was it for the right reasons? She prayed that God would help her know for sure. She had a decision to make about the rest of her life, and she needed to know.

Before leaving, she prayed for another small soul she knew would be in heaven waiting for her some day.

After twenty minutes, she blessed herself, rose from the *prie-dieu*, and walked out the side door.

She walked across the campus and up the steps of the residence, key in hand.

Something rubbed against her leg and caused her to jump with alarm. She looked down to see a nondescript stray cat, its back arched as it mewed and rubbed her ankle. Sister Carmelita always fed strays, and now they couldn't get rid of them.

She looked out across the campus. A light breeze brushed the leaves against the night sky. There wasn't a soul about. Other than the cat, that is. Scoping her surroundings was something she still did regularly. Once a cop …. Then she shut the door and opted for the stairs instead of the elevator to take her to her room.

As she walked down the hallway, she stopped outside of Sister Theodora's room. The door was open, and she could see Theodora sitting in a rocking chair in the corner reading her breviary. Music from a cassette player on her dresser was softly playing. It was Elvis singing "Fools Fall in Love." Theodora loved Elvis. Margaret warmed as she watched this beautiful woman who had come to mean so much to her. She chose not to disturb her, and instead went down the hall to her own room.

It had been an awful day, and at the end of it there was still a child out there, somewhere, and parents who were going through the worst hell imaginable.

The last thing Margaret did before going to sleep was utter a whispered prayer aloud in the darkness of her room.

"Jesus, Mary and Joseph, be with Alison tonight and with those who love her."

CHAPTER 8

Her "vacation" was becoming a tedious affair. The first day, she slept in. She spent the rest of the day cleaning her apartment, straightening closets, and doing other things that seldom got done because there just wasn't time when she worked. Well, there was time now.

On day two, after her morning jog around Washington Park, she showered and got in the car and drove to Jacksonville.

There wasn't anyone left for her in Jacksonville. Her dad had died following a severe stroke in 1990, and the only family members left were cousins she didn't know that well. So there wasn't much to go home to except memories. Yet it was still nice to go home again.

She parked on Mauvaisterre Street near downtown and just walked around. As she passed the corner of Main Street and College Avenue, she stopped for a minute at what was now an empty lot on which a new building was being erected. In her mind she saw once again the brick two-story structure that had housed the Morgan County Jail. It had been painted an odd shade of light green. In the yard next to it, where at one time had stood a gallows, she remembered grass and playground equipment. This strange juxtaposition was due to the fact that half of the second floor had served as a residence for the sheriff and his family until the new county building was completed and the jail demolished. It had been Margaret's home until she'd finished eighth grade.

Memories of playing there on the swing and sliding down the slide while men behind barred and screened windows watched her from above left her with an empty feeling now. Her dad was gone. Her mother, who had died two years after Margaret was born in a fiery collision with a semi on Route 67, was someone who, try as she might, she could never remember. Margaret had been too young. But she could still remember the countless, nameless faces staring at her, some smiling, and some calling down to her as she played in the yard below. Faces of men who, when they smiled, displayed gaps where teeth once had been. Or faces that were scarred, faces with empty eyes that betrayed even emptier hearts. For some reason they never frightened Margaret. She just accepted their presence in her life. In a strange way, the nameless men with holes in their teeth and in their hearts were like family. Later she drove past Illinois College and stopped and treated herself to the buffet at Vic's Pizza, and then drove to the Catholic cemetery. She passed through stone gates with carvings of the crucifixion and resurrection, sculpted in the 1960s by a British monk named Dom Hubert von Zeller, OSB. Her dad had had several books by von Zeller at home. Margaret had kept one after her dad died, though she never actually read it.

She pulled a few weeds from her parents' graves, and then knelt silently there. The sun felt good on her, and for the time she was there she felt a peace wash over her that she hadn't felt for ... well, she wasn't sure of the last time she had felt such quietness. Such hopefulness. There was such certainty in the midst of death.

As she headed east on her way home, she spied the bell tower of Our Saviour's Church. She passed the grade school where she had spent eight years of her life and then swung into the driveway in front of the Spanish-style church and parked. It was Saturday and, judging from the cars parked in front, they were hearing confessions before the evening Mass.

There was a time in Margaret's memory when confession had a clear and predictable feel to it. There was a large box—that was the only way she could think to describe it—with three doors. Behind the center door, the largest, sat the priest. The other two doors were for the penitents who, once behind them, knelt in a dimly lit, very small space until the sliding screen door opened and the process began. Confession wasn't for the claustrophobic.

On this day, however, the full force of reform was evident as Margaret sat in a straight-backed chair in a large room, hands on her knees, facing a priest with a wide smile and an even wider girth who bid her welcome and invited her to make her peace with God.

Margaret just sat there. That's what you get for waiting fifteen years between confessions. Whatever happened to "Bless me father for I have sinned"?

"Is there something I can help you with, ma'am?"

"No. Nothing. Look, I'm sorry. This is … this is a mistake. Thank you."

With that she stood up and walked out of the room. The large man sitting in the chair opened his mouth as if to speak, and then just as quickly shut it again and gave her a polite wave.

After her abortive attempt to make confession, she took Old Jack back to Springfield. It was a quiet and beautiful drive that took her past miles of cornfields and across green and rolling hills. But the quiet she had felt for however brief a time had dissipated. The pain and confusion that she had grown to live with now once again swirled about in the cavernous place that her heart had become.

Chapter 9

On Saturday Margaret awoke at six, got dressed and was in her prayer stall by seven forty-five for morning prayer and Mass. The sun cast a colorful glow as it filtered through the stained glass windows above the sanctuary and shone directly on the large crucifix suspended from the ceiling. After Mass, she stayed in her station for fifteen minutes and pleaded with God for the safety of Alison Corcoran.

If Abraham could convince God to spare a city from destruction for the sake of a few good men, surely she could convince Him to spare one young girl.

By nine forty-five, she was running through Washington Park. Her daily jog was an extension of her spiritual life and one of the reasons she disliked the winter months so much. She felt as close to the Creator surrounded by nature as she did in chapel. A stranger passing her on her run would never have guessed her station, because she now wore grey shorts, a loose-fitting tank top and Nike running shoes.

She was a block away from the convent when she heard the sound of another runner behind her.

"Good morrow, dear Sister." It was Tom Brightman. He was dressed in running shorts and a T-shirt. His arms and legs were well muscled, his chest taut. In addition to teaching religion, he also helped coach the wrestling team.

"Morning, Tom," she said. She stopped running and began to walk. He slowed and walked with her.

Tom Brightman lived in a one-story brick ranch that sat on the edge of the property, together with Brother Swartz and Father Reginald Milkowski. Tom was the only one who exercised. Brother Swartz's idea of exercise was walking to and from the refrigerator, and Father Milkowski had a serious heart condition. Daily Mass was about all he could muster.

"Great show last night," Tom said.

"Yes, I enjoyed it. In spite of everything."

"Yes," he said. "What a horrifying turn of events."

Neither spoke for the next half a block. Tom broke the silence.

"Santini had a heck of a day yesterday."

"I'm not surprised. I am sure that a lot of those kids are scared. I think we can safely assume that she just didn't just run off. If it can happen to a girl like her, it can happen to anyone."

"We need cheering up, dear Sister. Want to hear a joke one of my students told me yesterday."

"Do I have to?"

"Yes. Doctor's orders."

"First, who told you?"

"Jason O'Shea."

"Oh, dear," Margaret said. O'Shea, a burly wrestler with an infectious smile, was famous for his bad jokes.

"This guy goes to a dance and meets this beautiful redhead. They hit it off. After a while, the guy tells a joke and the girl laughs so hard her eye pops out! Instinctively, he reaches out and catches it. As he is standing there, looking at it, she says, 'Oh, my! I am so sorry. I have a glass eye.' He gives it back to her. She pops it back in and they continue talking.

"Well, as the evening goes on, they stay together and he ends up spending the night at her place. Next morning, she gets up and fixes him a great breakfast. The guy says, 'Say, you do this every time you meet a new guy?' 'No,' she says …"

"You just happened to catch my eye," Margaret said.

"You heard it?"

"About twenty years ago."

"You're a tough crowd, lady!" he said, as he waved her off and turned toward the rectory.

"Get better material, Brother!"

"Keep the faith, Sister!"

He did a left oblique and headed to his house. She noticed that, when he reached the parking lot, he stopped, bent over and placed his hands on his knees. When he arose, he shook his arm and started rubbing it.

"You okay, Tom?" She yelled across the parking lot.

He turned around, startled.

"Oh, yeah. Just winded. Getting old, I guess. Catch you later."

Before going upstairs to shower, Margaret went into the common room and turned on the computer to check her e-mail. There were a couple of messages from students. One had lost his notebook and forgot what the assignment was for Monday. Another wanted to know if he could turn in his paper that was due on Friday on Monday and still get credit. There was also one from a former student asking for a letter of recommendation to the criminal justice program at UIS.

There was also a note from Sister Agnes Ann Carpenter, the prioress. She wanted Margaret to stop by her office at her first opportunity. Margaret knew why.

Margaret had a degree from Illinois College with a double major in English literature and criminal justice—*magna cum laude*—when she became a candidate. The Order saw her potential, and encouraged her to continue her education. One of the areas she had to choose from was theology. The more she reflected on it, this seemed to be something that appealed to her. Her studies in English had focused on the Metaphysical poets, Donne in particular. An avid reader, she had always been enthralled by the poetry of Yeats, Hopkins, and T. S. Eliot, all of whom delved into intriguing theological notions.

She enrolled in the Master's program at St. Louis University. For two years, she commuted the ninety miles to the campus twice a week, and attended summer sessions. She was now completing her thesis and was fulfilling a vital role as one of the two theology instructors at Saint Dominic's, Brother Thomas being the other.

After two years, she took temporary vows. She was in what the Order called her period of discernment, a time during which she and the community would determine whether she was suited to the religious life. This period of discernment usually lasts three years, although it could be extended for up to three more years. Her period of discernment was drawing to a close. Margaret knew this was coming, but she didn't know whether she was ready to make her final profession, the final decision to dedicate the rest of her life to serving God as a member of the Order of Preachers. The prioress no doubt wanted to discuss her intentions.

Margaret had joined the Dominicans at an inauspicious time in the history of the order. Whereas in the 1950s there were about three hundred sisters in the Springfield order, stationed at the Mother House and at the dozen or more schools throughout the state and in a handful of other states, now there were fewer than fifty who were below the age of sixty. In fact, the average age of the sisters was sixty-five. Capital development in the past decade had been focused chiefly on expanding the infirmary, which housed more patients each year.

During her first year of novitiate, Margaret spent several weeks in St. Louis with other novices from around the country. Bringing young women from around the country together allowed for a community experience that would not be possible at their various convents with only one or two in a class. It saved her the arduous twice-weekly trek from St. Louis and allowed her to make some friends from among her fellow novices. She became close with several nuns from La Oroya, Peru, where vocations were actually on the rise. She continued to stay in touch with Sister Teresita, a moon-eyed Peruvian beauty whose faith made Margaret envious. Teresita was a truly holy child who thought nothing of sacrificing herself in service of the Church. Margaret prayed for that same tenacity of faith.

The paradox was that the church continued to grow in spite of the scandal of pedophilia that had threatened to bring it crashing down around the Vatican. Vocations had dwindled to the point where there weren't enough priests to serve the parishes in the Diocese. There had not been nuns in most of the Catholic schools for more than a decade, and many of the schools had long since closed their doors. The crop was growing in leaps and bounds, but the workers were few and far between.

Her former pastor in Jacksonville, Monsignor John Laughlin, once said in a sermon that religion was always one generation away from extinction. She sometimes thought it ironic that her call to the religious life brought her here at a time when the religious life had become almost an anachronism.

Sister Theodora had a different take on things. She pointed out that the Church had ebbed many times through the centuries. She cited the Church of the Renaissance, whose excesses had contributed to the groundswell of opposition that became the Reformation. She believed that the emphasis society placed on science had led to the erroneous conclusion that what we can't see we can't know and so people no longer believe they will survive life after death. Even some priests who preached eternal life had succumbed and sought their heaven on earth through sex. "Many have just stopped believing," Theodora said.

Margaret logged out, and went into the lounge. Sister Carmelita was sitting there reading the paper with Sister Clarence. The two were seldom apart, even though they constantly bickered. Carmelita looked at Margaret over the top of the City State section of the *State Journal-Register*.

"Lovely outfit, dear," Carmelita said with a good-natured grin. "Clarence, you and I must get one of those outfits!"

"You'd look like Humpty Dumpty," Clarence said.

"Somehow, the outfit seems to run counter to the rule," Carmelita said, disappearing behind the newspaper once again.

The "rule" was the Rule of St. Augustine. The rule had served as a guide to persons in the religious life for nearly two thousand years, and the Dominicans were essentially a monastic order. Chapter four of the Rule addressed chastity and admonished the sisters that "there should be nothing about your clothing to attract attention."

Margaret smiled, duly admonished, and then glanced at the coffee table and saw the front page of the paper. A headline announced the disappearance of Alison Corcoran.

There was nothing in the article that she didn't know. Sheriff Hargrove was quoted as saying that the investigation had not turned up any leads yet, but that they were tirelessly working to find the young girl and return her to her parents. He asked anyone who might know anything to contact his office.

The article featured a black and white picture of Alison. It was her her senior picture.

Margaret put the paper back on the coffee table, and went up to shower.

Chapter 10

It wasn't until Sunday morning that the Corcorans learned the fate of their daughter.

Margaret was sitting in the dining room at a table with Sister Theodora and Father Milkowski after Mass. Ron Swartz and two rosy-cheeked novices joined them.

Theodora always said that community was the essence of the religious life. The laughter from their table had an infectious quality and brought smiles to the others sitting nearby.

It was nine thirty when Margaret saw Sister Kathleen walk in through the front door. Her face was drawn and blanched and her eyes red. She walked over to where Margaret was sitting, and the group quieted.

"What is it, Sister?" asked the priest.

"I'm afraid I have bad news. They have found Alison."

"Alive?" asked Theodora.

Margaret turned her head from side to side, fighting back tears.

"Sweet Jesus!" Father Milkowski closed his eyes and made the sign of the cross.

"A fisherman found her this morning about six thirty," Jim Hargrove said. He had left his cell number with Kathleen and asked her to have Margaret call him.

"She was at the bottom of a ravine near the old Sertoma Club. Poor guy almost had a heart attack when he came upon her. Thing is, that's a fairly well traveled road near a lot of houses. Coming around the curve there you can see right down that ravine. Whoever did it wanted her to be found."

"How was she killed?"

"We won't know until the pathologist does the autopsy. There was a nylon stocking tied around her neck. It was tied so tightly that it had cut into the flesh about a quarter inch. But she may have been dead when he tied it. It appeared that her neck was broken."

"Was the body wet?" Margaret was thinking about Thursday night's thunderstorm.

"No."

"So it was deposited there after Thursday night, and given what you are saying about the site, possibly as late as last night sometime," Margaret mused. "Did you say a nylon stocking?"

"Yeah. And her hands were tied behind her back with one as well."

"Panty hose?"

"I would guess, but we won't know for sure until they are removed."

"Was she clothed?"

"She was naked as the day she was born. She only had one shoe on. The other was about ten feet away. There was a Saint D's T-shirt, a pair of shorts, a bra and panties scattered around the area."

"She wouldn't have been wearing nylons, Jim. Not with shorts."

"I know."

"So, why do you think the killer used nylons?"

"I would expect duct tape or rope or something like that."

Margaret jotted down the word "nylons" on a legal pad followed by a question mark.

"Gag?"

"Not when we found her."

"Any sign of sexual assault?"

"Couldn't tell. The only marks on her were some scratches on her arms, but there was no blood. Those might have been made rolling through the brush on her way down the hill. No obvious signs of sexual trauma. The pathologist will hopefully be able to tell us more."

"Have you spoken with the parents?"

It took a while for Jim to answer her.

"I watched that girl grow up, Margaret. You'll have to forgive me. Yeah. I just left there before I called Sister Kathleen. They are devastated."

"I can only guess. If there's anything I can do, please let me know. And I would appreciate it if you could keep me updated."

"Sure thing, kid," he said, and then the line went dead.

Margaret sat at the desk, tapping a pencil eraser on the legal pad. She turned to see Sister Kathleen standing in front of the television.

"Feel like going with me on a mission of mercy?" Kathleen asked.

I'd rather be dragged through cactus by wild horses, Margaret thought. "Of course, Sister."

It was a quiet ride to the Corcoran's home. The sun was bright, the weather comfortable; all in all it was a glorious day to be driving on Old Jack. Under any other set of circumstances, it might have been a pleasant outing.

"Here's the turnoff," Kathleen said as she approached an intersection marker.

About a mile down the blacktop Margaret noticed a jack rabbit lying in the road. Its hind legs were sticking straight up in the air and its head had been flattened into a stew of brains and dried blood. It was a pitiful sight. The smell worked its way into the passenger compartment of their LeSabre as they drove over it.

So, Sister, Saint Augustine was saying that evil was the lack of goodness?

Alison's question popped into her head. Those were among the last words she had heard spoken by a child who would never be in her presence again. She brushed a tear from her cheek, and then she noticed something on the right of the road.

"Stop a minute!" she said.

"What is it?"

"Please, just pull up."

Margaret opened the door and walked back down the road about fifty feet and stopped in front of a large tree surrounded by bushes, tall grass and wildflowers. Beyond it was an access road going between two fields from which light green sprouts had begun to show. She heard the car door close behind her. Kathleen walked up to where she was standing.

"This area is obscured enough that a car could have pulled in there and not have been seen by traffic coming from Old Jack. There's the access road that Jim was talking about. This is the place."

"But couldn't the car have been seen by someone coming from the subdivision?"

Margaret turned around and looked down the road.

"It was a gamble. Unfortunately, it paid off."

Chapter 11

Kathleen pulled into the circular drive in front of the Corcoran home, an imposing two-story brick structure that covered a half acre. There was a white Mercedes 300SL parked directly in front of the steps leading up to the front door.

Peter Corcoran met them at the door. He was a nice looking man in his forties, with hair lighter than his daughter's, but his olive colored eyes would have made paternity testing unnecessary. That a father and daughter could have the same color eyes—and such an anomalous color at that—created a serious problem for the familiar two-gene theory. To Margaret it seemed that God sometimes entertained himself by throwing a monkey wrench into our reliance on induction. Now Doctor Corcoran's eyes were red from crying. The man whose wealth and influence in Springfield were reflected in the mansion he inhabited had lost his only child.

"Sisters, thank you for coming."

Instinctively, Kathleen reached out and put her arms around the man, who laid his head on her shoulder and held on as though she was saving him from drowning.

"Our prayers are with her and you both," Kathleen said. Margaret marveled at the appropriateness of the remark. She envied people who could say appropriate things in the face of suffering. At funerals she simply was at a loss. Kathleen was good.

When he broke loose from Kathleen, he smiled at Margaret.

"Sister."

Margaret took his hand. Unlike Kathleen, she had never met the doctor so she let the hand hold suffice. "I'm Sister Margaret. I'm so sorry for your … loss."

What a stupid thing to say. That was something Mariska Hargitay would say.

"Alison's theology teacher! She really enjoyed you. Said you were 'cool.' Please come in."

The ceiling in the foyer rose to the height of the two-story structure, and opened onto a beautiful curving staircase that could accommodate workers carrying a fully assembled four-poster bed. They walked through the foyer into a very large formal living room lighted by eight-foot windows. As they entered, an elderly man dressed in a white shirt and gray slacks rose from a large leather sofa and smiled weakly. He had a thick mane of white hair and a white moustache.

"This is my father-in-law, Congressman Wheatley. Dad, this is Sister Kathleen, the principal at Alison's school, and Sister …"

"Margaret," she said, reaching out to the congressman for a polite shake. This time she kept her mouth shut.

A woman about the congressman's age, with white hair shaped by a severe permanent with nary a stray hair, entered from the kitchen. She was dressed in a loose-fitting dress that had probably cost as much as the foyer they had just passed through. She wore enough jewelry on her arm to fund the war in Iraq. The look on her face matched her permanent. Severe.

"This is my wife, Antonia," said the congressman. He pronounced it "Ahn ta KNEE ah."

"Pleased to meet you," Antonia said. "Shelley won't be coming down for quite some time," she added peremptorily.

"Understandable," said Kathleen.

"Please, sit," said Peter Corcoran. The sisters sat on a love seat across from the sofa. Peter and his father-in-law sat down almost in unison. Antonia stood at the end of the sofa, making no attempt to sit and drag out this visit. A vigilant sentry, she showed little expression. Margaret took her attitude for what it probably was—shock at having lost something so precious.

At least two minutes passed in silence. Punctuating the stillness at one point was the sound of the large grandfather clock in the foyer chiming the quarter hour. Margaret felt awkward, but Kathleen sat with the patience learned from years of dealing with persons in crisis. Oh yes, she was good.

It was Peter who, at last, broke the silence.

"I would like to establish a scholarship in her memory, Sister."

Kathleen smiled. "We can think about that later, Peter. Now we're here for you."

The man began to shake, and closed his eyes as the grief washed over him. The Congressman put his hand on Peter's shoulder.

They visited quietly for another ten minutes or so. It had all the elements of a pastoral call, appreciated but not productive. Margaret could sense that Peter was truly grateful for Kathleen's presence. Antonia, on the other hand, was truly grateful when they got up to leave.

"How do you do it?"

"Do what?" asked Kathleen as she drove down the blacktop.

"Know how to say the right things to people in pain. I never know what to say."

"You learn after saying the wrong things a few times."

Margaret smiled. "I remember going to a wake with my dad once in Jacksonville. I was maybe fourteen. It was an older woman, a cousin of ours. We shook hands with everybody and then went over to kneel at the coffin. My dad said, 'She looks good doesn't she?' I looked at him and said, 'Uh … Dad, she's dead!' He grabbed me by the arm and we left suddenly."

Kathleen laughed. "Your penchant for speaking your mind hasn't gone unnoticed at the Mother House either."

"You *think*? You seem to know Dr. Corcoran pretty well."

"Well, I make it my business to get to know the families whose generosity has made St. Dominic's what it is. Does that shock you?"

"No. It might if you weren't also caring toward the ones whose parents can barely scrape by."

"Thank you. I try. But yes, Peter has been on several committees through the years, even before Alison was a student. He was the driving force behind the state-of-the-art computer lab we have that is the envy of every public and private school in the area. He himself donated ten thousand dollars."

"Impressive."

"He also influenced several of his friends, doctors and lawyers, to ante up equally generous amounts of money. But the truth is, I actually enjoyed his participation. He is one of my favorite …"

"Donors?"

"I was about to say parents. He has a very good personality, and he is also a good looking sucker."

Margaret gave her a look.

"What? I am celibate, not dead."

"Did he also donate part of the infirmary? Now that you mention it, I saw the name Corcoran on a plaque in the hallway."

"That was his father, John Michael Corcoran. He was a doctor too. They say he was also a good looking …"

"Parent?"

"Yeah, that. There was a time when the infirmary was for sick girls, not dying nuns. St. Dominic's had a residence hall for girls who lived out of town, and the infirmary was for them. I am told we had several governors' daughters at St. Dominic's over the years."

"I remember reading about that somewhere."

"That all ended in the late seventies. They say Doctor Corcoran used to come and take care of the girls himself, in his spare time. In fact, there is a picture of him caring for one of the girls hanging in the hall of history."

Margaret vaguely remembered seeing that black and white photograph. She would have to look at it more closely.

"I worry for the Corcorans with the investigation coming up."

"In what sense?"

"Investigators in this type of crime always start with the people closest to the victim, to rule them out. In the case of a child they will want to rule out, say, sexual abuse by the father, for instance, as a motive. The mysterious disappearance may lend a great deal of suspicion there. It won't be pleasant."

"Surely, you can't think …"

"No, I don't think anything. But it has to be ruled out in any sort of investigation."

"Surely, Peter's prominence and reputation will minimize that sort of thing."

"Well, wealth and influence shouldn't give someone a pass in a murder investigation."

The words had barely left her before she realized how naïve that was.

"But he and the sheriff are close friends. Surely, the sheriff will buffer this somewhat."

Margaret thought about that for a few seconds. "Possibly. But their friendship may cause him to stay out of it personally. He's a straight shooter in that regard."

"I am wondering whether we should close school the day of the funeral."

"I suppose. I don't think that it would be a productive day."

"I will talk with Joe and Marty and get their opinion first thing in the morning."

"We've got time. The autopsy won't be until tomorrow, so the funeral will be toward the end of the week at the earliest."

"What a God-awful nightmare," Kathleen said.

"I suppose it could always be worse," Margaret said.

"I really can't imagine how," said Kathleen.

Chapter 12

He got the shakes about three thirty in the afternoon. He didn't want anyone to see. He hated it when this came over him. It had been a beautiful day and everything had been going so well for him.

Those awful green eyes. He saw them in his sleep and again now as he stared around the sparsely furnished room. They seemed to be barely visible, shining at him transparently.

But now maybe people would know. People would understand. People would see him and would know the secret he had carried with him all the years.

He would bring to light what had been hidden in darkness. Yes, he would do that.

But he couldn't think straight when his head hurt so bad that his arms shook. It was a shaking that started deep, deep down in his chest and then moved to his extremities. It would cause fear to swell in his soul and leave him cold, empty, hopeless. At times he saw slobbering, hirsute, unspeakable demons with black and empty eyes that nibbled on his toes and clutched at his ankles with blood-red claws, trying to drag him down into hell.

Abandon all hope, ye who enter here.

He was hiding in a closet.

They didn't notice him when he returned to the cabin, so focused were they on his sister. At first they were all laughing, his sister too. They kept getting her to drink out of a bottle of clear liquid, and the whole room smelled of booze. Now she was crying, and they had stopped being nice. It wasn't fun anymore. She screamed and one of them put his hand over her mouth, while the other one—his dad's boss from the fire department—undid his belt buckle and forced his sister down on the sofa.

Oh God, Bonnie! Bonnie! He couldn't do anything. He was too frightened. He realized that he had wet his pants.

Then the other one, the fat lawyer, dropped his pants and did something to his sister who was whimpering now. His ugly, naked fat ass was moving up and down and his sister was crying. The fat man finished just as someone else entered the room.

"Bring her here," the man said.

The man his dad called Sally pulled her up. She was naked from the waist down. He started to walk her over to the other side of the room when she swung around and struck at him and for a moment seemed to have gotten away. Then she slipped on something and her body sort of flew up into the air and then. … THUNK! It sounded like the coffee table had broken. Then it was quiet.

There wasn't a sound for about a minute. Finally, the fire chief knelt down next to her and then said, "Jesus! She's dead."

"She can't be!" the fat guy screamed, echoing the ten-year-old boy's own terror and disbelief. By now he had slid down onto the floor of the closet and buried his head in his arms. When he looked up through the louvered closet door he saw the face of a third man.

Those eyes.

The next sound was the voice of his father who walked into the cabin through the front door.

"What the fuck! Oh my God! Bonnie! What the fuck have you done to my daughter?"

He awoke from the dream in a start, almost falling out of bed. The room was dark. He had closed the blinds to keep the sun from entering into his private places and he lay down now on top of the bedclothes and waited for the discomfort to pass.

He had to be resolute. More sacrifices were necessary, as painful as they would be. It would take that. It was necessary in order to fill in the holes of his broken and shattered existence and bring to light a horrible injustice.

That girl. The one with the haunting green eyes, eyes like the man he saw through the louvered doors. Try as he might, he couldn't remember her name.

Chapter 13

It was dark and the air smelled clean.

He sat in a dark parking lot across the street. Waiting.

His fingers drummed on the steering wheel as he sat watching a group of young people dressed in black standing around outside the Qik n EZ. In his rearview mirror he could see, beneath the dozens of lights over the pumping stations, the one who was the focus of his efforts this evening.

Billy Matheson had just bought a coke and was standing in front of the convenience store with several of his friends. Unlike several of his friends, whose hair was long and stringy, Billy's hair—though dyed jet-black-- was cut above the shoulders. Saint Dominic's had rules about hair.

Billy hated that school. His mother was making him go there just because his grandpa had gone there. She was working three jobs to make it happen. The money his grandma had given them only went so far. So he went. It was important to his mother.

He was all she had now. The last guy she married drank and hit her a lot. She finally managed to break free of him and now she was home by herself. Billy had suffered through three different stepfathers in his fourteen years of life. He didn't remember his own father and his own father apparently never thought about him. He loved his mother, though. And he knew deep down that in spite of her problems she loved him too.

Black was the theme. Billy's eyes were accentuated with black eyeliner and eyebrow pencil; he wore a black T-shirt, black jeans and black canvas shoes. He wore a chain around his neck and there were posts through his eyebrows. Of course they came out during school. His piercings weren't as extreme as some; his friend Erik, who was making out now with Alice May behind the ice machine, had a ring in his nose. Alice May sometimes would attach a leash to it and walk around with him in tow.

These were his friends. This was his life. He was the only one who had the misfortune to attend a school where he couldn't dress this way and be who he really was during the day.

It was past ten, so Billy tossed his joint and waved his friends off. He didn't want the embarrassment of having his mother coming to look for him.

In the back of his mind he must have thought about the fact that none of his Goth buddies had mothers who would care. He tried not to dwell on that. At fourteen, you paid whatever price you needed to for acceptance.

Billy walked west on Washington Street. It was darker along this street but Billy had walked it many times at night. Nighttime was his favorite time of day.

He had about three blocks to go to reach his mom's apartment. The night was clear and cool. Hopefully the breeze would help dissipate the smell of pot that was probably in his clothes. He didn't want a scene when he got home. He was tired.

Traffic was light. Only a few cars passed him. One passed slowly and then turned into the empty parking lot of the Lutheran church a half block ahead. Billy didn't think anything about it.

As he passed the church, someone called his name. Billy turned and looked up the drive and saw him. "Hey," he said.

The man was up the hill of the driveway. The car was partially obscured by the church sign. The man was just dropping the hood.

"Thought that was you."

"What are you up to?"

"I just pulled in here because I heard a rattle under the hood. It's fine. Saw you walking by. Heading home?"

"Yeah. Don't want my mom to have a cow."

"Well, hop in. I'll drive you the rest of the way."

"That's cool. Thanks."

It wasn't until the car had pulled back out on to Washington Street that Billy noticed the man was wearing gloves.

He thought that was strange.

Chapter 14

At seven fifty on Monday morning, Joe Santini sat alone in his office. The day hadn't started and already his head was killing him. He had taken two aspirins, but so far they hadn't done a thing for him. And his day was going to be a doozy.

Sitting across from him was a senior girl who spent most of that time wiping away tears and sobbing. She was on the volleyball team with Alison Corcoran, and even though she and Alison didn't hang around together, she was upset. Scared. Who wouldn't be? Before the session was over, the subject had changed.

"My mom just won't leave me alone. She's always bugging me. It's not like I do pot or stuff like that, but I have to beg her to let me do anything."

The girl crossed her legs and pulled her navy skirt up ever so slightly, angling her leg toward the man sitting across from her.

"Mr. Santini, it's not like I am a child. I am a woman!"

Santini was accustomed to this. Some of the girls who came in for counseling were adept at manipulating. A good number of them came from privilege, and were used to getting what they wanted by batting their eyes at Daddy. Unfortunately, such behavior all too frequently carried over into their dealings with other men. He was in great shape, except perhaps for a little middle-age paunch that was creeping up on him, and his good looks, dark hair and dark eyes made him a target for adolescent crushes and sometimes out and out flirtation. It was a hazard of the job.

Teresa Hollings was letting out all of the stops. She was blonde, busty, tall, and leggy; the modest uniform of Saint Dominic's couldn't begin to obscure what she was toting around.

Joe had moved back to Springfield from Santa Fe six years earlier, bringing with him a beautiful wife, Connie, who was six months pregnant. Ever the good Catholic, he and Connie now boasted four children.

He left Springfield after graduating because he wanted to get away from the family. He loved his parents, but he sensed that he was living in the shadow of an uncle he knew, but was never close to.

His mother's uncle was Johnny Rigali, the godfather of Springfield.

Rigali made a good living in Springfield. He served the organization well in his hometown of Benld, an Italian enclave ever since the Capone era, and later as a made man in charge of the Capital city. Until his death in 1973, Springfield was his town. He ran gambling and high-class call girls out of the Lakehouse, a posh club near the lake. On the surface, it was a successful restaurant and ballroom where some of the most famous names in entertainment headlined, thanks to Johnny's connections in Chicago, New York and in other cities controlled by his friends. Behind the scenes, it was the nexus of a spectacularly successful criminal enterprise.

Uncle Johnny—the name by which Joe knew him as a kid—didn't look the part of a mobster. A small man—he stood only five foot six and weighed one fifty soaking wet—with a bald head and simple frame glasses, Rigali didn't live lavishly. He had built a modest home for himself, his wife, and their six children in an established neighborhood near Blessed Redeemer, his parish church. He mowed his own yard, trimmed the hedges, and chatted with the neighbors who all spoke highly of him. He drove a trademark 1962 Plymouth Valiant, which he had until his death.

Joe had heard all the stories. His uncle had been caught in Appalachin, New York, with other mobsters whose summit at the home of Joe "the Barber" Barbara was cut short because cops noticed big cars cruising through a town that was used to seeing tractors and pickup trucks. When New York officials called the cops in Springfield, they said that Rigali had no record and was a model citizen.

They were paid well to cover his ass.

His uncle had been a suspect in several murders in and around town, but people in Springfield benefited from an otherwise crime-free city—no one would dare to attempt a robbery in Rigali's territory—and some of the best entertainment and eateries in Illinois.

At the Kefauver hearings in the late fifties, Uncle Johnny's only comment was "I don't know how to speak it so good."

To his credit, he never invoked the Fifth Amendment.

Joe's mother and father were decent, respectable people who belied the stereotype of Italian as mobster—just like most Italian Americans. But Joe felt the need to separate himself, to just be Joe Santini, student at Notre Dame University, without the shadow of his infamous uncle or his minions.

He left Notre Dame with a master's degree and took a job counseling at a private school in Santa Fe, New Mexico. He was a good-looking guy who truly cared about the kids and they flocked to him—especially the girls.

All was going well until he met Gracie Caldwell, a sixteen-year-old high school junior with a laundry list of disorders. She easily could have passed for twenty-five. After that, it all changed.

Soon, he was in search of another job. He told his wife that his mother and father were older, and his sisters and brothers were shouldering the burden of caring for them. He needed to come back home. It was safe now that enough years had gone by to distance him from his infamous uncle.

When a job opened up in the counseling department at Saint Dominic's, where once he had been an honor student and the star on the soccer team, Joe jumped at the chance. Now he was director of the counseling department, he had a nice supplemental income from counseling on the side, and had twice turned down the chance to be assistant principal. Principal was out of the question. Saint Dominic's was the flagship for the Order. As long as there was a qualified religious, she would sit in the captain's chair. No matter. Joe was in his element. He was at the top of his professional game and quite content with his life.

Joe looked up at the girl, realizing that he hadn't heard the last few things she said.

"Teresa, have you talked with your mother about any of this?"

"She should know how I feel!"

"How can she know if you don't tell her? Like you are telling me? Saying 'she should know me' only deflects the problem."

Their session was interrupted by a knock at the door. Carol Oates, his secretary, stuck her head in.

"Call Sister Kathleen. Sorry to interrupt, but I have to leave for about half an hour and she needs to talk to you sometime this morning."

"Thanks Carol."

He turned back to Teresa, who had managed to pull the skirt up about an inch higher.

"Okay, tonight find an excuse to talk with your mom. Tell her we talked, and then explain how you feel. Then let me know how it goes."

She stood up and gave him a smile. "Thanks. I'll let you know tomorrow."

"Teresa?"

The girl turned back expectantly.

"To your mom, and to me and your teachers, even when you get to be a woman, officially, you will still just be a kid. Adults are funny like that."

She stopped smiling, and then walked out of the door.

"Not to put too fine of a point on it," Joe said softly to himself.

There was a knock at the door, after which it opened. It was Kathleen.

"Did you get my message?" She asked, clearly irritated.

He let out a breath. "Sorry. Yes. I forgot."

"Some parents have been pressing me to cancel school for the Corcoran funeral, whenever that is going to be. Marty thinks it would be best. I wanted your opinion."

Sister Kathleen had no problem making decisions. But she always solicited the thoughts of her team, and for this she was respected. Unlike her predecessor, Sister Angelica, she even listened to what they had to say.

He pointed to the stack of papers on his desk.

"Check out my appointments for this morning. The other counselors are just as busy. This was from before we found out what had happened to …"

"Alison?"

"I'm sorry. My head is killing me. Do we have any idea when the funeral will be? They will have to do an autopsy."

"Probably closer to the end of the week. I am just thinking that there won't be much point to having school that day."

He looked again at the stack of phone messages, some from frantic parents.

"Well, I can see what they are saying. How are we on days?"

There had been several closings during the year due to weather.

"We can afford one," she said.

"Then, I guess it's a no brainer. Nothing much will be accomplished around here the rest of that day."

"And I am pretty sure we won't be having a blizzard before the end of the year."

Chapter 15

Sheriff Hargrove had just picked up coffee after leaving his house in Sherman when the call came through. Instead of turning on Peoria Road to go to his office he stayed on the bypass and headed down Bruns Lane. As he drove, he put in a call to his chief of detectives, Ernie Jones, and told him to meet him at the scene.

Hargrove was growing tired. He was almost fifty-seven years old, and the hallmark head of thick red hair was now streaked with gray. Still, even though his wife was bugging him more and more lately, the last thing he wanted to do was hang up his badge and gun. Another election would be coming up in a year and he had the full support of the party—if not his wife—and he planned to stay in the game for at least one more term.

He drove past Wabash and Knights Road and found himself on a two-lane road bordered by deep ravines, rolling hills, farmhouses of varying architectural design, and trees that had probably stood there since before the Civil War. The developers hadn't made inroads here yet, but less than a mile away a commercial center stood, waiting for a road to connect onto this one. It was only a matter of time.

He saw the cruisers and the CSU van after he had rounded a curve and he pulled his car up on the side of the road and got out. He walked down one of the ravines and passed Deputy Rogers, who was walking up with some poles and crime scene tape.

"What have we got, John?"

"Dead kid, Sheriff. Another one."

"Morning, Jim." Tom Cross, the county coroner, spoke to him from his kneeling position at the bottom of the ravine.

"Tom." Jim moved closer. Two of the deputies stepped back, and then Jim saw the naked corpse of a very young boy lying face down.

Someone approached behind him, and Hargrove jumped.

"Jesus, Ernie! Honk, will you?"

"Sorry, Jim."

At six foot six inches, Ernie Jones easily stood out among the uniformed deputies crowded around the scene. He was in his mid-fifties and, although he could easily take down any one, his success as a cop was largely due to his warmth and charm. When Ernie smiled, he had a way of making people feel that it was all going to be okay, all facts to the contrary notwithstanding.

People who knew Ernie attributed his easygoing manner to his southern roots. Ernie was born in New Iberia on the Bayou Teche, Louisiana and boasted both Creole and Cajun blood. His mother was a quadroon who had grown up in Algiers. His father worked for the McIlhenny Company on Avery Island, where they produced Tabasco sauce.

Ernie joined the Army at eighteen, and spent most of his enlistment at Fort Leonard Wood in Missouri. Afterward, he worked in St. Louis at a variety of jobs until he took the exam to become a St. Clair County sheriff's deputy.

It was marriage that brought him to Springfield. His wife worked for the St. Clair State's Attorney as an assistant prosecutor. They fell and love and, shortly thereafter, she was offered a position with a law firm in Springfield that lobbied for the unions. After they'd spent a year seeing each other only on weekends, the new Sangamon County sheriff, a guy named Hargrove, hired him on a recommendation from the sheriff in St. Clair.

Springfield had a checkered history of race relations, particularly among law enforcement professionals. The city that laid claim to the Great Emancipator had been the site of an ugly, two-day race riot in 1908 in which two black men were lynched. Nearly a hundred years later, relations were still strained. Lawsuits were continually filed against the city by black officers claiming discrimination in hiring and promotion on the city force. But in the sheriff's office, Hargrove would have none of that. He boasted a fair number of well-qualified black deputies whom he had hired based on their characters, not simply because he needed to fill a quota, and Ernie Jones was one of Hargrove's most trusted men. Ernie had respect because he earned it.

"Oh, my," Ernie said. "A child. Lord help us."

Hargrove glanced up to the top of the ravine and saw Bill Templeton, a young detective he had promoted to the rank of sergeant on Ernie's recommendation. Templeton was a good cop—but Jim didn't like him. Templeton sensed it and kept his distance.

Hargrove turned back toward Tom Cross. "What do you know?"

"Dead a short time. I am talking hours. No rigor. Neck's broken."

"Is that a nylon stocking around his neck?"

"Think so. His hands and feet are tied with one as well."

Hargrove stepped in closer and surveyed the area. He noticed clothing strewn about, and then something caught his attention. The body was naked except for one shoe. He looked around and then saw the other one, about ten or twelve feet from the body.

This wasn't just a murder. Someone was trying to tell them something.

"We know who he is?"

"Name's William Matheson. He's fourteen years old."

Tom Cross held up the ID card for the sheriff to see.

It was a student ID from Saint Dominic's High School.

Hargrove walked back to where Ernie was standing.

"We're going to need some inside help."

Someone passing along the road had seen the congregation of cruisers and the CSU van and had called it in to a local radio station.

It wasn't long before an enterprising reporter from W109 pulled up alongside the road to get a jump on the story. A young, slightly plump but very well put together blonde got out of the car and started to walk toward the area that was now cordoned off by crime scene tape.

"Go charm her, will you Ernie?" said Hargrove.

"My pleasure, boss," said Ernie. But before he could get to the perimeter he noticed that she had already homed in on Templeton. Templeton was more than happy to keep her entertained. He looked down at Ernie and winked at him.

The sheriff didn't care who kept her at bay, frankly, as long as he could keep this from turning into a panic before the parents were notified and the school knew what was coming.

He pulled out his cell phone and dialed the number for Saint Dominic's.

"Someone please pinch me," Kathleen said. "What the hell are we going to do? We are going to have parents panicked, and kids scared to death."

"This doesn't make any sense," said Joe Santini. "I doubt those two kids even knew each other. He was a freshman; she was a senior. I doubt they ran in the same circles."

Margaret stood near the door. She was trying to place the Matheson boy. There were almost a thousand kids at Saint Dominic's. She taught all four years of theology, two classes for each. He must have been in Tom Brightman's class.

"Matheson was kind of a sad kid. Real quiet," said Marty Jeffers. "He never caused any trouble though. Pretty much stayed to himself."

"But two of our kids within a couple of days, killed in the same way," Kathleen observed. Someone is targeting our kids. We are going to have to respond to this. Any ideas?"

"We should call a parents' meeting tonight, in the auditorium," Santini said. "You and I address them. We can get someone here from the sheriff's office."

"Probably the sheriff himself," said Margaret. As close as Hargrove was to Peter Corcoran, she was relatively certain he would participate.

"We can address safety, and get parents and kids to tell us something, anything, that might help us figure some of this out," Margaret said.

Tom Brightman opened the door and joined the group. No one was sitting.

"Hey, Tom," said Kathleen.

"But if they're targeting our kids, I have to go back to what Joe said a minute ago. What's the connection? These two kids are like day and night," said Jeffers.

"At the meeting tonight, we need to let parents know that investigators will want to talk with their kids. If they have a problem with that they need to let us know. Have you seen Roy Walker?" Margaret asked, looking at Kathleen.

"He was in earlier, before the sheriff called," said Kathleen.

Kathleen blessed herself, and for a moment closed her eyes. Margaret had never seen her rattled.

"Parents should never have to outlive their children," Kathleen said. "And school principals shouldn't have to comfort parents whose lives have been torn asunder by some senseless act of violence. God, why have you given this cup to me? Okay. Enough self-pity. Go back to class, and don't say anything yet to anybody. They will be notifying the boy's mother. Joe, set up that meeting. Anything else?"

No one spoke.

"Everybody pray. Pray like you've never prayed before."

Sister Kathleen dismissed school at two in the afternoon, after making the sad announcement about Billy Matheson. She announced the parents' meeting for that evening at seven. Margaret asked the sheriff, who had no hesitation about attending and addressing their concerns. Kathleen knew how skillful Joe Santini was at communicating with concerned parents. She was quite comfortable in the course of action they had selected.

The hallways of Saint Dominic's were normally chaotic at the end of the day, between locker doors slamming and kids yelling at one another up and down the halls. It was a pandemonium Margaret had come to accept and even grown to love since coming here. Today no one spoke above a whisper; no one ran or slammed locker doors. She didn't see tears—very few knew the young man and it didn't appear that he had a lot of friends. Fear had closed its grip on Saint Dominic's.

As she walked down the stairway, she looked up and saw a young woman—a senior, she thought—who stood at her locker crying. She stood there alone. Someone, it would seem, missed Billy Matheson.

"The tragedy of this morning has brought us all down. However, please recall our appointment this afternoon. It is imperative that I speak with you."

Three thirty. Margaret hadn't forgotten, although she had prayed Sister Agnes would put it off, given the circumstances. Her e-mail message had squelched that hope.

Imperative. That was a key word in the vocabulary of every self-respecting prioress.

Margaret wasn't sure she was ready. What was she going to say?

Golly, Mother. You know, I am still not sure because I am feeling compunction for fucking another woman's husband, even though I loved the man and never did and never would have done anything to hurt his wife. Golly, is it possible that this whole vocation thing, as smoothly as it may seem to be going, is nothing but a long, drawn out episode of avoidance?

Her three years of discernment had gone too quickly, and there were too many ghosts that still hovered.

Chapter 16

Saint Alphonse Church was empty and the sanctuary light was beginning to outshine the light coming through the stained glass windows. Margaret had been here since four in the afternoon. It was now nearly seven.

Church was somewhere she always felt safe. Her dad had been an ardent churchgoer, a daily communicant. That started, she later learned, after her mother died. Every Sunday, she was awakened, told to bathe and pick out a dress. She and her dad drove to Our Saviour's on East State Street where they always sat in the third butcher block pew from the back on the right side of the main aisle for the eleven o'clock Mass.

She began every weekday at the eight o'clock Mass, sitting with her classmates. This was where they convened in the morning, and then all eight classes were marched across to the grade school to pursue their educational endeavors.

She didn't even get Saturdays off. Dad went to Mass, and so did Margaret.

Church was deeply woven into her character—so much so that, once she was in college, she made it a point to go to Mass every Sunday, and occasionally during the week at the Newman Center. Afterwards, she stayed to talk with God and her mother.

After she joined the sheriff's department, her church going became much more sporadic. She honestly couldn't recall the last time she'd gone to confession.

Now, her life seemingly at its nadir, she sat in the back of a darkened church, staring at the emaciated corpus that hung on an iron cross above the elevated altar, trying to understand how she had come to where she was.

She hadn't cried, really cried, since that night at the hospital. Now, the grief began to swell up inside her again, starting in her bowels and working its way up through her stomach. She slid from her kneeling position to a sitting position, her head in her hands, crying so loudly she wondered if she could be heard outside. She didn't care, though. She couldn't control it any longer. It took about five minutes for her cries to subside, to be reduced to a whimpering.

"Young lady?"

Margaret was startled and looked up toward the end of a pew. She saw a tall, nice looking Dominican nun with a concerned look on her face.

"Are you all right, honey?"

Margaret wiped her face with her hand. *God, I must be a sight.* She couldn't answer, but just nodded her head.

"I just brought over some flowers for the Mass tomorrow," the nun said. "I'm from the convent across the street. I am Sister Theodora." The nun extended her hand. Margaret reached over and took it. The hand was warm, soft, loving, caring.

"May I sit down?"

Margaret had regained her voice. "It's not necessary, really, Sister. I am okay now."

"Of course you are, dear," Sister Theodora said as she seated herself next to Margaret. "That's why you are crying your heart out in an empty church on a beautiful day when you could be out doing all sorts of other things. Things are just swell, right?"

Margaret actually laughed. "Right, Sister. Swell?"

"Swell. It's an anachronism from an earlier generation. Sort of like me."

Margaret smiled again. The nun was clearly someone she could like. "Thank you, Sister. I'm Margaret. Margaret Donovan."

Theodora thought for a moment, and then her eyes flashed recognition. "Oh, my! You're that policewoman! The one who took down that poor misguided soul at the Seven Eleven. I always read Police Beat."

"White Hen, actually."

"Seven Eleven. White Hen. They're all the same."

"Pretty much."

"The paper said your dad was Sheriff Pat Donovan, from Jacksonville."

"Yes. He was my father."

"And here you are, following in his footsteps. He must be so proud."

"Actually, Dad died some years back. A stroke."

"I read that. I am certain he is still proud. I knew him somewhat. I was principal at the high school in Jacksonville in the late seventies. You were just a wee thing. He certainly had a reputation as a tough guy, but the people in Morgan County—the elderly especially—kept him in office because they felt safe. He and Monsignor Laughlin were good friends. The Monsignor was a tough guy once, too."

Margaret remembered the frequent visits Monsignor Laughlin paid to their apartment above the jail. The two men would sit around joking and downing shots of bourbon. The tall, big-shouldered, chain-smoking priest with bright, steel-grey eyes had once regaled her with a story of how he, when a much younger man, had run with the bulls on their trek to the bullring in some town called Pamplona in Spain. But for all his bravado, she remembered seeing the Monsignor fight back tears during the homily at her dad's funeral.

"Yes, I remember," Margaret said. "Dad loved Father Laughlin. He wasn't really close to anyone else after mom died."

"How old were you when your mother died, dear?"

———

The nun and the deputy sat in the darkened church talking for more than an hour. She came very close to spilling everything. The nun made her feel that comfortable. She really felt she could tell her anything. Almost anything, anyway.

Theodora talked as well. Her given name was Mary Frances Hohmann. If she was a good listener, she got it honest, being the oldest of seven children born to a farm family in Alexander, Illinois. She had helped raise her five younger sisters; and later, after her mother died delivering her youngest brother, she became the female head of the household.

When she graduated high school, she announced her intention to go into the convent. She was a bright student who knew what fate lay in store for her if she stayed and married one of the persistent farm boys from the area. She had watched her mother change from a vibrant, beautiful woman into a haggard, unhappy crone who had little good to say to or about Mary's father. Mary wanted more from life. College was out of the question. She was a girl, number one. Number two, her father thought education beyond grade school was a waste of time—it had only been her mother's intransigence on the issue that saved her from having to quit after eighth grade.

Her father was angry at first. "Damned waste of a good-looking woman, if you ask me." Yes. A good looking woman who could go to bed and produce a passel of children and cook and sew and do chores and die young and wrung out.

Mary was, in fact, a beautiful woman. She was much taller than most of the other girls in her school, standing nearly six-foot tall. She had long, brown hair and hazel eyes. Her nose was straight and her cheeks prominent, her jaw firm and her complexion like that of her mother's prior to what life had done to her. The boys were all wild over her, but she knew better than most what that would lead to. Her mother had been pregnant with her when she married her father.

At least her father respected the Church and its religious and eventually found comfort in knowing that one of his children would be in a position to offer up prayers for his immortal soul.

Since making her final profession, Theodora had done remarkably well. She had obtained a master's in education, and later a PhD. She served as Diocesan director of education a number of years, and served as principal in high schools run by the Order in the Springfield diocese, Chicago and Louisiana. She had become what other women from her era could never have become outside of the convent, a true professional.

Her father finally told her how proud he was of her the day before he died at Passavant Hospital in Jacksonville.

Her premonition had been correct. Although she was the oldest, only one of her sisters was still living. One had died in an automobile accident. One lost a battle to cancer. Angelina, the youngest, died when a tractor rolled over on her (she was helping her husband put in the crop). And poor Evangeline, the sweet girl who always made Mary laugh, drank herself to death after losing a son in a hunting accident. The one remaining sister was happily married to a decent man and lived in Champaign, about an hour and a half from Springfield. Her only brother, Mark, was retired in Florida after a successful career as an investment broker. It saddened Mary that she was the only one who was still a Catholic. The Church was the one constant in her life.

Around eight thirty, they rose and the nun reached out and hugged her. She held Margaret tightly, and Margaret responded. Is this what it might have been to have been held by her mother, by someone who would love her unconditionally? It felt wonderful.

"Let me drive you home, Sister."

"Oh, I have a car. And it's only across the street. I used to teach here, and even though I am not connected with the parish any longer I still like to bring some flowers from the garden and place them on the altar. Father Greeley has come to expect them. He leaves the empty vase standing there. We're all creatures of habit, I guess—pardon the pun."

Margaret found herself smiling when Theodora spoke.

"Margaret, I am going to exact a promise from you. You must come visit me, and soon. We must continue our conversation. I would like to know you better."

Margaret shared that desire.

"I promise you, Sister."

As Theodora left, it struck Margaret that stopping at Saint Alphonse that afternoon wasn't something that just happened. She was driving by, and simply turned into the parking lot without so much as a second thought. Odd happenstance.

It was as though someone else had been driving that afternoon.

Margaret kept her promise. She visited Theodora at her convent in the evenings, and the two walked around the grounds, talking, laughing, and just enjoying the new friendship that had grown from their encounter at Saint Alphonse.

On the fourth visit, Margaret told Theodora the whole story. Well, almost the whole story. Theodora sat quietly, listening, never interjecting, never judging, never so much as moving until Margaret had unburdened herself.

"You must think me awful," Margaret said as she wiped away a tear.

"Nonsense. I do have a question, though."

"What?"

"What is the thing you regret the most?"

Margaret stopped and looked at her. It was a minute before she answered.

"Not the part about loving him, because I did. I really did. And since his wife never knew, we hadn't hurt her."

"Okay."

"I guess the thing that really bothers me is that I never wanted it any other way."

"What do you mean?"

"I mean, well, there had been other guys, but I never really wanted to take the chance. I didn't really want to be tied down, I guess. The thing about Eric was that he already was tied down. So he was ..."

"Safe?" Theodora finished her sentence.

"Yes. Safe."

"And your regret?"

"I wonder sometimes if I wasn't using him."

"I see."

Maybe I am starting to see too, Margaret thought.

"You wanted love, but for some reason not a commitment to a man."

"Perhaps," said Margaret.

Then what was it I was looking for?

Chapter 17

Margaret knocked on the door frame of Sister Agnes's office. The door stood open.

"Come in, Margaret." Agnes was a sixty-something woman with large hips and thin legs. She wore the modern habit: a navy skirt with white blouse and large pectoral cross. Her salt and pepper hair had recently been subjected to a severe perm. She wore black-rimmed glasses that just screamed, "I am the prioress!"

Her office was spacious and overlooked the parking lot. Various certificates and diplomas hung from the walls and a large Hibiscus sat in one corner by the windows.

"Sit down, Margaret. Thank you for coming. Awful things happening, Margaret. Those poor parents."

Margaret simply nodded.

"We'll get to that in a moment. September will mark the end of your third year of temporary vows. I have spoken with our Sisters throughout your stay here. You have truly made a contribution. Sister Kathleen is especially fond of you, and is very complimentary toward your teaching. Theology seems to suit you."

"Yes, Sister. I do enjoy my studies."

Sister Agnes paused. For a minute, she said nothing.

Margaret had always felt a bit uncomfortable around Sister Agnes. There was a good reason for that: Agnes had never cared for Margaret. Margaret was too independent, too much inclined to go off in her own direction and sometimes she made judgments that were questionable.

Margaret was popular with the students and with the parents too. All of the sisters who were able showed up to support the school teams, but Margaret took it one step further. She served as the school's liaison to the Booster Club Board. Whenever the Booster Club cooked hot dogs or steaks or chicken breasts, Margaret was just as likely to be working the grill as the board members. She was also known to enjoy a beer or two with them. It was unorthodox, but quite effective in building bridges with the parents. Still, Agnes couldn't help feeling that it could lead to a lack of respect for Margaret's station in life.

Agnes was nothing if not brutally honest with herself. She knew that, at some level, her problem with Margaret was that Margaret was a beautiful woman. Agnes was not an attractive individual.

When she entered the convent, she knew that friends—and perhaps relatives—were thinking that she had done it because she couldn't nab a man—or because she preferred women. In fact, Agnes had no such concerns and her orientation was quite normal. She was not of a passionate nature, and the vow of chastity was never a problem. Her vocation was very real, and it galled her that some may have thought it to be anything other than what it was—a choice based on a true love of Christ.

In the final analysis, Sister Agnes was able to put aside her personal feelings and acknowledge that Margaret had made a valuable contribution to the order, and would continue to do so if she decided to make her final profession.

"Your thesis, if I recall, has to do with Augustine's view of evil. You've seen your share of that, I would venture, before coming to us. I suppose we are seeing it up close now at Saint Dominic's. Anyway, any feel for what you want to do come September?"

"I really don't know, Sister. I am sorry, but I can't say at this time."

"Do you wish to talk about it?"

"I love it here, Sister. It isn't that. The community has allowed me to grow, and I feel a very strong tie to everyone here. This has truly been the happiest five years of my life."

"But?"

"I am struggling to understand whether my reasons for coming are what they should have been."

"Well, for whatever reason, you are here. That tells me something. But you are right about one thing. This is not a decision to be made lightly. You know your options. I would hope that you are not entertaining notions of leaving us, although that certainly is one option. We can, and frequently do, extend the period of discernment for another three years.

"It's up to you. We want you if you want us. I honestly believe you are where you belong. However, only you can decide that. Pray, Sister Margaret. Keep your heart open to God's will, and stay close to him. He will allow the way to be made clear."

"Thank you, Sister."

"Well, perhaps the current horror at Saint Dominic's will put your choice into perspective. It seems I have a somewhat unorthodox request from the Sangamon County sheriff."

Margaret sat up straight. "What is it?"

"Sheriff Hargrove telephoned me earlier today. It seems he wants you back. Not permanently, but on loan, so to speak. He thinks you can be of use in finding the person responsible for these horrible crimes. The sheriff is always respectful when it comes to protocol, and I admire him for that. I told him that I had no objection, which leaves the decision to you. Brother Thomas can cover two of your classes, and surely someone among us has enough theology to cover the others. Your study halls are no problem. We have coaches who can spare some time. Any thoughts?"

Margaret didn't answer. She sat across from the older woman, biting nervously on her lower lip.

"Well," Agnes said, "he said for you to call him if you wish to offer your assistance. This afternoon, if possible. Just let me know so

I can make the arrangements here." She offered a yellow sticky note with a telephone number on it. "I might add that it would give me great comfort to know that you would be able to provide assistance, provided of course that there would be no threat to your well being."

"Thank you. I have his number, Sister."

Chapter 18

At four thirty, Margaret turned into the parking lot behind the county building and pulled into a visitor's parking space. She walked up and knocked at the rear entrance, where a matronly deputy met her.

"I'm Sister Margaret. I am here to see Sheriff Hargrove."

The woman, in her forties, looked like Dame Judith Dench in a serious role. She wore a corrections uniform, but Margaret did not recognize her. She pressed a button to release the door lock, spoke with someone upstairs on her walkie-talkie, and then stepped aside to allow Margaret to enter. No smile, no words, no class. But Margaret chalked it off to the clientele the woman was used to dealing with.

"I know the way," Margaret said.

"Mmph," the deputy said.

Margaret got a visitor's pass at the front window, and walked through the steel door into the detective division. Little had changed since she'd worked there. There were seven desks, four of which were occupied by detectives who were on the phone or filling out paperwork. A radio was playing "I'm in a Sad Mood Tonight" by Sam Cooke. The oldies station WQQL—Cool 101.9—was still the station of choice in the bullpen. Several of the detectives recognized her, smiled, and gave her a wave. As she approached the bank of offices against the back wall, she noticed a young, good-looking man in a pink shirt who wore a striped tie loosened at the collar. He was on the phone as he saw her approaching.

He was tall, a little over six feet in height, with black hair combed straight back, deep blue eyes set wide apart by the bridge of a Greek nose that was alarmingly close to being too big. A line from Byron came to mind: *One shade the more, one ray the less had half impaired the nameless grace.* Every particular of his physiognomy conspired to make him unattractive, but their combination worked to bring about quite the opposite effect. His black eyebrows were arched, and his lips were full and blushed. He had the faint suggestion of a dark mustache and sported a fashionable day's growth of facial hair.

The detective made eye contact, smiled, placed his hand over the phone and spoke over his shoulder to someone. "Chief? The psychic's here." Then he returned to his conversation.

Margaret's eyes flashed angrily at the remark. *A good-looking asshole is still an asshole.*

"Margaret?"

She looked away and saw the large figure of Ernie Jones approaching, his arms extended. Ernie's smile always made any day seem better. He enfolded her in an avuncular embrace that she reciprocated, and kissed her lightly on her forehead.

"You're too pretty to be a nun," he said, still with that smile.

"And you're still full of shit, but I love you for it!"

"Jim is in my office. We were expecting you. Come on in."

She glanced over her shoulder at Detective Smart-Ass and treated him to another look. He smiled. *What a cocky little shit,* she thought to herself.

Sheriff Hargrove stood to greet her, and then gave her a welcoming hug.

"Welcome back, Deputy."

"Once a cop, right?"

He smiled, and motioned for her to sit down.

"Thanks for coming, Margaret. We need all the help we can get."

Ernie shut the door, and walked over to his desk. "This case has been assigned to Detective Templeton, and you will be working closely with him on it. You, uh, met him on your way in." He smiled.

"Detective Smart-Ass out there on the phone?"

"He grows on you."

"So do warts."

"Sister, a little charity would be in order."

"This is me, Ernie. You wanted me back, you got me."

The door opened, and Templeton walked in.

"Ah, we were just talking about you, Detective. Sister Margaret, this is Bill Templeton."

"I'm the psychic you saw out front," Margaret said frostily, half-heartedly extending her hand.

"Nice cross."

"It wards off evil spirits."

"Well," Ernie said, "I know you two have a lot to talk about, but we have an autopsy report on the Corcoran girl." He held up a file folder, and set it back down. "She died of a broken neck. Death was probably instantaneous. Quick. Efficient. Deadly. No sign of sexual molestation. In fact the girl's hymen was still intact."

"In this day and age, not bad," said Templeton.

Margaret ignored him. She had the feeling she would be doing that a lot.

"So the nylons," asked Margaret, "had nothing to do with her death?"

"Apparently not," said Ernie.

"Then why?"

"Well, that's the sixty-four dollar question," said Hargrove. "And the Matheson boy died in the exact same way—although the autopsy hasn't happened, Tom Cross is willing to bet a week's pay on it. Broken neck, nylon tied around it, nylons used to bind him. And there's one more thing that is too interesting to be a coincidence."

"Okay?"

"Both corpses had one shoe on and one shoe off. In both instances, the other shoe was found at approximately a forty-five degree angle from the body, ten feet or so away. My gut tells me it was deliberately placed there."

"The scene was staged?"

"I suspect this guy is trying to make a point. To tell us something."

Detective Smart-Ass spoke up. "We can't find any connection between the two kids. Matheson was a Goth, three years younger, and definitely not in the same class any way you look at it. Corcoran was rich, popular, and going places."

"Do you know if they had any classes together or any other connection at school, Margaret?" Hargrove asked.

"None to my knowledge. He was a freshman. Quiet. Not very well liked. Kind of a sad kid, really. Alison was … Alison was very well liked and involved in all sorts of things at school."

She turned to Ernie. "Have you checked for other cases with a similar MO?"

Templeton answered, "Yes, and no luck. I have run it through ViCAP and NCIC. Nada. I have personally phoned Menard, Morgan, Macon, and Montgomery Counties. I was on the phone with Champaign when you came in a few moments ago."

"I was sensing that, of course." Frosty again. Templeton raised his eyes to heaven and gave a little smile.

"What about old cases?" Margaret asked. The three men looked at one another and said nothing.

"Bill?"

"Haven't looked yet."

"I can do that," said Margaret. "Point me to a computer before I leave."

"Great."

"I have talked with the kids who were with Matheson the night he died," said Templeton. "They last saw him when he left them at Qik N EZ on Monroe and Chatham. He was heading west on Washington

Street. His friends are interesting. They all have metal in their faces and God-knows-where-else."

"Did the Matheson boy?"

"Come to think of it," Hargrove said, "I didn't notice it at the murder scene, but he might have."

"Okay, how do you want to use me?" Margaret asked.

Jones answered. "You are there, at the school. We would like you to keep your eyes and ears open and help us conduct whatever interrogations we might need to conduct there. Also, whoever killed these kids knew them. So it could be one of their friends. Or …"

"A staff member?"

"We have to entertain all possibilities. Someone was able to get close to these kids. We want you to nose around. We'll need you to provide Detective Templeton with names so that he can run a check on them."

"You want the nuns too?"

Hargrove smiled. "Not at this point."

"Okay." She bit her lower lip. "So you are looking at a man for this?"

"Well, according to Mike Crowley at the FBI, they are."

"They're in this too?"

"The second case caught their eye. Officially, they're not involved since neither victim was taken out of state. But Mike has offered his assistance."

"Shit," said Templeton.

"I don't mind working with Crowley. I plan to make use of one of his profilers. This is our case, but I will use all the help I can get. Margaret, I would also like you to work with Detective Templeton, when possible, in the field. He is going in the morning to talk with Matheson's mother. Also, I want you to call and go out to the Corcorans and talk with them some more. Follow your instincts, the way you always did."

"Just don't go wailing on any suspects," Ernie said with a smile. "I am getting you a cell phone and … I will have a service weapon issued to you."

"Oh, that will go nicely with my crucifix."

"You can use the gun to ward off the killer, and the cross to keep Templeton at bay," said Ernie.

"Are you going to wear the cross while you're working?" asked Templeton.

"What's the matter, Bill?" asked Ernie. "You afraid you'll turn to dust?"

Margaret asked, "You are planning on attending the meeting at school this evening, aren't you Jim?"

"Yes."

"I will be there."

"Okay," said Hargrove, "any questions?"

None.

"Bill, step out a minute, will you?"

Templeton rose, nodded at Margaret, and then walked out the door, closing it behind him.

"He's a prodigy, Margaret," said Hargrove. "One of the best we have. You okay working with him?"

"As I said, he grows on you," added Ernie.

She waved off the question with a motion of her hand.

"Let's get started," she said,

"It really is good to see you back here," said Hargrove. "We've missed you."

In a very brief conversation, Margaret arranged to have Templeton pick her up at the convent the next morning. Then she sat at an empty desk and began to search the database. She typed "homicide," "nylon stockings," "strangulation," "broken neck," and ran a search. Twenty case files showed up. She printed them off. Then she went to Google, and again ran the search terms, adding "Springfield" and "Illinois."

The first item returned was an article dating back to 1994 from the *State Journal-Register*. "Who Killed Bonnie Easter?" The byline read

"Ted Baker." She clicked on it, only to find that it was not available without a fee. Then she tried the library website and went into the reference section. The SJ-R was listed there, and when she clicked on it she was prompted for her library card number. She opened her purse and took her library card out of her billfold. She typed it in, ran a search under bylines for "Ted Baker," and the article came up. She hit print and pulled the nine-page article from the printer and stapled it together.

The article was about a murder that had taken place in Springfield in April of 1974. A young girl named Bonnie Easter was found at the bottom of a ravine north of the State Fairgrounds, naked, her arms and legs bound with what turned out to be her own nylon stockings.

Bonnie Easter had been a junior at Saint Dominic's High School.

She read down the list of cases her search had brought up from the archives. No mention of "Easter" appeared.

She returned to the archives and typed in "Easter," selected a drop down date of "Before 1980," and hit search.

Nothing.

Then she entered a wildcard—an asterisk—and selected "Before 1980."

Thirty-seven cases came up.

Among them she noticed the misspelled name "Ester," and clicked on it.

Two words appeared on the screen: *File missing.*

"Detective?"

Templeton looked up from his desk. He conveyed with a look the degree to which her presence thrilled him.

"Would you check something for me?"

"What?"

"Would you check with city and see if they have any files on a 'Bonnie Easter,' who was murdered back in 1974. See if we can get a copy of their case file, if they have one?"

Templeton wrote it down.

"Easter. No problem," he said. "You want me to bring it tomorrow?"

"Actually, I would appreciate it if you would have them fax it to me." She wrote down a fax number on a sticky note and pushed it toward him.

"Sure. No problem. Is there anything else I can do for you?"

"That will be fine, for now," she said. "I've got some reading to do at the public library."

Margaret turned and started to walk away.

"Sister?"

Margaret turned back to look at him.

"Don't forget. I need names."

"Names?"

"Teachers, staff members, everybody at Saint Dominic's."

Could it be someone that close?

She nodded, and walked out of the office.

Microfiche was once state of the art, but when you are used to the lightning speed of the Internet it seems that you have stepped back into the Stone Age.

Margaret sat turning a crank at the public library, viewing pages of ads and headlines and obituaries as they flashed by in her search for the articles about the Easter murder. The newspaper article she had printed off earlier contained no photographs; for those, you had to resort to the library and microfiche was the only game in town for papers going back that far.

Margaret felt at home in a library. In Jacksonville, the library was a block from the jail. On a summer's day, she would hop out of bed, go down and help her dad get breakfast ready, and as soon as they were back from Mass she would head down the street. The library was built in 1905 with money donated by Andrew Carnegie, whose beneficence to the tune of $40 million made libraries a reality for more than a thousand communities like Jacksonville from 1870 until 1917. It was a two-story stone structure with a wide stairway with steps that, after the passage of the ADA, would require a workaround in order to be compliant.

After a lady at the library told her about Mr. Carnegie, Margaret started including him in her nightly prayers.

The stacks on the second floor stood on glass floors. This wasn't uncommon in libraries built near the turn of the century, because the stacks in many were not adequately lighted. Glass floors allowed light from the lower floors through, and also helped reflect the light from the windows. In summer, they were cool. Margaret sometimes took off her shoes to walk barefoot as she rummaged through the stacks. It was her special world.

Here she fed her imagination with stories by Hemingway, Stevenson, Melville, Tolstoy, Dostoyevsky, and dozens of other writers. She would pick a book, check it out, and then return to the jail, climb up the tree in the side yard, nestle herself between two accommodating branches, and read until the book was finished.

Then she would hop down and go get another one.

Thus, by the time she reached high school, her erudition in any number of subjects rivaled if not surpassed that of most college graduates.

The library had been her window to a world far more expansive than the county jail yard in Jacksonville, Illinois.

There it was. The squeaking stopped when Margaret quit turning the crank.

A black-and-white photo, made grainier by the microfiche reproduction, showed what appeared to be a body, covered by a sheet, over which stood three serious-looking men. The picture identified them as Sheriff Durward Long, police chief Abraham Tomiczek and Ed Lacey, Sangamon County coroner.

There was a shoe, barely visible, but at an oblique angle from the body, behind the Coroner, about ten feet away.

She hit the print button, and then paged through and printed the entire article. She paged through for follow-up articles, printed them, and then placed the rolls back in their boxes.

Chapter 19

The parents' meeting lasted for more than two hours. Joe Santini was masterful in his ability to quiet the concerns of the more vocal parents. Sheriff Hargrove spoke candidly about the investigation, and how he was going to keep Sister Kathleen informed every step of the way. He encouraged the parents to talk to their kids and to let them know how important it was to inform his office of any little thing, no matter how seemingly unimportant, that might lead to the apprehension of the killer. He also advised parents and kids to be extra watchful.

"Know where your kids are at all times. Tell them not to go anywhere by themselves. Actually, for the time being—at least until we know more than we know now—tell them to go as few places as possible unless there are a lot of people there."

Hargrove mentioned that Sister Margaret, who was sitting in the front row, was a former deputy of his and that she had agreed to serve as a resource person. Several parents stared at her, and smiled. She wanted so badly to say, "I'm the psychic."

Later, Margaret sat in the common room at her residence near the computer, file folders and faxes spread out on the table.

The file from the police department consisted of only three pages. A note attached to the file indicated that the original case file had been stored in the "vault" because it was so bulky. The vault was in the basement of the old police station, which was subject to infestation and flooding. Records were in such a deplorable condition when the station moved to its current location in 1986 that they could not be handled and were destroyed.

Nothing had been microfilmed, save for a few pages of the autopsy and a list of persons who were interviewed.

The complaint, typed on an IBM Selectric, was filed at 7:00 AM on the morning after Bonnie disappeared by George Easter, Bonnie's father.

Bonnie's time card at the restaurant had been checked and she had clocked out at 8:26 PM

At the bottom of the report, it was noted that on the following Sunday the department was notified by the sheriff's office that the girl had been found dead in an unincorporated area not far from the fairgrounds.

Bonnie Easter had suffered a severe but not fatal blow to the back of her head and had been strangled with her own nylon stocking. She had had sex before she died. The faded autopsy report indicated that she had done so several times, with every orifice implicated in the activity. Unfortunately, DNA was a pipe dream in 1974 so there was no way of knowing with whom, or how many.

She turned to the *State Journal-Register* article that Ted Baker wrote in 1994. He had done meticulous research, interviewing anyone who had any connection with the case that he could locate; anyone who hadn't died, that is. As she read she cross-matched names against the paltry information in the case file that had arrived at the fax when she got home.

She checked the web site for the *SJ-R* and couldn't find Baker's name among the writers or editors in the "about us" link. She made a note on a legal pad to see where he had gone.

Bonnie had been a junior at Saint D's at the time of her death. Her father, George, was a fireman who had been promoted to captain and was in charge of public relations. Her mother had died when Bonnie was eleven years old. The article mentioned a sister named Irene who had graduated from Saint D's in 1969, but who apparently had since died in an automobile accident in Tennessee. There was also mention of a younger brother, although nothing was said of his whereabouts or even his name.

Margaret wrote, "brother?" on the legal pad and underlined it.

On the day she disappeared, Bonnie had left work at Wheeler's restaurant on South Grand and was last seen walking north on Eighth Street by another waitress whose boyfriend honked at her as they drove past the intersection. It was on a Thursday.

The only suspect ever seriously considered was twenty-eight-year-old Anthony Garcia, a dishwasher at the restaurant. Several of the waitresses told police that Garcia was always coming on to them. He had a temper and was given to cussing out the girls who would turn him down—as all of them apparently had at one time or another. "Creepy" was the word one of them used to describe him.

Garcia, it turned out, had a rap sheet that included assault, criminal trespass, and a variety of other transgressions that had landed him, at one time or another, in the county lockup.

Garcia was arrested, but police couldn't tie him to Bonnie any time after she left work. There was no evidence tying him to the body, so they eventually released him. The newspaper said that Garcia was serving a life sentence for kidnapping, rape and murder in a Wisconsin federal penitentiary at the time the article was written.

Baker's article indicated that the chief of police, Abraham Tomiczek, refused to talk with him. Tomiczek, a Polish immigrant, was quoted as saying, "Ain't gonna do nobody no good to revive that old horse. So I got no comment." *Quaint.* She did a quick calculation and determined that Tomiczek, who was said to be sixty-two when the article was written, would be in his late seventies now, if he were alive at all.

She wrote "Tomiczek?" on the legal pad.

The list of persons who were mentioned in the article, except for Tomiczek, were said to have died before the article was published.

They included Edward Jenkins, chief of the Springfield Fire Department in 1974. He died in 1984. Heart attack.

A key figure in the investigation, State's Attorney Gerald Brown, died nine months following the murder. He was found sitting in his Oldsmobile on Rutledge Street, north of Madison, one morning at four AM by a passing squad car.

Brown's car was running. There was a hose attached to the tailpipe that snaked around and into the rear window.

Brown's wasn't the only suicide. A year after Bonnie's death, George Easter was found hanging by the neck in a cabin he owned along the Sangamon River near Riverton.

Where were the kids?

Also mentioned was one Salvatore "Sally" Rigali, who was a family friend.

Rigali. The son of Springfield's famous godfather, who had died not long before Bonnie disappeared. Rigali's son had since joined his father in the family crypt at Oak Ridge, as Margaret recalled.

Another name jumped off the page.

Doctor John Corcoran, a well-respected Springfield physician, was interviewed because he was a "close family friend."

A philanthropist-physician, a mobster and a fireman? Not your usual social set, Margaret thought.

According to Baker, Corcoran died of cancer seven years after the murder.

"Who killed Bonnie Easter?" the article concluded, "Barring a deathbed confession, in all likelihood the murderer will have escaped his due punishment—at least in this life."

Margaret checked the police report's list of persons who had been interviewed and compared them with the names that Baker had mentioned in the article. She saw all the names mentioned in the article—except one.

There was no mention of Doctor Corcoran in the police report.

She had to find out where Ted Baker was now.

"Doctor Corcoran? Yes, I know who he was." Theodora was knitting a baby sweater. "For my grand niece," she said, holding it up for Margaret to see.

"That's adorable."

"So is she. Why do you ask about him?"

"Just curious. I know he donated the infirmary years back and gave a lot of money to the Church. He also treated the students here at the school."

"Why do you ask?" Theodora was quick to put people back on track. Always to the point.

"He is mentioned in an article I just read; an article about the murder of a Saint Dominic's student back in 1974. He was a family friend."

"Bonnie Easter." It wasn't a question.

"Yes."

"Tragic. I was serving in Jacksonville then, but I know how much it upset the sisters here at the time."

"So you didn't know the girl?"

"No. But the sisters told me that her fate was not surprising. She was always getting into trouble."

The newspaper article from the library quoted one of the sisters at the school as saying that they had no comment concerning the child. Margaret found that tantalizing. If you can't say something nice, say nothing at all.

"Did you have an opinion about him?"

"Is this the policewoman asking?"

"Yes. I guess it is."

"In that case, you know how I hate casting aspersions on anyone, let alone someone who has departed this earth."

Margaret bit at the cuticle of her index finger, something she did when she was nervous.

"You must stop doing that, Margaret."

Margaret, duly chastised, put her hand down on her lap. "Yes, mother."

"Sister Carmelita does not have such qualms, I might add," Theodora added without missing a stitch. "Before she retired, she was a nurse. She knew the good doctor quite well. I am certain she would have no reservations about sharing her opinions with you. God love her."

Theodora gave Margaret a mischievous smile.

Chapter 20

"So, Sheriff Pat Donovan was your father?"

Templeton's question was the first thing he said, other than, "Good morning," since he picked Margaret up from the parking lot.

She looked down at the seat beside her. There sat a wallet containing a badge, a cell phone, and a holstered Glock model 22. She picked up the badge and the cell phone but left the gun on the seat.

"You can keep the Glock. I might be tempted to shoot a couple of the guys in study hall, and you wouldn't want to be responsible for that."

Templeton didn't even smile. "Suit yourself."

"Why do you ask about my father? Were you acquainted with him?"

"No. But my dad knew him. I grew up in Chapin. Your dad hauled him in once on a DUI. Funny thing, though—Pop said he was a good guy."

"My dad had that effect on people. Even the ones he arrested."

"Guess the guy he pistol whipped didn't feel that way though."

Margaret looked at Templeton for the first time since getting in the car. *Don't let him get to you. He thrives on that.*

Margaret noticed a card clipped to the driver's side visor that had Reinhold Niebuhr's prayer printed on it: *Lord, grant me the Serenity to accept the things I cannot change, the Courage to change the things I can, and the Wisdom to know the difference.* Either Templeton was prayerful, or he was an alcoholic. He didn't strike her as the prayerful type.

As for the pistol whipping, Margaret knew the story all too well. Sometime in 1968, before Margaret was born and a few months after her dad had been elected county sheriff the first time, a Cadillac carrying four thugs from East Saint Louis was pulled over for speeding on Highway 67 south of Jacksonville. Her dad's was the first car to arrive after the deputy called for backup.

The driver wore a pimp hat and a lot of jewelry. Her dad was known to use the "N" word, even though he treated his black prisoners with respect. It is one thing to use *nigger* to denote a class, quite another when looking a human being in the eye. Her dad respected humanity, even though his upbringing leaked through every now and then in stereotypes.

The Jacksonville *Journal-Courier* reported that the driver of the car had smarted off to her dad, so he'd pulled his pistol and whacked him upside the head. The newspaper quoted him later as saying that the guy had resisted arrest and that he hoped that this would send a "message" to people like him to avoid Morgan County.

By "people like him," her dad hadn't meant black people. He had meant drug dealers. After the men were taken into custody, deputies found a box stuffed with heroin in the trunk along with several .357 Magnums and five boxes of ammunition. Three of the men, including the driver, had warrants for assault with a deadly weapon outstanding. Not a model citizen among them.

A few liberal professors from the two local colleges wrote nasty letters condemning the sheriff for his brutal treatment of the man, but the voters of Morgan County paid no attention whatsoever to their ranting. Pat Donovan was the kind of man they wanted guarding their back doors at night.

Her dad explained to her later that the man had taken a swing at him after getting out of the car, and that he had actually brought the man down with a thwack from his nightstick, not his pistol.

"But what the hell," he said. "The word got out not to screw with the sheriff in Morgan County, so I left it alone. If my reputation makes it possible not to have to use my gun, that's okay with me."

Still, Margaret always worried about the other edge of the sword: someone might come looking for him *because* of his reputation. She couldn't bear to lose her dad. He was her world.

"It wasn't quite like that," she said to Templeton. "But he didn't take any crap off people, that's for sure"

"So, is he why you became a cop?"

"Do I know you?"

He looked over at her. "What do you mean?"

"Did something I say imply that I wanted to share my life story with you?"

"Sorry."

He stepped on the gas as they passed Veterans Parkway on Old Jack Road.

"It's going to be a long day," he said.

"Sister, it's good to see you again." Pete Corcoran shook her hand and smiled. He looked more rested and better groomed.

His wife Shelley, on the other hand, looked like hell. Understandable. She shook Margaret's hand and then immediately sat down on the sofa.

"This is Detective Templeton of the sheriff's office, Doctor Corcoran. We are sorry to bother you at this time."

"*We?*" Peter Corcoran looked curiously at Margaret. "Sister, in what capacity are you serving, exactly?"

Templeton answered. "Uh … the truth is, Sister Margaret is—or, rather, before she entered the convent, was—a deputy sheriff. Sheriff Hargrove has asked her to assist in the investigation, given her close connection to the school."

"So, you requested this interview as a representative of the sheriff's office?" His eyes flashed.

"Forgive me, Doctor. It didn't occur to me when I phoned you yesterday, but yes, this interview was requested by the sheriff."

Shelley stood up. "I am leaving," she said, shooting Margaret a look that bespoke her grief and her animosity at having been interrupted in her mourning under seemingly false pretenses. She stomped out of the living room.

"I'm very sorry, Doctor. But we are trying to get any information we can on Alison's murderer. You may have some vital information that you yourself are not aware of."

"I suppose you want to know if I molested my daughter." Corcoran's anger was palpable.

"Did you?" Templeton asked, unmoved by the doctor's reaction.

Corcoran stood up. His face turned beet red. The situation was deteriorating quickly.

"Doctor," said Margaret, "that's precisely the kind of question that law enforcement needs answered to rule you out as a suspect." She couldn't believe she was stepping in to save Templeton, although she had to admire him for being unruffled by the situation as it was unfolding.

"Out of my house, *now*." He walked toward the front door leaving them on the sofa.

"Bonnie Easter. Did you ever know of a girl named Bonnie Easter, Doctor?" Margaret called out to him. He stopped and turned around. He took several breaths and then seemed to recompose himself.

"That was a girl who was murdered when I was a kid. What does she have to do with this?"

"We don't know for sure, Doctor. But she was killed in much the same way your daughter was. We are looking into a possible connection. Did you know her?"

"No. But my father may have known her. I think I met her father on one or two occasions. He was a policeman, or maybe a fireman, as I recall."

"Do you remember where you met him?" Margaret kept pushing the envelope.

"I think my father introduced me to him once at the State Fair. Dad ran into him when we went to the fire prevention building."

"Well, we're terribly sorry to have bothered you, Doctor." Margaret stood, and signaled Templeton to do the same. "We'll be leaving now."

"If Jim has any more questions, tell him to call my lawyer," said Corcoran.

"Oh, and Sister? I did not molest my daughter. I loved her. She was the only child I ever had or ever will."

A tear slid down his left cheek. Margaret had to fight back one of her own.

"What the fuck was that?" Templeton asked as they were getting back into his car.

"A newspaper article about the murder in 1974 of Bonnie Easter mentioned that Corcoran's father was interviewed during the investigation and that he was a family friend. I had expected him to say they met at the country club or at a cook out at one or the other of their homes. But a family friend that you 'run into' at the fair? Something's out of whack."

"You're assuming that some girl's murder thirty years ago had anything at all to do with this? That's a great big assumption if you ask me. Even given the apparent similarities. Maybe you aren't the only one in Springfield who likes to read old newspaper articles."

She hadn't asked him. But he had a very good point.

Angela Connors had been drinking. Heavily.

She was in her late forties and forty to fifty pounds overweight, and her hair was stringy. She smoked one cigarette after another and the apartment smelled of tobacco and cheap whisky.

Margaret wasn't sure anything would come of this interview. But since they were here, she forged ahead.

"We are so sorry for your loss, Mrs. Connors." Mariska Hargitay again. But Margaret really was sorry for this woman. Angela wore no makeup and her face was dirty and streaked with dry tears.

"Thank you," she slurred.

"Mrs. Connors," Templeton said, "do you know of anyone who would have wanted to hurt your son?"

"No. He had some strange friends. Other kids who felt like shit, like he did. He was into that Goth stuff, and I rode him about it. The piercings, the tattoos, the black hair and clothes. But none of those kids were bad kids. Just messed up like my Billy."

"Messed up how?" Templeton asked.

Angela looked at them blankly. "Take a good look at me, detective. Take a good look at my life. Can you blame him?"

Margaret reached over and touched the woman's arm. Angela gave her a strange look. Another human being hadn't touched her warmly for a long time—unless it was in the process of removing her underwear. Sex for some tenderness—that was a trade-off she had been making for years, but one that left her with nothing to show for it but an empty apartment and an empty heart.

"Mrs. Connors, was Billy having any trouble with anyone at school? With any teachers or any of the kids?"

"He didn't talk much to me, you know. But I know that those kids weren't nice to him. Stuck up bunch of shits with their fancy cars and rich parents. He wasn't good enough for them. I knew he shouldn't have gone to that school."

Margaret looked at the surroundings. The Lincoln Apartments were more than forty years old, and this apartment hadn't been updated for at least twenty years.

"If I may ask, how did you happen to send Billy to Saint Dominic's?"

"You mean, how could someone like me afford to send my son to that hoity-toity school, don't you?"

Margaret didn't answer. That was exactly what she meant.

"My mother left a trust fund for him to be used at that school. Last thing she did before she died."

"Was she an alum?"

"No. My dad was. Played football there in the early fifties. He got a scholarship to Notre Dame. He lived for that damned school."

"Really? What was your father's name?"

Angela took a drag off of her cigarette, and then downed the rest of the whisky.

"Jerry Brown. Lot of good it did him. He killed himself when I was eighteen years old. Took my mother's life too, eventually. And mine, truth be told."

Margaret's eyes lit up.

"Mrs. Connors? Do you mean Gerald Brown? The Gerald Brown who was once the State's Attorney?"

"One and the same." She held the bottle up. "Drink, Sister?"

"Alison Corcoran was the granddaughter of John Michael Corcoran. Billy Matheson was the grandson of the State's Attorney. Both of those guys figured, somehow, in the Easter killing. This can't be a coincidence." Margaret was fired up.

"Okay. I have to admit, that is too weird for words. So what are you suggesting? That whoever killed the Easter kid has come back and now is cleaning up the grandkids? Hell, the killer would have to be, what, in his sixties now maybe?"

"No. It's someone else. What if someone knows who killed her? Or at least blames those men and is now trying to get back at them?"

"But who?"

"I don't know. But I am concerned about something else right now."

"What?"

"There were more names in that case file. What if someone else's grandchild is on this guy's list?"

Chapter 21

It was a beautiful morning and Theresa Madison had her whole life ahead of her.

She kicked the ball as hard as she could and watched the goalie stop it before it went into the net.

"Damn," she said as the goalie kicked the ball back into play. She charged back into the fray, intent on getting another goal before the period ended.

At last the ball was kicked back to her. She watched as the goalie's body weight shifted slightly to the right, and kicked as hard as she could to the goalie's left. The goalie tried to shift back, but the ball blew past her as she fell to the ground.

Goal.

The whistle blew and a substitute came in for Theresa. She went back and sat on the bench, took a swig of water, and wiped her face with a towel.

"Nice job, Madison," the PE coach said. "I never could figure out why you didn't play on the team. You could have made a difference."

"Not my thing," she said as she reached for her water bottle.

"For not being your thing, you're sure a natural," the coach said.

Theresa had no intention of being a jock. Ever. It was bad enough having to suffer through PE class three times a week.

She was tall and athletic with the figure and face of a cover girl. Her shoulder-length hair was naturally auburn, now bleached blonde and tied back in a ponytail. Her eyes were the color of a crystal clear spring. She was—as Jeremy Mathers, captain of the football team and one of her many failed suitors once said—"drop-dead gorgeous."

But she didn't hang with jocks or cheerleaders. Her life was in her books. She got off on calculus and chemistry and biology. Her high came from solving for *x*, from dissecting animals to see what they were made of, and from organic chemistry.

Her father, a manager at Chase Bank, and her mother, a self-described homemaker ("and damned proud of it!"), had one other child, a boy, who was normal in every way but nowhere near as focused or as certain of where he wanted to be in his life. Theresa was driven.

"She was born with a plan," her father always said.

The only goal that mattered in her life was to make it to medical school—hopefully SIU. She had been accepted at the University of Illinois. She had four years of college to go, and competitive sports were not going to be a part of her experience.

Getting into medical school would take all of her time and energy.

It was just a matter of time.

At ten minutes before the hour, the coach blew his whistle and the kids started their trek back from the soccer field to the showers on the first floor of City High School.

The coach and several of the girls waved at him as they walked back to the school.

He had been watching Theresa the whole time from behind the fence. It was like seeing a ghost. This one was special. It wouldn't be long now.

It was just a matter of time.

Chapter 22

Sister Martha Grenoble was past retirement age, but refused to sit back and let people "wait on her." She had come to the Mother House from her last assignment in Crystal Lake, Illinois, two years earlier. Her entire forty-seven years of service had been in parish schools served by the Order, as teacher, then principal, and finally as librarian. "A busy mind wards off the clouds of dismay in later life," she was fond of saying. Statistics were with her on that one. Nuns with an active mental life, as a class, have a lower incidence of Alzheimer's. At seventy-eight years of age, Martha was as sharp as she had been at twenty-four.

She sat at her desk in the Alumni Office doing address changes in Excel when Margaret knocked at the door. Martha looked over her glasses. "Do come in," she said.

"Sister, I need your help."

"Well, I will help if I can."

"I think you can. I have a list of names here. Can you check the files to see if any of them have any connection to the school, or if they might have grandchildren in school now? It is urgent."

"Urgent? Oh my! I understand you are back with the sheriff's department now." She brightened. "You think one of our alums is the perp?"

Margaret had to stifle herself. Obviously Sister Martha watched too much *Law & Order*.

"No. We suspect a link between the victims and their grandparents."

Margaret looked to her right and then to her left for dramatic effect, then spoke in almost a whisper.

"Now please, Sister, this is in strictest confidence!" She knew that would get to her. It did.

"Oh, you can count on me. Yes sir-ee. These lips are zipped! I will do a name match against graduates and donors and friends of the school. How far back?"

"As far back as you can, but focus on the sixties and seventies. Let me know the minute you find anything? Call this cell phone number."

"Ten four!"

Margaret had made Sister Martha's day.

She didn't see him until she walked out of the door. She ran right into him. The collision knocked her back a bit, causing her to drop the stack of file folders she had in her hand, but the impact didn't faze Bill Pickering. It was like hitting a wall. He stood there without saying a word. His eyes were frightening somehow; they were a translucent green, appearing at once vacant and yet deep. Up close there was something that drew you into them.

"Oh, dear!" Margaret said, catching her breath. "I am so sorry, Mr. Pickering."

For what seemed like an eternity, Pickering didn't say a word. Then, finally, he said, "You need to watch where you're going."

"Yes, of course. Sorry." Margaret bent down and picked up the folders and replaced the scattered contents. To her surprise, he reached down and picked up a notebook that she had been carrying and handed it to her.

She looked at the shiny notebook cover as he held it out, and carefully took it from him and laid it on top of the file folders. She wondered how long he had been standing outside of the Alumni Office. Had he seen the file that was on top of the stack she was carrying?

It was his personnel file.

Chapter 23

"For Pete's sake, hurry along Clarence." Sister Carmelita was becoming impatient with her companion. "I'm older than you are, for heaven's sake."

"Only by minutes. Your disposition should improve with age, not deteriorate."

"Never mind my disposition. They're waiting. Can't you hear them?"

The sound of high-pitched barking could be heard down the hall of the retirees' home. The two nuns rounded the corner and saw two grey Shi Tzus who were jumping and yapping with anticipation of their visit from behind the doggie door.

One of the nurses at the infirmary had explained to the prioress that pets had a documented impact on the long-term health of older persons. The convent, with its increasingly older population, would greatly benefit from having one or two animals for the sisters to enjoy.

Clarence and Carmelita, both in their eighties, frequently behaved as though the dogs were theirs and theirs alone. They brightened as they saw the animals, and Carmelita held up two leashes and a bright play toy.

"There are my babies."

"Your babies? I'm here too," Clarence said huffily.

"I'm sure they are thrilled beyond belief! Come now, little ones."

Carmelita and Clarence were frequently seen walking the two animals around the grounds. The other sisters were indignant when they went to take the dogs, only to find that Carmelita and Clarence had beaten them to it.

Sister Kathleen had a story about the two and their dog walking that the parent of a freshman had shared with her. It seems the girl was sitting in study hall one afternoon when Sister Kathleen announced that no one was to leave their classrooms because the city police were bringing dogs in to sniff the lockers. Random locker searches had been protocol for several years now. After the announcement, the freshman girl happened to look out the window and see Carmelita and Clarence with Elmer and Elise—names chosen by Carmelita for the two creatures—tugging at their leashes. They seemed to be headed toward the main building.

"I can't believe it!" the freshman said to the girl sitting next to her. "Those nuns have trained those little shits to sniff for weed!"

Now the two nuns were walking across the campus with Elmer and Elise when Margaret saw them. It was a perfect opportunity to follow up on Sister Theodora's suggestion.

"Sister Carmelita?"

Carmelita stopped. "What?"

"Sister, may I have a few moments of your time? "

"In case you haven't noticed, I'm busy right now. Make an appointment."

"I would, Sister. But this is terribly important."

Carmelita handed the leash that was attached to Elmer to Clarence. "Think you can manage not to lose them both?"

"Go soak your head," said Clarence. Carmelita turned to Margaret.

"I see you've opted for a more conventional habit today," she said. "Okay. What's so important that it couldn't wait?"

"Come; sit with me for a minute." Margaret pointed to the concrete bench. Carmelita looked put out, but walked over and sat.

"Sister Theodora said you might be able to help me."

"Theodora? I thought she knew everything."

"Ahem. Sister, I understand you were a nurse in the infirmary."

"Yes. For many years. So?"

"Did you know Doctor John Corcoran?"

"Sure did."

"Sister, you may have heard that I am assisting the sheriff with the investigation into the two deaths recently."

Carmelita blessed herself. "Those poor children."

"Yes. Exactly. You know one of them was Doctor Corcoran's granddaughter?"

"Yes. But he's been dead for years now. What do you need to know about him?"

"What was your impression of the man?"

"Salt of the earth," Carmelita said. End of story.

Margaret had to be tactful. Carmelita wasn't about to spill her guts to her that easily. She didn't know her well enough. She tried a different tack.

"Sister, we have information to the effect that Doctor Corcoran was a friend of the family of a young girl from Saint Dominic's who was murdered thirty years ago. It is critical that we learn all we can because it may have a bearing on the murders we are investigating now. Sister Theodora said you were very knowledgeable, that you could maintain strictest confidence, and that you would be most willing to provide us with any impressions you might have."

She fudged a bit.

"She did, did she?"

"Yes. Can you tell me anything?"

The older woman thought for a moment before speaking.

"If you ask me, I suspect the good doctor had a hard time keeping that thing of his in his pants."

Margaret had to steady herself on the bench. "Oh?"

"Rumor has it—not that I ever listen to that kind of thing—that he still made house calls if the patient was female, good looking and open to treatment. If you know what I mean. Oh, he was a good-looking sucker, no doubt about it. He'd look at you with those green eyes, and I don't mind saying he made my heart flutter a time or two." She chuckled. "I suspect the good doctor may have had designs on me. Thank goodness the habit covered everything in those days. I was a looker when I was young, don't you know!"

"I'm sure you were. Sister, did you ever notice anything unusual in the doctor's behavior around the students."

Carmelita grew quiet for a moment. The question clearly bothered her.

"I insisted on being present whenever a doctor, any doctor, examined those girls. But the good doctor thought he owned the place, just because he donated the infirmary. In a way, I suppose he did. He wanted me to leave him alone with one of the girls once, and I refused. He stormed off. Next thing I know, the prioress calls me in and reads me the riot act for 'interfering' in Doctor Corcoran's treatment of the patients. So, from then on, I did as I was told. When he asked me to leave, I left."

"Do you really think he was doing things he shouldn't have been?"

"I prayed that he wasn't. But then one afternoon I walked in on him and one of the girls. I didn't know he was making rounds. Surprised the hell out of them. What I saw I couldn't put into words. He collared me later and warned me not to mention it."

"Did you do as he asked?"

"Absolutely not. I went straight to the prioress."

"What did she do?"

"She assured me she would talk with the doctor."

Talk with the doctor? How about calling the police?

"I guess times were different," Carmelita added, her mood softening for the first time since Margaret began speaking with her. For a moment, Margaret thought she detected a tear starting to form. "Not a day goes by I don't pray for that little girl I saw him with. I don't think Mother Beatrice did a damned thing. God rest her soul."

Margaret patted her hand. "I see. I am sorry to have bothered you, Sister. I am grateful for your time."

"That Easter girl? That's who you are talking about, right?"

"Yes."

"She was a townie. The girls who stayed in the infirmary were our residents. You knew that? We used to be a residential school."

"Yes."

"That girl was trouble, may she rest in peace. God forgive me, but the child was asking for trouble all along."

"Mind if I join you?"

Brother Tom stood at the table where Margaret sat in the cafeteria. She smiled, and motioned for him to sit down. She was half-heartedly working on a sloppy joe that she had picked up for lunch.

"Congratulations. I hear you are pulling double duty now." He put a napkin on his lap and opened a carton of chocolate milk.

"Thanks for covering my classes."

"Oh, no problem. I have to tell you though: the boys in class aren't any too thrilled."

She smiled. "Well, I'll bet the girls are going gaga."

"In my dreams. You enjoy being back on the job?"

"You know, it's funny. In some ways, it feels as though I never left."

"You were good at it."

"I don't know about that, but it is like slipping on a comfortable pair of old shoes. They still fit, you know?"

Tom took a bite of his sub sandwich. "Well, if you need anything, let me know."

Margaret noticed that Tom's hands were shaking slightly. He saw her looking, and self-consciously wiped his mouth and then looked down at his sandwich.

"Taking my classes for a while is plenty. I can't thank you enough."

For a few minutes they simply ate in silence. She looked down at the file folders on the table. She had extracted the social security numbers, dates of birth, names and all known addresses and had faxed them to the sheriff's office for background checks. Tom's file was on the bottom and was sticking out a bit. She subtly moved the pile so that his name didn't show.

"Tom, you once told me you were in the service."

"Yes. I served in Desert Storm. I was a Ranger."

"I take it that doesn't mean putting out forest fires."

He laughed. "Oil fires maybe. No. Rangers are the guys they send where no one else wants to go. A lot of times they don't come back."

He took a drink from the milk carton. His arm seemed to tremble. He set the carton down quickly and placed his hands in his lap.

"Interesting," Margaret said. "How does one go from that to being a religious?"

"How does one go from that and not become religious?" He smiled. "I found the Lord Jesus in Iraq during the Mother of All Wars. You see a few people get their faces blown off and you start thinking. You familiar with Hieronymus Bosch?"

Margaret brought to mind the horrid images set to canvas by the fifteenth-century ultra-religious Dutch artist.

"Yes. *The Garden of Earthly Delights*, I think, is the one that comes to mind."

"A triptych. Perfect example. Many of the images of hell came from the experience of warfare after the introduction of gunpowder. Europeans knew it well. Sadly, most of the killing was over religion. War provided a tactile image of hell. Although hell is really more frightening than that."

"More frightening than war?"

"Isolation is much more horrifying," Tom said. Margaret knew exactly what he was talking about.

"Hello," Sister Kathleen provided a much-needed interruption. She sat next to Tom. "Am I interrupting anything?"

"Margaret and I were planning an illicit rendezvous after vespers," Tom said.

"Well, you wouldn't be the only ones."

They both looked at her curiously.

"Apparently, our two novices were seen kissing in the hall this morning. It wasn't a sisterly kiss, but one of those deep, tongue-thrashing ones. Mother is busy now explaining why the convent may not be the best place for them."

The two rosy-cheeked novices, Margaret thought to herself.

"Well, two down—nun to go," said Tom. Kathleen rolled her eyes.

"I'm just saying, you girls need to be more careful recruiting," said Tom. "The brothers never pass out pamphlets in gay bars."

Margaret laughed. Kathleen did too, finally.

"And now I get to take your theology classes, on top of everything else," said Kathleen.

"Why?" Margaret asked.

Tom set his milk down. "I have some personal business I have to take care of," he said. "I am sorry. I will have to be gone for a few days."

"Perhaps I can take one of them back," said Margaret.

"Nonsense," Kathleen said. "I think I can handle it for a few days. I studied theology, too, you know!"

"I'm sure it will be an education," said Tom.

"For who?" said Kathleen.

"Whom," said Tom. "You're slipping."

They all laughed.

"Doctor Corcoran just called. The funeral is going to be Friday," Kathleen said.

Margaret put down her napkin. "Oh, dear. I'm not looking forward to that."

"Or to the next one. I haven't heard yet, but I am assuming it will be early next week. Have you heard?"

"No," Margaret said. "But I would imagine the autopsy is being done today."

"We were going to close Friday. That was before we knew there would be another funeral. Graduation's set, and I have only one day to work with. So, it looks like school will be held, and we will just excuse the students who want to go."

Margaret saw a girl walking from the cafeteria line looking for a table. It was the girl she saw crying shortly after the announcement of Billy's death.

"Sister Kathleen, do you know that girl?" Margaret asked. "The one walking over to the window." They watched as she passed several tables with girls seated at them and found one where there was no one.

"Erin Mosby. Senior. Quiet girl. Good student. She's on scholarship. A bit of a loner."

"Would you excuse me?" Margaret said, picking up her tray.

"Don't forget to meet me after evening prayer," Brother Tom said.

"In your dreams, Thomas. In your dreams."

Chapter 24

The county-issued cell phone rang as Margaret emptied her tray and placed it on top of the trash receptacle.

"Sister Margaret."

"This is Sister Martha."

"Yes, Sister. Did you find anything?"

"I'm sorry to say that I didn't. Other than Corcoran and Brown, none of the names you gave me track to any of our donors or alums. I really am sorry."

"Don't be, Sister. You have helped me more than you know."

Margaret had hoped to get lucky. It wasn't going to be that easy.

"If I can be of any more assistance, please let me know."

"Thank you, Sister. You've really been a great help."

She hung up and walked over to the table where Erin Mosby was sitting.

Isolation is much more horrifying.

Brother Tom's words ran through her mind as she watched the girl sitting alone, flanked by tables where other girls were crowded together.

"Erin?"

The girl looked up, surprised. She looked plain, with red, curly hair and freckles. Her uniform blouse needed ironing and her face was pockmarked by acne. She was startled, no doubt wondering what she had done wrong to have one of the nuns approach her table.

"May I sit down?" Margaret asked.

"Sure," Erin said. Margaret noticed that the tables around them quieted a bit, only to resume their previous noise level after Margaret sat down.

"I'm Sister Margaret."

"Yes, I know."

"Erin, I couldn't help noticing you the other day, the day that Sister Kathleen announced that Billy Matheson had died. You were crying."

Erin didn't say anything. A flurry of activity on both sides of them occurred as the girls at the nearest tables picked up their trays and left. Margaret pressed on.

"Erin, were you friends with Billy?"

"I used to live in the same apartment complex. I babysat him sometimes. He was sweet. He was one of the few kids around here who would talk to me. We had something in common there."

"I see. Did he talk with you about anything in his life? At home? Or about his other friends?"

"A little. His mom drank. He didn't get along with a lot of her boyfriends. She had a new one every few months, so he sometimes didn't like going home."

"What about his friends?"

"People thought Billy was weird, because of his hair and the way he acted and all. He hung with some kids who were into that Goth stuff. They treated him okay, so he dressed like they did. He fit in with them. Nobody here treated him very nice."

"Did anyone here ever hurt him, or threaten him?"

"They teased him a lot. Once, one of the boys pushed him out in front of the building and called him a name. But Billy turned around and socked him in the jaw. Kids left him alone after that."

Good for Billy.

"I understand you are a good student."

"I have to be. I am on scholarship. If my grades drop I lose it. My dad does okay but he can't afford to send me here without it."

Margaret didn't say anything for a minute or so. She was thinking about the cruelty of children toward other children. She was, momentarily, ashamed of the kids who so unthinkingly made the lives of children like Billy and Erin a living hell because they weren't as good looking, or as rich, or as popular as they were. Being different in high school made one a target, as Margaret knew all too well from her own experience. She had been different. Bookish. Smart. It wasn't until her junior year in high school that she had blossomed physically and socially.

"Thank you for talking with me, Erin. I appreciate it. Would you come by my classroom sometime? I would enjoy talking with you again. Anytime."

Erin looked at her suspiciously. "I guess. Sure."

"I would like that. And if you ever need anything, anyone to talk with, you let me know."

Erin brightened. "Thanks."

Chapter 25

"Jesus Christ, Johnny! We've got to get you out of here. Did they see you?"

The boy shook his head. He was still crying, sick at his stomach and saturated from wetting his pants.

"Johnny, you can't tell anyone about this."

"But Bonnie—"

"We can't help Bonnie now, Johnny. But if they find out you were here they will kill you too. You can't say anything to anyone. Promise me!" His father had him by both shoulders and was shaking him. "Promise me!"

Johnny had promised. And he had kept that promise faithfully. He'd buried it deep, so deep that it had only recently broken through the crust of his consciousness.

Until now. Now everyone would know. Everyone would be sorry.

The nun was a glitch he hadn't counted on. He knew she had been a cop, but he never expected that they would pull her directly into the investigation. She was smart. But so was he. He would have to play this very carefully.

But it was becoming harder and harder to think.

There was one more to go. She wasn't as socially diverse as Alison had been, or as inclined to walk the streets alone as the boy. She spent a great deal of time studying at home.

Frequently, she spent evenings at the public library. A dangerous place, the library, with dozens of homeless camping outside at night and going inside for air conditioning on hot days or warmth in the winter. These were the ones the shelters wouldn't take because they refused to follow rules, or because they wanted to stay high, or because they were convicted sex offenders. A girl shouldn't go there alone.

He knew exactly how he would go about it. He had rehearsed it in his mind a hundred times.

He swallowed two Vicodin. The drug still made him nauseous, but another headache was coming on. It was imperative that he stay on schedule. He was beginning to exhibit symptoms. He couldn't let the pain interfere with his thinking. Not now.

There wasn't much time left.

Chapter 26

"Doctor Corcoran was reputed to be a womanizer," Margaret said. "Fact: One of the sisters walked in on him and a student at the infirmary. Fact: Corcoran knew the father of the Easter girl, but their relationship was puzzling. Fact: Both the girl's father and the county prosecutor committed suicide shortly after the murder. Fact—and this is the fact of facts: the two victims were the grandchildren of Corcoran and prosecutor Jerry Brown."

Sheriff Hargrove, again sporting a Brooks Brothers suit, looked at his watch. He was meeting his wife at five and it was now almost four.

"Do we have any other grandchildren potentially on the hook here?"

"Great question, boss," said Templeton. "The psychic here is already running that down."

Margaret bit her lip.

"Good," said Hargrove. "Did you get the staff and teachers' names collected up for background checks?"

Templeton told him he had brought the names, social security numbers, and dates of birth and addresses of the Saint Dominic's staff members Margaret had collected back to the office. They had been sent to the local FBI office.

"You two make a good team," said Ernie, who was standing next to Hargrove's desk. "I thought you would have killed each other by now."

"I'm a changed woman, Ernie," said Margaret. Templeton rolled his eyes.

"And I'm a white man now," Ernie said.

There was a knock at the door, and Tracy stuck her head in.

"Agent Renfrow's here, Jim."

"Bring her in."

Tracy glanced at Margaret and rolled her eyes. Margaret looked at Ernie, but Ernie just smiled.

When agent Renfrow walked in, the men rose from their chairs. Renfrow was over six feet tall, with chestnut hair tied back into an efficient ponytail. She had high cheekbones, chocolate brown eyes and a small straight nose. It was plain to see why all the men in the room were smiling. Margaret was trying to remember the last time every man stood up when she walked into a room. Renfrow was wearing a skirt that was a bit too tight and a bit too short, but she had the figure for it. She wore a navy blazer over a light blue blouse. On the jacket was a gold-plated FBI lapel pin.

"Margaret, I'd like you to meet Special Agent Jane Renfrow of the FBI."

"Pleased to meet you, Sister. Call me Jane."

Margaret stood and shook her hand politely and then sat back down. The others resumed their seats.

"I've been discussing this with Mike Crowley, the special agent in charge of the FBI here in town," Hargrove said. He has been most helpful and has offered the expertise of Agent Renfrow, who is a trained profiler."

"Is the FBI getting involved?"

"Not officially," Renfrow answered. "We're just helping out. Mike has the utmost respect for Sheriff Hargrove—I believe he and you play poker occasionally, Sheriff?"

Hargrove nodded and smiled. "He cheats." Everyone laughed.

"That may be. But, frankly, he is glad you're in charge of this investigation," Renfrow continued. "We are simply offering to provide any support you may need."

"Detective Templeton and Margaret have been busy," Hargrove said. "Why don't you fill her in?"

She listened quietly as Margaret and Templeton reviewed the findings from their interviews during the day. Agent Renfrow crossed her legs, which made her skirt hike up and caused Templeton to lose his train of thought. Men were so easily distracted, Margaret thought.

"So, we may have another target out there," Ernie said.

"Yes," Margaret said. "And right now it doesn't appear to be one of our students."

"Well, the odds were against that," Ernie said. "If everything you have surmised is true, and this is some sort of whacked out vendetta over a murder thirty years ago, I would expect that at least one of those kids would go to a public school."

"If there is another target, he or she may not even be here in Springfield," Agent Renfrow chimed in.

"I've got a guy running those names," Templeton said. "Hopefully we can find birth records that might help us zero in."

"We've got to put a priority on that," Hargrove said. "I will give them to Agent Renfrow as well."

"Agent Renfrow," Ernie said, "would you share your insights with the detectives? You don't mind if I refer to you as 'detective,' do you Margaret?"

"That's why you're paying me the big bucks."

"Well," Renfrow began. "I have been to both of the murder scenes and reviewed the photographs and autopsy reports."

"They've finished the Matheson autopsy?" Margaret interrupted.

"Yes. This afternoon. The results were as we had anticipated. No sexual assault. Broken neck. Nylons for show. Identical MO."

"Excuse me, Agent Renfrow, for interrupting."

"No problem," Renfrow said. Her look told Margaret otherwise. She didn't like being interrupted. Templeton never took his eyes off her.

"As I was saying, we are probably looking for a white male, in his thirties or forties, possibly with military training. The neck breaks were without hesitation and death probably instantaneous. The individual may have difficulty engaging in sexual activity, either due to some physical or emotional trauma. He is intelligent, perhaps more intelligent than the average, and is very bold. It took some nerve to commit that murder on a road which, however sparsely traveled, still carried the risk of detection. He moved efficiently and quickly. We are looking at a very dangerous man."

"How do you do that?" Margaret asked.

"Do what?" The agent looked at her strangely.

"I am always amazed at how you profilers can be so confident of your observations."

Hargrove smiled. He knew Margaret was jerking the agent around. The convent hadn't changed her that much.

"You're not the only psychic here," Templeton said.

"I assure you, Sister, these observations are well founded."

"I don't doubt that. I am just amazed, that's all."

"Is there anyone so far who might meet that profile?" Ernie asked, steering the conversation back on course.

Margaret immediately thought of Tom Brightman.

"Well, yes," she said. "One of the Dominican brothers at the school served in Desert Storm."

"That certainly fits," Renfrow said.

"Of course, he has been a religious since 1995, and just came here a few years ago from Ohio. There is nothing in his file, other than his military experience, that would cause me to suspect that he could do something like this."

"Torquemada was a religious too," Templeton said.

Margaret let it pass. "And of course there is the question of motive. We don't have one."

"We need to interview him," Hargrove said.

"Absolutely," Margaret said.

"Well, we have a couple of problems," Templeton chimed in.

"Okay. What?" Ernie asked.

"The background on Brightman didn't come up with anything. Can't get his military stuff, though. The Army isn't that cooperative."

"I might be able to help with that," Renfrow said.

"Great," said Templeton. "Brightman was born in North Dakota—although we can't verify that as of the moment—raised in Wisconsin, joined the military after college, and then—as Margaret said—found religion. But two other names came up."

"Who?" asked Margaret.

"The janitor. William Pickering."

"What about him?" asked Ernie.

"To begin with, Pickering isn't his real name. His real name is William Scarpelli. Seems he has a rap sheet back in Indiana dating back to the eighties. Criminal assault. He apparently served a couple of years for cutting up a guy in a bar fight in Indianapolis, and was on probation for five. But going back before that, he was found guilty of statutory rape. And … there's more."

"Well, don't keep us in suspense, deputy," Ernie said.

"He was in the Marines for two years. Dishonorably discharged. Needless to say, his application for employment was a complete fabrication. Including his social security number. His fake social security number suggests it was obtained in Illinois. His real soch was issued in Indiana."

"Mother Beatrice seems to have run a pretty loose ship," Margaret said.

"Not necessarily. That file goes back to 1990," Templeton said. "That's when he was hired. The National Child Protection Act wasn't passed until 1993, and IAFIS was just in its infancy. The background checks were pretty cursory. There were no Indiana addresses given—he neglected to provide that information, surprise, surprise—and there were no fingerprints taken. In those days, people just placed a few calls to law enforcement offices in the communities listed on their resumes. He didn't list Indianapolis, or mention Indiana at all."

"That having been said," Templeton added, "the information we obtained said that he had an aunt living in Springfield."

"Sister Beatrice," Margaret said.

"Bingo. That's how he got the job, and she would have known."

Margaret was beginning to have serious doubts about the omnipresent Sister Beatrice.

Hargrove looked puzzled. "If there was nothing in his personnel file and if he is using a different name, how is it that you were able to find out all of this?"

Margaret answered, "I bumped into Mr. Pickering today and accidentally dropped a spiral notebook, one with a glossy cover. He picked it up for me. It occurred to me that perhaps his fingerprints might be useful, so I called Ernie and he was good enough to run by and get it."

"Nice job, Donovan," Hargrove said. "Get him in here, Ernie. Don't spook him. See if he will come in tomorrow morning. Let's see what he has to say for himself."

"And the other problem?" Margaret asked Templeton.

"Joseph Santini. It seems that he left Santa Fe, New Mexico after the school he worked for convinced a couple of well-connected parents not to bring charges against him for diddling their daughter."

The color disappeared from Margaret's face.

"You can't be serious."

"You've been a nun too long," Templeton said. "One thing this job teaches you is that things—and people—aren't always what they seem. But it gets better."

"Better? Or worse?" asked Margaret.

"Depends on your point of view. One of the names mentioned in the original police report is a Salvatore Rigali."

"Rigali? I know that name," said Renfrow.

"You probably do. His father was John 'the Chairman' Rigali, Springfield's godfather until he died in the seventies," Templeton said. "Salvatore was his son and heir apparent. Fortunately, he wasn't as smooth as his old man and ended up in Marion on a murder wrap. In

1979, somebody put him out of circulation using a shiv made out of a duct-taped dinner fork while he was taking a shower."

"What does he have to do with Joe?" Margaret asked.

"Salvatore was Santini's cousin."

"But Joe would have just been a kid."

"Yeah. But with mob families, blood is thicker than water. In any event, we now have two reasons to talk to him, don't we?"

Deputy John Rogers was the first to arrive at the home of William Pickering. He waited out front for another cruiser to pull up behind him. When he saw Bill Costello get out of his car, he got out and the two walked up to the one-story house that was two blocks from Saint Dominic's in an older, run-down part of Springfield.

Pickering lived in a clapboard house with loose gutters and peeling paint. The porch consisted of a concrete stoop.

"Some janitor," Rogers said as they knocked on the door.

"Hmph," Costello said. Costello never said much about anything.

They could hear a television playing inside, and the front door was open. Rogers knocked again.

Pickering came into view. He had a can of Bud Lite in his hand and was wearing a T-shirt and boxer shorts.

"Mr. Pickering?"

"Yeah."

"May we talk with you a few minutes?"

"You're talking."

"Yes. Well, sir, we have some questions, and we need you to come down to the office to clear them up."

"Questions about what? I'm kind of busy here."

Costello smiled. Pickering gave him a look that caused the smile to disappear.

"Tomorrow would be fine, sir," said Rogers.

Pickering didn't say anything for about a minute. The two deputies simply stood there, waiting in silence.

"It'd have to be after four," Pickering said, finally. "I work for a living."

"First thing in the morning, Mr. Pickering. Eight sharp. County Building, Room 121. I'll tell the sheriff to expect you."

Pickering slammed the door without further comment, leaving the deputies standing on the stoop.

"Think he'll show up?" Rogers said.

"Hmph," said Costello.

Pickering's sink was filled with dirty dishes. The half-empty beer can that he tossed into it cracked a plate that was on top of the pile and sprayed beer on the wall and the dirty curtain above the sink.

"God damn sonofabitch!" He exclaimed, hitting the cluttered countertop with his fist.

He went into the living room, dropped into the recliner and put his head in his hands.

"Mother fuckers!" he said, as Judge Judy screamed at a plaintiff on the TV in front of him.

"God damned mother fuckers!"

"My God! He's worked here for more than fifteen years. He's a bit odd, but we've never had any problem with him."

Sister Kathleen was reading a copy of the report concerning Pickering or Scarpelli or whatever his name really was.

"At the very least, I will have to be convinced not to fire him. Statutory rape?"

"We don't know the details yet. The Indianapolis police report is on the way," Margaret said. "But he apparently has a violent streak."

"What do I do now? What do I do about this?" Kathleen was sitting on a bench in the atrium. She was clearly agitated. Marty Jeffers was standing nearby.

"Nothing right now," said Margaret.

Tom Brightman walked up with several books under his arm. Roy Walker was walking with him.

"Hey guys," Jeffers said.

"Hey, Marty."

"Nothing right now? We have a janitor who could pose a threat to our students and I am to do nothing?" Kathleen was clearly flustered.

Joe Santini had now joined them. It was about ten minutes before four in the afternoon, and they were all about to bring the day to a close.

"Templeton and the FBI are going to question him tomorrow. We will know more about him by then. Just keep an eye on him until then," Margaret advised.

"Who are we talking about?" Santini asked. Margaret was feeling a bit edgy with the audience they had attracted. She had caught Kathleen in the atrium when she entered the main doors and had expected to talk with her alone.

"It seems our janitor has a record."

"Sister Kathleen," Margaret interrupted, "just sit tight."

"Sister Margaret, there was a message for me when I finished my last session today from the sheriff's department," said Santini. "What's that all about?"

Margaret blushed. "Joe, they are just going down the list of faculty and staff to rule out everyone."

"Just relax, Joe," said Jeffers. "I got called earlier. I went in already this afternoon. It's nothing."

"So, I guess I will have a message too," said Tom.

"Probably. It's routine stuff. Really," said Jeffers. "Margaret, while you were playing cops and robbers we had tons of excitement here."

Tom chuckled.

"Tom and I saw a couple of freshman boys across the street on some private property smoking this morning before first bell," Jeffers said.

"So we decided to take a walk over there. Well, they spotted us before we could get a good look at them and took off with those cigarettes still in their mouths. They jumped the fence over by the grade school and took off down Washington Street. We decided to take it easy."

"I could have caught them," Brightman said. "But the coach has a bit too much inner tube going for him."

Jeffers waved him off. "Besides, we had a clear-cut way of identifying them. They were wearing their uniform pants down low and their boxers were showing. One's was blue with yellow polka dots; the other's was red with white stripes.

"So after first bell, we went into three homerooms and asked the boys to stand up. Got them in the third room. Caught them by the shorts! They will be spending Saturday morning in detention."

Such simple crises. Margaret was sorry that she had traded the likes of them for the horror she was involved in now.

"Well, okay," said Santini. "I'm out of here. I will call them in the morning. Good night."

Margaret was feeling some guilt. She wasn't just a cop. This was different. She was in an untenable position here. She feared for Joe Santini, in particular. He was truly gifted. She liked him and respected him. What was this going to mean for his career? She now had something else to pray about during vespers. It had never occurred to her that she might be ruining the lives of those she cared about.

Theodora was working on the sweater in her room when Margaret came by. The sound of Elvis singing "Tender Feeling" drifted softly into the hallway. Her door was open, an unspoken invitation for her friend to drop in anytime she wanted.

"May I come in a minute?" asked Margaret.

"I always welcome it," said Theodora. "Please." Theodora set down her knitting, turned her tape player down, and moved over to her rocker.

Margaret entered the room and sat down. She didn't speak.

"You look worn out," said Theodora.

"Just worried."

"Guess being a cop wears on you, huh?"

"It never dawned on me that I would be putting the people closest to me in jeopardy."

"I don't understand."

"They are questioning everyone. Someone might get hurt as a result. And I will have had a part in it."

Theodora sat back, her hands folded in her lap. "Margaret, this is incredibly ugly. That ugliness cannot help but splash back on us. It isn't your doing."

"Maybe not. But I'm part of it, and I will be partly responsible."

"We're all part of everything, Margaret. You know your friend John Donne? He was right. We are part of the main."

Margaret smiled. It was remarkable how well this woman knew her mind after these few years. "I've been thinking a lot lately about the last conversation I had in class with Alison Corcoran."

"What about?"

"We were talking about Augustine. She was, quite intelligently, discussing the problem of evil. As though she was beginning to understand. As though she could understand."

"You know, Margaret, I always am amazed at why people discuss the problem of evil as though it is something imponderable. It isn't, really."

"What do you mean?"

"Evil isn't the problem. Evil is an incontestable and omnipresent fact of our existence. I think we need to change the question around a bit. The question shouldn't revolve around how we explain evil, but rather how we explain goodness."

Margaret sucked in her lower lip, contemplating what her friend was saying.

"Remember when we saw *Miss Saigon* at the Sangamon Auditorium a few years back? I love that beautiful song that says something about a song played on a solo saxophone. In the midst of a dark world, that sound was all there was to tell those young people that love goes on.

The problem to consider isn't the darkness, or the evil in the world. It's the little things, the goodness that pops up out of nowhere. That is what we must focus on. That is where we find God."

Margaret was having a difficult time finding that at the moment. But she hoped Sister Theodora was right.

Chapter 27

It was midnight and Bill Pickering couldn't sleep.

The small TV sitting on a folding table provided the only illumination, a grey-green glow that shone on Pickering as he sat drinking his tenth beer.

He had gone through a pack of cigarettes since the cops had been at his house. A haze of smoke hung in the air in spite of the window air conditioner that was humming in the bedroom.

He was alone. He had been alone for more years than he could remember. Since coming to Springfield, he at least had a job. His aunt, the prioress at the time, had offered him a life, a job and a way to straighten himself out years ago.

Sister Beatrice knew all about the trouble he had been involved in, but she helped him anyway. Then she left him. Death took her, just as it had taken his mother years before that.

Death hadn't taken his father soon enough.

Now, as he sat in the chair, he slapped his head with the palm of his hand. He had done that since he was a child. He had been taught well. His father used to pound on his head with the flat of his hand whenever Bill did anything to irritate him—which was frequently. Now, Bill punished himself.

His father would be proud.

He deserved it. He always deserved it.

And why hadn't he heard from *him*? It had been over a week now. Whenever he tried to reach him at home, he wouldn't answer. When he saw him at school, he would turn and go the other way.

He was always protective of his position, and Bill had never done anything to threaten him in that regard. Maybe if he threatened to divulge a few things, he might get his attention.

His life was about to come crashing around him. What if they knew? He had a feeling they did.

That god damned nun.

He got up and walked into the kitchen. When he turned on the light there was a rope sitting in the middle of the kitchen table.

Bill Pickering was not going to make that appointment the next morning.

Chapter 28

"Excuse me?" Jim Hargrove set his coffee cup down and sat back in his chair. "You'll have to forgive me. I just thought I heard you say you were resigning to go into the convent." He shook his head rapidly side to side and then rubbed his eyes. "Okay. Now what was it you wanted to talk with me about?"

"Jim, I'm serious."

Margaret's life had settled down after the White Hen Pantry incident and her career was back on track. She had been promoted to detective and had exceeded Hargrove's expectations on the job.

There was something markedly different about Margaret that was apparent to anyone who noticed, to anyone who knew her at all. Hargrove and Ernie had both seen it. Whereas before she was driven, now she was resolute but more patient with herself—and others. Something was going on inside her head and—whatever it was—it was working.

Hargrove assumed she had worked through her grief and found closure. Leave it to Margaret to ride the pendulum as far to the other extreme as she could, he thought as he sat tapping a pencil on his coffee cup.

"Jim, I have been Catholic all of my life. Not necessarily a good one, but it's part of who I am. It's in the grain. My dad was a devout Catholic, a daily communicant. I went to Mass every day of my young life, in grade school and on weekends with dad. So this is not something out of the blue."

"I knew that about your dad. He gave me a St. Jude medal years ago. I'm a Baptist, but I wear it even today."

"The patron saint of lost causes and cops."

"Not sure why he gave it to me. One of those reasons, I suppose."

Margaret smiled. She loved Jim Hargrove. She knew that the feeling was mutual. It sometimes got in the way of how he related to her as a deputy. He favored her, and so had to be tougher on her so as not to let it show. It showed, nonetheless.

"Margaret, are you sure you're not just … "

He stopped, not sure of where he was going—or whether he really wanted to go there.

"Running from something, Jim? The thing with Eric?"

"Yeah."

"I have a lot of things to learn about myself. A lot of questions to answer. But I can tell you that I have found a new sense of belonging, and a new sense of who I am, since I have been visiting the convent. I have attended two vocation weekends, and there is something there for me, Jim. This has been going on for months, and I feel alive again. I feel full again. I don't understand the thing with Eric, but you yourself said once that I should look closely at what that was all about. Why I was content with the way things were? Maybe I knew that this was what was really coming and didn't want to commit."

"Knew?"

"Sensed. I don't know."

"You mean you sensed that God was calling you?"

"I feel that God is inviting me in and I want to go. At this time in my life, even though I can't verbalize it precisely right now, I want to go with all my heart."

Neither of the two friends spoke for a minute or two.

There was a knock at the door and Tracy Polanski stuck her head in.

"Jim, there's a—"

"Go away!"

"Yes, I just wanted to tell you I was going away."

The door closed. Margaret had to stifle a laugh.

"She's going to miss you," Hargrove said.

"I'm going to miss her too," Margaret said.

"What about me? You going to miss me?" Hargrove smiled.

"A little. Promise to call me every now and then and yell at me?"

"Get out of here, Donovan. I've got work to do. I have to find a new deputy."

He stood up, and Margaret walked over and hugged him. "Thanks for everything, Jim. And I will miss you."

The sheriff didn't like to let his emotions show, and fought back a tear.

"Good. Now I've got things to do."

―――――――

"I desire to enter more fully into the Order of Saint Dominic," Margaret said in reply to the question that had been asked by the prioress as part of the initiation ceremony.

The day was glorious, the garden of the Mother House resplendent with annuals and perennials that exploded into many colors. An outdoor ceremony was conducted for Margaret—the only woman seeking to enter the novitiate—and four lay associates.

Margaret's heart was filled during the Eucharistic celebration as she stood now wearing the head covering of a Dominican and sang the Hosanna. She wished her father and mother could have been here. In her heart she knew they were there watching, loving, understanding. At one point she turned to see Sister Theodora. She had come to love this woman who had taken the place of the mother she never knew.

Sitting next to Theodora were Jim Hargrove and his wife. Jim smiled and gave her a thumbs-up sign. Next to them sat Tracy Polanski with her husband and four kids. Behind them she could see John Rogers, and several other deputies. Ernie Jones and his wife both smiled at her. These people were her extended family.

Margaret felt blessed.

"Go in peace, to love and serve the Lord," said the priest at the end of the Mass.

Margaret said, and truly meant, "Amen."

Chapter 29

Bertie Higgins was on the radio singing "Key Largo."

The morning light softly illumined the room as he kissed and held her and came into her and filled her. To be loved. To be held close. To be wanted. Needed. Desired. Filled. Respected for who she was. Understood. This is what she was looking for. The sex was the culmination of the search for acceptance, and she was enjoying it. Yet, she knew it could only take her so far.

As she came, tears came too. La petite mort. *A beautiful agony.*

As Higgins faded to a commercial, she lay stroking the hair of her lover. Margaret had missed him so much.

"Do you love me?" she whispered.

His head lay on her breasts. He moved. He tilted his head toward her and started to speak but the words never came.

It was Bill Templeton's face.

"Oh God!"

Margaret sat up in bed. She took her head in both hands and pushed her hair back, then looked at the clock on the nightstand. It was five in the morning. She lay back down and tried to go back to sleep. And hoped she wouldn't dream any more.

Part Two

The Hound of Heaven

You have made us for Yourself, and our hearts are restless until they rest in Thee.
—*Saint Augustine*

Chapter 30

The low country in April was already beginning to get muggy, presaging the drenching summer humidity that made Charleston and the surrounding area infamous.

Ted Baker sat at his desk in the offices of the Charleston *Post and Courier* at eight o'clock in the morning finishing up a story. For six years, he had been the *Post*'s crime reporter. He had a reputation as an investigative reporter who pulled no punches.

His tightly written and piercing questions aimed at city and police officials in Springfield had ruffled more than a few feathers during his tenure at the *State Journal-Register*, causing the paper considerable grief. But his style hearkened back to the type of writing that made newspaper reporting exciting. His childhood hero was Mike Royko, the two-fisted, hard-drinking reporter for the *Chicago Daily News,* and later for the *Chicago Tribune.* Nowadays, Ted claimed, papers hired milquetoast writers out of college who simply attended court hearings and reported on what they observed. Few of them knew how to follow their gut, how to dig around in places where they shouldn't and unearth the real skinny of a story. They showed up at eight and walked out at five. Not a good way to uncover the real truth.

He left Springfield after a row with the publisher over a story he'd written about an alderman who was caught *in flagrante* with the wife of a police captain. The indiscretion had placed a murder investigation in jeopardy. The wife, it seems, was a suspect and was using the hapless public servant as an alibi. The mayor had had enough of the scandal and intimidated the publisher into shutting Baker up. Baker told the publisher to fuck off, left town and within two months had found a home in Charleston with the *Post and Courier*. This paper appreciated hard-hitting journalism.

The story he was finishing up concerned a brutal murder that had taken place two years before. John Salvo, a bank manager from Philadelphia, his wife and two small children were walking to their car from a restaurant near the French market when they were approached by Jefferson Washington. Washington had been out on parole for a year after serving five years for armed robbery. It was later determined that Washington was high on crack at the time.

Washington produced a gun and demanded money. Salvo stepped between Washington and his family and reached for his wallet. Washington spooked and pulled the trigger. The bullet entered Salvo's heart and the bank manager fell to his knees, then onto his face. Washington reached down and took a Rolex watch off the dead man's wrist and ran, leaving the family screaming in terror.

The story didn't end there. Washington was charged with first-degree murder in the death of Salvo and was awaiting trial at Perry Correctional, a level-three facility in Pelzer. From there, Washington used his phone privileges to conduct a campaign of terror against the Salvo family. He had also made calls to family and friends to obtain telephone numbers and addresses of prosecutors. He allegedly telephoned several former associates and asked them to murder the prosecutors.

Baker had actually tracked down one of the associates—a gangbanger named Kenneth Kane, or KK—and managed to get corroboration. KK was threatening and uncooperative. At one point he said he would cut Baker into little pieces, but Baker didn't back off. Baker cited him as a confidential source, and promised to return the favor some day. He had lied through his teeth, saying that Washington himself had given him

KK's name. Baker was the kind of guy who did whatever was necessary to get a story.

Baker's story was a scathing indictment of what he called "a corrupt system" that would provide phone privileges to a man charged with a brutal crime and then, after learning what he was doing, allow the privileges to continue. The story was going to raise a ruckus. That was what Baker liked to do.

His phone rang as he was finishing his final edits.

"Ted Baker."

"Mr. Baker. My name is Margaret Donovan. I am working with the Sangamon County Sheriff's Department in Springfield."

"Yes."

"You used to report for the *Journal-Register* here in Springfield, didn't you?"

"Yes. I was crime reporter there for a number of years."

"I have some questions about an article you wrote in 1994. Is this a convenient time, or would it be better if I called back?"

"Bonnie Easter?"

"Yes. Do you remember that story?"

"Ms. Donovan, I will never forget that story. But can I ask why you are interested in this case all of a sudden? Nobody from your office seemed to care much before."

"We are investigating the murder of two students at St. Dominic's High School. We have stumbled on some information that suggests a possible link to the Easter killing."

"Okay. You've got my attention. What do you want to know?"

Baker went through the story, which was essentially a rehash of what she had read. It struck Margaret how well he remembered the details. But the most interesting information had to do with the information-gathering process.

"The sheriff's office had nothing. So I went to the police. There was a brief report, and a list of items that were originally in the file. But they were missing when I got permission to go through the box."

"I saw the report," Margaret said. "Pretty perfunctory. Where did they say the other information had been sent?"

"To the State's Attorney. It was like pulling teeth to get that box from the State's Attorney when I wrote the story. But I finally got permission."

"What did you find?"

"Well, it was what I didn't find that intrigued me. I had seen an inventory at the police department, which listed some jewelry and her clothing. There may have been blood on the clothes. If there was blood, there was possibly DNA, so my heart was beating a mile a minute when I opened that box."

"What was in it?"

"Another inventory list, a photograph, and a wad of packing paper. That was it."

Margaret exhaled loudly. "What was the photo of?"

"It was an old black-and-white photo of the Easter family. There was the dad, Bonnie, her sister and her younger brother. That was it."

"Were there names of the kids in the file?"

"Only the sister's name. The sister has since died."

"You mentioned a boy in the article."

"Were it not for that picture, I wouldn't even know he existed. I only mentioned it in passing because there was no indication of his name or his whereabouts after the murder. I guessed he would have attended Blessed Redeemer School at the time of the murder. It was a dead end. I called Blessed Redeemer but there was a fire in 1983 that destroyed many of the records. No trace of any child named Easter."

"Do you think the photograph is still at the prosecutor's office?"

"No."

"How do you know for sure?"

"Because it somehow made it into my coat pocket."

"You stole it?"

"So arrest me. Whoops! Statute of limitations. Guess you can't."

"And where is it now?"

"I am looking at it even as we speak. I still have the file in my desk. I told you I would never forget this case. The police and the prosecutors in Springfield have. They forgot it very soon after it happened. I didn't."

"Any chance—?"

"I will scan it and send you a copy this morning. Do you have e-mail?"

Margaret gave him her e-mail address.

"Anything else you can tell me?"

"There was a cop, a Terence Crawford, who was retired when I did my article. His name appeared on a list of policemen who were involved in the investigation. At that time, he was living in the Presbyterian Home, so I paid him a visit. He shared some concerns."

"What were they?"

"He said that rumors were flying. Apparently the Easter girl's dad was a sycophant who liked to surround himself with influential friends, hoping to get a boost. Did you ever see that movie *The Apartment*? The one with Jack Lemmon and Shirley MacLaine?"

"Yeah. About the guy who worked his way up the ladder by giving his bosses the key to his apartment for their trysts?"

"Yeah. Easter bought a cabin around Riverton somewhere. He went into hock to get it. He supposedly made it available to his boss, the fire chief, and thus came into contact with some of the more powerful folks around town."

"Would any of them have been Gerald Brown?"

"Crawford mentioned him specifically. And another big name in Springfield."

"Doctor Corcoran?"

"Bingo. There were stories about parties that Easter would throw, to get those folks together around him. All the while, he was racking up favors and secrets."

"Was Bonnie involved in any of this?"

"Possibly. Crawford said the girl was wild as a March hare. 'Easy' was the word he used. She would do anything to please Daddy, to get his attention."

"You didn't write about much of this."

"I'm not crazy. It's all hearsay. I was only able to corroborate the Corcoran connection. Besides, Crawford died of a massive stroke the same week the story was scheduled for publication. How much of it was an old man spouting off to make himself seem more important than he was? I didn't know for sure.

"I see," Margaret said. "It's interesting, because the children killed this week were grandchildren of two of the men you mentioned. Corcoran and Brown."

"Yeah?"

"We are concerned that there may yet be others, and we are trying to figure out who he or she might be."

"You have the list of those involved in the investigation, right?"

"Yes, and that is what we are working on."

"Is Abe Tomiczek still alive?"

"The police chief?"

"Yeah. He was a cantankerous old bastard. He refused to talk with me. Almost physically threw me out. The quote I got from him wasn't spoken, it was screamed. If any of what Crawford told me was true, I think Tomiczek knew about it. He and the fire chief, Ed Jenkins, were good friends. He was hiding something, I would bet my life on it."

"I will definitely find out. What was your take on the suspect? The dishwasher."

"What I could glean was suggestive, but they were never able to pin the murder on him. No evidence of any connection other than the place they both worked. Nobody could put them together. Of course, they may have been barking up the right tree all along. He was given life for kidnapping and murder. Maybe he actually did it."

"But then why these recent killings? Two with this connection can't be a coincidence. There has to be a link."

"As crazy as it seems, they just might be a coincidence. There is always that possibility. Do you know if Garcia is still alive?"

"No. Everybody else in this case is dead. But I will find out."

"If I can be of any further help you let me know, honey."

Honey. Margaret smiled.

"I'll be waiting for that picture, Mr. Baker."

Chapter 31

Margaret's cell phone rang as she walked through the atrium. "Sister Margaret."

"Pickering didn't show up." It was Templeton.

"Let me call you back." Margaret walked into the office area and knocked on Sister Kathleen's door.

"Good morning."

"Have you seen Bill Pickering?"

"Why, no." Kathleen stood and walked toward the door. "Angie? Have you seen Bill Pickering this morning?"

"No. He hasn't been in here."

"Check around, will you?"

"Sure thing."

Kathleen turned back to Margaret. "What's wrong?"

"He didn't show up at the sheriff's office this morning for his interview."

After several minutes, Angie hung up the phone in the outer office. "Sister Kathleen? No one has seen him yet this morning."

Margaret pressed the call back number on her phone and walked out of the office.

"Templeton."

"Pickering's not here. I'll meet you at his place."

"Stay put. I'll call you."

"I'm on this whether you like it or not."

"Jesus. I'll pick you up. I'm heading for my car right now."

Light rain was falling from the slate grey sky as Templeton pulled up in front of Pickering's house. He and Margaret stayed in the car until they saw Deputy Rogers pull up behind them. Then they got out.

Templeton waved Rogers around to the back of the house. He turned to Margaret. "Please stay in the car."

"Templeton, don't let the cross fool you. I'm still a cop. I've done this before. Now get on with it."

Templeton closed his eyes and shook his head. "Okay."

As they walked up to the door they noticed Pickering's green Chevy pickup in the driveway.

"Well, he didn't leave in his truck," Margaret said.

Templeton walked up to the stoop. Margaret stood off to the left. Templeton knocked. "Mr. Pickering? This is Detective Templeton, sheriff's office."

No answer. Templeton knocked again. Still no answer. Templeton opened the screen door and tried the door. Locked. Then, slowly, the door opened. There stood Deputy John Rogers. "The back door was open," Rogers said. "I found Pickering."

The three walked through the living room. It smelled of beer and putrid cigarette smoke. The television was on. They walked through the doorway into the kitchen. The smell of excrement greeted them.

The sight that awaited them was stomach wrenching. To the left of the kitchen table, suspended by a rope that came from the top of the closed door to the basement, was the body of Bill Pickering. His right leg was extended at an oblique angle from his body, his left leg bent at the knee. He was clad only in a T-shirt and boxer shorts. His face was pale and he was bug-eyed. His tongue protruded slightly through darkened lips. It was a face that one might encounter in a Bosch painting.

Margaret saw a piece of paper on the floor, next to the chair. There appeared to be writing on it.

Margaret blessed herself.

"Guess that's that," said Templeton.

Strange, piteous, futile things. Those children had to die. Now I must die.

The note from the kitchen floor was now encased in plastic. Margaret read it over and over, trying to make sense of it. Around her there was a flurry of activity. Lab techs from the city were going over the living room and kitchen, and the Coroner was working with people from the pathologist's office in the kitchen.

The thrust of the note was clear. Pickering was responsible for the two murders, and now he had ended it.

There was something about the phrasing that intrigued her. She took out a pen and copied the note in a small notebook.

And why? Why did those children have to die?

Templeton walked up to her.

"Well, so far it looks pretty clear cut. The preliminary findings are that this is just what it looks like. We were closing in, and the guy offed himself."

"Sure seems that way," said Margaret.

"Let me guess. You're getting vibes. You're not satisfied?"

"No. No vibes. There's just something about that note."

"Well, let's head back to the office. You can commune with your spirits about that along the way. Guess you won't be hanging around much anymore." He seemed elated.

Margaret's eyes flashed.

"Were you born obnoxious, or do you work at it?"

"It's part of my charm," he said.

Then, Sister Margaret spoke her heart, casting aside all pretense of her new station in life.

"Fuck off, Templeton."

Chapter 32

Joe Santini did something he seldom ever did. He took a day off.

He spent some long overdue time with his kids, fixing breakfast and getting them ready for school. It allowed his wife an opportunity to sleep in, something she seldom had the chance to do.

Joe loved his family. They were why he worked hard, and did counseling on the side. It allowed his wife, Connie, to be at home with the kids. She had always protested, saying that she would be glad to help out by taking a part-time job but he knew she was only offering out of love. She loved being a full-time mom and wife, and he felt it incumbent upon him to make this possible.

The older kids were in school, and he sat at the kitchen table holding Caitlin, his two-year-old, and watching four-year-old Constanza color.

"She's asleep," Connie said. She reached over and brushed Caitlin's black hair with her index finger.

Connie was wearing a terry-cloth robe. She walked over to the counter and poured a cup of coffee, then turned around and leaned against the sink. Connie, too, was Italian, and Joe couldn't help thinking she was even more beautiful today, after four kids, than she was when he had first met her in a Psych class at Notre Dame. She was taller than

Joe by about two inches, with an athletic build, an olive complexion and large, brown eyes that had lured him the first time he saw her.

"What are you doing, pumpkin?" she asked Constanza.

"Coloring. You like it, Mommy?"

Constanza held up her masterpiece, a brightly colored rendition of their home, Mommy, Daddy, her three siblings and herself.

"That's beautiful, honey," Connie said.

"I'll put it on the fridge with the others," the proud four-year-old said, getting up and walking to the other side of the room.

"I'll go put this one down," Joe said.

Connie pulled out a chair and sat down with her coffee. Constanza came back to resume her artistic endeavors.

"Sweetheart, would you go into the living room and color. Daddy and I would like to visit. I don't get to visit with him much, and you've had him all morning. Okay?"

"Okay, Mommy. I like having Daddy home. Why can't he be home all the time?"

"What, you don't like having me here anymore?"

"No, Mommy. I want you both home."

"Give me a kiss," said Connie, reaching over to accept what was gladly given. "Thanks honey."

Joe returned and sat down.

"Good morning, handsome."

He reached over and kissed her on the cheek.

"So, tell me, how is that after—gosh, at least a year—I am honored to have you in my home on a school day?"

"I just needed some time off."

"Never stopped you before."

"Yeah, well we haven't had two murders in a long time."

Connie sipped her coffee. The two sat in silence for several minutes.

"Okay," Connie said. "Now you want to tell me what's bothering you?"

"The police want to question me. I telephoned them this morning, and I am going in this afternoon."

"Okay. I imagine they are questioning every male in or around that school. A hottie like you is going to be on their list." She smiled and rubbed his arm. "Got something to hide, handsome?"

He sipped his coffee. She sat waiting for a reply that never came. Her smile disappeared.

"Joe? Is there something I need to know?"

Chapter 33

Pat Donovan had been fond of saying that if you don't like the weather in Illinois, wait five minutes. It will change. Margaret remembered that as she and Templeton drove across town to the county building. The morning drizzle had stopped, the sky had gone from gray to blue, and the temperature was rising with the humidity. By eleven o'clock it was eighty-five degrees and rising. But it was only April, so snow could be in the forecast for tomorrow.

Gotta love the Midwest.

Jim and Ernie were waiting for them in the sheriff's office.

"I'm gonna hit the john," Templeton said. "Be right there."

"Same here," Margaret said.

Margaret put down her handbag, and then walked to the restroom.

As she left, she saw Jane Renfrow walking toward Ernie's office. She was wearing a beige, sleeveless blouse and a dark brown, flowing, calf-length skirt. She walked more like a model on a runway than an FBI agent on a case.

Renfrow stopped at the door as Templeton came out of the men's room.

Margaret drank from a water fountain and watched as the two stood in the hallway, laughing and talking.

She bit her lower lip and turned back toward Ernie's office and did her best to wish away what she was feeling.

There was neither rhyme nor reason for what she was experiencing. But in matters of the heart she knew that was often the case. She had for so long put away such thoughts, and had not even gone out with a man since Eric's death. There was nothing to recommend Templeton to her as an object of desire. He was rude, cocky, self-assured, and sarcastic. Or was it sardonic? No, sarcastic. Her Greek led her to that, since the word sarcasm came from the word for flesh. His sarcasm could be biting.

Yes, he was good-looking. He was unquestionably intelligent, and could be charming when it suited his purposes. His eyes also betrayed a hurt that ran deep—something that drags a woman, who is by nature a nurturer, right into a man's lair. At times it seemed he wanted to punish others for the pain he felt inside.

She had tried to avoid his gaze whenever possible. She remembered the rule of Saint Augustine: *Seeing a man is not forbidden, but it is sinful to desire them or to wish them to desire you. And whoever fixes her gaze upon a man and likes to have his fixed upon her must not suppose that others do not see what she is doing. She is very much seen, even by those she thinks do not see.*

Still, there was no escaping the emotion she felt when she saw Templeton engrossed in conversation with Jane Renfrow.

She felt jealousy.

"Morning, Jane," she said as she walked past them. "You coming?"

"Hi, Margaret. Be right there," Renfrow said.

Margaret bit her lip and felt her face go flush.

Get a grip, Margaret. Get a grip.

"I think this might be it," Templeton said.

"Sure looks that way," said Jim. "I asked the pathologist to put a rush on this one. He may even be able to get to it this afternoon. The preliminaries look good for suicide. What do you make of the note?"

Templeton responded, "It says what it says."

"Any question that it's his writing?"

"We've got some people looking at it now," said Renfrow.

"There were some notes scrawled on his refrigerator that seem to match his—how shall I put it—indescribable printing," said Templeton. "He wrote like a seven-year-old."

"He matches the profile," said Renfrow.

"Margaret?"

All heads turned toward her.

"Yes?"

Hargrove pulled his chair closer to his desk. He was looking dapper; it was another Brooks Brothers day. He had a meeting scheduled with a reporter from WICS this afternoon to discuss the investigation into the murders.

"You agree about this guy?"

Margaret bit her lip. He recognized that trait and he knew that she was having some doubts.

"Looks like it," she said. "Let's wait and see what the evidence tells us."

Hargrove folded his hands, elbows on his desk. He was hoping the case would end quickly, if for no other reason than to bring some quick closure to his friends, the Corcorans, before they buried their daughter. Still, he didn't want to close the books on a case too quickly. It sure looked as though this might be it, but there was something bothering Margaret. He respected her instincts. She had been one of his best, even better than Templeton.

"What do you *really* think, Margaret?"

"If nothing funny shows up in the autopsy, I'll feel better. There's something about that note, though, Jim. Something familiar. I really think we need to continue with the investigation until we're sure."

"What's funny about the note?" asked Templeton.

"The first line, for one thing. I've heard it before, or read it. I want to find out where and how Pickering might have come up with it. It may be nothing; it's just something I need to understand in order to feel better about this.

"Say the janitor is the guy, and that all the pieces fit. We need to continue digging to find out why. What did this guy mean when he said those kids had to die? What are they to him?"

"He may have been a whack job," said Templeton. "As long as we have the who, the why can take its sweet time if you ask me."

"You still think this has something to do with the Easter killing?" Ernie asked Margaret.

"I think we need to examine it closely. I talked to Ted Baker this morning, the reporter who used to work at the *SJR*. He didn't publish it, but he learned that there might have been some involvement by some prominent Springfield people—among them the grandparents of the Corcoran girl and the Matheson boy—in that girl's death. But nobody is or was talking."

"Okay," said Ernie. "But how does the janitor fit in?"

"Not sure, Ernie," Margaret said. "But Baker said that there were three kids in the Easter family. Bonnie, and an older sister. Both of them are dead. But there was a boy, too. He was younger and he dropped off the radar. Baker didn't even mention him in the article because he couldn't find anything about him."

"So, maybe somehow he ended up in Indiana?" Hargrove offered.

"He was Sister Beatrice's cousin," said Templeton. "So was Easter related to Sister Beatrice too?"

Great question, thought Margaret. She made a mental note to check into that.

"Come on, Ernie," Templeton continued, "this whole Easter connection is still speculation."

Ernie rubbed his hand across his mouth and sat back in his chair. "But why does a janitor, after seventeen years at that school with no reported problems—even if he did have a rap sheet going back a few years—kill two students out of the blue?"

"Who knows? The guy lived alone. He drank like a fish. I can't wait to see his blood alcohol level. Who knows what else they'll find in him? The place smelled like a brewery," Templeton said.

Hargrove had been in law enforcement too long to leave so many unanswered questions on the table.

"Okay. Right now, all the facts point to this guy," Hargrove said. "Why he did it, or whether he did or didn't have any connection to Easter, are things we just don't know. Maybe we won't ever know. The Easter connection should be followed up, and Margaret, you seem to be in a good position to do it. So keep digging. But if you don't find a connection, if this is just a coincidence, and all the evidence points to the guy as the doer, we might not be able to answer those questions."

"So are we going to keep moving on this?" Ernie asked.

"It's an open case until the evidence convinces me otherwise. Margaret, keep digging. Templeton, keep trying to locate other potential victims just to be extra-cautious."

What if the janitor isn't the guy, Margaret suddenly thought to herself. What kind of a maniac were they up against if he wasn't?

"How's the trace of other potential targets going?" Ernie asked Templeton.

"We are stalled. The best bet was Ed Jenkins, the former fire chief. We tracked a son, but he is dead. They are looking through birth records, but so far no luck; and if there was a kid born somewhere else, in another state, Accurint is little better than a crapshoot. Especially with a name like Jenkins.

"Are we going to continue with the interviews too? We still have a couple from the school, that Dominican, and Joe Santini. Santini called earlier to schedule a one o'clock today."

"Yeah, let's finish them up. Let's proceed as though nothing has changed, at least until we get more hard data. Margaret, you do whatever you have to do."

"I'd like to be in there when you talk with Joe Santini," Margaret said.

"Not a good idea," said Templeton.

"He's right, Margaret," said Ernie. "He might be less inclined to talk openly in front of you. To you he's a peer."

"Can I observe?"

"Sure. You can sit in but I don't want to let him know."

"Fine. Joe's a good man, so take it easy."

"I'll be my nice charming self," Templeton said.

"That's what I am afraid of," Margaret said.

"I will participate, if you don't mind," Renfrow said.

"Fine with me," said Templeton.

I'll just bet it is, thought Margaret.

"There are two others I would like to talk to," Margaret said.

"And they would be?" said Hargrove.

"Abraham Tomiczek, for one."

"The former chief of police? Why?"

"He refused to talk with Baker, or with anyone. Baker thinks he knows something and isn't telling. Tracey tracked him down. He's at a nursing home in Sherman."

"Who else?"

"There was a guy named Garcia. He was a dishwasher at the restaurant where Bonnie Easter worked. He's up at Oxford, Wisconsin, for kidnapping and murder."

"Well, there you go!" Templeton said sarcastically. "Sounds to me like they had the right guy pegged for the Easter killing after all."

"Oxford's federal," Renfrow said. She turned to Margaret. "If you like, I can set up a teleconference from our office. That way we won't have to drive the five or six hours."

We?

"If you don't mind, Margaret, I would be glad to sit in on Garcia. I'm in this until I know it's resolved to the best of our abilities."

Templeton looked away.

Margaret suddenly had a new appreciation for Jane Renfrow.

Chapter 34

Joe Santini sat in one of the interrogation rooms, his hands folded on a long wooden table. He was dressed casually, in jeans and a tan polo shirt. He looked at the clock and noted that it had been five minutes since detective Jones had invited him to have a seat and brought him a diet 7-Up.

Ernie had put Joe somewhat at ease. Ernie was good at that. He had asked Joe how the football team was looking for next year, could name the top seniors who were moving on to college and was speculating about who best would fill in for them. After about five minutes, he excused himself and told Joe that detective Templeton and agent Renfrow would be in shortly.

Templeton was watching from the room next door on closed circuit TV. He liked to leave them sit alone and sweat, to make them a little uneasy about what was coming. Perhaps he would get some signal, some sign that the subject was nervous about something.

Margaret walked in and saw Templeton watching the screen. Jane Renfrow walked in behind her.

"Sorry, Bill," Jane said. "I got a last minute call from the SAC."

"No problem," Templeton said. "It just gives him time to sweat."

"Let's go," Jane said, and the two walked through the doorway and into the interrogation room.

Before Joe's interview, Margaret had called the Mother House and spoken with Sister Grace, who served as assistant to the prioress several days a week. She inquired about Sister Beatrice. Grace had been at the Mother House for more than thirty years, and didn't even have to check the records on Beatrice.

"Beatrice was no relation to the Easter family at all, dear," Grace told her. "Beatrice hailed from Saint Augustine, Florida. Had there been any relationship, it would have been evident at the time of that unfortunate girl's death. Beatrice was not fond of the child, because she was a discipline problem. Don't get me wrong, she grieved for her as she would for any child under the circumstances. But, related to her? Absolutely not."

Grace had admitted that Beatrice was related to the janitor, and that she had hired him to help her sister. But when Margaret inquired about the false personnel records, she clammed up.

After a few moments, Margaret pushed.

"Sister, the man is dead. Sister Beatrice is dead. Her nephew may have been responsible for the deaths of the two kids from Saint Dominic's. I, of all people, would not want to create a scandal of any sort, or to besmirch the memory of Sister Beatrice. This is you talking to me. By doing so, it may make talking to the sheriff unnecessary."

The line was silent for a few seconds.

"Beatrice loved her younger sister terribly, but the poor woman had all sorts of problems. She was a horrible mother to that boy, and then when she died he was left with his father. That was the worst thing that could have happened. He had always loved Beatrice, and when a job opened up she brought him to Springfield. She herself had put the file together to protect him. And, of course, she was the prioress."

And the Catholic Church is not a democracy, thought Margaret. She saw Beatrice's behavior not that different from the many bishops who moved pedophilic priests from parish to parish. *They were, after all, the bishops.*

"She wanted to help him escape his past. She would have been horrified to think that he would do something like this. Are you certain he did it?"

"It looks that way, but we won't know for sure for a while. Sister, you have been very helpful. Thank you. And don't worry about this."

"I'll pray for that poor man. At least he is with Beatrice now."

Very likely, thought Margaret. Then she silently begged forgiveness for such an uncharitable thought.

Margaret sat contemplating the significance of this information as Templeton and Renfrow shook hands with Joe Santini and sat down.

Beatrice was no relation to the Easters, and so it was unlikely that Pickering was the boy in the picture that awaited her at the convent. This meant that either the Easter connection was a coincidence—or Pickering wasn't the one who killed them.

But, if Pickering was murdered, whoever killed him went to a lot of trouble to turn the spotlight in Pickering's direction.

She glanced at the clock, and realized that the pathologist was probably opening Pickering up right about now.

"So, you are forty-two years old, married, four children." Templeton was reading from his notes. "Go, Notre Dame."

Joe smiled, but Templeton didn't.

"Mr. Santini, we are questioning anyone who knew the two students who were killed recently. This is routine. We have to rule out everyone so that, when we do find someone who looks good, we won't have any question marks. Do you understand?"

"I think so. My wife watches a lot of *Court TV*."

"That's about the only thing on TV any more that's any good," Templeton said. "Speaking of TV, this is being videotaped."

"How will it be used?"

"Well, it could become evidence if you were to turn out to be the murderer. Otherwise, it will probably sit in a drawer for twenty years. You didn't kill those two kids did you?"

About as subtle as a hammer to the forehead, thought Margaret.

"Of course I didn't."

"Were you acquainted with the two students who were murdered? Alison Corcoran and William Matheson?"

"I knew Alison. I was her counselor. The Matheson boy was assigned to another of the counselors, but I was acquainted with him."

"Let's talk about Alison. She was a pretty good-looking girl, wasn't she?"

"Yes. She was a beautiful girl."

"What kind of problems did she come to you about?"

"A lot of kids with problems at home or at school sometimes find their way to the counseling office when they need to talk to someone objectively, and we encourage that. We lost a student to suicide a year ago, and so I make it a point of having an open door policy. Alison, however, never came to me except to discuss her class schedules and to ask for help deciding about college. I never counseled her about anything personal. She was a kid who pretty much had her act together."

"She never came on to you?"

"Never. Alison wasn't that way."

"Girls do that, though, sometimes? Come on to you, I mean."

"It sometimes happens. It never happened with Alison."

"Do you ever respond when they do, Joe?"

Joe's face turned red and he tilted his chair back on two legs.

"Never mind," Templeton said. "So, you are not aware of any problems Alison might have been having at school, or at home, or anywhere? No one had ever threatened her, or there were no boyfriends causing her trouble? No one stalking her?"

"As I said, I didn't know that much about her personal life. But I don't ever remember seeing Alison with any one particular boy around school. She was popular, and attractive, but as far as I know she wasn't dating anyone regularly."

"Know why anyone would want to kill her?"

"For the life of me, I can't imagine why anyone would want to hurt her. She was not only a good student; she was an exceptionally nice person. She came from money, but she never looked down her nose at others who didn't. She was one of our best."

"What about the Matheson boy? Was he one of your best?"

"I didn't counsel Billy, but he was frequently in the principal's office and our office. Usually, it had to do with uniform violations. He was into this Goth stuff, and he wasn't permitted to wear black to school or to wear jewelry in his piercings. Sometimes, he would forget and leave them in—or deliberately leave them—and then argue with a teacher about his individuality. But, from talking with his counselor, Mrs. Matthews, I learned that he had some serious problems at home."

"Drugs?"

"None that ever showed up at school. But Mrs. Matthews suspected he was doing marijuana. Unfortunately, a lot of the kids are doing that—even at school."

"How about Alison. Did she?"

"Not that I know of. But then, a lot of nice kids are doing it these days."

"Any idea why someone would kill William Matheson?"

"Some of the kids picked on him because of his black hair and his non-conformity. There was a fight once outside of school. No one saw it or intervened, but one of his friends told me about it."

"Who was that?"

"Erin Mosby. She was one of the few friends Billy had at school."

Templeton wrote the name down. Margaret listened with interest. Erin had told her about that fight.

"You think that could have escalated to murder, Mr. Santini?" asked Jane.

"Highly doubtful. Kids have fisticuffs at school without it turning into murder. Besides, I would imagine you have already talked with the kids in question."

"Ever worry about Billy becoming violent?" Templeton again. You know, showing up some day with an Uzi or a shotgun, like at Columbine."

"It never occurred to me with Billy, although he fit the pattern. We have been on the alert for some years now. That's why we lock the doors and have metal detectors. Even schools like Saint Dominic's are taking precautions nowadays. But no one ever mentioned anything to suggest that he was a worry in that regard."

Templeton turned some pages in his notes. Jane sipped her Coke. Joe sat perfectly still, his chair once again on four legs.

"Did you ever hear of a girl named Bonnie Easter?" Templeton asked.

Joe didn't answer right away. "Yes. But, I can't remember the context."

"She was a student at Saint Dominic's in 1974. You were only about nine years old. She was murdered."

"I do recall hearing something about that, now that you mention it."

"Are you related to her in any way?"

"Excuse me?"

"Are you in any way related to the Easter girl?"

"No. Absolutely not. Why?"

"Could there be any other connection?"

"I don't see how."

"Okay. Let's talk about Sally Rigali."

Joe let out a deep breath. "He was my cousin. He's dead. He was older than I was, and I barely knew him."

"Well, he was questioned about the Easter murder. Knew nothing about it. Except he was always present at parties that the Easter girl's father threw at his cabin in Riverton."

"Okay. So, what does that have to do with me?"

"Maybe nothing. Maybe everything."

"Look, my parents are decent, hard-working people who don't have people whacked and who raised me to be decent as well. My uncle

Johnny was a guy who gave me quarters, and his kids were often at family gatherings. I have spent my whole life trying to get out from under the shadow they cast over my life—over my parents' lives. But, other than family stuff, I never had anything to do with them. I haven't seen Sally in years, and I only learned that he died in the paper."

"Did you go to his funeral?"

"No. My mom did. You want to question her?"

Joe was starting to chafe.

Good for you, thought Margaret.

"Well," said Templeton, "I only have a few more questions. Would you like another soda pop?"

"What I would like, detective, is to get back home with my family. So, what are your questions?"

"Fine. Tell me about Grace Caldwell."

Santini went whey-faced. Even though he had feared this would come up, and had tried to brace himself for it, his reaction was obvious even to Margaret who was watching it on closed circuit.

"What about her?"

"Well, I called that school in Santa Fe and talked with a—let me see—Ted Quigley. He has apparently been a counselor there for a lot of years. Real talkative guy. He told me you left that school under a cloud of suspicion. Apparently, this Caldwell girl's parents were threatening to sue the school because you took advantage of their daughter. Was she a beautiful girl, too, Joe?"

It was at least two minutes before Joe responded. He swallowed the last of his drink before he spoke.

"Grace Caldwell had been assigned to me for three years. If you ask around at Saint Dominic's, you will find that I require students to switch counselors every so often, unless there is a very good reason not to. It helps prevent students from becoming too closely bonded to a counselor."

"And this was because of Grace Caldwell?"

"Yes, in part. And, it's just good practice."

"So you don't want your counselors diddling the beautiful girls?"

"That never happened, Detective!" Joe shouted and slammed his fist down on the table. Margaret jumped. The interrogation room became very quiet.

In a very calming voice, Jane spoke. "Doctor, could you tell us what did happen?"

To her consternation, Santini's emotions turned from rage to anguish and he began to sob loudly with his head in his hands. Templeton and Renfrow just looked at one another.

In the next room, Margaret was feeling sick to her stomach. Joe Santini was her friend. The nun overruled the cop in this situation. Hargrove was right about not putting her in that room. She felt Joe's agony deeply.

"Mr. Santini?" Renfrow again. "Do you want to take a break?"

He waved her away and tried to compose himself.

"No. It's just that I anticipated this, so I took off work today so I could tell my wife. I have never kept a secret from her in all the years of our marriage, and today I had to tell her. It broke my heart."

"Why did it break your heart?"

"Because I have been lying for years to the one woman who means the world to me. That's why, agent Renfrow. That's why."

"Well, if you didn't do anything, why hide it from your wife?" Templeton asked.

"Shame, detective. And the fear that, even though I know I didn't do anything, in the back of her mind she might have that nagging suspicion. I love her too much to have her thinking that about me, to live with the unspoken pall of doubt draped over our marriage."

"That's touching, Joe," said Templeton. "But do you want to tell us what happened?"

"Quigley is a jerk. He's just a counselor. Aaron Peterson is the head of counseling."

"I was told he was out on an extended sick leave," said Templeton.

"Quigley had no business talking to you about this."

"Well, sometimes people like to answer questions asked by law enforcement officials. Why don't you try that?"

"In her junior year, Grace was running with a bad crowd. I think she was into drugs, but I couldn't prove it. Her grades were plummeting. I was working with her to try to find out what was going on. I think she was trying to get back at her father, who never had time for her. He was some big shot in Santa Fe, and his idea of raising a kid was to give her everything she could possibly want—except his time.

"I saw the danger signals. It was as you said, detective: some of the girls quickly learn how to manipulate you, and the good-looking ones are walking dynamite if you aren't careful. I always have been careful. It is my goal in life to help them become decent human beings, not to sleep with them.

"One morning in a session, Grace blatantly asked me if I would like to have her. She said it, just like that. That was the last straw. I assigned her to another counselor, and explained that it wasn't in her best interest to see me anymore."

"What did she say about that?"

"She was furious. She cried. She screamed at me in the office and it could be heard outside. Then she stormed out."

"Did you tell anyone?"

"I told my boss. You really should talk with him."

"We will," said Renfrow. "Whenever we can. Then what happened?"

"Next thing I know, the school is being threatened by her parents with a lawsuit. The principal, wanting to avoid a scandal, discussed it with me and suggested that it would be best if I moved on. The Caldwells dropped their threats, and then next year donated another twenty PCs for the computer lab.

"I was young. I was too ashamed to tell my wife. I should have trusted her. I know I have to live with the fact that I didn't and pray that she will forgive me. The last thing Grace Caldwell said to me was, 'You'll be sorry.' I was. And I am again. My wife is now wondering if she can ever trust me to be honest with her. And if this comes out, my job might be in jeopardy."

"But, if it's as you say, how could they fire you?" asked Templeton.

"When it comes to children, and the abuse of children, we are so protective that even to be accused of something like that casts a doubt on your character. People think that if there's smoke, there's fire. No one takes chances like that. I know priests who won't go anywhere near a kid any more, won't hug them when they need it, won't even play ball with them, because they don't want people looking, pointing, and thinking. You can never defend yourself, even when you are proven innocent. People just figure that the evidence wasn't sufficient, not that you didn't do it. I know, detective. I teach in a Catholic school that is a flagship for a church plagued by scandal. Oh, the nuns would be charitable. I could stay on as a counselor, perhaps, for a cut in pay. Then, if word got out, my part-time counseling would dry up. You say that tape will be in a drawer for twenty years? Well, this was supposed to be off the record in Santa Fe, too. But you found out. Who's to say where that tape will end up, detective? Even though I am innocent. And I am innocent. I had nothing to do with the deaths of those children."

When the interview ended, Margaret knew in her heart that Joe Santini had nothing to do with the murders of Alison Corcoran and Billy Matheson.

She knew, too, that there wouldn't be a record of that interview.

Chapter 35

"God damn it! What did you do?" Templeton got into the car and slammed the door.

The outdoor temperature had risen to eighty-nine degrees. The sun had heated his car's interior such that Margaret was waiting with the car doors open until the air conditioner could be turned on.

"That tape is blank!"

"I haven't the slightest idea what you are talking about. When you finished, I shut the recorder off. Maybe you didn't have it set to record properly."

"And maybe gremlins got into the anteroom. You realize you have impeded an investigation and you could be brought up on charges?"

"Ridiculous. Don't go blaming me for your own ineptitude."

Templeton pounded on the steering wheel.

"You couldn't have recorded over it. There wasn't time. So you switched it. I'll find it. This was a big mistake. A big mistake."

"That system is antiquated. We got that about a year after I started with the department, and except for the addition of a few VCRs, it has been the same. Don't blame me. You need better equipment."

"It's a sin to tell a lie, Sister. And you are guilty as hell. I'm returning you to your convent, and then I am coming back and having a long talk with Hargrove about your suitability for this kind of work."

"Are you telling me that you like Santini for this?"

"No. Not at all. He didn't kill them."

"Then why, in God's name, are you so bent out of shape over a tape that didn't come out?"

"Liar, liar, pants on fire," he said as he squealed out onto Capitol Street.

"That's juvenile," she said. "But I suppose I should consider the source."

"Don't go all holy fucking roller on me. You aren't a nun in this car. You are a cop. You have to live by the same rules I do and it pisses me off that you feel you can do any damned thing you want and get away with it."

"Okay. I'm done. Just take me home. I've never known anyone so bullheaded in my life."

"Sister, you have no idea how much pleasure I am going to get by dropping you off. And I won't be picking you up again. I will make sure that Hargrove understands that."

A call came through just as Templeton turned south on Lincoln. There was a disturbance in the Fairhills Mall parking lot. A city car and an emergency transport were on scene, but backup was requested from any car in the area.

"Well, I am going to have to delay my pleasure for a while and be a cop. It will do you good too," Templeton said. "Might help you remember whose side you're on."

He swung into the parking lot and saw the lights flashing on an emergency transport. There was a city police car there, and about thirty people were crowded around parked cars near the County Market.

Templeton pulled up and got out. Margaret got out and followed him.

From where she stood, she could see a man screaming and being restrained by two policemen. The man wore a shirt and tie. His face was bright red and tear-streaked. The noise he was emitting was one of pure horror, like something Margaret remembered from old scary movies she would watch on TV.

She walked around the parked cars and saw a late model BMW, dark blue, with the rear door standing open. An EMT was kneeling over something with his back turned to her.

Templeton distracted her as he walked up and gave an assist to the two officers. Soon they had the man seated on the ground, still wailing but at least under control.

Margaret turned back to the BMW.

The EMT stood and, for the first time, she saw what he had been working on.

A child, who appeared to be less than two years old, lay on his back on a blanket. His color was unnatural, red and purplish, and his eyes wide open. His mouth was frozen open in a cry that had gone unheeded, a cry that would go on forever in the minds of those who loved him. Margaret's stomach turned, and she placed her hand over her mouth.

"Mother of God," she said—and blessed herself.

"Had to be a hundred and twenty degrees in that car, Sister," the EMT said. He was perspiring heavily from attempts to resuscitate the boy.

"Heard the guy tell them that his wife had called because she couldn't pick him up at the sitter's. Guess the sitter got sick. He had to interrupt his busy schedule to get the boy. Wife also told him to pick stuff up at the store. So, he parked here and went into the store. Was on the cell phone the whole time. Guess he forgot about the time, since he was working on some big deal. I think he's a pharmacy rep or something. Well, he forgot about the time, all right. And this is what he has to show for it," the EMT said, pointing to the child. "People just don't realize how fast a car can heat up. Hyperthermia has to be a horrible way to die."

Margaret looked back at the man, who was still sobbing. One of the city guys stood next to him, patting his shoulder. God would need to intervene dramatically in his life to allow him—and his wife—to overcome this. She couldn't imagine the horror he must be feeling now, or the agony that would continue to haunt his existence.

Then she noticed Templeton.

He had walked over and had seen, for the first time, the child lying on the ground. The EMTs were placing the boy in a body bag for transport, but the scream on the boy's face was still frozen in its fruitless appeal to the sky—a sky that reflected back into eyes now dead.

Templeton's face was drained of all color. He lost his balance for a moment, and had to steady himself against one of the parked cars.

"Hey. You okay?" Margaret asked.

He waved her off and then turned and rushed back behind a pickup truck. She could hear him throwing up.

"Can't blame him," the EMT said. "I want to myself."

Margaret walked behind the truck. Templeton was wiping his mouth with a handkerchief, and was leaning up against the tailgate.

"Give me your keys."

Templeton didn't argue. He simply handed over the keys.

A cooling breeze now whispered through the outdoor seating area at Sonic, where Margaret and Templeton were sitting at one of the tables. He took a sip of 7-Up while Margaret sat quietly nursing an iced tea.

"Thanks," he said.

"Feeling better?"

He sat the drink down. "You don't have to nurse me. I'm fine."

As he looked at her now, her eyes seemed more open, more radiant. More inviting. Her brown irises hovered beneath her eyelids, almost seeming to cross slightly as she focused her attention on him. There was a quick intelligence behind those eyes. He had thought her somewhat attractive before, but now—as he looked directly at her for perhaps the first time—he was thinking how beautiful she was. He was having a visceral reaction that was spreading to his groin.

Jesus Christ! This is a nun.

"Look," Margaret said. "I am calling a truce. Okay. Maybe I am a bitch on wheels, and maybe you are a self-satisfied, arrogant SOB."

"Charmingly put."

"You said it yourself. When I'm in that car, I'm a cop. Well, my partner is hurting. So, yes, I do have to take care of you."

"Fair enough. You ready? I'm fine."

Margaret wasn't ready.

"That was a horrible thing. I have never seen anything like it. I hope to God I never do again. Those poor people," Margaret said. "You've been a cop for a long time, Bill. What happened back there?"

Templeton had started to slide over to stand up, but then scooted back and set his keys on the table top with a clink. Attached to the keychain was a large coin on which was embossed what appeared to be the Serenity Prayer. Embossed on the back, in small letters, was the name "Cumberland Heights," which she knew to be an alcohol rehab center in Nashville, Tennessee. Her earlier impression of him was thus confirmed.

"I have," he said.

"You have what?"

"Seen that before."

Margaret spread her hands apart on the table.

"It wasn't hyperthermia. It was a drowning. It was my little brother. He was about six. I was eight. His name was Christopher. Where we lived in Chapin was sort of on the outskirts, and there was a farm pond across this field where we used to go fishing and swimming. One day—it was a hot day in July—I went to take a dip and he tagged along. We went in the water and splashed around. It was pretty shallow up to a point, so I wasn't worried about him. Anyway, I got distracted by something. I think it was an airplane going over. I was always crazy about airplanes. When I turned around, I couldn't see Chris. So, I remember getting out and hollering at the top of my lungs for help. Somebody. Anybody. Probably about like that poor kid screamed today. But there wasn't anybody around. So, I did the only thing I could think of. I ran home. It took over an hour for us to get back there. My dad and some of the neighbors went in and found him in about five feet of water."

He stopped talking. Margaret was overcome by sadness for this man, whose bravado she now knew to be a mask that covered a very vulnerable little boy who was still in a great deal of pain. She watched as a tear began to slide down Templeton's cheek.

"When they dragged him out, he looked so ... like he was just asleep. I remember going over to hug him, to make him get up. My dad grabbed me by the hair and threw me down on the ground. 'You killed him!' he said. 'You killed your brother and you will rot in hell.'"

Bill looked up and, for the first time since they had arrived, looked at her directly. Entreating? Seeking judgment? She wanted desperately to place her hand on his, to comfort him in some way.

"Bill, you didn't."

"Yes," he said, picking up the keys. "Yes, I did. But thanks for the thought. Let's go."

Neither of them spoke during the ride back to the convent. As he pulled into the circle drive behind the chapel and stopped, she reached for the door handle and then turned back to look at him. He was looking directly into her eyes. Their gaze coupled in mid-air and in the moment. There were no words but much was being said. The intensity was frightening to her but she couldn't look away.

He finally broke the silence.

"What I said earlier? Forget it. I'll be back to get you again."

No! No! Go and never come back.

"Thanks," she said.

Then she went straight to the chapel for a conversation with God about what was going on in her heart, hoping she could find some relief for the guilt she was feeling at this moment for any number of reasons. One of which was the cassette tape buried in the bottom of her bag.

Chapter 36

The photograph wasn't very clear. It had been a black and white to begin with, and it did not reproduce well when scanned to jpeg. Baker had sized it for e-mail, which made the resolution less than optimal.

The photograph showed a family grouping. George Easter stood in the center, flanked by two young girls. Margaret compared the one to his left with a photo in the 1974 Saint Dominic's yearbook. Even though younger, Bonnie was the taller of the two girls and appeared physically more mature. Her breasts were well developed and anyone looking at the photo would think her to be much older than sixteen. She was much prettier than her older sister, who was shorter and rather plump. The face Margaret saw in the yearbook was angular, with high cheekbones and clear, intense eyes. She could break hearts, no doubt.

In front, seated, was a young boy. He might have been anywhere from eight to ten years of age. He was very thin and his hair was cut close. He and his father both wore short-sleeved shirts, so the picture had been taken in a warm season. His face wasn't clearly visible, but he wore an anomalous smile. The other three appeared to have just come from a funeral.

"Why can't you ever smile?" her dad used to ask her whenever someone would take her picture as a kid. Margaret remembered how frustrated he would get when trying to snap her photo, at home or on vacation.

"I'm ugly, Daddy!" she would say.

"You can't be ugly, Margaret. You're my daughter—and you are the spitting image of your mother. She was beautiful and so are you."

Margaret always hated that expression, 'spitting image.' It made her think of someone who spat as her photo was taken. The thought just made her less inclined to smile for the camera, and would send her father into a spasm of complaining.

She smiled now, remembering the little drama that had played out with her father on a regular basis as she grew up. Now she looked at what could have been, should have been, a happy photo of a family. But it was so sad.

The photograph appeared to have been taken on a front porch, with the four of them posed in front of a bay window. Whoever snapped it had no feeling for lighting, because the sun was coming from the side of the house and left shadows on the left sides of their faces, further obfuscating the image.

She couldn't see anything in the face of the boy that looked familiar. It was too dark, too faded, and too old.

She dropped the photograph on the desk and took a sip of her Diet 7-Up. It was too late for a Coke; the caffeine would keep her up half the night.

What was going on in the Easter family? How could it be that an entire family could just vanish from the face of the earth? One, to a horrible death at the hands of a person or persons unknown; the father to suicide; and the other daughter—the only one of whom there was any record after the double family tragedy—to a traffic accident.

Where was that little boy? Did he even have a name?

And could he have anything to do with the recent murders—or was Margaret just chasing a ghost?

She wondered if this was the only ghost she was chasing.

The events of the day had thrown her together with Bill in a way that had left her reeling. She sat now analyzing. She did that to a fault.

She smiled now, remembering how her dad used to tease her about thinking too much.

When she took biology at the Catholic high school in Jacksonville, she learned that each one of her legs was comprised of thirty bones. She became obsessed with this, and wondered how something so complex could work together in harmony. Pretty soon, the more she thought about it, the more self conscious she became about walking—and started to limp.

"Hey, gimpy!" her dad said one day as she walked home from school. "What's with the limp?"

"What limp?" she asked. She honestly wasn't aware of it.

That had set her dad off into one of his imitations of Marty Feldman as Igor in *Young Frankenstein* ("What hump?"), which made her laugh in spite of herself. Her dad would hunch over, roll his eyes and shuffle along beside her. It was embarrassing how he would carry on. She had seen him get the prisoners to break up in their cells in such a manner. She came out of it quickly, though, and soon became aware of her tendency to overanalyze.

But she never quite stopped doing it.

Sometimes focusing on all of the parts has a paralytic effect, and you have to move forward with faith that it all will work, she decided. Still, she sometimes failed to follow her own advice.

Like now.

What was she doing?

For more than five years, she had been happy. Happier than she ever had been in her life. Then why the hesitation about making her final profession?

And now—to make matters worse—she was still experiencing shock waves from what had occurred in the car between her and Templeton. She had experienced a reaction to him unlike any she had felt since—well, since Eric. It started in her chest and radiated to her breasts and groin and seemingly wanted to engage her tear ducts in the process. As obnoxious and as maddening as the man was, there was something about him that attracted her. Yes, he was great looking, and when he wasn't busy being an asshole he could be affable, comical and engaging. He was unquestionably intelligent and, thus, good at his job; it was easy to see why Ernie was bringing him along.

Margaret closed her eyes now, mortified by the clear understanding that for a brief moment in time she had wanted to tear off his clothes.

"What am I doing?" she said aloud to herself.

Her cell phone rang. She pushed the button on her phone. "Donovan."

"Hargrove. I am faxing the pathologist's report of the autopsy to you as I speak."

"Okay. Thanks." She clicked off, and turned to see paper being ejected from the fax machine. She walked over and began reading as the paper was coming out.

Cause of death: Cardiac ischemia due to neck compression. Manner of death: *Pending further investigation.* The pathologist was waiting for the results from toxicology. That would take several weeks.

His hesitation in deeming suicide the manner of death had less to do with any concern that someone had deliberately done this to Pickering than it did with Pickering's motivation. The cause of death was not in question. The hyoid bone was not fractured, and if someone had strangled Pickering it most likely would have been. His heart had stopped because the rope had exerted pressure on his carotid arteries. What was in question was whether Pickering had done this to end his life or to get off.

This would not be the first case of erotic asphyxia to end up in the pathologist's office this year. Although the circumstances didn't clearly point to it—in fact they were leaning toward suicide—they wanted to completely rule out any other possibilities.

Anal fissures indicated that Pickering had engaged in sex with other men for a long period of time, probably years—but not immediately before death. Toxicology would determine whether any recreational drugs were present.

Preliminary blood work had indicated a blood alcohol level of .25—more than three times the legal limit. However, this would require confirmation from the laboratory as well, given the problems associated with obtaining an untainted blood sample post mortem.

There were other interesting observations on the chart.

For one, there was a cut on Pickering's neck, below the right jaw line, indicating that a sharp object had been pressed against the skin. It was a small point, which could indicate the point of a knife. However, it could as easily have been a razor.

There was an old straight razor found in the bathroom that Pickering used for shaving. It had the initials "TNP" on one side of the handle. The other side of the handle was missing. A family heirloom? A razor left by a lover? No one could say, but it could very well have caused the cut that was noted in the report.

"So, where does this leave us?" Margaret asked Jim Hargrove. She had reached him as he was preparing to leave for a fundraiser.

"Well, nothing in that report tells me that this isn't the guy," Jim said. "The pathologist isn't wavering between suicide and homicide; he just wants to verify that it was a suicide and not an accident."

Margaret didn't respond.

"The report ties with the evidence the city guys found in his place. There was semen found on the bed sheets—probably going back a number of years. I don't think he ever changed the sheets. There are a variety of different contributors based on the initial analysis. Obviously the findings about his sexual preference weren't a surprise. Only question I have is, did this guy go out entertaining himself or was someone else in on the games? If so, then we may have a manslaughter charge against someone—you still there?"

"Yes," Margaret said. "I'm just thinking."

Hargrove let out a deep sigh. He knew what that meant.

"Maybe a boyfriend was playing the game with him, Margaret."

"Maybe."

"Well, if you ask me, I think we can stand down. If something else turns up, then we'll put more manpower on it."

Or if someone else dies, thought Margaret.

Chapter 37

As was her custom, Margaret prayed late that evening in the chapel illumined only by a pinpoint of light from the sanctuary lamp. Thick stone columns met in pointed arches high above, from which the crucified and bloodied savior inclined his head in her direction, fixing his gaze on her as she knelt beneath him.

She prayed for the family of the child who had died so tragically that day. Where was the good? Where the evil? Try as she might, she could never understand.

She also prayed for Bill Templeton. How long had he been carrying this pain? She thought of her own father, how he had been everything to her, and she to him. Even though she hadn't known her mother, she had wonderful memories of a loving man who had cared for her and given her so much. Why are not all children so blessed? Why is it that so many children do well simply to survive their parents? Where is the good in that?

Her personal experience of evil, in her work and in her heart, was what had bogged down her thesis. The problem wasn't the age-old question of why, if God is good, does evil exist. Her problem was why, if God is good, couldn't human beings sense it anymore? Where do they go to see it? They should be seeking that goodness the way ants swarm toward bread dropped on the grass, the way moths fly headlong into light bulbs, the way piglets fight for the open teat and children turn instinctively to a mother's breast. It seems that we humans, the only ones who can reflect, languish rather than seek out that comfort. And now, we tend to accept the conventional wisdom that says that comfort simply isn't there. All we have are the hard facts of existence, where the soul dies with the brain and the wheel keeps turning and churning forever and ever. No Amen.

Where to people go to see it? When she was young, they went to church. They saw it in the priests and religious who embodied it. It was there for her to see.

Now the religious were dwindling, and priests were more likely to be viewed with suspicion than reverence.

Where, indeed, does one seek God? Or was it that God was seeking, and our job was to answer? Had the world shut out the possibility of His signal getting through, the way trees and hills interrupt the signal of a cell phone?

She recalled a poem she had read many years ago, from a book in her father's library, about a soul running from God. She could still remember the first few lines:

> I fled Him, down the nights and down the days;
> I fled Him, down the arches of the years;
> I fled Him, down the labyrinthine ways
> Of my own mind; and in the mist of tears
> I hid from Him …

She prayed for understanding of her own heart. She was trying to deal with the emotions that had erupted earlier as she looked into Bill's eyes. Those emotions still churned.

The autopsy results could mean an end to the search for the killer of Alison and Billy. For now, she resolved to continue her investigation. The two interviews that she had planned she could do without Bill, without having to look into his eyes and stir up those feelings again. She knew she had to resist any occasion of sin, and fought with herself because part of her didn't want to avoid it.

She wasn't a cop any more. She had left that behind her. It was time to move on, put her hand to the plow and not look back. This diversion had muddied the waters of her life again.

But what about those feelings?

Why would God send those feelings if they weren't good, if they weren't supposed to tell her something? She prayed for help in understanding what this meant about her, about her decision to become a religious, to give her life to God. Was this a test—or was it an intervention?

Was she deserving of this life of service? Or was she running from the guilt that she still carried deep within? Margaret's was a soul in pain. The time to answer these questions was drawing nearer. She would have to make a decision.

Finally, she had to question her own integrity. She knew all too well that people could lie with alacrity, even and especially to themselves. Was she honestly praying that the investigation would end, and thus her association with Templeton?

Or was she praying that it wouldn't?

It struck her as she walked past the cemetery gates on her way back to the residence. It was starting to rain and the wind was picking up. She stopped walking as the words came back to her.

"Strange, piteous, futile things."

The words from Pickering's suicide note. She knew she had seen them somewhere before. She ran to the residence, up the steps, past the two cats drinking milk on the front stoop ("Damn it, Carmelita!"), and into the front door, which had not yet been locked for the night.

She went to the library, which consisted of one whole wall of the common room, floor to ceiling, with approximately one thousand books, many of which the convent had received when the junior seminary in Springfield closed. They were in some semblance of order, as one would expect in a convent. Religion (mostly), philosophy, great works of literature, and—yes—poetry. She couldn't remember the author or the title, but she knew it would be a small book. Her father's was a narrow tome. Unless it was in an anthology, in which case it would take some time.

She was just about to go to the computer and Google the first line when she spotted it. She pulled it off the shelf and sat down in the large armchair in front of the library shelves.

The Hound of Heaven, by Francis Thompson.

She opened to the first page, and saw the words that had come to her earlier: *I fled Him, down the nights and down the days.*

She read the entire poem, recalling as she did how she had borrowed it from her dad's library and spent a summer afternoon reading in the tree next to the jail. This poem was considered by some to be one of the greatest religious poems ever written, and the Catholics were especially possessive of it since Thompson was, himself, a Catholic. It told the story of a man addicted to opium who finally realized that he was fleeing the only one who could bring him peace and happiness—God.

She stopped when she found the stanza:

> Strange, piteous, futile thing,
> Wherefore should any set thee love apart?
> Seeing none but I makes much of naught" (He said),
> "And human love needs human meriting:
> How hast thou merited—
> Of all man's clotted clay the dingiest clot?

She bolted from the chair and walked, almost ran, down the hallway and up the stairs. She noted that Theodora's door was closed, and then looked at her watch. Theodora seldom went to bed before eleven. But she proceeded to her room and pulled out the accordion file where she had stored all the case information.

She read again all of the personnel file and notes taken by Templeton regarding Pickering. He had never finished eighth grade. There was no indication of his having completed a GED during his period of incarceration. Yes, his family had been Catholic—his aunt was a nun—but from all indications his mother had long ago strayed and the church was not a part of his upbringing. The most he had been exposed to was during the years at Saint D's, and she had never seen him in chapel except to sweep up.

Then she remembered something else. She remembered that the poet, Francis Thompson, for all the adulation paid him by Catholics, was truly a dark character. She went back down to the common room and switched on the computer. She sat now in the chair in front of the desk barefoot, her right leg folded under her.

She typed "Francis Thompson" into Google.

Francis Thompson may have been the author of a compelling poem about the flight of a soul from the love of God, but he was among the most troubled of men. A seminarian who failed at the priesthood, and who later studied unsuccessfully to become a surgeon, Thompson was addicted to opium and lived on the streets. In 1888, he lived in the wharf district of Whitechapel. A failed relationship with a prostitute led him to hate all of her ilk, and he possessed a surgeon's knife that he would proudly show off for friends.

It is ironic that Francis Thompson, author of what is considered one of the greatest poetic expressions of faith, was among the suspects in five unsolved murders in 1888 in Whitechapel, attributed only to a man known as Jack the Ripper. At least one writer insisted that Thompson was the most likely suspect.

Strange, piteous, futile things.

Margaret was now more certain than ever that Pickering was not the killer. The words may have been in his hand, but they almost certainly did not come from his mind. Those words sprang from a spiritual experience, however muddled and horribly confused, and from a person who had encountered those words in a moment of reflection, perhaps years earlier. Perhaps even from a person with a religious background. And, if the killer knew of Thompson's background, perhaps there was a double message there. Maybe—but one thing of which she was certain was that the killer of Alison Corcoran and Billy Matheson was still out there.

She had to keep going, regardless of the risk to her soul and to her vocation.

Chapter 38

It had been several weeks since the doctor had shown him the images of his brain. The doctor pointed to a seven- or eight-centimeter mass in the frontal lobe. It was inoperable. He did not reply when the doctor explained that chemotherapy and radiation might prolong his life, but that the prognosis was bad even with those treatments. He had six months, at most, and his last days would be painful.

He popped another Vicodin. He knew it wouldn't help much, but anything was better than nothing. Had the cancer brought back the memories? He had buried them so deep that they never surfaced to eat away at his psyche. Not even in dreams. Now, those memories swirled about in his head, and he feared sleep because the horrific scene replayed itself over and over again. He was so tired. It was becoming more difficult to think clearly, and he had to think clearly. He had to finish what he started. He could never talk about it, so he decided to let the grandchildren tell the story. In this way, his sister's death would be avenged.

He had spent a lot of time on the Internet, and learned about the complexities of the human brain. There was a place there, called the amygdala, which housed traumatic memories. This part of the brain was not conscious of the passage of time, such that whenever a memory was recalled, even from decades past, it struck the consciousness in such a way as to make it fresh, eternally present, throbbing with a Proustian clarity that caused one to relive the pain anew with each passing moment.

The disease had awakened those memories, and they gave him as much pain as the headaches. He could take pills for the latter, but the trauma seemingly knew no end.

Now he was again that ten-year-old boy, hiding in the closet, watching Sally throw the naked body of his sister over his shoulder and walk out on the porch. He heard a trunk lid close, and watched as the other men stood in the doorway. The police chief was there now talking with them. The fat lawyer, still naked, sat against the wall, crying. The doctor with the green eyes looked down at the man and shook his head. The police chief said, "Get a grip, Jerry. Can you keep your god-damned mouth shut about this, or should we have Sally take you along with her?"

The Vicodin began to work. He popped another one. He hated what he had done and what he still had to do. He had cried when he rolled that beautiful girl down the embankment.

He had to kill Pickering. Pickering couldn't understand why he couldn't come over any more. He knew that the investigators were looking at the janitor, so he decided that a sacrifice would buy him time to finish what he had started. Pickering, like many others whose names escaped him now, had provided a needed outlet. For as many years as he could remember, he had an almost priapic sex drive. He would sometimes masturbate two, maybe three times a day. Another man made it more pleasurable, but he could and frequently did just shift for himself. It helped him make it through the day. It helped him get through life. Now, however, the desire was no longer there. Was it because of what was going on inside his brain? It didn't matter. He had to finish what he had started before he died. He was not going to go for treatment. Why prolong what had become a living hell? *But before he went, everyone would know what those men had done.*

He had held a knife to Pickering's throat and made him write the note. It was an inspired message. He then stood him up and threw the noose around his neck. The rope was draped over the closed door and tied in a double hitch to the doorknob on the other side. Still holding the knife, he pushed down on Pickering's shoulders, fully expecting him to resist.

To his surprise, Pickering didn't fight. Instead, he looked up at him the way his old dog did years ago when he took him to the vet's to put him to sleep, just before he handed the animal over. It was a look of trust. It was as though he was saying he understood. He understood that it was something that had to be done and that it would be better—for everyone.

Pickering's look sliced through him like a knife. Something buzzed in his brain momentarily and he wondered what, in God's name, he was doing. He watched helplessly as the man slid down the door, and started to die with no effort whatsoever to stop what was going to happen. It was as though his body was simply rejoining the spirit that had ceased to exist meaningfully years before. A tear formed in his eye as he watched this man die and, after he felt for a pulse, he had to fight the urge to throw up.

Pickering had knowingly and willingly allowed his life to end.

He cried again as he remembered the event. He wasn't this kind of a person. He had always been a good person. He had studied for the priesthood, and had served his country with distinction. He had lived a good life.

That was before the dreams and the memories resurfaced. He had never forgotten Bonnie. She came to him in his sleep. Bonnie had brought him back to Springfield because she and her father were all the family he had now that his adoptive parents were gone. But he had managed to place the horror of that night somewhere deep in a place where it wouldn't break free. Until the headaches. Until the thing grew in his head. It was making it harder and harder to concentrate. He didn't have time to waste.

He had spent an hour afterwards wiping down every surface in the apartment that he might have touched any time he had been there. He didn't need fingerprints showing up. DNA would take time, and they didn't have his anyway.

He had been thinking clearly then. It was getting harder, but he had to try to keep thinking.

There wasn't much time left.

Chapter 39

Bill Templeton was dying for a drink.

He had a decent apartment on Koke Mill Road on the west side of town. It was furnished simply. The place had a sitting room, a dining area off the kitchen, and one bedroom. That was all he needed.

He was watching Nancy Grace and reading.

It had been two years since his last drink. He wasn't about to break that record. It was now a matter of sheer willpower. He knew that was dangerous; his weekly group leader was always reminding him—and the others—that they didn't have the strength to do it alone. Only the God part of the brain—reliance on the power that was greater than all of us—would give him the strength.

Unfortunately, Bill had never been a big believer. His parents took him to church sometimes—usually his mother because dad had come in late drunker than a skunk—but it was more rote than religion.

He remembered the smell of the wood and cast iron chairs that were bolted to the floor of the First Baptist Church. The seats folded back when they weren't being used, and they weren't very comfortable. He kept squirming, which caused his mom to shush him—and his dad to smack him on top of the head on those Sundays when he attended.

The preacher was a fat man with a bad comb over and big brown glasses whose suits never seemed to fit him. His sermons were interminable and unintelligible, at least to a boy of his age. For the life of him, he couldn't understand why people would subject themselves to such an experience willingly.

After eighth grade, he quit going. His mom was too tired to argue, and his dad had stopped going long ago.

He could count on one hand the number of times he had been in a church since. He could not comprehend why someone like Margaret would give up her life for religion. He hadn't been able to shake the feelings that she had evoked earlier in the day. Why in God's name he had opened up to her he couldn't understand either. He had never talked about his brother before. It was like a splinter that had worked its way deep under his skin, still hurting, still causing him anxiety. It was still there—but for some reason he had opened up to her.

Was that it? Was the emotional outpouring the source of his feelings for Margaret? Had he, by sharing, transferred the feeling of elation to her person somehow and confused relief for attraction?

No. That wasn't it. He had been attracted to her the minute he saw her. Her eyes were alight, her face more beautiful for being unadorned. No religious attire, however modestly cut, could conceal her anatomy. He was experiencing a physical response now just thinking about it.

It wasn't right.

She had sensed it too. He knew it.

Jesus Christ! She's a nun.

He could really use a drink right now.

Since day one he had thought that Margaret was on the wrong track with the Easter thing. He had repeatedly made his opinion known. Nonetheless, he now sat reading the case file and all of the articles that had been written about the Easter murder.

He kept thinking that it made no sense. He read again the Pickering autopsy report, and knew that the pathologist was a few tox reports away from deeming it a suicide. Which meant that Pickering was the killer. Which meant all of this was a waste of time.

It occurred to him that, if Pickering was the doer, Margaret would disappear from his life. Part of him didn't want that, in spite of the impossibility of the situation.

Sure, he would love to jump her bones. What was going on in his boxer shorts gave ample testimony to that. But there was something more. He had jumped a lot of girls through the years, and could take them or leave them. He had no trouble finding another. But he just wasn't looking that hard these days.

The sense of calm that had come over him looking into Margaret's eyes was something he had never experienced. His own mother never made him feel that way. Margaret looked deeply into his eyes once this afternoon, and his soul was reeling from the encounter.

It was a good feeling. He didn't want to lose it, no matter what the cost.

So, he was now poring over all of the documents that he could find. He had even stopped by the State's Attorney's office and asked to see anything they had. There wasn't much. But copies of what they had now sat on his coffee table.

He was playing 'what if' games.

What if Bonnie Easter had been sexually molested by a few of Springfield's finest? The names in these files of men who were questioned read like a who's who of the town's best—and worst. There was the prosecutor himself, Jerry Brown—fat, inclined to drink too much, and rumored to be corrupt. Then there was the fire chief, Ed Jenkins, who racked up favors over the years from other corrupt politicians until he got a nice cushy job.

Then there was the connection revealed by the *State Journal-Register* about Doctor Corcoran.

He was the only one that didn't seem to fit. But there was a lot that wasn't in the file.

And lurking in the shadows was Sally Rigali.

What in God's name was Rigali doing in this file? He was listed as a friend of the family.

Some friends the Easters had.

What if Margaret was right? Let's say that the younger Easter boy had witnessed what happened to his sister. Okay, so his dad does whatever he can to get him away, someplace where the others would never find him and hurt him, or kill him. The kid grows up, eventually cracks, and decides to take it out on the grandchildren of the men who killed his sister. Was something like that possible?

He looked unsuccessfully for any mention of a viable suspect for the girl's murder. The dishwasher was a scumbag, but not a shred of physical evidence put him anywhere near Easter except at work. But there was that pesky conviction for rape and murder. Maybe the dishwasher had gotten lucky with Easter.

But, even if one were to suppose that the Easter killing was connected, that the lost son had come back like a ghost to claim revenge on the grandchildren—to cause the sins of the fathers to be visited upon their children—why would Pickering have died? What connection did the janitor have with all of this?

"And a special thanks to you …" Nancy Grace was signing off.

He shut off the TV. "You're welcome," he said, and got up to go to bed.

It was three in the morning when Templeton awoke and sat straight up in bed. He threw off the covers and went into the living room. Flipping through the papers on the coffee table, he found the police report on the crime scene investigation at Pickering's rented house. This was the fourth time he had read through the report, but something had just now awakened his curiosity and brought him out of a dead sleep. So he read it again.

After about ten minutes, he set the papers down and sat back in his chair, where he brought his hands together in the attitude of prayer and moved his fingertips up to his lips. There were no usable prints found at the scene. There were some smudges, but almost every surface and object that could be dusted for prints was clean as a whistle. The place was a dump, but there wasn't a fingerprint anywhere. What sort of person, inebriated almost to the point of being unconscious and intent on hanging himself, would first go around and clean every surface in the house?

"Margaret, dear girl, you just might be on to something," he said aloud to himself as he turned off the light and went back into the bedroom. He was smiling. *He would have to telephone her in the morning.*

Chapter 40

The face behind the barred and screened window kept changing.

"What you reading, little darling?"

Margaret looked up from her perch in the tree where she was reading The Hound of Heaven, *and finally located the cell window from which the voice had come.*

"Margaret. Margaret. Sitting in a tree."

The man was smiling. He wore a badge. It turned into a spider and crawled over his shoulder.

When she looked back a few minutes later he had morphed into an infant, his mouth frozen open in a silent scream, his eyes hollow, his teeth sharp and dripping with blood. In his right hand he held a severed liver.

"Must thy harvest fields be dunged with rotten death?"

"Margaret. Margaret." He started to pound on the window screen.

The pounding on her door awakened her.

"Margaret?"

She looked at the LED on her clock radio. Four thirty.

She threw the covers off and padded over to the door.

When she opened it, she saw Theodora leaning against the doorsill. She was bent over and holding her side. She had no color in her cheeks.

"Come in! What's wrong?"

Margaret put her arm around her and led her in. She sat her down on the bed, and then helped her lay back.

"The pain. I have been having a little lately, mostly in the evening. But this—it feels as though someone has impaled me. And ... there's bleeding—"

"I'm getting dressed. We're going to the hospital."

Margaret sat in the patients' lounge at St. John's emergency room. It was seven in the morning, and she had thus far consumed six cups of vending machine coffee. The TV was tuned to CNN, the volume set low, but Margaret paid no attention to it.

There were several other persons milling around the waiting room.

At five thirty, two young black girls who smelled of weed and alcohol came in, crying and carrying on about a young man who had been brought in with a head wound. Two police officers were in and out, alternately questioning the girls—who were not very cooperative—and the nursing staff. Now, the two girls were pacing the floor.

An older man sat against the window reading a paperback novel.

She had telephoned Sister Agnes by six, after the paperwork was finished and Theodora was comfortable in one of the rooms. The doctor had come in and Margaret went to the waiting room, where she still sat doing just that: waiting. She had run out of *Newsweek* magazines, and was now turning the pages of a *Field and Stream*.

"Sister?"

Margaret looked up to see a white-haired nurse, clad in a yellow and blue smock with a stethoscope draped around her neck. "Yes?"

"They have come back from X-Ray, but they are going to send her up for additional tests. It will probably take another hour or so."

"How is she feeling?"

"She is uncomfortable, but the doctor has given her something for the pain."

"Thank you."

"Sister, come with me," she whispered.

Margaret put the magazine down and followed the nurse through the automatic doors, down a long hallway, and into a small, nicely appointed lounge. There she saw a Bunn-O-Matic with freshly brewed coffee, leather chairs and a long sofa. The TV on the wall was tuned to CNN. The hospital must get a deal on CNN coverage.

"You will be more comfortable here. The waiting room out front gets a little hectic sometimes."

"Thank you so much."

"And I see you're drinking that crap from the mud machine. You'll appreciate this coffee more."

"No doubt." Margaret smiled and walked directly over to the coffee maker.

"I know you are worried about Sister Theodora. This may seem a strange question, but are you related to her by any chance?"

Margaret smiled. "No."

"You look alike. I'll keep you informed." The nurse walked out and closed the door.

It sometimes bothered Margaret that people treated her and other clerics specially. There were others in the waiting room who would doubtless enjoy more privacy and better coffee. The irony was that clerics are supposed to live their lives in service to others, but others seemed to go out of their way to serve them, to make them comfortable, to treat them differently. It was a vestige of a time, perhaps, when clerics were of a higher caste, and deference to them was expected. Or maybe people thought that their kindness to one of God's servants would be remembered on the Day of Judgment.

Now, however, it didn't bother her that much. She was grateful for quieter surroundings, and for the real coffee that she now held in her hand. She blew on it, and sipped it quietly. And prayed.

Chapter 41

Theresa Madison brushed her teeth and checked for pimples. She knew she was great looking, and she figured it would serve her well in her career. She jealously guarded her complexion.

"You need to eat something, Theresa," her mother said.

Georgiana Madison, called "Georgie" by her husband, was a pretty woman, short in stature, with shoulder-length black hair that required coloring once a month so as not to show the gray. She had done her best to maintain her figure over the years, and had managed to keep it within bounds. She was self-conscious about her hips and thighs, which had always been her trouble spots. When she was younger and more active, she had managed to keep them at bay but time and gravity were working against her.

It had been eleven years since she had moved back to Springfield. She missed the many attractions that St. Louis offered: Forest Park and the Muni Opera, the Fox Theater, the great restaurants on the Hill, and the many other cultural offerings. But it was good to be back in Springfield, where she and her husband had lived since Chase had purchased the old Mariner's Bank. She was content. He was a good man, a good father to Theresa—whom he had adopted when she was four—and to Aaron, their child together, who required a great deal more patience.

Georgie stood at the stove in her nightdress where she poured pancake batter into flawless circles onto a round Calphalon griddle. The batter hissed as it hit the pan and the smell spread from the griddle to the kitchen and eventually to the entire house.

Theresa's younger brother was sitting at the table doing his homework. Unlike his sister, he waited until the very last minute to do his assignments. He was more laid back and less anal about his schoolwork, and his grades showed it. His teachers were always on him about how his aptitude didn't jibe with his accomplishments. He laughed it off and simply enjoyed himself. There was only one Type A personality in the family, and he certainly wasn't it. That distinction rested safely with his sister.

"Find any pimples?" Aaron said to his sister as she sat down and waited for the plate that would soon be set in front of her piled with pancakes.

"I see you finally decided to open your books. Are you going to graduate or spend another year in eighth grade?"

"Bitch."

"Aaron! You apologize to your sister right now. I will not have you talking to her like that! I mean it. You will be grounded for life if you don't."

Aaron sneered at his sister. "Please accept my heartfelt apology," he said. "I can't imagine what came over me."

"You can't help it. Mom and Dad never did find out who your real parents are."

"Where's Dad?"

"He had to go in early today. He is leaving for Chicago later, and had some things to finish up," Georgie said as she set a plate in front of Theresa.

"Aaron, the bus is pulling up out front," his mother said.

"Yeah. You don't want to be late for class, since you are all prepared and everything," Theresa said.

Aaron piled his papers up and threw them in his backpack, and ran out the front door.

"See you later, honey!" Georgiana said.

"He really is a little creep, Mom."

"Shut up and eat your pancakes." Georgie kissed Theresa on top of her head.

Theresa ate her pancakes and in five minutes she was in her car on the way to school.

She parked two blocks away on a side street off Walnut, and walked to the side entrance.

As she neared the building, she was startled to see him. He had walked up from behind one of the parked cars in the teachers' lot.

When she recognized him, she smiled with relief.

"How you doing, Theresa?"

"Fine, thanks," she said. Then she walked through the doorway.

How did he know my name? The question occurred to her, but she quickly dismissed it.

He bit his lip as he watched her walk down the hallway. He kept watching until she disappeared down another hallway to the right.

"Have a nice day," he said quietly to himself.

Then he turned and walked away.

Chapter 42

"She's in here," the nurse said, opening the door for Sister Agnes.

"The nurse said they are still running tests," Agnes said, sitting on the sofa.

"Yes, apparently so," Margaret said.

"You said she was experiencing stomach pains?"

"She was holding her abdomen and she said the pain was quite severe. She had lost her color and was feeling quite faint. I almost called an ambulance, but then decided that I could get her here faster in a car. I'm glad I did."

"I stopped by the front desk to make certain that there were no questions. I brought her breviary," Agnes said, handing the small black prayer book to Margaret. "Do you intend to stay?"

"Unless there's a reason why I shouldn't, I plan to stay at least until we know something. Maybe longer, depending. I am in hopes that she will be coming home."

"No reason not to. She needs someone with her. I need to go back, however. The Corcoran funeral is at ten and there are some things I need to take care of first."

Alison Corcoran's funeral. It has slipped Margaret's mind.

"Oh dear. I forgot about that, with all of this."

"Don't fret. Sister Kathleen and I are going, and many of the other teachers. Under the circumstances, it is quite understandable."

"Thank you, Sister. I really think I should stay with her."

"Well, I for one am glad you are here. She feels very close to you."

"The feeling's mutual."

"Yes. Well, if you need me for anything, take my cell phone number." The prioress and the school principal were the only ones assigned cell phones. Agnes wrote the number down and handed it to Margaret.

The door to the lounge opened. A young doctor walked in wearing scrubs.

"Sister Margaret?"

Margaret stood. "Yes, I'm Sister Margaret. This is Sister Agnes, our prioress."

As prioress, Agnes had signed authorizations to be informed of any matters pertaining to the health of the sisters. Theodora had signed an authorization for Margaret when they brought her in.

"I'm Doctor Scalini, Sister," the doctor said, reaching for Agnes' hand. He was in his early thirties with dark brown eyes, dark curly hair and prominent cheekbones. He was a handsome young man. He looked more native-American than Italian.

"Sisters, we're going to keep her for a day or two. I'm sorry to say that I have bad news."

Theodora had cancer of the liver. The long-range prognosis was poor, Doctor Scalini explained. At the most, she would survive a year. Probably not that long, because the disease had progressed too far by the time she experienced symptoms.

"How does something like this just happen?"

Doctor Scalini explained that, according to Theodora's chart, she had contracted hepatitis some years back when she was in Louisiana. She went through a grueling course of treatment and there was no reason to believe that she hadn't gotten through the worst of it.

"In some cases—and I fear that this is what has happened with Sister Theodora—the hepatitis stays dormant and then develops problems later in life," Scalini said.

"What about a liver transplant?" Margaret asked.

"There is a range of possibilities for treatment, Sister," Dr. Scalini said. He told her he was referring Sister Theodora to an oncologist. Capitol City Clinic had several top-notch people who could outline a course of treatment. "I have a call in to them."

"Does she know?" Sister Agnes asked.

"Yes."

"What did she say when you told her?"

"Well, she said that if she was going to have to be here for any length of time she was going to need her cassette player."

Margaret lowered her head to conceal her smile.

"And, she said that if you were still here, Sister Margaret, she hoped you would come upstairs for a little while after she gets settled."

Margaret had to compose herself in the women's restroom before going up to the Oncology floor. The nurse told her that it would take about twenty minutes for them to get Sister Theodora to her room.

She was sitting in a chair beside the hospital bed now, the picture of composure. She wasn't fooling anybody, least of all Theodora.

Sister Agnes visited for a few minutes, and the three of them prayed the Our Father.

After Agnes left, the hospital chaplain came in and performed the sacrament of healing, what older Catholics used to call the "last rites." The sacrament might have gone PC, but the import was the same.

Theodora was dying, and sooner than later.

Theodora's sister lived in Champaign. Margaret asked if she wanted her called, but Theodora asked her to wait. She said that if she felt better later she could call her herself.

Now, Theodora dozed lightly and Margaret sat watching the beeps and the various readings on the instruments attached to her friend.

Theodora wore no veil now, and her short, salt and pepper hair was neatly combed back. Margaret had combed it for her. Theodora looked peaceful now, unlike when she had appeared at Margaret's door early in the morning. Then, her face had been contorted with pain. Now, she was once again the woman whose visage had for so long brightened Margaret's life.

Margaret's cell phone rang. She reached into her purse and looked at the number. It was Templeton. Her heart raced when she saw the number, and she thought about just letting it ring.

She changed her mind. "Sister Margaret."

"You may have been onto something all along."

"Why?"

He explained that he had read all the reports again, and how it disturbed him that there were no usable prints found at the scene. Margaret stood and went out into the hall, closing the door behind her. "I have to admit, that one got by me. I must be slipping."

"That's why they call me the prodigy!"

She smiled.

"You sound funny. You okay?"

The asshole Templeton, she had come to expect. The arrogant Templeton, she had learned to ignore. But the sensitive Templeton? This was something she hadn't experienced.

"I'm at St. John's. One of the sisters, a good friend of mine, became ill last night and I have been with here since very early this morning."

"I'm sorry. Anything serious?"

"Yes. I'm afraid so."

"Well, you want to call me back or something?"

"No. No, I am fine. What else?"

"Well, Renfrow has a teleconference set up later with Oxford. Can you make it?"

"What time?"

"She said around three."

"I should be able to do that."

"She will sit in on that with you. She learned that he is dying of cancer. They moved him to medium security a year ago. But he can talk. Wants to, in fact."

Cancer. The rain falls on the just and the unjust alike, she thought to herself.

"I thought we could go to Sherman tomorrow sometime and interview Tomiczek. If you don't mind me tagging along."

Margaret closed her eyes. It was the last thing—and the only thing—she wanted. God forgive me. "That's fine."

"So, see you later?"

"Yes. Thanks for calling."

"Oh, there's one more thing."

"Yes."

"I don't know how much difference this makes, but we have had interviews with everyone whose name you came up with from Saint D's—except one. Brightman has never called in to schedule one."

"Really? I know he knew about it. He was leaving town, but I thought surely he would have called you and set it up by now."

"Nope. Let me follow up on that."

"Yes. Thanks. That's probably for the best."

"I am going to the Corcoran funeral in a little bit. I gather you aren't going to be there?"

"No. I have to run some errands for Sister Theodora to get some of her things."

"I'll keep you informed. Later."

Margaret flipped the phone shut.

Tom Brightman knew about the interviews. Why hadn't he called to make arrangements to go in before he left?

Curious, too, was Templeton's change of heart about the case.

She went back into the room to see Theodora sitting up and wide-awake.

"How are you feeling?" Margaret asked.

"Much better."

Margaret sat down and took her friend's hand. Several minutes passed with no words spoken. No words were needed. A nurse walked in wearing a pink smock with Disneyland characters printed on it. She was in her mid-forties and heavy-set, with short brown hair. "I just want to check a few things. That okay?"

"It's your hospital," Theodora said.

"Oh, my! I wish it were my hospital. I would give myself a raise!"

The nurse flipped a switch, which started up the automatic oxygen LED reading once again.

"These things are touchy," she said. "Can I get you anything, Sister?"

"No, honey. I have everything I need."

"They will be coming to get you in a little while for some more tests."

"How many more tests could there possibly be?" Theodora asked.

"Oh, plenty. They have been waiting for you, Sister!"

"I feel so special."

The nurse left and closed the door.

"You don't have to stay," she said to Margaret.

"Well, since they are coming to take you away shortly, I will go back to the residence and gather up a few of your things."

"Don't forget—"

"Your Elvis tapes. I know." They laughed. "As soon as I leave here, I am going to get them. You need anything else?"

"I am just going to rest. You go do … whatever it is you do."

Margaret stood up and kissed her on the forehead. "Theodora?"

"Yes?"

"I love you."

A tear could be seen working its way out of the corner of Theodora's eye. "Elvis tapes."

Margaret laughed. "Elvis tapes. I'll be back after a shower."

"That would be especially nice."

Margaret turned to go to the door.

"Margaret?"

Margaret turned around.

"I love you too."

Chapter 43

Bill Templeton made a point of going to Alison Corcoran's funeral. He was less interested in the ceremony than in seeing who was in attendance. He had come early and slid into a pew toward the back next to Roy Walker. Roy turned and nodded to him.

Every seat in St. Alphonse was taken, and people were standing in the rear and in the vestibule. The bishop, a small man with a less than powerful voice, was the chief celebrant. There were two concelebrants—the pastor, Father Greeley, and a priest who was a nephew of the Corcoran's who had flown in from Africa where he worked in the missions. The bishop wore a microphone that broadcast his voice for everyone's sake as he performed the rites in the vestibule. Then, the concelebrants, led by altar servers and lectors, followed the casket draped in white up the aisle to the front where it would remain for the funeral Mass.

The St. Alphonse choir was in fine form, and was accompanied by a contingent from the Saint D's band. Incense swirled about, causing more than a few in the congregation to cover their noses and fight off fits of coughing. As the smoke inclined heavenward, sunlight beamed through the large stained-glass windows and shone directly on the box that contained the mortal remains of Alison Corcoran.

Peter Corcoran stood rigidly in the front pew, his wife at his side. She held a Kleenex to her mouth and her face was flushed from crying. They did not hold hands or touch. Next to her stood her father and mother.

The Corcorans were highly regarded in the community. Seated in the first few rows—directly behind the family—were local dignitaries, including the mayor, several members of the county board, and Sheriff Jim Hargrove and his wife. A large contingent of Saint D's students was present, two of whom were serving as lectors.

After the opening prayers and the two readings, the bishop walked over to the lectern to the accompaniment of the choir singing "Alleluia."

"The Lord be with you."

"And also with you."

He held up the large book, and turned from side to side in a studied motion and with an appropriately serious demeanor. He had something of the consummate showman about him. It had lent an air of credibility to him in the media when he struggled during the first two years of his episcopacy to overcome a series of scandals involving several priests under the dubious leadership of his predecessor. He communicated an air of calm in the midst of the storm of public opinion that, for a time, had threatened the faith of the people and had a serious impact on Sunday collections. Now, the settlements had been offered and accepted, and things were slowly returning to normal in the diocese. Rome had sent the right man in to quell the storm.

"A reading from the Holy Gospel according to John.

"Martha said to Jesus, Lord, if you had been here, my brother would not have died...."

At one point during the Gospel reading, Bill turned and saw a tear sliding down Roy Walker's cheek. He was touched by the display of emotion. Bill leaned over and said, "These things are always tough."

"She was just a child," Walker said, wiping the tear away. "Just a child."

The homily was a boilerplate exhortation to faith in the face of death, belief in the promise of resurrection, and the comfort afforded by the sacraments of the Church. Every now and then, the bishop—no doubt mindful of the generosity of the Corcoran clan to the Church and all its works—made passing reference to the exemplary Catholic family from which Alison sprang. The bishop deftly pulled this off without crossing the line to sycophancy.

Erin Mosby, who sat alone in the back pew near the vestibule, heard not much of what the bishop was saying. She was sad as she observed the church full to capacity, the cadre of priests and the numbers of choir members and musicians crowding the sanctuary area.

She wondered what Billy's funeral would be like the following Monday. His father was not a community leader. His mother lived on the margins of society. She cried when the casket processed past on the way to the altar, thinking about how Billy's send off would compare. She wondered how many of the kids from Saint D's would even come.

CHAPTER 44

"The body of seventeen-year-old Alison Corcoran was laid to rest this morning, five days after her body was discovered in an unincorporated area of the county," the radio announcer was saying. "The sheriff's office has indicated a connection between the murder and the apparent suicide of William Pickering, a janitor at Saint Dominic's Catholic High School, where Corcoran was a senior. The investigation is still ongoing."

Margaret had just pulled out of the parking lot of Circuit City. There she had purchased a four-gigabyte iPod nano and six Elvis CDs. She was returning to the Mother House, where she planned to upload the CDs to the computer and sync them to the iPod. She knew Theodora would be thrilled to be so high tech, and to be able to listen to Elvis without having to worry about whether the tape player was turned up too loudly.

As she drove up Chatham Road a thought occurred to her. She marveled that she hadn't considered it before. She drove past the turnoff to the convent and kept going to the north end of Springfield. Soon she was driving down Monument Avenue on her way to Oak Ridge Cemetery.

Springfield residents will proudly tell you that Oak Ridge Cemetery, the site of the tomb of Abraham Lincoln, is second only to Arlington

National Cemetery in the number of annual visitors. It was here that the murdered president was interred in 1865, and where his much-maligned widow, Mary, was laid to rest by his side after she died in 1882. Their three youngest sons are buried there as well. Lincolnophiles the world over have been coming to Springfield in pilgrimage for decades, and the number continues to grow now that the Lincoln Presidential Library and Museum has opened.

She pulled into a parking space next to a small, gray stone building near the entrance and got out of the car.

"Easter. Let me see."

Inside the cemetery office, a fifty-something man in a white shirt, blue pants and suspenders, pored over plot maps for about three minutes. "Here it is! Bonnie Jean Easter. Died 1974. I'll show you how to get there on this plot map."

It took ten minutes for Margaret to find the burial plot. She had driven past the place twice, failing to discern the difference between the curves in the road and the lines on the map. It lay in an older part of the cemetery, shaded by large oak and maple trees, about three hundred yards northeast of the obelisk of the Lincoln tomb. When she found the right spot, she parked and began walking up a hill.

She was suddenly aware of eyes trained on her.

She stopped and slowly glanced at a large family tomb to her right. There, his eyes intently wary of this approaching human, sat a fox, burnished red in color with white on his front and a white-tipped tail curled alongside him. He was beautiful, his fur like velvet, his eyes like something dark and dreamy. Neither fox nor nun moved for at least a minute.

Then, almost more quickly than her eye could perceive, the creature vanished from sight, retreating to the row of trees behind the tomb.

She moved on and walked down a row of stones.

At last she saw it.

It was a wide, rectangular marble stone with rough-hewn edges, the name EASTER boldly carved on the surface. Beneath the surname, in smaller letters, were the names George—1940–1975; and Bonnie Jean—1958–1974.

This was such a peaceful and beautiful part of Oak Ridge. The stone and its surroundings beguiled the onlooker into contemplating timelessness and peaceful repose. Yet, it stood over a child who had been brutally murdered and a father who had died by his own hand in the wake of her death.

But there was something else that captured Margaret's attention now. She looked from side to side, and noted that the dates on the other stones were all roughly from the same decade. She saw no adornment on any within her view. Flipping open her cell phone, she checked for bars and then dialed. She got Templeton's voice mail.

"Bill? This is Margaret. Tell me I'm crazy, but I found no indication that there was anyone left from the Easter family in Springfield. Well, I'm out here at Oak Ridge, at Bonnie's grave. And I'm staring at a vase, filled with water that has two fresh and beautiful red roses in it. Fresh roses, Bill."

The fox suddenly scampered past her and scurried down the hill, causing her to jump. She let out a deep breath as she watched the creature disappear into the brush on the other side of the road.

"Bill. It's him. He's here."

Chapter 45

Jane Renfrow walked up to the security desk as Margaret was clipping on her visitor's badge.

"Hi. I understand one of the sisters is ill."

"Yes. I'm afraid so."

"I'm sorry to hear that," Jane said. She had a way of saying it that actually made you believe she was.

They walked to a bank of elevators and Jane pushed the button. She looked like an advertisement for Macy's. Her skin was flawless, her hair shining. Her hands were manicured, her nails coated with a dark red polish. She wore a loose flowing tan skirt, navy blazer and fashionable pointed-toe shoes with three-inch heels. Margaret wondered if Jane had a fashion-coordinated Glock under that blazer.

She wouldn't blame Bill, or any man for that matter, for wanting to climb all over Jane. It hurt, however, to think that he might want to do just that. Standing next to her, Margaret felt like a frump.

When Margaret had left Theodora a few minutes prior, she was sitting up in bed, reading her breviary, with the earphones of her new iPod tucked neatly into both ears. She was smiling. She had telephoned her sister, who told her that she was going to be coming sometime next week. Theodora protested, but to no avail. It helped for Margaret to know that Theodora had others beside herself who cared for her.

She wouldn't die alone.

It made Margaret more conscious of the fact that she, herself, was alone in the world.

Alone, that is, except for God. He is supposed to be our All. But is He enough?

Did not Augustine say, "Our hearts are restless till they rest in Thee?"

"If you don't mind me tagging along," Templeton had said to her.

You mean now or for the rest of my life?

"He's quite ill." Jane's voice interrupted her reverie.

"I'm sorry?"

"Garcia. He is terminally ill with cancer. Perhaps you can appeal to his heightened sense of mortality."

"Yeah. A heightened sense of mortality. There's a lot of that going around lately," Margaret said as she stepped off the elevator.

Reality for Tony Garcia was filtered through pain.

The cancer that had started in his colon had eaten its way through that part of his anatomy already traumatized by the brutality he had encountered when he began prison life. Now it had spread to his liver and lungs. Life in prison had become a death sentence. He never prayed, but if he had he would have prayed for a private session with Doctor Kevorkian.

He caught a glimpse of himself in flat-screen TV as the guard wheeled him into place in the teleconference room. He looked like a wraith. He weighed in at ninety-five pounds. He had weighed 198 when he was sentenced. His hair had long since been eaten away by the chemo and his left eye sagged. Occasionally he would joke with the guards about selling his photograph to be used on Halloween cards, but that it would be too frightening.

Now, he sat facing the two television screens, one on which he could see himself very clearly, and another that showed a room in some FBI building in Illinois. The room was empty now, but in a few minutes the people conducting the interview would be visible.

A nun? He told the prison officials to fuck off when first asked to do this interview. Dying gives a man some rights over his person he figured. But when they told him that one of the deputies was a nun, something still alive, still curious, still struggling inside of him was overcome with intrigue. What the fuck? Sure, he would do it. It might take his mind off the numbing effects of morphine and the intermittent moments when soul-shattering pain racked every inch of his body. He sat now, holding an oxygen mask to his face, an IV tube in his arm. Waiting.

What else was there to do? Life for Anthony Garcia was nothing but waiting.

He had grown up in St. Louis. His mother, a Mexican girl who had found her way to El Paso, had married a drifter in South Texas and lived with him in San Antonio, where they lived until Tony was four. She threw the drifter over for a truck driver and moved to St. Louis. The truck driver was gone a lot, and that was good. When he was home he drank and frequently took his frustrations with life—which were many and varied—out on Anthony's mother. Anthony learned to stay away from the goon, whose name was Ralph, because he sensed that Ralph was missing a few screws and held a grudge against him for some reason. Namely, that Anthony sprang from the loins of another man and Ralph viewed life through very primal lenses. "You're not my fucking kid, Tex-Mex!" was how he so charmingly put it when he was drinking.

Thank God for that, Anthony thought—although he never dared say it aloud.

As luck would have it, Ralph didn't make it home one night because his tractor-trailer overturned on a lonely stretch of highway in Kansas. Ralph had been drinking in the cab—to no one's surprise, least of all Anthony's—and failed to right his rig after having to brake to avoid hitting a farm truck that had pulled out onto the highway hauling a load of hay.

No tears were shed in his mother's house.

Anthony's mother worked at a White Castle and could barely afford to feed and house the both of them. Her looks had been complicated by scarring from the beatings she had received from Ralph. She was overweight and in ill health.

When he was eighteen, he kissed his mother good-bye and headed north, eventually landing in Springfield where he stayed for ten years, working odd jobs, getting into trouble, and eventually washing dishes at Wheeler's restaurant.

Where he met the subject of today's interview—that little cunt Bonnie Easter.

"Mr. Garcia, I am special agent Jane Renfrow, FBI."

She was a looker. If he could get it up any more, it would have been standing proudly at attention. The thought brought a weak but genuine smile to his face.

"This is Sister Margaret Donovan. Sister Margaret is acting as a deputy with the Sangamon County Sheriff's Office."

This was getting very interesting, Garcia thought.

"They're deputizing nuns now?" he asked, lifting the oxygen mask aside. Then he laughed out loud.

Jane ignored his comment. "Mr. Garcia, we would like to ask you some questions concerning the time you spent in Springfield some years ago. Specifically, when you were a dishwasher at Wheeler's restaurant. When you were there, you worked with a young woman named Bonnie Easter. Do you recall that?"

Garcia coughed, and pulled his mask off again. "They tried to pin her murder on me. Yeah, I remember that."

"What can you tell me about her, Mr. Garcia?"

"I can tell you she was a little cockteaser. She was always waving it in my face. For that matter, she waved it in every guy's face that came along. But if you tried to take her up on it, she froze up like nobody's business."

"Mr. Garcia, thank you for talking with us," Margaret said.

"Fortunately, you caught me on a day when there wasn't anything else going on, Sister. I was able to clear my schedule for you."

"I am just going to ask the question, Mr. Garcia. Did you have anything to do with Bonnie Easter's death?"

"Fuck no."

"Her death was not all that dissimilar to the one for which you were convicted, Mr. Garcia. Why should I believe you?"

"I don't give a fuck whether you believe me or not. Yeah, I did that broad, the one they sent me here for. She was another little cockteaser, and I was drunk and horny. Ever get horny, Sister?"

No one spoke for a minute. Margaret simply looked directly, intently into the camera, seemingly impervious to Garcia's insulting manner.

"Why do you think they suspected you, then, Mr. Garcia?"

"The fucking sheriff, Tomiczek. He had me in his lockup for a bunch of stuff before, and I was convenient. He didn't want anyone to start sniffing around in other places."

"Like where, Mr. Garcia?"

"Well, for one, that fat fuck of a prosecutor. I saw him and her together in the parking lot after work one night. He was rubbing his hands all over her shoulders and back, and she wasn't fighting him off."

Jerry Brown. Margaret wrote his name down on a legal pad.

"Did you ever see her with anyone else?"

"Yeah. There was this fancy doctor, Cockrell or something like that."

"Corcoran?"

"Yeah. Corcoran. He came into the restaurant a lot, and she always waited on him. One night, she actually sat in the booth with him. Hell, old man Wheeler would never let a waitress do that with a customer. But he never said a word when Bonnie sat with that guy."

"Mr. Garcia," asked Jane. "Did you ever know anyone named Rigali?"

"Sally Rigali. Hell yes. He was a mean sonofabitch. He used to come in the place too. She knew him."

"Bonnie?"

"Oh, yeah. Well, too, by the looks of things."

"Mr. Garcia, is there anything else you could tell us that would shed light on anything that might have happened to Bonnie Easter?"

"What the hell is this anyway? Don't tell me that you are just now getting into checking out a murder that took place, what, thirty years ago?"

"There are other murders, sir; more recent ones, and they may be related," Margaret answered. "Did you ever see Bonnie's sister or brother at the restaurant?"

Garcia coughed. It was about a minute before he responded.

"Yeah. Little kid. About ten. He would come in sometimes."

"Do you remember anything about him?"

"Yeah. He was crazy about his sister. His eyes lit up when he would spot her, and he always ran up and gave her a big hug. He was a sweet kid."

A sweet kid? An oddly sensitive observation coming from someone so calloused by life, Margaret thought. Perhaps the humanity had not been completely drained from his heart.

"Mr. Garcia," Jane said. "You're dying. Were you to admit to the Easter murder, it would make little difference to you, considering your situation. It might, however, allow you to end your life with some sense of contrition. Please, tell us again. Did you kill Bonnie Easter?"

"Fuck no, Agent Renfrow. You're a great looking broad, you know that? You make a good point, though. I have nothing to lose, do I? That's why you should believe me. Not that I give a shit whether you do or not. I'm done here."

"Thank you, Mr. Garcia," Margaret said. They watched the security guard, who had been seated behind Garcia, stand up and walk toward the camera. Then the screen went black.

"Jerry Brown keeps popping up," said Margaret. She and Jane were sitting at a table outside of a coffee shop on Sixth Street.

"I did some checking on Brown," Jane said. She was cutting into a piece of key lime pie. "I learned that we had a file going when he committed suicide. He was a high roller, into some people big time for gambling debts. Cases would come to him and, somehow, he would find insufficient evidence to proceed to trial. He was especially close with the Rigalis. His intemperance was a well-documented fact in Springfield, for alcohol and for women."

"Not exactly a looker, from what I have heard," Margaret said.

"Don't have to be if you have a fat wallet."

"True enough."

"You know, Margaret, the janitor just may have been the guy."

"No, Jane, I don't think so. You heard what Garcia said? About the brother who was crazy about Bonnie?"

"Yes."

Margaret related her visit to Oak Ridge Cemetery. "The only thing is we can't find anything about this little kid. No one even knows his name."

"I have been running checks, but we haven't found anything either."

Margaret smiled.

"What?" Jane asked.

"I just remembered. There is an old nun in the infirmary at the convent. Her name is Sister Jean Marie."

"So?"

"She taught at Blessed Redeemer in the seventies."

"You think—?"

"Yes, I think."

"Who needs the internet when you have a Sister Jean Marie?"

Chapter 46

Sister Jean Marie was thrilled to have young Sister Margaret drop by. Jean Marie was eighty- something, and she wore a hospital gown as she sat in a chair next to her hospital bed, but she had her veil on her head. She was reading from her breviary when Margaret walked into the room. The twinkle in her eye was irrepressible.

Margaret showed her the grainy photograph.

The old nun smiled.

"Johnny."

"Johnny?"

"Yes. He was such a sweet, loving little boy." Sister Jean Marie spoke with an unmistakable Southern drawl. She hailed from Lafayette, Louisiana. She handed the picture back to Margaret.

"What happened to him? Do you know, Sister?"

"No. He just left school quite suddenly. It was after that horrible thing happened to his sister. He loved his sister dearly."

"We can't find him, Sister, and it's terribly important that we do. Do you have any idea where he might have gone, or even if he is still alive?"

"I haven't seen him since 19—when was it? 1974?"

"That was the year his sister was murdered."

"Yes. Well the school records would—no, never mind. There was a fire wasn't there?"

"Yes."

"They had relatives somewhere. I remember, now, having to send his records to his new school."

"Where was it?" Margaret asked, impatiently.

"Well, that's what I'm sitting here trying to remember, dear!" Jean Marie said. "It takes a while for the old synapses to start firing. Don't get your shorts in a wad!"

"Sorry, Sister."

"Wisconsin."

Margaret looked at her, and remembered something.

"Wisconsin?"

"Yes. As I recall. I sent those transcripts to a school in some place, Wisconsin."

"Do you recall the school, by any chance?"

"Don't push your luck, young lady. I'm doing well to remember the state."

"God bless you, Sister!" Margaret said, patting her on the hand.

Margaret ran to her room, and pulled the files off of her dresser.

She found the file on Tom Brightman.

Tom Brightman had graduated from high school in 1982.

In Milwaukee, Wisconsin.

He would have been ten years old in 1974.

Brother Tom Brightman—Johnny? If he had witnessed his sister's murder, then his father would have done anything to get him away from Springfield. Perhaps even gone to the trouble of changing his name. Perhaps, giving him the name of his new family.

Where are you, Tom? Where the hell are you?

She picked her cell phone up and dialed Bill's number.

"I'm on my way to the priest's house now. Father Milquetoast, or something?"

"Milkowski," Margaret said. "He might know where he is."

"We'll see. I'll call you later."

Bill had done some research on Brother Tom Brightman. After graduating high school, Brightman had entered Loyola University in Chicago. He graduated with a degree in Psychology. He went on to get a master's degree and then joined the army, where he served with distinction during Desert Storm. After leaving the service, he entered the Dominican Order and at first had studied for the priesthood. He later changed direction for reasons unknown and instead took vows to become a brother. He taught theology at Ohio Dominican University for a couple of years and completed a doctorate. Three years ago, he was assigned to Saint Dominic's, where he taught and assisted the wrestling coach.

Information from several sources listed his birthplace as Fargo, North Dakota. The FBI was having a problem verifying that information, however. He had no rap sheet, not even a parking ticket. But he was trained to kill as adeptly as he has been trained to teach theology. He fit the profile. All of which could be cleared up if he had come in. Unfortunately, he was nowhere to be found.

Bill turned off of Monroe Street and swung into a parking space in front of the priest's house. He got out, walked up to the door and rang the bell. Father Reginald Milkowski opened the door. He was tall, but appeared frail. He was dressed in black slacks and a white long-sleeved shirt.

"May I help you?"

Bill showed the priest his badge. "Yes, father. I'm Detective Templeton with the sheriff's department. May I speak with you for a few moments?"

"Certainly." Father Milkowski stood to the side, inviting Bill to enter. They walked into the living room. The priest pointed to the sofa, and then sat down on a large armchair next to the window.

"How can I help you, detective?"

"I need to talk with Thomas Brightman. Do you know where he is?"

"I am afraid he isn't here."

When a Dominican begs the question, there is something up, Bill thought. He repeated the question.

"Well, I am not really at liberty to say, detective."

Bill was getting impatient. Unlike the Catholic cops who worked with him, he was not accustomed to showing deference to the clergy. He had investigated too many of them to assume anything about their sanctity.

"Why is that, Father?"

"Because it involves a very private matter. He hasn't even told me the whole story."

"Look, Father, I don't want to seem abrupt, but we are in the middle of an investigation into the murders of two of the students here at Saint D's. He was supposed to talk with us, but he has failed to do so. I need to find him, and quickly."

"Surely, detective, you don't think that Brother Tom is implicated in this horrible mess."

"I don't think anything, Father. But we do have to talk with him."

Father Milkowski was tapping the arm of the chair with his fingers, looking down to the floor.

"I can only tell you that he is in ill health. He left here for an appointment at the Veteran's Hospital in Danville. I don't know for sure when he will return."

"Do you know what he is seeing them for?"

"No. And I wouldn't tell you if I did. I don't believe they will tell you at the hospital either. For that matter, they probably won't even inform you whether he is there. Privacy laws have become quite draconian in that respect."

Bill made a note to call Jane. If anyone could override HIPAA privacy laws with the Veterans Administration, maybe the FBI could.

"Surely it wouldn't be a violation of privacy if I were to call him on his cell phone," Bill offered.

"If he had a cell phone that would be a wonderful solution to this problem. However, Brother Tom doesn't. He did say he would check in, but he hasn't done so and, really, there is no reason for him to."

So much for that.

"Have you noticed anything strange about his behavior lately, Father?"

"Well, it has been obvious to me that he is not well. He doesn't have the same sparkle I am used to seeing. He hasn't really been himself lately, now that you mention it."

The priest was right. Bill hit a brick wall when he contacted the Veterans' Hospital in Danville. They refused even to acknowledge that Tom Brightman was, would be or ever had been treated there. Bill called Jane and asked her to pull some strings. She promised to get back with him, but didn't hold out much hope.

Chapter 47

As Bill drove back to the office, he went off route and ended up driving down Edwards Street toward the State Museum and the Capitol complex. He slowed down as he neared Boone's, a restaurant and bar on the corner of College and Edwards. He pulled into a parking spot across the street and shut off the engine.

He closed his eyes and fought off the temptation to get out of the car, walk across the street, sit down at the bar—the bar where he had spent so many hours of his life until two or three years ago—and have just one drink. The devil on his shoulder was telling him that one drink wouldn't hurt. It would taste so good. He waited for the angel on the other shoulder to argue the point, but for some reason no voice was heard. He was squeezing the steering wheel so hard that it hurt his hand. Sweat was pouring off of his face.

God, he wanted a drink. He would have killed for a drink.

Bill had left high school and joined the army just to get away from the nightmare he called home. He was stationed at Fort Leonard Wood in Missouri. After basic training, he was looking forward to training—as the recruiter had promised him—as a mechanic. He always loved tinkering with cars. He learned the lesson that many recruits had learned over the years: recruiters will say anything to fill their quota.

After a series of aptitude tests, instead of being trained as a mechanic, he was sent to the Criminal Investigation Division, or CID, where he was trained as an investigator. Although at first he was miffed at this assignment, which he would never have chosen for himself, in time he came to like the work. And he was good.

When his time was up, he re-enlisted and became an investigative supervisor with the CID. He had a gift for sniffing out patterns that other investigators never noticed, and had a long list of solved investigations to his credit.

When he returned to Illinois, he joined the sheriff's department, where his supervisors quickly noticed his abilities. After two years, he was promoted to detective. That was when things started going downhill.

The reason was a woman.

He had never been seriously involved with anyone until coming back to central Illinois. There he met Sylvia Patterson, an assistant federal prosecutor. She had legs that wouldn't quit, tits that begged to be squeezed, and long blonde hair. For several weeks, she fucked his brains out.

Unfortunately, for him it was more than sex. He had fallen for her. Hard.

Then, one evening when they were having dinner at Bauer's restaurant in the Vinegar Hill Mall, several of her buddies from the office happened by the table. The more they talked, the more he sensed she was embarrassed.

She was a prosecutor and he was only a street cop.

It wasn't long before she somehow was just too busy to go out. She had a meeting, or she had to prepare for court, or whatever.

Finally, he stopped over at her apartment one evening and she announced that she simply couldn't see him anymore.

He got angry, and she got angry, and he walked. Fifteen minutes later he walked into a dive on Adams Street that had a great jukebox.

Then, every night after work he was in some bar getting smashed, picking up women and waking up alone and feeling like shit every morning.

His drinking didn't start with getting dumped by Sylvia. It began when he was twelve years old. Later, in high school, he discovered that alcohol was the drug of choice for teenagers in west central Illinois. A cultural phenomenon known as the "laker" is familiar to anyone who grew up in the Jacksonville area. This was a weekend affair that saw dozens of young people from high schools around the area parked around Lake Jacksonville with kegs and cases of beer. Sometimes, kids would be there from Friday night through Sunday morning. It was the thing to do to fight off boredom in a small town.

The army curtailed his drinking somewhat; but eventually the old pattern reemerged and after work he would gather with a group of his buddies from the CID at a local watering hole.

It had never interfered with his life, until he moved to Springfield. Here his life was unraveling. Jim Hargrove and Ernie could see it, and tried to talk to him.

He assured them there wasn't a problem. He was fine.

Then one night that all changed.

Bill was investigating a series of home invasions on the north end. He got paged one evening after he had downed about six boilermakers at Boone's and was informed that they had a suspect in custody. He needed to go to the office and assist in the interrogation.

Thinking he was just fine, he jumped in the car and drove to the station. When he pulled into the parking lot, he drove over a trash basket and crashed the car into the rear of the building. He was unconscious when he was found, bleeding from the head. He hadn't been wearing a seat belt and had hit the building at twenty miles an hour

Ernie and Jim managed to keep the incident from blowing up in Bill's face. Ernie Jones knew that it would take a pain greater than any pain Bill had ever experienced to get him to climb out of the hole he was in. Ernie decided he would become the biggest pain Bill had ever known. He was on Bill's case every minute he was around him.

One evening, Ernie followed him in to the locker room and was reading him the riot act about how he had screwed up on an investigation when

Bill turned and took a swing at him. That was a big mistake. Ernie hooked his arm and swung him to the floor.

"You feeling like a bad motherfucker now, boy?" Ernie put his knee in his back and then pulled him up and sent a shot to his solar plexus. Bill went down in a heap. "You going to keep going until you fuck yourself over good? Someday maybe I will come see you outside the public library when you are living there with the rest of those folks who sold it all. But if you do end up there it won't be for lack of my trying. I am going to stay on you, and kick the shit out of you if need be, until you see the shit hole you crawled into for what it is and start getting out of it, or until you quit. And if you quit, you die. But I got to tell you this, boy. You are so goddamned close to losing this job that it may be out of my hands."

Ernie walked out, leaving Bill sobbing on the floor. He crawled over to the bathroom on all fours—he was a man reduced to moving like an animal—and threw up.

Faced with losing his job and whatever was left of his self-respect and dignity, he had finally reached bottom. The next morning, he walked into Ernie's office.

"You look like shit," Ernie said.

"I want help, Chief."

Ernie looked at him intently, and then sat back in his chair.

"How bad?"

"I can't do this anymore. I want to get my life back, my job, and I want to feel better."

"If you mean that, I'll help," said Ernie.

He spent three months in rehab in Tennessee, at a place that Ernie had recommended. Ernie had read about it in an article about Johnny Cash, his favorite singer. It was expensive, but the county health plan helped somewhat. It still cost him several thousand dollars. Ernie lent him half of it.

Now, his career was on the fast track, and he hadn't had a drink for two years. He attended meetings each week and had support from others in his condition that was invaluable. Not to mention the fact that Ernie was always looking over his shoulder, waiting to strike. Ernie had become the father he wished he'd had growing up.

But the thirst never subsided. It was killing him now. Was it a coincidence that a woman had come into the picture again? Was the need to self-medicate generated by a fear of falling for a woman it was impossible to have?

As he sat in his car, he remembered Margaret's eyes. They were brown and deep, and so calming. He had wanted to take her face in his hands and kiss her forehead, her cheeks, her nose, and her lips. He had wanted to tear her clothes off and take her right there in front of the convent.

This was crazy. He was falling in love with a nun. But he couldn't make the feeling go away. He was terrified that he was setting himself up for a fall, and he didn't know if he could handle another one. There was something very different about this one, though. True, she was beautiful and he was physically attracted to her. But something about her had gotten inside of him. He had always beaten around the bush in group about what had happened to his brother, but he never broke the surface in any of those discussions. Even in therapy in Tennessee he was reticent to go there for fear of dredging it up again and having to face the pain.

But it had all come pouring out when he looked at her. It hurt like hell, and still did. But it was out. She had reached into his core and had shaken him at the foundation. It still hurt, but somehow he felt that a valve had been opened in his heart that had relieved decades of pressure. She did that. Somehow, she did that. No one had ever made him feel secure enough to reach down and tear it out of his heart.

He glanced again at Boone's, a turn-of-the-century grocery store that had been converted into a trendy after-work spot. He saw couples walking in, laughing; and customers sitting at the bar flirting with the waitresses. He saw himself two years ago.

At long last, the angel on the other shoulder materialized and reminded him he wasn't that man any more. And, as good as that drink might taste, Bill had no desire to be that man again. He turned the key and pulled away from the bar and headed back to the office.

Chapter 48

Erin Mosby sat on a concrete bench under a flowering magnolia tree waiting for Sister Margaret.

She had gone into the reception area an hour earlier to ask for her, but the woman there had said that Sister was not in her room. Instead of leaving, Erin had walked around the grounds for a while and then simply sat. The grounds were alive with colors and the smell of magnolia blossoms. The sound of the light breeze shuffling the trees had an almost mesmerizing effect on her. She felt something here she had seldom ever felt. Happy.

Erin studied very hard, and the results of her efforts had placed her in the top ten percent of her class. At first, she did it because she was on scholarship and had to study to keep it. Then, in time, the habit of study had incorporated itself into her character so that now it had become second nature. She was University of Illinois bound and headed somewhere in her life. She just wasn't sure where.

She was growing more and more impatient with living at home. She wasn't the kind of kid who caused problems for her dad. She certainly had little or no social life, and never went out with boys. None had ever shown any interest in her. She was all he had since her mother died. That was nice, in a way, but in another way it was a burden. She so wished her father could find someone else to lift that burden from her shoulders.

Erin was eight years old when her mother, Clarice, died following a long bout with cancer. Her mother had been alive with humor, and involved in Erin's life every step of the way. She volunteered at the grade school, and was the life of Erin's home. Erin's dad, a bookish computer programmer, was quiet, decent and very withdrawn. Clarice's death drove him more and more into himself, and even though there was no question that he loved Erin, there wasn't much to give. Instead, he clung to Erin and made her the focal point of his life.

Erin lived each day with the memory of the last weeks of her mother's life. Clarice had wanted to die at home, so the front room was converted into a hospital room. Erin sat holding her hand every morning and every evening, begging her mother not to go. She began each day at school at Mass, where the children convened, asking God not to take her mother away. She watched the life drain out of her father's heart as he stood by the bed. Her mother couldn't hear. God didn't listen. On a beautiful day in May, Clarice left Erin and her father alone. She would not be there to tell her daughter about boys, to teach her all of the things that mothers teach daughters about doing their hair or prettying themselves up. The soul of the Mosby home had departed, leaving Chuck Mosby a shell and condemning Erin to an arid existence.

Sister Margaret, the pretty nun she knew only from seeing around campus, had touched her heart in the cafeteria that day, and she wondered whether she had meant what she said about coming by sometime. Probably not. She was probably just being nice, and would be too busy for someone like her. Now she was feeling silly, and was just about to go to her car when she saw the door to the residence open.

Margaret checked her messages and learned that a young woman had stopped by. When she returned to her room, she looked outside and saw

Erin Mosby sitting across from the residence hall. She ran down the stairs and walked outside just as Erin stood up and started to walk away.

"Hello, Erin. How are you?" She called.

"Fine, Sister."

"I understand you were looking for me."

"I just wondered if I could talk with you sometime." Erin only looked her in the eye briefly, and then looked down. Her red hair was in tangles, and her complexion was in need of much attention. She wore faded jeans and an old shirt and tennis shoes. Erin's academic performance was stellar, but her personal hygiene reflected a low self-esteem. The sadness in this girl was palpable.

"Well," Margaret said, "I have a few minutes now. Why don't you come inside?"

"Sure."

Margaret walked up the steps and into the residence. She led Erin into the common room and sat down near the library shelves.

"What is it, dear?"

"I went to Alison Corcoran's funeral today."

"Oh my, how sad."

"Yeah, it is sad. I didn't know her. She wouldn't have given me the time of day, but I felt sad about her and all."

"Yes?"

"Well, Sister, Billy's funeral is Monday. The church today was full, and there were priests all over the place. It made me sad to think that Billy's funeral is probably not going to have anyone there."

"I see."

"No one knew he existed. He is dead, and no one cared about him when he was here and no one will care enough to remember him now that he's dead. It just makes me sad."

"Erin, is it Billy you are talking about—or yourself?"

"What?"

"I sense you are feeling quite alone, and that you have felt that way for some time."

"Uh, yeah. That pretty well sums up my life."

"Erin, I don't know what anyone will do about Billy's funeral. I do know that we have no control over what others do. The only thing any of us can do is what we think is the right thing. But I will tell you this."

"What?"

"I will be there. In fact, if you would like, I will be there with you."

Erin's face brightened, showing the potential for beauty that lay beneath the pain and years of unintentional emotional neglect. "Would you?"

"I promise you," said Margaret.

The two sat for a few minutes without talking. The soft breeze stirred the leaves above them, and the silence was only periodically marred by the sound of cars passing.

"Erin?"

"Yes?"

"Do you have a little time?"

"Sure."

"Well, would you like to go with me to evening prayer? It's quite beautiful. The sisters chant the prayers. And then, if you would like, you could have dinner with me in the dining room."

Erin Mosby did something Margaret had yet to see her do. She smiled. "Sure, Sister. That sounds awesome."

Chapter 49

Erin loved evening prayer. The sisters' voices carried the antiphonal prayers upward into the stone arches and they bounced back down creating a surreal experience that was truly unique. She had never heard anything like it.

She thought it odd that they called the narrow cubicles they stood in *prayer stalls*.

She was sitting now at a table in the dining room with Sister Margaret, eating a plate of spaghetti with meatballs, garlic bread and a small salad with bleu cheese dressing. It tasted so good. It reminded her of the spaghetti sauce her mother used to make. But that was in another world. One she visited now only in her dreams.

"I have heard that you are like a deputy sheriff or something?" Erin slurped a long piece of spaghetti.

"Yes. Sort of. I used to be a deputy, before I was in the convent."

"Awesome. Did you ever shoot anybody?"

Margaret laughed. "No. Truth is, I never had to draw my gun in the line of duty, thank heaven. Most policemen don't, in spite of what you see on television."

"Are you helping the sheriff find whoever killed Billy?"

"Well, I am trying."

"Could I help?"

"Well, I'm not sure how."

"I'm pretty good at figuring things out. Really."

Margaret looked at the girl. She was basking in the small amount of attention that Margaret had shown her, and her demeanor had changed in a very short time for the better. Her eyes were brighter, and she was looking at Margaret when she spoke. It was amazing.

"I don't know whether I can really talk about it with anyone, honey. There are rules."

"Well, just tell me something you are having trouble figuring out. See what happens."

Margaret sipped her coke, placed it on the table, and folded her hands together. "Okay, let's try this out. We are trying to find someone. She may be a high school student—although we aren't really sure any such person exists. She would have been the granddaughter of a man who died quite a few years ago. We are trying to find out if he had children. Well, he did. He had a son. But the son died. We have not been able find any evidence that the son had any children, and we have pretty much reached a dead end."

"Is this person in danger of being murdered, like Alison and Billy?"

"That is the concern, yes."

"I presume that the sheriff uses Accurint, or some other such utility?"

Margaret's mouth fell open, and she looked at Erin with wide eyes.

"Why, yes, as a matter of fact I think they do. They use quite a few different search engines. How do you—?"

"I have no life, Sister. I am quite good on the computer, and I can pretty much find anything. As for Accurint, it's a subsidiary of Lexis-Nexis, the legal research company. They have a very good program for locating people. If there is anyone like that, I am sure they would have turned up."

"Okay."

"Unless …"

"Unless what?"

"Well, let's say this son got somebody pregnant before he died. Did he die young, and suddenly?"

"Yes, he did."

"Well, if he died before he could marry the mother, the child could have been born—here or in another city—and been given the mother's name. That would make it hard to trace if you are operating with more conventional assumptions."

"I see what you mean. What exactly do you do on a computer, anyway?"

"I'm a State Scholar, Sister. I do know my way around those things."

Erin pulled her cell phone out of her purse, and pressed a speed dial button with her thumb.

"Dad? I'm visiting with Sister Margaret at the convent, and she wants to show me something. I will be home later. There's some soup left from last night in the fridge."

Pause.

"Good. Finish it all, because I will have to throw it out if you don't. And there's a strawberry pie from Schnuck's there too."

Pause.

"You found it. Figures. Love you." She clicked off. "He is going to have to learn to take care of himself sooner or later. I won't be there come fall.

"Now, I saw a computer in that room where you live. Can I use it for a little while?"

"Got it!"

Erin had been typing at the keyboard and checking information for about half an hour before she perked up with the announcement. She hit the print button, and a sheet of paper began to wend its way through the HP three-in-one on the table.

Margaret sat in the chair at the end of the table, marveling at how quickly Erin could type.

"How?"

"It's complicated. I tapped into a search engine that is used by the courts to track fugitives."

"How?" Margaret felt like a five-year-old in kindergarten, pestering the teacher to explain how cows give milk. The roles of teacher-student had been flip-flopped in a surreal fashion.

"I'd rather not say. Anyway, I typed the Lewis guy's name in there and there is a relationship utility that links people to any known persons with whom there was ever any contact. Financial, usually. You know, like rent payments, bank accounts, bills going to the same address but with different names. That sort of stuff. This is really good because it goes back to the mid-eighties. Ages ago, don't you know?"

"Wait a minute. You just hacked into a government database from a computer here in the Dominican convent?"

"Relax. I masked the IP address. They think I'm in Alaska."

"Erin, you are scaring me."

"One thing my dad could teach me was computers. I learned fast."

"I would have thought our folks at the sheriff's office could have done this sort of thing. And certainly the people at the FBI."

"Remember what I said about assumptions? They may have assumed they were looking for someone who was married. I found several names that did not match the family's name. One of them was a girl named Georgiana Hawthorne. She lived on Glenwood here in Springfield. I did some searching, and tracked her to St. Louis. There, she gave birth to a little girl seventeen years ago. The baby was named Theresa."

"So, we are looking for a Theresa Hawthorne."

"Wrong assumption. People meet other people and fall in love. She apparently met a guy in St. Louis named Gregory Madison. They got married, and he adopted the little girl."

"Theresa Madison. You're sure?"

"Would I lie?"

"So, she's in St. Louis?"

Erin handed her the piece of paper. "Wrong again. They live here in Springfield. He is an officer at the Chase Bank. They live in Panther Creek."

Margaret was speechless. She sat looking at the paper, and then looked up at Erin.

"What?" Erin said.

"If you're right about this, then whoever we are looking for has to be as good at computers as you are. Or have access to people who are."

"I would agree."

"Then we might just be ahead of his game." Margaret pulled out her cell phone. "Erin, I think you have a future with the FBI."

"Awesome!"

"A high school kid found this out? Jesus Christ!" Hargrove threw down the pen he had been using to write up a report. "What the hell do I pay these people for? Got an address?"

Margaret read the address to him.

"Ernie!" Jim screamed across the office. Ernie had just walked by. "Where's Bill?"

"He is getting something to eat. What is it?"

"Come here!" He handed the note to Ernie. "The girl we have been looking for. Her name's Theresa Madison. Her dad's a vice-president at Chase Bank. Get Bill on the horn, and get him out there now! You still there, Margaret?"

"Yes." Her ears were stinging a bit from Jim's screaming.

"You busy?"

"I'm on my way!" She hung up.

"Are you going? Can I go?" Erin asked.

"No, honey. I'm afraid not. But thank you so much. You might have saved someone's life."

Erin looked a little down. Margaret stopped for a minute.

"Would you like to come over again this weekend some time?"

Erin brightened. "I'd love to."

"I will call you when I have some time."

"Promise?"

"I promise."

Chapter 50

Theresa was sitting at a table on the third floor of the public library working on a report for advanced biology. She had been writing it for several weeks, and she wanted to put the finishing touches on it before it was due Monday.

There were several people sitting by the microfilm readers, and a scruffy looking man sat half-awake in one of the chairs near the newspaper rack. He was one of several homeless who had made a home of the library when it was open. They never bothered her, however, and she paid them little attention.

It was ten minutes before eight, and it was getting dark outside. The library would close shortly, so she took one more look at the journal she had pulled down from the periodicals shelf and then closed it.

She walked down the three flights of stairs and out the front door. Several homeless persons sat on the concrete planters outside on which were stacked their belongings. These persons chose to camp outside the library rather than to go to a homeless shelter because shelters had rules. No alcohol, no weapons, and no drugs. The library had no such rules. If any were convicted sex offenders, the shelters wouldn't take them. How many predators lurked here was anybody's guess.

Theresa walked to her car, which she had parked in a spot down the street across from the old post office.

"Oh, shit!" she said as she reached for her keys.

Her left rear tire was flat.

She looked around. It was dark, and no one was around. She saw only shadows in the distance lurking under the overhang of the library. She hated to call her father, but she didn't want to let any of those people near her. The library was closed. She set her books on the trunk, and reached into her purse.

"Looks like you have a little problem," someone from behind her said.

She was startled, and turned quickly to see who was standing there. Her first reaction was fear.

Then, seeing who it was, she let out a breath and dropped her phone back into her purse.

She smiled.

"Think you could give me a hand?"

The man smiled back.

"No problem."

Chapter 51

Margaret's cell phone rang as she was walking to the garage. It was Bill. "Margaret? I'll pick you up on the way."

"I can drive."

"I'm about three blocks from the parking lot. You're riding shotgun."

"Okay." She hung up, and then turned and ran back toward the main parking lot. She arrived just as Bill turned in. He swung up beside her and she jumped in.

"What's this about some high school kid finding all this stuff out?"

"It's true. One of our students was over and wanted to help, so I posed the problem and she figured it out."

"The old man is really hot. I have had a couple of people on this. They probably slacked off a bit after Pickering took himself out. It's not like they don't have other things to do."

"Should I call the Madisons and alert them we are coming?"

"No. It will just drag things out and we'll be there before the conversation is over."

It was a little after eight, and Georgie was watching *Larry King*. Gregg, her husband, was in the garage.

The doorbell chimed and Georgie walked over to answer it.

"Mrs. Madison?" There stood a nice looking young man holding a badge ... and a nun.

"Yes?"

"I'm detective Templeton from the sheriff's office, and this is Sister Margaret."

"Let's see, the policeman's benevolent society has joined forces with the Salvation Army in an effort to cut costs in their fundraising activities, right?" Gregg Madison appeared at the door, having come in from the garage. Margaret might have laughed, had there been time.

"Mrs. Madison, this is important," Bill said. "It concerns your daughter, Theresa."

"Theresa! Oh my God! Is she okay?"

"Yes. It's nothing like that. Is she home?"

"No. She isn't," said Georgie. She was clearly shaken. Margaret knew she needed to do something to settle her down.

"Mrs. Madison, I know this seems a bit odd. But, I am actually acting as a deputy to the sheriff's department. Might we talk with you alone for a moment?"

"What the hell is going on here?" Gregg asked, clearly growing impatient.

"Well ... there isn't anything I can't talk about in front of my husband," Georgie said.

"Theresa was born in St. Louis, is that correct?"

"Look, unless you tell us what this is about, this isn't going any further," Gregg put his foot down. He pulled out a cell phone. "You wait out front. I am calling the sheriff's department."

"Theresa's grandfather used to be the fire chief in Springfield, is that right, Mrs. Madison? Please. Her life could be in danger," Margaret pleaded. Gregg put the phone down.

"Yes, he was," Georgie answered slowly. "But I don't see ..."

"Two young people were murdered last week. They were both grandchildren of persons known to Theresa's grandfather. There is a concern that this is more than a coincidence. Theresa is the granddaughter of former chief Jenkins, is that correct?"

"Oh God," Georgie said. "Please come in."

"Where is Theresa now?"

"She is probably on her way home," Gregg said. "She goes to the library to study of an evening. It closes at eight."

"Could you call her?"

"Sure thing." Gregg dialed her number. Seconds went by.

"Theresa. Dad. Call me right away." He clicked off. "It was her voice mail."

"What kind of car does she drive?" Bill asked.

"It's a 1999 Mustang. Dark green."

"Know the plate number?"

"Yeah. QTEE 89. You don't think she's in immediate danger, do you?"

"We hope not," said Bill. "We are just being cautious."

"Theresa is adopted, is that correct?" Margaret asked.

"Yes. But she doesn't know it. Gregg is her father. We agonized over whether we should or shouldn't tell her. Frankly, we decided there was no real reason at this point," Georgie said. "Did you say those children were the grandchildren of the chief's friends?"

"Yes," said Bill.

"Who were they, if I may ask? Those friends."

"Doctor Corcoran—not Peter Corcoran, but his father—and Gerald Brown."

"I see."

"Did you know Chief Jenkins, Mrs. Madison?" Margaret asked.

"Enough to keep my distance. He couldn't look at a woman without his eyes dropping to her chest. There was something primitive about the man. I was living with his son, and he couldn't keep his eyes off me. It was a bit frightening at times."

Gregg dialed his cell phone again. Nothing.

Bill pulled his out. "It's me. Send a car to the library. Ask around. Theresa Madison, seventeen years old. She is driving a dark green, '99 Mustang, license plate QTEE 89. Get an APB out. Call me."

"Oh, dear Lord." Georgie closed her eyes, and leaned against the wall.

"Let's sit down," said Gregg. "Honey, come here."

They walked into the large sitting room off the foyer. Five minutes went by, during which not a word was spoken. Finally, Georgie broke the silence. "Theresa is an honors student. She is going to the U of I in the fall. She plans to be a doctor."

"You must be very proud," said Margaret. "She sounds like a wonderful girl."

She noticed Theresa's senior picture sitting on a table near the staircase.

"So this is Theresa?" Margaret asked.

Georgie walked over and picked up the photo, holding it to her breast. "Yes. Isn't she beautiful?"

"She certainly is."

"She is so lucky. I am so lucky," she said, taking Gregg's hand. "Gregg loves her like his own."

"She is my own," Gregg said. "I'm the only father she has ever known. She will be here in a very few minutes. She always comes home right after leaving the library."

Bill's cell phone buzzed. "Templeton."

Margaret watched Bill's face as he spoke. She sensed by the way his expression changed that the news he was hearing wasn't good. He flipped his phone off, and then turned slowly to the Madisons, who were holding hands on the sofa.

"What is it?" Georgie asked urgently. "They found her, right?"

"I'm afraid not. Your daughter's car is parked about a block from the library. With a flat tire."

Georgie put her hand to her mouth, and a look of sheer terror overcame her.

"Officers are looking everywhere around the area."

"Jesus Christ!" Gregg Madison stood up. "What is going on?"

"One of the deputies spoke with a woman outside the library, one of the homeless who lives there. She said she saw a young woman walk away from the library around five after eight. She later looked up, and saw that young woman about a block away walking with a man. She couldn't describe the man, but she knew it was the young woman."

"Someone is bringing her home. That's it!" said Georgie.

"But she would have called," said Gregg. "She would have called me."

Bill looked down at his hands, which he had folded in front of him. "I'm afraid they found a cell phone several blocks from where her car was found. It had two missed calls on it from this number. I am sorry, but it appears that Theresa may have been abducted."

Margaret's heart sank. The scream that came out of Georgie Madison sent shock waves through Margaret's spine.

Chapter 52

There were four city cars and several unmarked cars outside the library. Their flashing lights cast eerie strobe-like shadows of the homeless against the library walls, some sitting, others walking back and forth, several standing in a group watching the drama that was unfolding in the street.

Bill pulled up behind one of the unmarked vehicles. He recognized it as Ernie's. He and Margaret got out and walked over to the Mustang that was the center of attention.

Ernie was talking with a woman. She was gesticulating as she spoke, and Margaret heard her say, several times, that she couldn't see the man clearly. The woman wore torn jeans and a tank top that had probably been discarded in a Goodwill box. Her hair was stringy, her face pockmarked and red. She smelled of cheap booze and a half-smoked cigarette was between her tobacco-stained fingers.

Ernie turned and walked over to Margaret.

"I'm tired," he said. "Retirement can't come fast enough."

Ernie was always telling the guys in the office how his time was almost up and how much he was looking forward to moving to Louisiana and opening up a bait shop in the Bayou Teche. He did look tired. This case was wearing him down.

Margaret's heart was beating so fast that her head hurt. She was angry. Angry that they had come so close, only to find out that the animal that had killed the two kids from Saint D's was one step ahead of them. Whoever he was, he had to be smart enough to track down Theresa Madison. It was no easy task.

"Any ideas?"

"No. That lady only saw the girl walking away with some guy she can't describe. They turned down Monroe and were walking toward the Municipal Building. The fountain kept her from seeing where they went."

"What are we doing?" asked Margaret.

"There's an APB out on the girl's car, but the car is here. Since we don't know how they left here we're up against a wall."

"Get an APB out on Brother Tom Brightman. We can run down his license plate," said Bill.

Margaret's anger was mounting to a frenzy, and she felt tears coming. She could only think of the Madisons clinging to one another. What horror they must be experiencing.

"The city guys are all over this, looking everywhere for anything suspicious," Ernie said. "The sheriff has called in extra guys and they are on it."

Margaret turned and walked back to the car. She pounded on the roof of the car so hard that her hand hurt. Her hand would be bruised in the morning.

"Jesus," said Bill. He looked over to the car. "I guess I better get her home. There's not much more we can do. How in the hell do we begin to know where to look?"

"Guess the janitor was a red herring."

"Yeah. I think the pathologist needs to take a closer look."

Ernie slapped Bill on the back and returned to the group of officers who were going over the Mustang. He stopped and turned back toward Bill. "The tire was slit. Probably a hunting knife or something else big with a serrated blade. It was sharp and he was strong."

"Great," said Bill, as he walked back to the car.

"Let me get you home," he said to Margaret.

"Home? You mean so I can get a good night's sleep? While another child may be dying and her parents are battling the worst thing any parents can ever dream of?"

"Margaret, get in."

She did. He started the car and turned east toward the capitol building. Margaret's head was pounding. She hit her fist against the door again.

"Take it easy on my car," Bill said. "That's county property."

"Is there something funny about this?" she screamed.

He was letting her problem become his, and getting frustrated, the very thing that he had been told not to do in his years of therapy. He had intended to turn toward the convent, but instead passed Monroe Street and kept going, turning finally into Washington Park. The broad, tree lined avenue was dark and theirs was the only car on the road. He came to a turn and swung up near the park pond and pulled the car over. She needed to get it out.

"No. Nothing's funny. I feel as bad about this as you do."

Margaret glared at him, and then opened the door and started walking toward the park bench near the pond. She sat down, dejected, angry and hurting.

Bill let out a breath, opened the car door and slowly walked over to where she was sitting. He stood behind the bench for a minute, and then walked around and sat down next to her.

"Did you get a look at the photo of Theresa?"

"Yes," he said.

"I had to look twice. Except for the hair—Theresa's is longer—she could pass for Bonnie Easter."

"That might work in her favor," Bill said.

The next few minutes passed in silence. Margaret sat watching the lights from the park pavilion shimmer off of the pond and listening to the waterfall from the fountain in the center that kept the water from growing stagnant.

"Evil."

"What?"

"I am supposed to be writing my thesis about evil. It's all so academic, the way the religious deal with it in nice, metaphysical terms. But it's all bullshit. Evil is the absence of good, said Saint Augustine. As though by coming up with a nice formula we can categorize it, understand it, set it on the shelf and go on with our lives. But it's real, and palpable, and frightening. And the worst part is, it's in each of us."

"I am afraid you are a little over my head here," Bill said.

"Am I?" Margaret stood up suddenly and, without warning, swung and struck him hard on the shoulder. He jumped up and looked at her like a wounded animal.

"What the fuck is wrong with you?"

"You know about evil, don't you? You know how heartbreaking it is. Isn't that why you drink?"

Had she kicked him in the groin, it wouldn't have hurt as much. He glared at her. "I'm outta here."

She moved quickly to block his exit. "Don't you walk away from me!"

"That's exactly what I am doing, lady! You can stay here or go, I don't give a shit."

She took both fists and began to pound on his chest. He caught her hands in his and held them. She looked up at him with eyes wide-open, eyes that flared. "Damn you! Don't you walk away from me! No matter how badly I want you to!"

Then, she kissed him. Hard. He let go of her hands and she put her arms tightly around his shoulders and held the kiss the way a drowning person clings to the lifeguard, threatening to take him down with her.

He grabbed her and kissed her back. His tongue went deep as he clung to her, partly out of passion and partly because he wasn't sure she wouldn't haul off and smack him again. Then he grabbed her arm and walked back to the car. He opened the back door and pushed her in. He got in after her. They kissed for five minutes, her hands running over his face, his hair and down his chest. Then she stopped.

She removed the cross she was wearing and placed it in the front seat.

Theodora awoke suddenly and sat up in bed. The light was coming from the hall through the doorway, and the dim light over the bed was on. She looked around and saw the IV stand and the bedside table. She reached over and picked up her watch. It was two thirty in the morning.

Margaret was very much on her mind. She sensed an anxiety, not unlike when she was still at home and one of her siblings hadn't returned from a night out with friends. But why she felt anxious concerning Margaret she didn't know.

She blessed herself and picked up the iPod. She put her earphones in and pushed the play button and picked up where she had left off earlier in the evening, with Elvis singing "Tender Feeling."

Chapter 53

Occasional chatter from the radio, an occasional passing car and the sound of a hoot owl broke the stillness as the two lovers lay entwined peacefully in one another's arms. For a blessed few minutes, whatever evil their lives were immersed in was kept at bay.

The radio played out a drama on the east side of Springfield in which a woman awoke to find a naked man lying next to her, kissing and touching her. She had no idea who he was. She screamed and dialed 911 on her cell phone as the terrified fellow threw on his jeans and ran out of the house in time to confront a cruiser pulling in the driveway. As it turned out, the young fellow had come home drunk and walked into the unlocked front door of what he thought was his house. It was the house next door. Afterwards, she recognized him and didn't file charges. The man's wife had been roused from a sound sleep, however, and didn't believe his story for a minute.

Margaret was awake now, and chuckled to herself as she listened.

"People never cease to amaze me," said Bill, awake now as well.

"I guess I have not only broken my vow of chastity, but have also committed a host of other sins," Margaret said.

"How's that"

"One. I'm a nun. Two. We're not married. Three. Assuming you are married, the church teaches that the only way to have sex that isn't sinful is when the man ejaculates inside the woman."

"Sounds like you hit the trifecta," Bill said.

"Oh, there's more."

"Spare me. I'm a Baptist."

"Baptists don't sin?"

"You know the old story. The Protestants don't recognize the Pope. The Catholics don't recognize the Protestants. And Baptists don't recognize each other at the liquor store."

She laughed softly as she gently rubbed her hand on his chest. "I suppose that if I died now I'd go straight to hell."

"Seems more like heaven to me," he said, stroking her hair.

"That's the funny part. Right this moment I don't really feel that guilty."

"Maybe the church should learn to pick its battles," Bill said. "This is such a powerful human energy; it's almost insanity to try to stifle it."

"Some of the saints felt that way, too," she said. "Saint Augustine, before he committed to Christianity, couldn't stop either. He prayed to God to make him chaste—but not just yet."

"You would have to shoot me to enforce that."

She looked up at him. "Yes. I suppose you come out here all the time."

He laughed. "Honestly, it has been about a year since I've been with a woman. And that wasn't the most memorable experience."

"Why?"

"Because it was just sex. I interviewed this girl at the Qik N EZ on North Grand after a holdup. She was cute. She was sending signals, and I was receiving. After work, we went to her place and had sex. I never saw her again. I can't even remember her name."

"So she really was quick and easy, huh?"

He chuckled. "Probably why they hired her."

"So, you're not into casual sex, detective?"

"When I was a little younger, maybe. No more. Except with nuns. Show me a nun and I will have my pants down around my ankles before you can shout 'Hosanna!'"

Margaret laughed out loud. It felt good to laugh. She was more relaxed than she had been for quite some time. She luxuriated in the peaceful moments in his arms.

"There was someone I was very attached to when I first came back here," Bill said after a while.

"Do you want to talk about it?" Margaret asked quietly.

He did want to talk about it. Strange, he thought. He had never wanted to before. He told her the story of Sylvia Patterson.

As she listened, she wondered if he was about to have his heart broken all over again.

"Bill, I am so sorry about the way I behaved earlier. And the things I said. I don't have any explanation, really. I just hope you can forgive me."

"A few more rounds with you might go a long way toward easing the trauma I suffered. It'll be tough, but I think I can overcome it."

"I'm serious."

"I know. You are forgiven. It has been an awful couple of days for both of us."

"I can't stop thinking about that poor girl and her family."

"Yeah. I know what you mean. But you know, you do have anger management issues."

"Oh, really?"

"Yeah. Ernie told me a story about you and how you went off on some kid in a corner store, took his gun away and then beat the shit out of him."

"Well, you know how it is. Don't ever piss a woman off."

"He pissed you off?"

She was silent for a few moments.

"He had shot a cop, and I kind of came unglued."

"Oh. Well, that might do it."

She sat up. "About ten years ago, I was having an affair with one of the deputies. He was killed after a routine traffic stop."

Bill thought for a minute. "Eric Thompson?"

"Yes." Now she became anxious. "Please, his wife did not know about us, and I wouldn't want her ever to find out. Promise me you won't tell. Promise me."

"I promise. Really. Besides, I never knew him. I just heard about what happened."

"Can I trust you? How do I know you aren't going to be in the locker room tomorrow telling the guys about the size of my boobs?"

"Because if I did, you would find out and I'd never get at them again. I mean it; I'm not going to say anything."

"It devastated me, but I couldn't let on. I was totally alone. And just when I thought it couldn't get worse, it did."

"How?"

"I have never told a living soul what I am about to tell you. Not even my confessor or the worthless therapist I went to for a while. I wanted to, believe me. You have no idea how much it hurts to have something like this rooted in your psyche, wrapped so tightly that it can't be extricated, like some inoperable tumor."

"Actually, I think I do."

"Three weeks after he died, I started throwing up in the mornings. After the second day, an EPT confirmed my worst fears."

"Oh, boy. What did you do?"

"What do you think I did? I am a Catholic. Okay, sometimes not a very good one, but I am still a Catholic and I would burn in hell if I did anything besides commit to having it."

"Okay."

"Two weeks later, I miscarried."

A car drove by. Bill reached up and brushed the back of his hand against her face. He felt tears rolling down her cheeks.

"There is no sin in that," he said. "That was God's doing, by your own reckoning I would guess."

"Yes. It was. But it helped me put the whole thing with Eric in perspective. It made me wonder why it was that I was content to be in what turned out to be a fairly long-term relationship with a man I couldn't have, and had no intention of trying to have for myself."

"I'm not sure what you are saying."

"I was playing around, passing the time, getting my fix of love and affection—and sex—but something else was going on inside of me. In the years that followed, I came to believe that I was actually being called to something else. I had mistakenly thought that being a cop was it. But it was something else entirely."

Bill just listened quietly.

"I adored my father. He was a tough guy and a great cop, but the essence of what he did was to help people live their lives and be better. The people he arrested respected him, and some even came to like him. He taught me to shoot a gun, he took me with him when he cruised around the county, and I felt like the biggest little girl in the world. But he also raised me in the Church, and made sure that I knew where the reality of my life really was. He planted this religious consciousness into me very deeply. As I grew older and was trying to figure out what I wanted to do with my life, I naturally felt that being a cop was what I was destined to do."

"What changed?"

"I did. After the miscarriage, I came to understand the thing with Eric for what it was. Delaying the real decision I was meant to make. And when I lost that baby, it hit me. God had brought me low. I was alone. I had no one to turn to but Him. It startled me, woke me up."

"Are we talking about destiny here?" He spoke the word disparagingly.

"Yes. That may be exactly what I am talking about."

"I'm not a big believer in that."

"You're not alone. Look around. We have reduced humans to biology and psychology. We learn from conventional wisdom that when the brain dies, the soul, or the mind, or whatever, dies too. We are thought of as a complex arrangement of DNA, fiber, flesh and excrement. And out of that we are supposed, somehow, to find dignity? What I don't understand is why a sense of purpose—call it destiny if you want—is such a threat. But it must be, because no one wants to even consider it a possibility any more. So, even if God is speaking to us, we not only don't hear, we've shut out the possibility of receiving a signal."

"And the thing about being a nun?"

"I eventually realized that I had mistaken the cop's uniform for the calling, instead of what lay behind it. Being where I could best serve others."

"So, you switched uniforms?"

"Literally and spiritually. And the past years have led me to believe that I was right. With some reservations."

"And now?"

"Oh, God. Now—God forgive me—I just want you to kiss me."

He did. Gently. Repeatedly.

"I could easily fall in love with you," she said.

"I think I have already fallen in love with you."

They nuzzled each other for a few minutes, and listened to the breeze kick up outside and toss the branches around. A park policeman drove by slowly and hesitated. Then he spotted the sheriff's star on the plate and drove on past.

"You aren't the only one sharing deeply imbedded secrets."

"Meaning?"

"I was in therapy for months, and then in group sessions. I go to meetings every week. It keeps me grounded. There are different levels of trust in those places. No matter how close you get to a therapist, there are things that you just don't break open too far. The thing about my brother? It came up, but I always moved on quickly. It was frustrating for my therapist in Tennessee, because he knew there was a bombshell down there. You're the first person I have brought it up with. I don't know why. There is something about you that just made it okay. It felt like I had something cut out of me that had been all tied up in my gut and that would go with me to the grave. I never stopped blaming myself. I always thought my dad was right."

"And now?"

"For some reason, I don't feel that way anymore. While I always understood intellectually that it wasn't my fault, it wasn't until I looked into your eyes and sensed your kindness and understanding that I knew it was true. That it really is possible to let go, and let God."

"The AA mantra?"

"Yes. After I went to bed last night, I slept a dreamless sleep. I never saw my brother's face once. It's as though he moved on."

"Or you did."

"Yeah. Maybe I did."

They were quiet for another twenty minutes. Bill's heart was filled to the brim. The thought occurred to him that he might not be able to keep this beautiful woman in his life. He had lost the last one, and it had caused him to spin out of control, to lose his grip on life.

This woman was different. The other woman had used him. True, he had used her too. But there was never anything in that relationship that raised him up. Margaret had, in a very short time, made him more than he had been. He felt that he was a better man.

And he knew, now, that he would give his eyeteeth to keep her forever. But he also knew, deep down, that he would be a better man with her in his life or without her. He reached down and kissed her gently. And they pleasured one another one last time.

Chapter 54

Peter Corcoran was in a fog during most of Alison's funeral. He heard the Bishop intone prayers over the coffin, and he could smell the pungent incense. He watched the long box that held what remained of his only child as it processioned down the aisle. At the time, he was in a dissociative state.

He had never felt so alone. His wife Shelley hadn't said more than two words to him since Alison's death. He had given her Valium to calm her down initially, when she was hysterical. Then, the hysteria was replaced by moods ranging from euphoria to withdrawal and utter silence. He might find her watering flowers in her garden and humming a show tune one minute, and a half hour later she would be sitting in an armchair in the living room staring off into space. He had never thought of his wife as the type of woman who, under any circumstance, would suffer from suicidal ideation, but now he was concerned.

His in-laws were still at the house, which only enhanced the gloom. Her dad was bearable, but Antonia could bring a circus clown to tears. She had never liked Peter. She felt he wasn't good enough for Shelley. It didn't matter. He held his temper and kept his mouth shut. It was easier that way.

This morning, he left at seven and headed for the clinic. It would be a relief from the pain that oozed from every corner of his home and the awful hole that was in his heart. It was overcast as he drove in, but even had the sun been shining brightly it wouldn't have broken through the darkness he was living in.

"Daddy, push me please!"

A memory came back of a sunny day in the back yard when Alison, or "Allie" as he called her, sat impatiently in her new swing waiting for him to give her a much needed push. He could see again her beautiful eyes—his eyes—and that smile that always brightened his life. He could still smell her hair. He pulled the car over to the side of the street at one point and broke into tears. It took him several minutes to compose himself before he started back toward the clinic.

Once in the office, he walked past the front desk. The clerks noticed him coming in and all stood up.

"Good morning, Doctor," said Gladys Hitchens, a pretty file clerk. Two nurses and an X-Ray tech spoke to him as well. He knew they were concerned, but he felt awkward as he sensed that they pitied him. He didn't want to be pitied. He wanted his daughter back. But that was not an option. Dead is dead. His life, or the happiest part of it, had ended.

He thought of his wife, once so vital and beautiful. They had been so in love, but that had been slowly changing for years. In time, she succumbed to the mythos of being a doctor's wife, and luxuriated in her position in society and seemed to live only for the new things she could buy. Her shopping sprees had been costing a fortune for years, but her ardor in the bedroom had disappeared long ago. Their once vital love affair had degraded into ennui and tolerance for one another's idiosyncrasies. He never heard it said, but he was certain that his mother-in-law was thinking, "I told you so" to Shelley every chance she got. He latched onto work the way a drowning man grabs for a life raft.

He sat at his desk with a cup of coffee, and reviewed files that his nurse had placed there. A new referral sat on top. He took a sip, and opened the file. Doctor Vito Scalini had referred the patient to him from St. John's. The diagnosis was hepatocellular cancer. Prognosis poor. He spent some time reviewing the test results. It appeared that Doctor Scalini's diagnosis was on target. He glanced up to the tab at the top of folder. The name on the file was "Hohmann, Mary Francis." In parentheses underneath the name was written "Sister Theodora—Dominican Order."

Margaret hadn't slept at all and now she felt like hell. She felt like a zombie as she stood in front of the mirror in the bathroom. It was after three when Bill had dropped her off in the parking lot. She looked at her face, which was red from Bill's whiskers, and ran her fingers around the dark circles under her eyes. Her hair was a wreck. She looked like a wild woman who had been had several times. In fact, she had been had several times.

A rush of shame washed over her and she closed her eyes and leaned against the sink.

"Margaret Donovan. What were you thinking?"

She remembered how her father had reacted when he had caught her smoking a cigarette behind the house when she was fifteen years old. She had thrown it down the minute she spotted him coming around the corner, but he had seen it.

"I'm sorry, Daddy!" she said. And she was.

"I'm sorry, Daddy," she said to herself in a whisper as she looked again at the wreck that was her face. Her pain doubled when she glanced at the pectoral cross that lay now on the sink. She looked at the silver corpus of the Savior who gave his life to expiate sin and the realization flooded her heart.

What in God's name is wrong with me?

She showered and dressed for the day. Morning Prayer would be in half an hour. She just had time to get to the chapel and catch Father Milkowski. She would have to make a good confession before she took the host.

Chapter 55

Theresa Madison awoke with a horrible headache.

The first thing she noticed was that she couldn't move freely. Her hands were bound behind her with something that had no give. It felt like duct tape. Her feet were bound tightly as well, and her feet were attached to her wrists forcing her into a painfully uncomfortable position. She winced as a cramp formed in her right calf, and tried to extend her heel to fight it off. Little movement was possible, however, so the cramp caused her a great deal of pain before it finally subsided. She had to breathe through her nose because a strip of tape covered her mouth, and her breathing was becoming more labored with each wave of pain.

After the cramp passed, it occurred to her that she was still fully clothed. Only her shoes were missing. She was fairly certain she hadn't been molested.

Yet. But she had no way of knowing what the man had in mind.

She was lying on a mattress on the floor of a room that had high windows. It was a basement room. The room was dark, but there was light coming through a louvered door that, once her eyes adjusted, made it possible to make out the features of her dungeon. The walls were painted concrete block, and she could see floor joists, wiring and air ducts on the ceiling above her. To her right there was a small room with what looked like a sink and an old toilet.

The mattress smelled of something. She wasn't sure what it was, but it was quite unpleasant.

She tried to remember what had happened after the library.

Her car had had a flat tire. Then, he came by and she accepted his offer of a ride.

She would never have thought anything about accepting it from him. She had thought herself very lucky.

They had walked for about a block and then got into his car. It had been parked right in front of the police station, directly across the street from Saputo's Italian restaurant.

They had turned south on Ninth Street and had gone about half a block when her cell phone rang. Suddenly, he swung the car over to the side of the street and put something on her wrist. She screamed when she realized that it was a pair of handcuffs. She reached for the door, and that was all that she remembered.

From the pain she was feeling in her head, she surmised that he had struck her.

She remembered something else now that ratcheted her fear level even higher.

Before he knocked her out, he had asked her why she was fighting him.

And he called her Bonnie.

She was terrified, and was trying to keep from crying. She could only breathe through her nose, and if her nasal passages became stuffed up she would suffocate. She was also fighting the urge to throw up. Her heart was beating so loudly that it heightened the pain in her head with every pounding beat.

She knew she had to overcome all of her physical reactions in order to remain calm.

To survive.

Her breathing had just about returned to a near-normal level when, from somewhere upstairs, came the sound of a scream that seemed to come from a tortured animal. It certainly didn't sound human. Then she heard a thud on the floor above her. Her bladder emptied.

The pain had rendered him prostrate. He lay now on the sofa in his living room holding his head. His breathing was labored and he fell onto the floor. He crawled over to a table and reached for a bottle. He unscrewed the cap and drank the brown, bitter-tasting morphine. No time to measure out the drops. In a few minutes, he sat against the wall, bottle in hand, and caught his breath.

Only a couple more days. Bonnie's birthday was Monday. This would be his birthday present to his sister. His beautiful sister. She loved him. His memories all flooded back. He pictured his aunt, his dad's sister Angela, and her husband. They could have no children, and were eager to have him come live with them. He had no idea that it would be for the rest of his childhood. How had he managed to put it all out of reach, buried so far down that the dreams and memories only recently had come back?

He grew up in suburban Milwaukee, where he played little league baseball, basketball, and football like so many other kids. He loved his aunt and uncle, and had taken to calling them mom and dad. No one ever thought otherwise, and they, of course, couldn't have been happier. He had even taken their name. Soon, all memories of the horrors he had witnessed at the hands of people he knew were soon banished into that record room of the brain where one could only hope that time would have the same effect that water and infestation has on records kept in vaults.

Not so. The dreams started coming again, and then the headaches. Then, the diagnosis.

He had been granted years of reprieve from the guilt. He didn't do anything to help Bonnie. The anger—he wanted to kill those men. The conflicted feelings about his dad, who knew who killed Bonnie and did nothing.

He would keep the last one downstairs until he needed her. She would be special. She would be the messenger. She, like the Corcoran girl, was beautiful and full of promise. Like Bonnie had been. Bonnie's life had been taken, and she had been tossed out like so much garbage.

People who think they can get away with things like that don't understand that the mark of Cain is carried by future generations. He had learned that in seminary.

He was there two years when the rector found him and another boy in his shower. He quietly transferred to a small college in Missouri, where he graduated with a criminal justice major and a computer science minor. Then, he enlisted and was able to use his computer skills as a telecommunications expert during Desert Storm.

He had lived a good life. An exemplary life. Well, for the most part. Before the dreams of death found him and left him no choice.

"I love you, Bonnie!" he said aloud, as he buried his head in his hands and sobbed uncontrollably.

Almost directly beneath where he sat, a young girl lay in the darkness terrified for her life.

Chapter 56

Margaret pulled into the parking garage at the hospital and walked to the main entrance. It was beginning to sprinkle a bit, but was still very warm. She had called and spoken with Ernie to see if there was any news about the Madison girl. Nothing. She flipped her phone shut and punched the elevator button.

"Oh, excuse me!" she said after walking into Theodora's room and seeing a man talking with her. The man turned his head.

It was Peter Corcoran. She closed the door and walked to the family lounge down the hall. She poured herself a cup of coffee and sat on the sofa. She was the only one there at the moment. In about five minutes, she heard footsteps and then saw Peter Corcoran standing in the doorway. She stood.

"Sister? Sister Theodora has given authorization and has requested that I speak with you. May I?"

"Certainly." She moved back and sat. He sat on the other end of the sofa.

"I won't pull any punches. Your friend is dying."

Margaret closed her eyes and then reopened them and looked directly at Peter. "How long?"

"Well, this type of cancer doesn't usually give people more than a year, and that's with chemo and radiation. In this case, it has begun to spread, so I would say that you will be lucky if she is still here six months from now."

"What about treatment?"

"She has refused it."

Tears began to roll down Margaret's cheeks.

"She told me," he continued, "that the cure, in her case, would be worse than the disease. It is very painful, and for the two to three months it would buy her probably not worthwhile."

"Will she suffer?"

"Toward the end, especially if it spreads to her spine. We can help with the physical pain. The spiritual pain is something that I think she has licked already, and that's frequently the worst. She is a truly amazing woman. Very strong and resolute."

Margaret smiled. "That she certainly is. How about quality of life, I mean for how long?"

"She can go home today, if she wants. She can continue to function normally for some time. Then, she will have to go to infirmary. She will receive good care there. I will visit her myself, regularly."

"You're very kind," Margaret said. Theodora would be able to see the new Lincoln Museum again. Margaret could even take her to Graceland.

"You are very close to this woman, aren't you?" he asked.

"I never knew my mother," Margaret said. "So, yes. Sister Theodora sort of became that mother when I came to the convent. It will be difficult letting go of her."

"I know something of having to let go," he said.

Margaret watched the man look down at his shoes, and felt for him deeply. Instinctively, she reached over and placed her hand on his. He didn't move. He seemed to welcome the warmth of her touch. He seemed to need it.

"Doctor, please accept my apologies," she said. "The last time we met, I angered you. It has been an awful time, and I am so sorry if I made your pain worse."

"Nothing could make my pain worse, Sister," he said, pulling his hand away. "I was angry at everything and everybody. I realize you were only trying to help. No apology needed."

Neither spoke for several moments. He never made a move to get up and leave.

"Sister? That day, you asked about the Easter girl."

"Yes."

"I didn't know her. I was in eighth grade when she died, and she came from another parish. But I remember some things."

"Yes?"

"My father wasn't really very close to me. It always made me wonder if there was something wrong with me. He was always working. Or something. My mother drank a lot. Eventually, she died of cirrhosis. It took years of therapy for me to realize that there hadn't been anything wrong with me, but rather with him. With them. He and my mother fought a lot. In time, I began to realize that they were fighting about other women. I guess my father never knew a woman he didn't like.

"I remember them fighting about the Easter girl. Apparently, Mom got wind of the fact that this girl was always at the cabin where my dad hung out, in Rochester or Riverton or somewhere like that. She wasn't very kind about it, calling the girl a slut and a whore and everything else. They didn't know I overheard it."

"So, your father did know the girl?"

"I suspect there was more than that to it."

"Why?"

"When I went through mom's house after she died, trying to figure out what to auction and what to keep, I found a poem that someone had written to my dad. It was on lined school paper, and the handwriting was a young person's. It was a love poem. At the bottom it was signed, 'I will always love you—Bonnie.'"

He paused.

"Do you think my father might have had something to do with her disappearance?"

He had been frank about Theodora, and he deserved the same. Somehow, out of the chaos of a marriage marked by infidelity, corruption and alcohol abuse, this man had turned out to be a thoroughly decent human being.

"Yes. We believe that there is a distinct possibility."

He sighed. "The sins of the fathers?"

Margaret was quick to reply. "Are not always visited upon the children! You are truly a good man, Doctor. You have God and your own integrity to thank for that."

He stood up. "Thank you for those kind words, Sister. Unfortunately, my hard-wired integrity didn't help Alison."

Theodora sat up eating her breakfast.

"I asked Doctor Corcoran to prepare you for my early demise," she said matter of factly. "I didn't ask him to hurry it along, but it would seem that he is conspiring with the kitchen staff to do just that. I'd offer you some, but it is atrocious!"

"It's the thought that counts," said Margaret.

"And this is coming from a woman who will eat anything!" Theodora added.

Theodora pushed her tray table away, continuing to clutch her plastic coffee cup. She placed her napkin on the tray, and then repositioned herself in the bed.

"I am happy, Margaret. Death doesn't frighten me," she said.

"I envy you that," said Margaret. "I hope that someday I can be as philosophical about it."

"I believe in what my religion teaches, Margaret. Death is not the end. I don't need to debate it; I don't need to convince you or anyone else. I don't need to concern myself at all. It is what it is, and there has never been any question in my heart. So, you see, I am simply taking the last step—or perhaps it will be another first step, who knows?"

Margaret smiled.

"Is that funny, dear?"

"No. I was just remembering a story my father told me once about his friend Monsignor Laughlin."

"The Monsignor? I can only imagine."

"He and my father came to Springfield for dinner once. They went to the old Saint Nicholas—best Cantonese food in the state, dad use to say. Anyway, the waitress knew the Monsignor. Called him by his first name. An attractive, middle-aged woman, dad said.

"Dad said the waitresses in Springfield all knew Monsignor, from when he was chancellor over here. Monsignor was a hopeless flirt who loved to bedevil them. Anyway, he and this waitress had a long, fun-filled conversation and then, when she walked away, dad said the Monsignor watched her walk all the way to the kitchen.

"Then he turned to my dad and said, 'You know, Pat, if I die and there's nothing, I am really going to be pissed!'"

Theodora had to put her hand up to her mouth to keep from spitting coffee all over the sheets. "Oh my, he was one of a kind!"

"Did you ever regret …?"

"Regret what, dear?"

"I mean, did you ever want a husband and kids? Did you ever think about things like that? I mean, wanting a man to cling to at night, and someone to come home to, to talk to and share your life with?"

Theodora put down her coffee cup. "There was a boy in high school I was sweet on, and he was sweet on me. Bobby Thornton was his name. We dated for over a year. Of course, in those days girls didn't strip down and do the nasty at age fourteen on the first date. But, we fooled around a lot in his car when he would take me places. It was thrilling for both of us. I really cared for him, and he truly wanted to marry me when we graduated.

"I had never let on that I had been thinking about the convent. I suppose I hadn't because I wanted to explore this part of life a bit. Who knew? I might have changed my mind. I didn't. When I announced my intentions as graduation approached, he was very angry. I am afraid I broke his heart.

"I still think about him every now and then. My sister told me that some years after graduation he married a girl who lived in the next county and they had seven children. He is happy, I think. And, so am I. Part of me will always love him, will always wonder what it might have been like. But I knew where I was going. And I went."

Margaret sat looking out of the window. The sun had replaced the morning clouds, and a bird had landed on the windowsill. He sat there for a moment and then he flew off.

"Did you ever have a hard time maintaining your vows, Sister?"

Theodora thought about this for a moment. "I assume the one about poverty isn't what you are referring to. You have always been marginal about the obedience part. So, it must be the vow of chastity to which you are referring."

Margaret smiled.

"Thank God we women don't become aroused at the drop of a shoulder strap the way men do. I should think this convent would have been a revolving door through the centuries, otherwise. At times, there were temptations. I found myself very attracted, in every way, to a young priest when I was in Louisiana. He was good-looking. My God was he good-looking. Smart, funny, and very, very nice. We weren't alone on too many occasions, but it was all I could do when we were to keep from grabbing him and dragging him off into some dark corner."

"Why didn't you?"

"For what would have amounted to a few minutes of pleasure—maybe about fifteen seconds since he probably hadn't done it before—I would be throwing away a lifetime commitment. Yes, I was tempted. But I managed to keep my vows. As it turned out, it was probably a false alarm. He was later sent to prison for having it off with some of the altar boys."

"What if you hadn't?"

Theodora looked at Margaret, trying to read between the lines. Her mouth came open, but they were interrupted by a knock at the door. There stood Bill Templeton, dressed in a blazer and tan slacks, holding a bouquet of fresh flowers. "Good morning," he said.

Margaret stood up, feeling her face begin to go flush. "Sister Theodora, this is Detective Templeton. I forgot he and I are going to interview someone this morning. I told him to pick me up here."

"Pleased to meet you, detective," Theodora said, her eyes sparkling. "Margaret, you didn't tell me your young detective was so handsome."

Bill blushed. "These flowers are for you, ma'am. Sister! I'm sorry."

"Ma'am is just fine, young man. They are lovely. Please set them on the windowsill." She looked up at Margaret and smiled.

"Well, we should be off," Margaret said. "I'll be back later."

"Nice to meet you, young man. Be careful, both of you. Oh, and Margaret?"

Margaret turned back to look at her.

"The question you asked me? If I hadn't, I would have had some very tough things to think about before I continued my life's work."

"That was sweet of you," Margaret said.

"She's a friend of yours. It just seemed right."

"Hold on a minute," she said, and then walked up to the desk. A young ward clerk looked up and smiled.

"Excuse me, but when will Sister Theodora be able to go home?"

The girl checked the chart. "Doctor Scalini will be up to see her sometime this morning. She can go anytime after that."

"Bill, when will we be done, do you think?"

"Depends on Tomiczek. But I am certain we could be back by twelve or twelve thirty."

She turned back to the nurse. "Would that be okay?"

"Certainly."

"Thanks." She flipped open her cell phone. Is Ernie there? This is Sister Margaret."

Bill watched her standing there, looking as beautiful as ever. And all without makeup. Less than six hours before, they had been making love.

"Ernie? Listen, if possible, could you have a squad car at St. John's around twelve thirty? Sister Theodora is getting out then. I would like to surprise her with a ride in a squad car."

Bill could hear Ernie's raised voice coming from Margaret's phone.

"I know we're not a taxi service, Ernie. Do it for me?"

Ernie was always a sucker for Margaret, Bill thought. He knew that there would be a car waiting. But then, who wasn't a sucker for Margaret?

Chapter 57

Abraham Tomiczek sat in a large sitting room near the window in his wheelchair. An oxygen tank sat next to him, attached to a nasal cannula. He had suffered from emphysema for three years and he would probably die of it.

He had smoked up to three packs of cigarettes a day for over thirty years, and even now—if he could convince one of the orderlies with a ten spot—he would sneak out to the courtyard and smoke one.

Tomiczek had come to the United States from Austria in the thirties, and ended up in central Illinois, where he worked at a variety of jobs. He cleaned stalls for a farmer in Alexander, Illinois for a few years, and then moved to Springfield where he went to work for Sangamo Electric.

When the police department advertised for candidates, he took the test and passed it. He met the physical requirements easily, and ended up patrolling the east side of town.

Tomiczek had learned politics from his father, who had once been mayor of the village he was born in, and soon he had worked his way through the ranks of the department.

In 1970, when the chief of police stepped down after a much-publicized romp with his secretary, Abraham Tomiczek became chief of police.

After all, he had the backing of one of Springfield's most prominent citizens: Johnny Rigali.

The glory days of the mob in Springfield were waning, but Johnny Rigali still maintained a stranglehold on illegal activities in town. Tomiczek was a practical man, and he knew that a man like Rigali could do a lot for a community like Springfield. There were plenty of girls to service the politicians from Chicago, and Rigali kept them clean. His girls had Blue Cross, and he paid for monthly checkups. He always had satisfied customers who could count on his discretion. He still ran gambling out of rooms in the rear of some of Springfield's finest restaurants and clubs. As long as no one interfered with his business, Rigali was an asset. In fact, crime in Springfield was never lower than it was when the Rigalis were in charge. No one dared commit an armed robbery in town. It stirred people up, and Rigali liked things quiet so that his businesses could flourish behind closed doors.

Rigali and Tomiczek had had an understanding ever since he was a patrolman. He knew what doors not to open, what citizens not to bust, and every month a nice envelope was delivered to his house that made life in the Tomiczek home very pleasant indeed. People might have wondered how it was that Tomiczek had an outboard at the boat club on a policeman's salary, or how he could afford a country house at Matanza Beach. No one ever asked.

As for Rigali, everyone understood how much of an asset he could be. An old woman who lived across the street from him had been troubled by kids stealing her Christmas lights from the fir tree in front of her home. She complained to Rigali's wife. No one bothered the woman's lights again. Tomiczek often wondered what happened to those kids, whoever they were. But, as was frequently the case, he never asked. Yes. Rigali had been good for Springfield.

Not so with Sally. He did as much as anyone to cause the mob's influence in town to dissipate after his father's death. He was a loose cannon. It was good that he had died.

But after that, everything changed in Springfield. No more envelopes.

Springfield was ready for Tomiczek to go. It was a new world. Gone was the heyday of the mob in Springfield, and Tomiczek was a reminder of an older way of doing business.

The town was as glad to be rid of him as he was to be out of it.

All Tomiczek had now were memories. His wife had long ago walked out on him, and his children never came to call.

Some of those memories would have sickened a normal person. Not Abe Tomiczek.

Who was responsible for the headless corpse discovered in a cornfield in 1971, later identified as Mike Carroll, a competitor of Rigali's in the jukebox business? Abe knew. The crime was unsolved.

And that business with the Easter girl? He knew all about that too. Crime unsolved.

But those envelopes had gone a long way to making his life very comfortable. Abe was more than happy to take those secrets, and countless others, to his grave with not a whit of guilt.

It was around ten o'clock by the clock on the wall when Abe saw a car pull into the parking lot. It was unmarked, but he knew it was a cop car. He saw a man get out, and then a woman. It wasn't just any woman. It was a nun.

He had to take a piss. He took off his cannula and wheeled himself out and down the hall to the restroom.

He spent about ten minutes just sitting. He was breathing hard, and couldn't muster the energy to get up. Finally, he pulled himself up and dropped back into his wheelchair, and backed out of the stall. An orderly was washing his hands in front of the mirror.

"How you doing Abe?" the orderly said.

"Just fucking great," Abe said as he pushed the automatic door opener. The orderly chuckled to himself.

Abe had just wheeled back into the room when he saw the cop and nun. They were sitting on a sofa in the middle of the room, and when they saw him they both stood and walked toward him.

"Mr. Tomiczek?"

"Who wants to know?"

Bill flipped his id wallet open, showing his sheriff's department badge. "I'm detective Bill Templeton, Sangamon County Sheriff's office. This is special deputy Margaret Donovan. Sister Margaret Donovan."

Abe laughed, and started coughing. He waved his hand, and then wheeled over to the window and attached his cannula. Bill and Margaret followed him.

"What brings you out here?" Abe asked.

"We'd like to ask you a few questions about the murder of Bonnie Easter."

Abe thought about what the detective had just said. He didn't answer.

"She was murdered in 1974, when you were chief of police."

"I know when the fuck she was murdered. What do you want?"

Bill pulled two folding chairs away from a card table and moved one toward Margaret. They both sat facing Tomiczek.

"You were involved in the investigation. You arrested a man for that murder."

"Sure did. Greasy spic named Garcia."

"We have reason to believe that Garcia didn't commit the murder."

"Who gives a shit? We couldn't hold him. No physical evidence." He spat the words out as though they offended him. Could he have been arrogant enough to expect the courts to hang a crime on a man simply because he said the man did it?

"Did you have any other suspects?"

"Nope. I think he got away with murder."

Nothing was said for about a minute. Margaret was biting her lip. She wondered how a man like Tomiczek could ever have been thought trustworthy enough to head up a police department.

"We have a theory, Mr. Tomiczek," she said. "We'd like to know what you think of it."

He looked at her with spite, and then looked away. He spoke to Bill.

"Women had no business in my department. Let alone nuns. You letting these broads run things in the sheriff's office now?"

Margaret was infuriated.

"Look, Tomiczek, we didn't come here to hear you spout your Neanderthaloid view of men, women, and life in law enforcement." Her voice had grown loud, and several nurses in the hall stopped to listen.

Neanderthaloid? Not bad, thought Bill.

"We think the girl was murdered, or that she may have died accidentally, while being subjected to what could have been nothing less than a gang rape by some very connected people. Among them was Sally Rigali. I am sure you knew the Rigalis, Mr. Tomiczek? It wouldn't surprise me to learn that you were on the Rigali payroll."

Bill's eyebrows went up at that. Now Tomiczek was looking at her. If he had had the strength, he would have reached over and strangled her. He started to cough. The fit lasted about half a minute.

"You fucking bitch. Go fuck yourself."

"No, it's you who are fucked, Mr. Tomiczek. The minute we are able to tie you in any way to this. Why don't you just tell us what you know? You don't have long anyway, so what do you have to lose?"

"I arrested the sonofabitch who killed her. End of story. It ain't my fault that the namby pamby justice let him go."

"I'll just bet that enraged you, too, didn't it? You couldn't get anybody else to hang it on, but your buddies all went free. How much did you get for that, Mr. Tomiczek?"

A nurse walked over and stood by anxiously. Bill put his hand on Margaret's knee.

"Look, Mr. Tomiczek," Bill said. "This murder is connected to the recent murders of two St. Dominic's students. We are trying to find the suspect. We believe he may be Bonnie Easter's brother."

The look in Tomiczek's eyes went from feral to fright. His color drained and his coughing resumed.

"I am afraid that this can't continue," said the nurse. "You are making him ill."

He can choke to death as far as I am concerned, thought Margaret.

"Please. One more minute," Bill pleaded. The nurse nodded, but stood by warily.

"Mr. Tomiczek, did you know the Easters?"

"I knew the father. He was a fireman."

"Did you know the children?"

"Not well. I saw them around."

"And the boy? Did you know the boy?"

Silence.

"Mr. Tomiczek?"

"I forgot about the boy. Yeah, there was a kid. He was younger. I never knew what happened to him."

Bill looked at Margaret. She was glaring at Tomiczek. The nurse looked at her watch.

"Well, thank you Mr. Tomiczek," Bill said. Tomiczek gave no response.

"Mr. Tomiczek," Margaret said. "Did you help cover up the murder of Bonnie Easter at the hands of Ed Jenkins, John Michael Corcoran, Gerald Brown and Salvatore Rigali?" She couldn't leave without hitting him between the eyes.

Tomiczek didn't cough. He didn't even look at her. He simply stared out of the window. Finally, he turned to the nurse. "Get me the fuck out of here."

"Anger management. Ever hear of it?" Bill said as he got in the car.

"I don't care. That bastard is guilty as sin. And what's pissing me off is not only that he knows damned well who killed Bonnie Easter, but he thinks he is going to get away with it."

"He has gotten away with it. We can't prove anything."

"That's why I'm pissed off. There's a little girl buried in Oak Ridge Cemetery who could be raising kids now if someone hadn't used her and tossed her away."

Bill looked at his watch. "We have some time. Want some breakfast? I don't know about you, but I am badly in need of some carbs."

Chapter 58

Margaret and Bill sat at a corner table at a restaurant in Sherman not far from the nursing home where they had interviewed Abe Tomiczek. Bill had consumed three eggs, two sausage patties, hash browns, toast and two pancakes. He was just finishing his orange juice.

Margaret smiled. Her breakfast had been somewhat less extravagant: one egg, toast, a slice of ham and a side of grits. Her father had introduced her to grits once when they visited a cousin in South Carolina, and she had really liked them. She ate them with butter. Some people put syrup on them, but there was something about the texture and bland taste that appealed to her.

She was sipping coffee. His repast finished, he looked up at her.

"What?" he said.

"I was just wondering if you were going to eat the table cloth."

He laughed. "Told you I was hungry. You of all people should understand why?"

She blushed.

"I'm sorry," he said. "I didn't mean …"

"It's okay."

"Are you okay?"

"I'm fine," she said, and sipped her coffee. She really meant it.

"I was worried that you might be upset."

"Upset? No. Confused? Yes. Worried? You betcha."

"Worried about what?"

She put her coffee cup down, looked around to see if anyone was paying attention to them, and then reached around and took his hand under the table. "Bill, I needed you last night but I had no right, and what I did was wrong on so many fronts. I have to work it out, and so do you. The God I worship wouldn't punish two people for finding comfort in one another, especially after what we have been going through. I am just not certain where to go from here."

"Where could it go? I know where I would like it to go. But I don't want to set myself up."

She didn't want to set him up either. Who was she kidding? She already had. He had taken a nosedive because a woman jilted him once before and now he had fallen for a woman who was probably going to do the same thing. She was agonizing over that possibility.

"Bill, I don't know where it will go. I don't know where I will go."

He nodded and squeezed her hand.

"But I want you to know one thing. What happened last night wasn't just about sex. I wish it were. That's something I haven't felt in years. Frankly, I don't know that I have ever felt that. I care very much for you. I just don't want to hurt you."

He didn't say anything. Finally he removed his hand and started playing with the saltshaker. She looked at him and loved him intensely at that moment.

"I'd better get you back to the hospital," he said.

"The hospital! I forgot!" she said. She flipped open her phone.

"I've got to call Ernie and make sure he will be ready!"

———

A crowd had gathered at the entrance to St. John's.

The attraction was a sheriff's car that was sitting directly in front, lights flashing. Deputy John Rogers stood at attention next to the car awaiting a special passenger. Bill stood next to his car, which was directly behind the cruiser. He had the light flashing on the dashboard. It made quite a spectacle.

Eventually, the double doors hissed and Margaret came out wheeling Sister Theodora to the car. Theodora had a teddy bear in her lap and a small bag with her belongings. Two nurses accompanied them.

"Oh, my goodness! These people probably think I'm a dangerous felon!" Theodora said. She was laughing.

The nurses were cracking up. One of them was checking out Deputy Rogers. Rogers smiled at her.

Margaret opened the door, and then helped Theodora out of the chair and into the car.

"Watch your head!" Margaret said.

"Just like on *Cops*, right?"

"John, can you ride with Bill? I will drive."

Rogers looked anxiously at Bill. Bill smiled and nodded.

Bill pulled out first, with Rogers riding shotgun.

Margaret put the cruiser in gear. She took out a CD and put it in the CD player above the radio. In a few seconds, Elvis was going to town on "Burning Love."

Soon they were cruising down Ninth Street, causing heads to turn the whole way.

"Whatever you do, don't touch the shotgun," Margaret said.

Carmelita and Clarence were walking Elmer and Elise across the campus when the motorcade turned into the parking lot off of Monroe Street. They both stopped. They saw the first car pass, and then they saw the cruiser. The lights were still flashing. Inside they saw Margaret behind the wheel and Theodora in the passenger seat. Theodora waved. The dogs tugged at their leashes, but both nuns stood with their mouths open.

"Don't tell me they've deputized Theodora too," said Clarence.

"Hmph! Remember when it used to be quiet around here and all we did was pray?" Carmelita asked. "You know? Before it turned into Dodge City?

"Come on Elmer. Let's go."

Chapter 59

Theodora felt like going to evening prayer, and Margaret went with her.

The dietician, after consulting with Doctor Corcoran, fixed Theodora's meals to specification. This wasn't a problem, since there were more nuns on a special diet than a regular one. Father Milkowski joined them at the table that evening, along with Brother Swartz.

Margaret walked up to get more iced tea. Sister Kathleen was filling her glass.

"She's feeling fine now," said Kathleen.

"Yes. She is happy."

"Are you okay?"

Margaret looked at her, wondering about the import of the question. Her conscience was working overtime. It took her a second to put the question in perspective.

"Yes."

Kathleen patted her on the shoulder, and then walked out of the dining room.

"Dear, you don't have to pamper me!"

"I didn't realize I had been," Margaret said.

"Well, let's put it like this. You have been attached to the hem of my garment since I got home. Now, don't get me wrong. I dearly love you. But I am not helpless—yet. I have a few good months left in me, and I can shift for myself, as Thomas More once said."

Thomas More had said that as he walked to the gallows, thought Margaret.

"Okay. I am sitting down. I am doing nothing."

She thought about what she had just said.

"Look, if you'd rather be alone …"

"Nonsense! Sit. Let me put these things away. I swear. Two days in the hospital and you brought me enough stuff to last a week."

Theodora finally sat in her chair.

"Whew! All of a sudden it hit me. I guess I am more tired than I realized."

"I should go!"

"Not so fast. I still want to talk. If you have time."

"Of course."

"My sister is coming on Tuesday. She is going to stay for a few days."

"That's wonderful."

"I have so many things to do to prepare. You know, in a way, there's something nice about knowing when it's coming. It's like planning for a trip. You can schedule the things you need to have done so that, when you leave, no one else will have to worry about it while you're away."

Margaret could only marvel at what was going on here. Theodora was thinking about her death the way most people think about a vacation. She could feel pressure building behind her eyes and soon they were leaking. Theodora noticed.

"Oh, my dear. I didn't mean to upset you."

Margaret shook her head then wiped her eyes.

"I just don't have your strength. I certainly don't have your faith," Margaret said. Then she started sobbing.

Theodora reached over and took Margaret in her arms. Margaret put her head on the older nun's shoulder and cried for several minutes. Theodora rocked her and patted her gently on the back until her sobs subsided. Margaret sat up and wiped her eyes.

"This is all wrong. I should be comforting you," she said.

"I don't need comforting. You, I fear, are a wreck. And I don't think it's all because of me, if you don't mind my saying so."

Margaret was starting to compose herself. "Whatever will I do without you?"

"You'll do just fine. You will have the strength you need. You just have to believe in yourself and trust in God."

"Let go and let God."

"Yes. Precisely. The folks at AA have got something there."

"Sister, I have broken my vows."

Theodora didn't so much as bat her eyes at that.

"As though it's not written all over your face, dear. The young detective, I can only presume."

Margaret nodded her head.

"And so, now what?"

"I don't know."

"I think you do."

"What do you mean?"

"Things like this throw everything into such confusion. Once you clear up the fog they stir up, you can see things clearly. Your Achilles' heel my dear is, paradoxically, the very thing that makes you such a wonderful nun. You feel too much. After meeting you, I quickly lost count of the number of times I watched you, in conversation with persons, reach over and touch them. You simply cannot control the need to reach out, to touch, to encourage and make people feel better. I don't know where that comes from, although I suspect it's in your genes."

Margaret could remember one occasion when her dad brought in a black man who was quite drunk. After sobering up, the man sat in his cell weeping. Margaret was with her dad that morning when he went up to check on the man. Her dad opened the cell, sat on the bunk next to the man, and placed his hand on the man's shoulder. That man talked to her dad for fifteen minutes, and her dad listened. Really listened. The man walked out of the jail later with a smile on his face.

Margaret wiped her face. "Oddly enough, I am not ready to give up on this. It's almost as though, instead of pulling me away, the experience actually made me realize that this is precisely the right place. I have often wondered whether I was here because I was running from something. That bothered me. Terrified me. Now, I know that I am not running from life. I embraced life, and can continue to embrace life."

"Well, you will have to put parameters on how you go about doing that, Margaret."

Margaret smiled, and then let out a laugh.

"Am I making any sense?" Margaret asked.

"I think so. But, I feel a 'but' coming."

"What if I break his heart? He had it done to him once, and now here I come. He is a recovering alcoholic."

"You'd like to walk away from this feeling no guilt, no responsibility. Is that it?"

That stung. Theodora meant it to.

"Oh, God. You're right."

"This is your life, dear. You have to choose the path you think is the one God meant you to take. If that means marrying your young detective and having children with him, then so be it. If that means staying the course you have chosen for yourself here, then do it. If you make a choice of this magnitude based on fear, fear of how someone else might react, then you are setting yourself up for a life of misery.

"This young man. Is he strong? I mean, emotionally."

"I don't know. He has suffered, and is struggling to overcome many demons."

"I left my demons behind days ago. But consider this. If he isn't strong enough to deal with your having loved him and then moved on, then I suspect that he wouldn't be strong enough to sustain a healthy relationship with you in another context."

"So, if he is the perfect man, then I should feel okay about leaving him behind?"

"Precisely. And if he isn't, you'd want to leave him behind without a second's thought."

"Life can be such a paradox at times."

"Now, if you don't mind, I have had a long day." Margaret reached over and kissed Theodora on the cheek. Theodora reached out and gave her a hug. "The ride home was a hoot!" she said. "Thank you for making my homecoming special. And Margaret?"

"Yes?"

"Don't settle for listening to an old fool like me. Pray. God has the answers. Listen. He will speak to you. Don't ever forget that."

Margaret went to the chapel at nine. She shut off her phone so as not to be interrupted.

She knelt on the *prie-dieu* with her head in her hands. She prayed that God would protect Theresa Madison. She prayed for a miracle. Too many lives had been ruined, and she could only hope that this would turn out differently.

At ten o'clock, she was still on her knees and her heart was beating rapidly. A stanza from the *Hound of Heaven* became a part of her prayer—*You don't know how little worthy of any love I am.*

Tears filled her eyes. At times she spoke aloud, and her pain echoed off the walls. "Why did you put me in this position? I left all that behind me years ago, and then I was thrown right back into it. I know. I know. It wasn't you that did the thing, it was me. If you sent this to test me then I failed and failed miserably. And now it has all turned into disorder, and I may have brought pain to a man that I have come to love. *What do you want?*"

The last words were almost shouted. She sobbed until her stomach clenched.

"My father is there with you, isn't he? Whenever I did something I wasn't supposed to, he was always strict but I never doubted that he loved me. He said that he never had to punish me too much because I was always harder on myself. He was right. Now I don't know where to go, what to do.

"I was a cop and then I walked away—for *You*. Now I am right back where I started and I have to ask myself all over again what I want. No. *What you want.* How can I ever come back to you after what I have done? I needed him, and he was there. I fell into his arms and I enjoyed every minute of it. Can I live without that?

"Dear God in heaven, help me understand what you want, and what I want, and help me find my way."

She knelt for another half hour until she had grown calm. As she blessed herself, another line from Thompson's poem came suddenly to mind.

Rise, clasp My hand, and come.

Unable to sleep, Margaret was sitting in the common room at eleven watching an old movie.

The movie was in black and white. She watched a man walking across the foggy moor, and then saw a large hound rise to the top of one of the hills, its face aglow. The man watched in horror, and then tried to outrun the beast but to no avail. As the action cut away, the dog overtook him.

Margaret's cell phone rang. She looked at the caller ID, and pressed the green button.

"Hi."

"I took a chance. I was afraid you would be asleep."

"No. I'm watching some old movie with Basil Rathbone. The Hound of something or other."

"Baskervilles. *The Hound of the Baskervilles.* Sherlock Holmes."

"It reminds me of the poem that I found. The one that whoever killed the janitor worked into the suicide note. It came from a poem by a guy from England. *The Hound of Heaven.*"

"Not a commonly known poem, I would gather."

"Whoever used it was familiar with it. Catholic, would be my guess."

"Well, in Springfield, that narrows our list of suspects to, oh, I don't know, sixty thousand people. Good work."

She smiled. "At least you are still an asshole."

"Part of my charm."

"Anything turn up with Theresa Madison?" She knew the answer, but it still helped to ask the question.

"That's why I called you. Nothing."

Is that the only reason you called me? She smiled. "And the APB on Tom?"

"Nothing. We're batting a thousand."

"All of a sudden I am very tired," Margaret said. "I am terrified that Theresa is going to turn up tomorrow. It was a Sunday when they found Alison."

"And when they found Bonnie Easter," Bill added.

"Yes. I can only pray that I am wrong."

"Margaret?"

"Yes."

"I just want you to know that I wasn't just saying that last night."

"Saying what?"

"That I was falling in love with you. I just wanted you to know it was special. You are special."

Margaret closed her eyes and swallowed hard. "I know you weren't just saying it, Bill." *God knows I know that.*

Chapter 60

Theodora was up early and was in her prayer stall for Morning Prayer and Mass as though nothing had changed. She ate a good breakfast, and was in very good spirits. If Margaret hadn't known better, she would have thought the cancer was all a bad dream.

At eleven o'clock Margaret remembered her promise to Erin. She picked up her phone and called her. She asked if Erin would like to come and visit for a few hours. It took Erin twenty minutes to appear at her door. They ate lunch in the dining room with Theodora and Kathleen. Afterwards, they went for a walk.

Margaret couldn't help noticing Erin's complexion, and the chronic mess that was her hair. Finally, she brought it up.

"I'm not much into that kind of thing," Erin said.

"Well, you're a young woman. You need to take care of yourself."

She winced after having said that, because she was afraid Erin would take it badly. In fact, Erin stopped walking. "My dad doesn't know anything about that stuff, and I don't have a bunch of close friends here. So I just don't bother. It's all, I don't know, so complicated."

Margaret got an idea. "Come with me," she said, and she led Erin toward the convent garage.

A father couldn't do the things a mother could. Margaret knew that all too well. Things had been fine when she was younger. She usually dressed in blue jeans and short-sleeved shirts. Then, in high school, she had to wear a skirt, blouse and a blazer. Unlike Erin, Margaret eventually became more outgoing and had several girl friends who taught her all the tricks. Her father wasn't crazy about her wearing make-up, and the school had rules against too much of it. But on weekends, she and her friends were not to be held back. To her dad's credit, he didn't say much—unless she really overdid it. He knew his shortcomings when it came to raising a girl, and he let her be who she was.

She was lucky. Now, she needed to pass some of that luck on to Erin.

For over an hour, Margaret helped Erin pick out the basics at a Walgreens down the street. She picked out a good acne soap, some makeup base, eye shadow, eye liner, blush, brushes, face scrub and mask, concealer—all of the weapons that any self-respecting high school girl should have in her arsenal. Erin was fascinated by all of the various articles of make-up—but she protested loudly when Margaret put it all on her charge card.

"Nonsense," Margaret said. "What do I have to spend my money on? Let me do this."

"I thought you guys were supposed to be poor."

"We take a vow of poverty, that's true. But I am not destitute. I get paid for teaching."

"What about being a cop?"

"Hmmmm. You know what? I never asked about that. I think they owe me a bundle. All the more reason I should spend some, right?"

The next stop was *Custom Cuts*.

Margaret waited patiently after turning Erin over to one of the stylists with orders to do something special with her. In an hour, the tousled head of hair had been replaced with a stylish cut that told Margaret she was on the right path.

They stopped for ice cream on the way back to the convent, and then went to the common room.

There, Theodora, Carmelita, and Clarence joined them. The four of them molded and sculpted and painted Erin such that, when they were finished, she didn't recognize herself.

Clarence and Carmelita fussed at each other, as usual.

"Go easy on that eye liner," Clarence told Carmelita at one point. "You don't want her looking like something out of the Egyptian Book of the Dead."

"What would you know about putting on eye liner?" Carmelita fired back. "The only time you probably ever used it was at Halloween—as if you had to work at making yourself scary."

"Shut up. Hand me that sponge. Don't talk to me about scary. They have to escort the novices past your room so they don't faint when you first walk out in the mornings."

"You two act like you were real sisters," Erin said.

Margaret and Theodora looked at one another and did their best to keep from laughing out loud as they worked on Erin's fingernails.

"They are really sisters," Theodora finally said. "Twins, to be precise."

"I got the brains," Clarence said. "She is the runt."

"I got the looks and the charm," Carmelita said.

"Not to mention the facial hair," Clarence retorted.

When they finished with the makeover, tears rolled down Erin's cheeks when she looked in the mirror.

"You're smearing it!" said Clarence, harshly. "Stop crying!"

"Sorry!" Erin said. "It's just that, I look so …"

"Beautiful?" said Clarence.

"I don't know if I would say that."

"I would," said Theodora.

"You'll be the belle of the ball at the prom, dear," said Carmelita.

"I'm not going to the prom," announced Erin. The room suddenly became silent.

"Way to go, big mouth!" Clarence said under her breath. Carmelita scowled at her.

"Well, you're not only smart, you're absolutely beautiful, child," said Theodora. "Come Monday, you'll be breaking hearts all over the place."

For once in her life, Erin felt that way about herself too.

It was after five o'clock when Erin pulled into her driveway. She and her father lived in a duplex west of White Oaks mall, near a small pond. As she walked to the house, two geese were sitting in the yard. They ignored her.

She walked into the house and dropped her keys and the sacks of cosmetics on a marble-top table near the front door. Her father was sitting at the kitchen table working on his laptop. She walked in and sat down in the chair opposite him.

"Hi, honey," he said, still typing. He had yet to look up. Erin didn't say anything, and finally her dad looked over the screen and saw his daughter for the first time since she had walked in. His face went white. He placed his hands on the table and just stared.

"Daddy?"

"Erin? You look … different."

"Different how? Different good or different bad?"

He took a deep breath before answering. "You look like … your mother. You look lovely."

She jumped up, walked around the table and kissed him.

"Thank you, Daddy," she said, a huge smile curving across her face, and then walked through the living room and down the hall to her room.

Her father's eyes followed her. He felt as if he had just seen a ghost.

Chapter 61

Margaret went to chapel again at nine, and then returned to the residence. She said good night to Theodora, who was crocheting and listening to her iPod, and went to bed.

She slept soundly until her alarm went off at six.

After Morning Prayer and Mass, she grabbed a quick bite, and then walked over to the school. Walking through the side door, she passed two students who had arrived early for morning detention. Down the hall, she saw Roy Walker making his morning rounds. She started to speak, but then realized that it wasn't Roy. It was a young officer she hadn't seen before. The officer smiled. "Good morning, Sister."

"Good morning. Is Roy sick?"

"I don't know. I have been here for a couple of days. I just go where I'm told."

Margaret laughed. "I know how that goes." She walked past the office complex and up the stairs. Arriving at the counseling office, she knocked on the door. Joe Santini opened the door.

"Could I talk with you for a moment?"

Santini wore a long-sleeved shirt and a Notre Dame school tie. He stepped aside, and motioned for her to come in. Margaret walked in and placed her bag on the table against the wall.

Joe started stacking files that had piled up on his desk onto the same table. He didn't speak.

"Joe?"

He stopped. "Look. I know you had to do it. I know you had to put me on that list."

"I had no idea that you would have to go through that."

"How could you? I didn't tell you. I didn't tell anyone. Even my wife. Now, things are pretty chilly at home. I can't blame her. You'd think that we would have had a stronger relationship than that. At some level, I think she believes that maybe there was something to it."

He looked at her. "I am assuming you know what I am talking about?"

She nodded.

"So, what can I do for you?"

She noticed several boxes sitting on the floor behind his desk. Some had books in them; others were waiting to have books placed into them.

"What are you doing?"

"Well, I am going to talk to Kathleen this morning. Now that the cat's out of the bag, I can't very well pretend that it didn't happen. The potential liability to the school, if any future accusations were to be made, would be devastating. I am prepared to turn in my resignation."

Margaret sat down in the large armchair in front of his desk. Joe sat down in his desk chair. "Joe, if Kathleen were to ask for that—and I don't think she will—I would only ask that you have her talk with me."

"How would that help? Besides, the problem remains. If this becomes public information, and it's now on the record, the school is vulnerable."

"Well, that's just it. There really is no record."

Joe rubbed his hand over his mouth. "No record? They videotaped it. I can just see it on *Dateline* TV someday."

"Actually, the only records of that interview are some notes that were scribbled down by the lead detective. And, of course, that videotape."

Joe opened his hands in supplication, and then returned them to the desk.

"As for the notes, I have an in with the lead detective. He isn't really that detail oriented. I suspect they could easily be lost."

Now Joe was leaning in. "What are you suggesting?"

"And as for that tape, well … I might have fibbed a little bit. You see, that tape was never found after the interview."

"Never found?"

"It got lost somehow. I might add that the chief of detectives followed up by talking to the head of the counseling department in Santa Fe. He not only corroborated everything you said but also pointed out that the man who leaked that to them did so out of spite. I understand he is no longer a counselor there."

Margaret reached over and picked up her book bag. She reached inside and pulled out the videotape and dropped it on his desk.

The color drained from Joe's face.

"Isn't this … illegal?"

"Oh, I wouldn't say *illegal*," Margaret said. "That is a bit harsh. Besides, they should know better than to try to turn a nun into a cop. Nuns are going to err on the side of mercy every time."

Santini picked up the tape and felt it, the way a bibliophile might gently feel a rare book. Then he sat it back down on the desk.

"Margaret, I don't know what to say. I am still going to tell Kathleen. I have to. I will never feel secure in my job if I don't."

"That's fine. Remember, I will support you. And I could probably convince the sheriff and the lead detective to support you. Sister Kathleen is fair, and she knows how valuable you are."

"I appreciate that."

He stood up and walked out toward the main office. "Coffee?"

"Please."

When he returned, he sat down. "Is this why you came by?"

"Actually, there is something else. "This"—she pointed to the videotape—"is actually sort of a quid pro quo. Do you have some time this morning? I really need to talk to you."

He glanced at his calendar. "I have an eight thirty, but I can shift it to someone else. Will now do?"

Chapter 62

Margaret had been to counselors before. She had tried going after Eric's death, but she never felt comfortable with the people her insurance steered her to. It just didn't fit. Joe Santini was different.

She told him everything. As she did, she found herself reaching for Kleenex from the box he placed near her on his desk, and soon a pile of the discarded tissues covered her lap. When she was done, she sat silently. An hour had passed.

"Wow," Joe said. "You have been carrying a lot of weight on your shoulders."

She nodded.

"What do you want to do?"

"I'm not sure," she said.

"I don't believe that," Joe said. "I think you know very well what you want to do."

"Yes, I would love to stay in the order, but I don't see how I can."

"You can quite easily. You just do it. More coffee?"

She shook her head.

"Well, I need some. Excuse me." He walked outside and closed the door. She could hear him talking to Carol Oates, asking her to shift his next two appointments to another of the counselors. Then, he walked back in and sat down. "What are you feeling?"

"What do you mean?"

"I mean, when you are faced with a crisis like this, you have an emotional reaction of some sort. Fear. Guilt. Anger. Sadness. Happiness. Shame. What are you feeling?"

"All of those."

"Not good enough. Tell me which ones. Name them."

"Fear."

"What are you afraid of?"

She was growing impatient with herself. She was afraid of so many things; she didn't know where to start. "I'm afraid of hurting Bill."

"And how would you hurt Bill?"

"He loves me. If I stay, I'm afraid he will be devastated."

"Being devastated is a choice. You have a choice to make too. You can't live his life. You can only live your own. What else are you afraid of?"

"Staying."

"Ahh. What frightens you about staying?"

"I don't feel … good enough."

"Why?"

"Because I am so … I just don't know whether I have what it takes."

Please Daddy, don't take my picture.

"Why do you feel that way?"

She looked at him curiously. "I don't …"

"Don't tell me you don't know. Why do you feel that way, Margaret? Reach back. Go back to your childhood. When you first remember feeling like that? The first time."

Margaret thought about that for a minute. Then she looked directly at Joe.

"I was four or five, I think. I had just made a new friend. She was one of dad's deputies' children. I can't remember her name. We were playing in the yard while our dads were doing something inside. Then, she asked me where my mom was. I wanted to cry, because I didn't have one. Well, instead, I told her that my mommy worked, and that she had to go to work real, real early in the morning and didn't get home until really late at night. She said that was awful. So I told her that Mommy always woke me up when she got home and read to me and hugged me before she went to bed. It shut her up."

"But how did you feel about it?"

"I remember feeling abandoned."

"Where was your mother?"

"She died shortly after I was born. It was an accident."

"But you still felt abandoned."

"I didn't know what 'dead' meant. But I sure knew what 'gone' was. All I knew then was that I didn't have her, and maybe at some level I felt it was my fault. That—"

"If you had been a better girl, she wouldn't have left?"

Margaret had been teary eyed several times up until now, but his remark was like a hit to the solar plexus. She put her head in her hands and cried.

After about two minutes, she wiped her eyes. "Sorry."

"Don't be."

"I'm not a child any more. This is ridiculous. I don't understand."

"I disagree. We are all five-year-olds inside. Or six-year-olds, or ten-year-olds. Or whatever age it was that our lives took a hit."

Like Johnny Easter, she thought to herself.

"It's true that our feelings are often set by the time we are five, and sometimes when we start out feeling that we are somehow responsible for things it stays with us. The child feels something that may not square with reality, but it is her reality. And, as Wordsworth said, 'the child is father to the man.' Or, woman—as the case may be. And so now, you are not worthy."

Margaret smiled. "You may be right."

"Only you can be the judge of that; I am not seeking affirmation. But let me ask you this: do you feel that God is calling you? Do you believe that deep down in your heart of hearts?"

Margaret's eyes came alive with a new light. The hound was at her heels, and she was running frantically away, when all she had to do was to let him overtake her and relax her restless heart in his embrace.

"Yes."

"And are you smarter than God?"

"Don't be ridiculous."

"I'm not. You're the one who said you were not good enough. So, you are content to get seconds from another woman's husband. And you are content to sit there and tell me that, if God is calling you, he must be mistaken about your worth."

Another blow. Truth hurts.

"But you broke the pattern, didn't you?"

"How?"

"The detective. He is, when he isn't bludgeoning suspects in the interrogation room, a charming man—although I didn't get to see that side of him. He is handsome, and—most importantly—available. His heart is free. You could have him if you want. You spoke of your jealousy of the FBI agent, but he is interested in you. And you willingly accepted his affection. So, tell me how you weren't worthy of it when, at some level, you were competing for it.

"The truth is, Margaret, I have seen a lot of religious come and go in this place, both as a student and as a faculty member. Some are good, some are mediocre, and some are downright worthless. You are one of the best nuns I have ever seen come through those doors. And why, do you suppose, that is?"

She shook her head.

"Because you are so human. The fact that you care for this man, truly and deeply, is not a showstopper. And never mind what happened between you. If anything, it will make you a better religious because you know the depths of human love, and human suffering, in a way most of these women never will. The only reason to walk away is if you really don't want this for the rest of your life. And, for some reason, I don't think that is the case."

He looked at his watch.

"I will be glad to meet with you any time you need. And I hope you will come back. Unfortunately, if I pass off any more students, the counselors will have me strung up."

Margaret smiled. She gathered her Kleenex in her arms and stood, dumping them in the wastebasket by the door. "Joe, thank you. You don't know how much I appreciate this."

"Thank you, too, Margaret."

He walked over and put his arms around her and patted her on the back gently. She hugged him back, tightly. Then he opened the door and showed her out.

After she left, he started taking books out of the boxes. He would talk to Sister Kathleen later just to clear the air. But for some reason, he knew that it would all be okay. As he unpacked, he was whistling.

Chapter 63

The bell rang as Margaret walked out into the hall. Students scurried out of the rooms to their lockers and into the restrooms. She had to maneuver her way down the hallway in order to keep from being knocked around.

As she neared the stairs, she stopped. She was standing outside of the boy's restroom. A familiar odor wafted into the hall. Margaret shook her head, and then turned and walked directly into the washroom.

"Oh shit!" said a boy who was washing his hands. "Morning, Sister," he said loudly as he threw his backpack around his shoulders and made for the exit.

Margaret set her book bag on the sink, walked to the last stall and pushed the door open. There, standing on the commode, was Calvin Martin, a sandy-haired junior with a face full of freckles, blowing the smoke from a joint up the cold air return. When he saw Sister Margaret, his eyes almost popped out of his head. He threw the joint into the bowl, jumped down and reached for the handle.

"Ouch!" he hollered. She had his wrist tightly in her hand, and easily pulled it up and behind him.

"Ah ah!" she said, backing him against the wall. She reached down and tore off a sheet of toilet paper and handed it to him. "Retrieve it."

He shut his eyes for a moment, and then reached down and pulled out the joint. She took it from him.

"Step outside, please."

He stepped out of the stall and stood against the wall.

Suddenly the door burst open, and a big, tow-headed student walked in. Exercising the quick perception and agile reflexes only possessed by adolescents, the boy immediately sized up the situation and did an about face. "Nun in the bathroom!"

Another boy, walking in behind him, said, "None of what? Oh. *Nun.* Uh, good morning, Sister. Cal." Then he exited quickly.

Outside, Margaret heard one of them say, "Don't nuns have their own bathrooms?"

"Perhaps we should step outside, Calvin."

He gladly followed her. She grabbed her book bag and led him to an alcove between the lockers.

Martin was on the football team. He had a good GPA. Margaret knew he came from a good family, who would undoubtedly curtail his extracurricular activities severely if they ever caught him doing something like this. They may have been the last parents in the world to adopt the attitude that "Sister is always right." He was a decent kid. Decent kids smoked joints. It was a fact of high school life.

"Do you know what this is?" she asked, holding the folded Kleenex up to his eyes.

"A joint?"

"Only a joint? Look closer."

He was dumbfounded. He just stared at it as though it would somehow miraculously reveal something seen only to her, something that could extricate him from this situation.

"That," she said, "is a two week suspension. To start with."

"Aw, come on, Sister."

"That's just to start with. Then, there will be the meeting with your parents, and the grounding. It's possible that you could end up sitting on the bench for an undetermined length of time next season. Your senior year."

Martin closed his eyes. He could see his entire high school career going down the tubes.

Margaret reached into her book bag and pulled out a wallet. She flipped it open to reveal the deputy's badge. "I am sure you have heard that I am a fully empowered deputy sheriff here in Sangamon County. You have committed a crime. You know I could haul your ass downstairs and call for a car to come get you?"

"Okay. Okay. I'm sorry. Whatever. Please, let's just get it over with."

Margaret put the badge back, and then tucked the joint and tissue safely inside her book bag.

"Evidence," she said. "You know, Cal, you're not a bad kid."

He was looking at her like a dog waiting for the rolled-up newspaper to come down on him. He didn't know what to do, what to say.

"We might be able to work something out. Of course, it would require your complete discretion."

A ray of hope presented itself to him. "Sure, Sister. Anything. Name it."

"You would have to promise never to tell a living soul. If you did, and I found out, I would have to take whatever action necessary."

"Sure. What?"

"Do you have a date for the prom?"

"What? Yeah."

"Oh. Whom are you taking?"

"Molly Ivans."

Molly Ivans, a junior, was a great looking girl and a good student as well. She could get any number of prom dates. "Cancel it."

"Cancel it? It took me weeks to get up the nerve to ask her. I can't just—"

She reached into her book bag.

"Cancel it. Right. Done. Is that it?"

"No. As a matter of fact it isn't. I have another girl in mind for you. Do we have a deal, Mr. Martin?"

Margaret kept her promise.

She sat in the front pew of St. Alphonse with Erin and Angela Connors. There were precious few family members in attendance, but the church was nearly full with students from Saint D's. She wanted to give them the benefit of the doubt; she hoped they were there out of respect for Billy Matheson, and not simply to get out of school.

Angela was dressed nicely in a light blue suit. She had had her hair done. But the ravages of alcohol and cigarette smoke and a life of continual bad choices, in men and in addictive behaviors, was showing on her face. She seemed detached. Somehow, Margaret felt that Angela had been detached for years.

Erin sat stoically through most of the service, until the priest came down to the coffin and sprinkled it with holy water. She started to sob. Margaret took her hand and squeezed it tightly.

Afterwards, Margaret drove with her in the procession to Oak Ridge Cemetery. They laid Billy to rest across the road and about fifty yards down the hill from where Bonnie Easter was buried.

As Father Greeley was saying the final words, she marveled at the evil that had made this day possible. She remembered throwing pebbles into the lake at Nichols Park in Jacksonville one day when she and her father were there for a department picnic. Each pebble would form concentric circles starting from the center where the rock dropped in, and those circles would continue to replicate and move outward until they disappeared.

So it had been with a crime committed thirty years ago. Circles of suffering were still emanating from that one act. And it wasn't over yet.

How long, O Lord? How long?

As the priest shook Angela's hand, Margaret saw the fox pop its head out of a row of trees bordering the cemetery property.

Then, as adroitly and as silently as he had appeared, he slipped out of sight.

Chapter 64

Daylight could be seen coming through the basement windows, even though they had been obscured with black paint. Places where the paint had dried and chipped admitted enough illumination to allow Theresa's dungeon to be seen in all of its squalor.

The floor was of concrete, and there was a drain in the room. Theresa sat now in a chair, tied with her hands behind her back, her feet bound to the bottom of the chair. He had released her several times to allow her to go to the bathroom, the small facility off of the main room that made the worst service station restroom look palatial by comparison. He had brought her McDonald's on one occasion, Arby's on others. He had not spoken a word to her.

She had no way of knowing what time it was. She wasn't even sure how long she had been here. She had gone to the library on a Friday. One—no two—nights had passed. Or had it been three?

It had been about five minutes since she heard his footsteps upstairs, followed by the sound of the back door closing and the key sliding a deadbolt into place. Then she heard a car start.

She was sitting in the chair looking at something in the corner. It appeared to be a piece of broken glass. The chair she was tied to was an old, tubular steel kitchen chair with an upholstered back and seat. She could move it by pushing herself forward or backward. He was never gone for too long, but she couldn't just sit there anymore and wait for him to decide whether he was going to rape or kill her.

She had to do something.

She pushed, moving the chair inches at a time, aiming for the corner of the room. It took ten or fifteen pushes to get near where the glass lay, but now she had the problem of how to get ahold of it. She tried to scoot the chair around into a position where, when it fell onto its side, she wouldn't hit her head against the cinder block wall. Ten minutes had passed. She was perspiring. It was cool in the basement, but there was no air moving. The smell in the confined space continued to make her nauseous. Then, she slowly rocked the chair. Finally, she pushed it over. A bright light exploded in her head as it struck the concrete floor. She had tried to stiffen her neck to keep that from happening, and had succeeded somewhat, but the blow she took was still painful, and she blacked out.

She had no idea how long she had been unconscious. When she opened her eyes, she was looking directly at the piece of glass. Only it wasn't a piece of glass. It was a remnant of a piece of clear, hard plastic, like that used to encase computer peripherals, that requires scissors or hacksaws or dynamite to get open. She wanted so badly to cry. But she was tired and her head hurt so much. Her eyes went shut. She fought the temptation to sleep, after having hit her head.

To no avail. In a very few minutes, Theresa was dead to the world.

It was six thirty when he walked back through the back door. He had a grocery sack in his arms and in his other hand a Hardee's sack.

He set the bags on the kitchen table, and lifted out a small, angel food cake. He unwrapped it and put it on a plate. Then, he reached into the drawer and took out a box of birthday candles. He carefully placed seventeen candles around the perimeter of the cake.

He then walked over and unbolted the door to the basement. He picked up the cake and the Hardee's bag, and walked down the stairs.

Theresa was jolted awake when she felt her chair being righted. She opened her eyes and found herself staring directly into his eyes. She couldn't tell whether his look was one of anger, or pity. He just looked at her, and then he placed his hand gently on the side of her head where she had struck it when she fell. There was a raised place, and it stung a little when touched.

He stood up and backed away. Then he reached down and pulled up his pant leg. When he came back up, he held a large knife with a serrated blade. Theresa's eyes betrayed her terror, and she started making pitiful animal noises from behind the duct tape.

He reached over, took her by the shoulder, and then bent down and slit the duct tape that had been holding her feet to the chair. She let out a breath of relief. Then, she decided she had had enough. Her feet were free, and almost instinctively she swung both feet upward and nailed him in the groin.

He screamed and doubled over—and dropped the knife. He dropped to his knees and held himself, breathing heavily for over a minute.

She was still attached to the chair and, except for her feet, unable to maneuver. The knife sat on the floor about a foot from her, and he knelt two feet away. It had been wasted effort, one that, in all likelihood, was going to cost her her life. But it sure felt good.

He grabbed the knife and stood up. She closed her eyes and waited. She felt him grab the back of the chair, and waited for the darkness to take her. She was ready. There are, she had decided, worse things than death and oblivion. But, to her surprise, instead of slitting her throat, he reached down and cut the tape binding her wrists. Then he reached over and pulled the tape off her mouth. She relaxed her arms, and then rubbed them to bring back the circulation.

He stood looking at her." Bonnie? Why did you do that to me? Don't you love me?"

Theresa stopped being merely afraid. Now, her fear-o-meter had jumped to sheer terror.

Chapter 65

Spring was Margaret's favorite time of year. She and Theodora went for a walk after dinner. It was a beautiful evening. Sister Agnes had eaten with them in the dining room, and Margaret made an appointment to talk with her the next day. She would bare her soul, once again, and she prayed that Sister would understand. She remembered what Kathleen had said about Sister Agnes and the two novices, who were no longer in the community. But that was different. Or was it?

She hadn't talked with Bill, and she wouldn't until after meeting with Sister Agnes. She was fairly certain of the outcome of that conversation, but she wanted it out of the way before she saw him again.

"You're feeling chipper this evening," Theodora observed.

"I might say the same for you."

Theodora smiled. Margaret wished she had known her when she was younger. She must have been a beautiful girl; she was certainly a beautiful woman now. She was the picture of health, and Margaret knew better than anyone that the health sprang from her soul. If anyone was ready to go to God, whenever God chose to call, it was Theodora.

They walked past the Gothic chapel, with its rounded chancel, wide transept with the side doors, and the long nave. It was a smaller version of St. Denis Abbey, but it had outlived the ability of the order to maintain it. Margaret couldn't imagine the hole that would be left in the campus when it came down. But come down it would. Such is progress.

They walked past the cemetery, with its angel that stood watch over the gate, and neither spoke their thoughts. They both knew that, in the not too distant future, Margaret would be visiting with Theodora under the watchful eye of that angel.

It was growing dark by the time they approached the main campus near the residence hall. Margaret noticed a vehicle with its lights on turning into the main gate. She watched as it veered away from the main parking lot and into one of the parking spaces near the priest's residence. She stopped walking. "Sister, go on back to the residence please."

Theodora looked alarmed. "What is it?"

"Please, just go." Margaret reached into her pocket and pulled out her cell phone. She had dialed Bill's number before Theodora had taken three steps.

She got his answering machine. She dialed another number.

"Sheriff's office."

"Bill Templeton. This is an emergency."

"He's tied up at an accident scene. Can I have him call you?"

"This is Sister Margaret Donovan. Find him. Get him, and some backup, out to the priest's residence at Saint D's. Tell him Tom Brightman is here. I'm going over there now, so they had better hurry."

Bill had just sat back down in his car after helping with a bad accident on Koke Mill Road. A teenage girl whose license was four hours old was doing about fifty in the Ford Mustang her father had bought her and had apparently reached down to answer her cell phone and lost control of the car. It careened into a Buick LeSabre with an old couple in it. They probably never knew what hit them. The front end on the driver's side was crushed, along with the eighty-four-year old driver.

The car swung around and struck a utility pole on the passenger side, killing his wife. The girl was in critical condition.

The kid was in too bad a shape to give a ticket. But he knew she would get one. Or worse. She had made a choice, kid or no kid. Her life would never be the same.

God, he hated this. It never got any easier.

He got a call from dispatch as soon as he got back into the car.

"Templeton."

"We have been trying to reach you on the radio."

"I was out of the car. It was a little intense out here."

"You have a phone don't you? We tried that several times too."

He reached for his cell phone.

"Shit!" The battery had died.

He reached down and connected it to the car charger and turned it on. There were four missed calls.

"It died. What the fuck do you want?"

"Sister Margaret Donovan called. She said Tom Brightman just came back. We have sent a car."

"Get hold of Special Agent Renfrow at the FBI. Have her meet us there." He clicked off and backed out, almost colliding with a Jeep Cherokee that was going around one of the cruisers. The driver flipped him off. Then he swung around and headed north on Koke Mill Road toward Old Jack, his light flashing and his siren piercing the silence of the spring evening.

Margaret walked across the parking lot. She watched as Brightman slowly got out of the car. He stopped and looked around him. He must not have seen her coming. She had not yet gone past the trees that lined the edge of the rectory yard. She kept walking slowly, watching him. He opened the back of the car and pulled out a duffel bag. He placed it on the ground, and then reached in for something else. She couldn't see what it was.

By now, she was within thirty feet of him. He picked up the duffel and a large suitcase, and began walking toward the house.

"Hello, Tom."

She must have alarmed him. He stopped and put the duffel bag back on the ground. His arm was shaking.

"Margaret?"

She was now about fifteen feet away. "Where have you been?"

"Away."

"Where have you been, Tom?"

"Look, I don't really feel like talking now. How about tomorrow?"

She moved closer. His arm was still shaking.

"Tom, I need to know where you have been."

He was growing edgy. His look was one bordering on anger. She moved closer. A cruiser swung into the driveway, and then pulled into the parking lot. John Rogers jumped out of his car, gun drawn.

"Sheriff's Department. Sir, drop the suitcase and put your hands in the air."

Tom looked from Rogers to Margaret, and put the suitcase down. "What is going on here, Margaret?"

"Do what he says, Tom."

He raised his hands in the air. Rogers stepped behind him. "Up against the car, sir."

Once Tom has assumed the position, Rogers holstered his service weapon and frisked him and removed his wallet and car keys from his pockets. He cuffed Brightman's right hand, then pulled it around and cuffed his left hand behind him.

"Nothing but these," he said, holding up the keys and wallet he had removed from Brightman's pockets.

"For God's sake, Margaret," Brightman pleaded. "Please tell me what this is all about."

Another car pulled into the drive, and swung into the parking lot, screeching to a halt behind Rogers's cruiser. Bill jumped out and quickly noticed that Rogers had the suspect under control. He holstered his weapon and walked over to the rear of Brightman's Monte Carlo.

Two more cars pulled in. Two more deputies got out of one of them.

Jane Renfrow, wearing blue jeans and a bulletproof vest, stepped out of the other car.

Margaret walked up to Rogers. "The keys."

Rogers handed them to her and she threw them across the car to Bill. He walked up to the trunk, and slowly opened it. Margaret held her breath and said a Hail Mary.

There, in the trunk, was a box of books and a spare tire.

Chapter 66

He had been sitting on a folding chair watching her for more than ten minutes.

Theresa sat with her hands flat on her knees, her feet together, in the chair to which she had been taped for most of the day.

The only sound came from outside as cars passed. The light was gone from the window. A single bulb suspended from the ceiling that was operated by a pull chain lighted the room.

He had stopped holding himself but he was still hurting. Gone was the anger from his eyes, replaced with an emptiness that caused Theresa to wonder if he was conscious.

Suddenly, his head came up and he looked at her directly once again.

"Now, we have things to do," he said.

He stood up and walked over to the table where the cake was sitting. He took a book of matches from his pocket and lit all seventeen candles. The cake gave off an eerie glow that cast moving shadows against the wall on the other side of the room.

He then reached down and pulled something out of the bottom drawer of a small, metal file cabinet. She couldn't tell for sure what it was at first, but then she realized that it was a cassette recorder. It looked to be an old one. She hadn't seen any like them at Best Buy or

Circuit City. The only ones she was familiar with had small tapes. The tape he was holding in his hand was larger, like her mother used to use to play music in the car. Her mother was the only one she knew who had to have a cassette player instead of a CD player in her car.

He put a tape into the player and placed the machine on the floor near Theresa's feet.

"I know you're not Bonnie," he said.

She didn't know whether that was good or bad.

I'll be anyone you want. Just don't kill me.

"But I know they will believe it when you tell them. I want you to tell them what happened. You see, I can't."

He reached into his back pocket and pulled out several sheets of folded lined paper that had been torn from a spiral notebook. There was writing on the front and back. It looked like the writing of a child.

He handed them to her and reached down and turned on the recorder.

"Read these out loud."

She looked at him expecting more of an explanation, such as one might get from a more rational person. Then she remembered that she wasn't dealing with a rational person and quickly looked down at the papers before her.

The writing ranged from small, cursive scribbles that were difficult to read, to large, block printed letters that seemed to want to fall over the edges of the paper.

"Read!" He said, his voice agitated.

She read.

> They killed me.
>
> My little brother saw it all. He had been bad and hid in the closet off of the living room because he wanted to see what happened at the parties when dad had his friends over. It was Mr. Brown the fat lawyer and Dad's boss Jenkins. They were there.
>
> So was Uncle Sally my dad made us call him that and the doctor with the funny eyes.

Sometimes women and girls would come to the house when they were there and they would play music on the stereo and me and Johnny would play down by the boat docks but my brother wanted to see so he had snuck in.

No girls were there. Except me.

Sally and me were making out. He was cute and I liked him. I liked the doctor too. They were nice to me. I didn't like the fat lawyer or the chief. But the doctor and Sally were always buying me things and dad said it would be good if I showed them a good time. I didn't mind and kind of liked it.

Sally and me went into the bedroom. We came out an hour later and everyone was drunk. Dad wasn't there for some reason and then the fat lawyer starts pulling at me and trying to kiss me and Sally is laughing and saying don't be a prude and then the fat lawyer pushed me down and started tearing my clothes off and Sally helped him while the chief and the doctor watched and laughed. The fat lawyer finished and the then chief and the record player was playing something by the Doors and then they picked me up with my clothes off and tossed me to the doctor. People are Strange. I think that was the song.

But I fell and hit my head and my brother didn't help me and he will have to die because he didn't help me because he was bad. My dad came in and saw what they did and cried and tried to hit them but they held him and then he sat while they carried me out to the car.

My brother could never tell because my dad said not to or he would die and then later the police man the chief told him the same thing because if he told anyone he would die and then they sent my brother away. He knew they would get away with it because even the police chief had come out later and done nothing.

I want everyone to know who killed me and my brother and my brother has come back to make them suffer by taking away their grandchildren and now—

"There's no more," she said, turning the paper over. She panicked because she was afraid that he would grow angry if she didn't go on. "There's no more!"

Silence.

He didn't move. The thought went through her mind that he had gone unconscious. His eyelids were drooping and he had no affect. She looked carefully to see if he was breathing.

She moved her feet slowly and then set the papers down on the floor, watching him to see if he reacted to her movement.

Nothing.

Then, slowly, she stood up from the chair. Her legs were weak and in pain, but she was determined to stand. She finally managed to stand and then her eyes moved to the stairs. She could not tell if the door to the upstairs was open or not. Was it locked? She would have to find out and the only way to find out was to go up there.

His eyes opened.

She let out a gasp as he jumped to his feet.

"What are you doing?" he asked.

She started to move but he rushed over and grabbed her by the shoulders. She took his forward movement and fell back into the chair, but she pulled at him at the same time. The chair fell backward and she struck her head again and saw a bright light, but the fall brought him down on top of her and she kicked with all of her might. When the chair stopped he kept going, flipping over onto his back on the concrete floor.

Free, she jumped up and ran toward the stairs.

He caught her arm as she started up, but she was not going to go down without a fight. She swung around and punched him in the face as hard as she could and then pushed him and kicked him in the knees. He dropped to the floor but he still had a tight grip on her ankle so that she couldn't pull away.

She looked up and saw a hammer hanging on the wall going up the stairs. She grabbed for it and swung it at him but missed. Then she dropped on the stair, his hand still clutching her ankle. Now she found momentum and this time she brought her arm up high in the air and brought the hammer down on his right forearm.

The scream that came from him scared her half to death. She had heard the bone snap and she knew that something had broken in his arm. He rolled away for a moment, and she wasted a valuable few seconds trying to determine what to do next. Then she pulled herself up and turned toward the upstairs door.

She felt a wrenching as he grabbed her arm and pulled on it, sending her flying down the stairs and crashing onto the concrete floor, dropping the hammer and sending the tape player skittering over behind a cabinet.

When she looked up, she saw him raise his left arm in the air. He had picked up the hammer. She screamed and thrust her arms upward to ward off the blow.

Everything went black.

He was on his knees holding his arm. He could see bone coming through. The pain was actually a welcome relief from the pain in his head.

He looked down at the girl. Her arm was bent badly. Blood was pooling under her head.

"I'm sorry," he said. "I'm sorry any of this had to happen."

He reached down and brushed his hand against her cheek gently, not mindful of the blood that he was smearing. She was Bonnie again. Tears were running down his cheek as he regarded her tenderly. He remembered her smile and how warm he felt in her arms.

"Bonnie, why did you have to leave me? I loved you so much." He struggled to his feet and limped up the stairs and into the kitchen. Soon it would all be over.

He would suffer no more and Bonnie could rest now in peace.

Chapter 67

The tremors had begun slowly. Before they started, he had experienced difficulty ordering his thoughts. He noticed it first when he was grading papers one evening. He had written the same comments twice on a student's paper, on separate pages.

When he found it difficult to swallow, he visited the ER at St. John's where he underwent a thorough physical and was subjected to a variety of tests. He was there until after one in the morning.

Then the doctor dropped a bombshell.

It appeared to be the early onset of Parkinson's.

A week later, he called the Veteran's Administration Hospital in Danville and requested a workup, after having his records sent there. He didn't want to do it in Springfield, and as a veteran he was entitled to the care.

He had become quite depressed. The doctor at the VA confirmed the diagnosis, which hadn't helped his mood.

When he left, he couldn't come back. Instead, he drove to Mahomet, to the home of a friend with whom he had served in Desert Storm, and stayed there. He didn't want to be around anyone, and his friend respected his need for privacy. He even had room in his garage for Tom's car.

Tom looked tired. He *was* tired. He sipped coffee, and the tremors seemed to corroborate his story. Ernie, Bill and Margaret sat on the other side of the long table in the interrogation room. Bill and Ernie stood and left the room, leaving Margaret sitting with Tom. Jane Renfrow had decided to sit out the interrogation. She was in the observation room.

"Shit. I thought sure he was the guy," said Bill.

"Well, it's a damned good story. We can get his authorization to check it out. But I think this is a dead end," Ernie said.

"Jane?" Bill said. "What do you think?"

"Well, for one thing, our guys finally ran down a birth certificate. North Dakota was having some problems with their data. They are struggling like everyone with Homeland Security over the national ID regulations."

"Homeland Security? Aren't you guys on the same team?" Ernie asked.

"In a parallel universe, maybe—but not in the Bush Administration. Brightman was born in Fargo. No doubt about it. And, just to drive in the last nail, while you guys were in there, I telephoned the friend he stayed with in Mahomet. He teaches at the U of I. He said that Brightman was with him the whole time."

Ernie and Bill slowly turned and walked back into the interrogation room.

"Brother Brightman, Sister Margaret can take you home," Ernie said. "I am sorry for the inconvenience. Especially under the circumstances. You have my sympathy."

"I don't want your sympathy, detective. I want to go to bed."

He turned to Margaret. "How could you possibly think this of me, Margaret?"

She felt like crawling under the table. But, more than that, she knew that much valuable time had been wasted. And the killer was still out there.

Ernie spoke up. "Brother Brightman, please don't be too hard on Sister Margaret. You fit the profile to a T. Right age. Military background.

And, you hailed from Wisconsin, where we think the killer may have grown up. When you disappeared, we didn't know what else to think. I regret that you didn't talk with us before you left. All of this would have been avoided."

Brightman exhaled and looked down at his hand. "I am afraid I was preoccupied. Scared to death, actually. You're right, Mr. Jones."

If not Tom, then who? Margaret was only half listening to the conversation that was taking place. She was transfixed. Something kept nagging at her.

Suddenly, it struck her. She remembered the encounter she had had in the hallway at school earlier in the day.

"Bill, have you talked with Roy Walker lately?" She blurted out. "He wasn't at school today."

Bill looked at her, ignoring her apparent *non sequitur*. Brightman, however, was paying close attention.

"Roy?" he asked.

"You can go, Brother Brightman," Bill said as he began to rise. "Thank you for your time."

"Wait," Tom said.

"Yes?" Bill sat back down.

"Well, I don't want to needlessly subject anyone to what I have gone through. But, you said the person you are interested in came from Wisconsin?"

Margaret was sitting on the edge of her seat now. "Yes."

"Well, Roy and I have talked at times in the past. He doesn't have much of a personality, but he is affable enough when you engage him. He was more so after he found out that I had gone to school in Milwaukee."

Three pairs of eyes were riveted on Brother Brightman now.

"Roy Walker grew up in Waukesha, Wisconsin."

"He's not listed," Margaret said, flipping frantically through the phone book.

"This is Detective Sergeant Templeton, sheriff's office," Bill was saying. He had reached the charge desk at the police department. "Look, do you have Roy Walker's home phone number?"

Margaret and Jane stood by waiting. Ernie had walked Tom out to the lobby.

"Okay. Thanks."

Bill hung up and dialed a number. He stood there for over a minute and then clicked off. "No answer. Jane, let's go."

Ernie walked back in.

"We're out of here. Ernie, get a couple of cars to 1224 Walnut."

He turned and looked at Margaret. He was expecting her to insist on coming along, and he was ready to fight her off. He knew there might be gunplay and he wasn't going to give in to her this time.

But Margaret didn't say anything. She just looked at him, her eyes pleading with him—for what? For understanding? He couldn't tell. He couldn't think about it now. There wasn't time.

"Margaret, take Brightman home, and keep trying to dial this number." Bill handed her a slip of paper.

"Okay," she said. She didn't argue. She was content to leave the door crashing to the ones who had done it more recently. This time, she knew she would just be in the way.

She wasn't that woman any more.

Chapter 68

It took five minutes for Bill to reach the address on Walnut Street. He pulled up in front of the house and he and Jane jumped out just as two cruisers pulled up from the other direction. Both deputies got out and stood near their cars, guns at the ready.

The home was a half-century-old traditional Craftsman bungalow with a low sloping roof and a second-story dormer. Concrete steps led to a porch that spanned the front of the house. The house was not well kept up. The light blue paint covering the clapboard siding was badly chipped in places, and the lawn was unkempt.

Bill walked up and had just set foot on the porch when an explosion from inside the house caused the window in the door to rattle.

"Get down!" he yelled, running back down the stairs and diving behind one of the cruisers. Jane followed, and ducked down behind the other car with the two deputies.

"Shots fired. 1224 Walnut Street. Officers on the scene." The rookie deputy's hands were shaking as badly as his voice as he called for help on the radio. The four crouched behind the cruisers for about two minutes. No other sound came from the house.

"Sounded like a big gun," Bill said.

"He's a cop. They carry Sigs."

"Yeah. He was military too. It could be something bigger."

Another minute passed. Some people across the street had stepped out on the porch to see what the commotion was all about. Jane held up her badge. "Police! Get back in the house."

She turned to see a cruiser screech to a halt at the north end of the intersection and position itself across the street to prevent traffic from coming through. A quick turn to the right told her that the same precaution had been taken at the other end of the block. There were two cars there—a sheriff's vehicle and a city car. Sirens could be heard coming from blocks away.

"We need to wait for the quick response team," she said to Templeton.

"Yeah. And by the time the bus gets here with all those boys in their fatigues, that girl could be dead."

"If she isn't already. Wait, Templeton!"

He looked at her. "Last I heard I was the detective in charge. You are just consulting. Or has that changed?"

"Wait, Bill. Follow procedure."

"Fuck procedure!" he said. He jumped up and darted around the cruiser and up the stairs.

"Oh, Christ!" Jane said. She turned to the two deputies, who were still crouched behind the car. She hoped the rookie wouldn't wet his pants. "Watch our backs," she said to the rookie. You," she said to the other deputy, a tow-headed three-year veteran named Andy Greider. "Go around back."

Andy looked over the cruiser, and then darted off to the right and between the two houses.

Then Jane ran around and positioned herself behind the trunk of a large pin oak tree to the right of the porch, her gun raised and ready to cover Bill, who, by now, was standing to the side of the front door.

He nodded to her. She moved quickly up to the porch and positioned herself on the opposite side of the door. She nodded, and Bill cautiously pulled open the aluminum screen door. The front door had glass in a fan-shaped aperture near the top and appeared to be of solid wood. He tried the door. Locked. It would probably cave in easily, but then he had tried to crash through old, seemingly flimsy doors before that had stood quite firm.

He couldn't waste time thinking about it. He came round and kicked hard on the door.

It gave a little but didn't break open.

"Shit!" He kicked it again.

This time, the wood on the doorjamb splintered and the door swung back. He rushed in and crouched, scanning the room with his Glock in both hands.

Jane stepped quickly in behind him, and scanned the other direction. The room was empty. The air was stale, and smelled of cordite.

"Clear!"

He moved quickly across the room and stopped at the side of the door leading to the kitchen. Jane moved to the other side. He swung around and went through the door. And stopped in his tracks.

Jane walked up next to him. Then she saw it too. The rear wall and part of the ceiling of the kitchen was splattered with blood and bits of brain matter. On the floor, between the kitchen table and the stove, Roy Walker lay on his back, his eyes wide-open. His service weapon was in his hand.

Bill kicked the gun from his hand and across the room. Then he reached down and felt for a pulse. Finding none, he holstered his weapon.

"Keep looking," he said.

By now, Andy had come in through the back door. He walked to the front door and signaled the rookie to come in.

Bill checked the back bedroom, and another room next to it that must have been a den. There was a small desk with papers strewn about and a computer next to the window.

Jane checked the bathroom and then went upstairs. She quickly came back.

"Clear," she said.

Andy walked over to a door opposite the kitchen table. It had a chain on it and a deadbolt lock. Bill walked over, his gun drawn again, and Andy opened the door. It led to the basement. Bill slowly descended the stairs, his gun moving from right to left, with Jane about four steps behind him. When he reached the seventh stair step, he stopped.

"Oh, no," he said. He put his gun away and walked over to where Theresa Madison lay on her back. Blood had pooled under her head, and her arm appeared to have been broken. Badly broken. He saw bone protruding through the skin and blood. Lots of blood. He reached down and felt for a pulse.

"She's alive!" he said. "Get the EMTs here fast."

"They're already out front," Andy said.

"Don't just stand there! Get them!"

Jane looked around the darkened room and saw a birthday cake with candles that had burned all the way down. A bloody hammer lay on the floor near the stairs. Some papers were scattered about and there was something rectangular over by the wall. She walked over and reached down to examine it. It was a cassette recorder. It was still running.

Margaret hung up the phone. She had just pulled into the parking lot near the rectory when Bill called.

"What happened?" Tom asked.

She looked at him. "Roy Walker is dead."

Tom blessed himself. "And the girl?"

"They took her to the hospital. She was badly injured. Apparently, she was struck one or more times with a hammer. They don't know."

"Mother of mercy."

Margaret closed her eyes to staunch the tears. Surely one of those children would be allowed to live. Surely God in his mercy would draw the line somewhere to end this insanity.

"I'm going to chapel," she said. "I'll just leave the car here."

"You mind if I come?"

She shook her head.

As she and Tom walked across the campus, she hooked her arm through his. His arm was trembling. She could only pray that all of this would end well for Theresa Madison.

There was at least one thing to be thankful for—the nightmare was finally over.

Chapter 69 - Epilogue

Bill Templeton turned into the parking lot at St. Alphonse Church and parked near the entrance around three thirty in the afternoon.

He hadn't heard from Margaret since the day after they found Walker and the girl.

"I will be gone for a couple of weeks, Bill," she had said. "I am going to Saint Louis for a retreat."

"Okay."

"I will talk with you when I get back."

He had wanted to say more, but he hadn't. Like, "Am I ever going to see you again?"

Why hadn't he said it? He asked himself that question every hour of every day since. He knew that it was because he didn't want to hear the answer.

It had been two weeks to the day. This morning, she had left a message on his phone to meet her here.

It had rained all day, and a fine drizzle was now coming down. The temperature had dropped ten degrees since the previous day so he hadn't shed his blazer. Springtime in Illinois was always a varied experience.

He looked around the empty parking lot and then walked up to the doors of the church.

In the days after they took Theresa Madison out of the house on Walnut Street, all of the pieces that could be put together had been. Bill had been buried with paperwork. The death of Roy Walker may have closed not two, but three investigations—one more than thirty years cold. The press was having a field day, and the sheriff's office was looking pretty good. Jim Hargrove was a shoo-in for another run at the job now, much to his wife's chagrin, and had been parading around, as Tracy Polanski put it, like the "cock of the walk." Bill wanted to ask her what that meant, but was somehow afraid to.

Roy Walker was, indeed, John Easter. He had been sent to live with his aunt and uncle in Wisconsin by his father to keep him out of harm's way. After his father killed himself, they adopted him and he took the name Walker. "Roy" was a nickname that he had picked up in high school, and he adopted it as his official name later on.

He had graduated with honors from high school and entered the Oblates of Mary Immaculate. He had spent three years there, and then left suddenly. Investigators had reason to believe that he had been caught engaging in homosexual activity with another seminarian, but that was only speculation. Evidence in his home corroborated his sexual preference, and it was determined that he had, in fact, engaged in a relationship with Pickering at some point.

Found among his belongings, along with the pornography, was a small book entitled *The Hound of Heaven*.

There was still insufficient evidence to place Walker at the scene of Pickering's death, and the cause of death was officially deemed a suicide. Bill was fairly certain, however, that Walker had killed him, perhaps to throw them off track, perhaps because Pickering knew too much. Walker was, after all, a cop and knew how to cover his tracks. The lack of fingerprints—any fingerprints—was telling. The pathologist, however, could only judge on the evidence he had—not the evidence he didn't have.

Walker enlisted after leaving seminary and served in Desert Storm. This had been another uncanny similarity with Brightman. They never met in Iraq, however. Walker worked in telecommunications behind the lines and never saw action. He was discharged honorably.

Sometime after leaving the service, Walker ended up back in Springfield. He took a class at Lincoln Land Community College and worked at a variety of jobs before making application with the Springfield PD. He had been a beat cop for several years before he applied for the position of Resource Officer at City High School. His career as a cop had been unremarkable, but he was well thought of by his superiors. He had few friends, however, and was thought to be a bit odd by his fellow officers. Still, he was considered competent and reliable.

It made sense, in retrospect, that Walker could have been so well informed about the investigation—the sheriff's office thought nothing about sharing details with him; Bill had done so himself. It was also clear how he could have tracked down the grandchildren of Bonnie's killers. He was skilled with a computer, and they had found a great deal of information on a Dell Inspiron that was in his bedroom.

The tape recording and the notes that had been found in the basement told a horrifying story of a child's life torn apart by the worst kind of betrayal. If it was to be believed, his own father was complicit in his sister's death. He had played up to influential people, spent money to entertain them, and even encouraged his daughter to entertain them. Bill would like to think that Bonnie's father hadn't had the type of entertainment in mind that they had engaged in, but the results were the same.

It appeared that the father had covered up the murder. He had filed a missing person's report the next day, but the new information clearly placed him at the scene. His part in his own child's death had probably led to despair and to his suicide.

It also appeared that Bonnie Easter might not have been dead when she was taken out of that cabin. Bill reviewed the remnants of the original autopsy report and noted that death was due to strangulation. Did she revive in the trunk of Sally Rigali's car? Then Rigali must have strangled her. Someone did, and if the letter left by Walker was to be believed Rigali was the one who had carried her out of the cabin.

Of course, the problem was that Roy Walker, or John Easter, was not in his right mind. The autopsy revealed a primary brain tumor of the frontal lobe that had grown rapidly. They obtained his medical records and found that he had been diagnosed as terminal some months before the first murder, but had refused treatment. The brain is still largely a dark continent, but the pathologist noted that damage to the frontal lobe affects the moral center of the brain and thus behavior, sometimes even making normally decent persons prone to violence.

Given the size of the tumor, the pathologist marveled that the man was functioning at any level. Had he not killed himself, Roy Walker would surely have died within weeks. Perhaps sooner. And very painfully.

Bill was bothered by the fact that, were it not for the brain tumor, Roy Walker might have continued to live a quiet life and no one would have died. All in all, he had been a decent man. Who do you blame for something like this? He concluded that answers to those kinds of questions were best left to theologians.

The evidence on the taped message and the handwritten pages implicated Abe Tomiczek in the cover up. Bill met with the State's Attorney, but the prosecutor had reservations about going to court with it. Bill tried to convince him to haul Tomiczek in for questioning, if for no other reason than to shake the old bastard up. Nothing had been decided yet, but Bill wasn't holding out much hope. He could only wish that the old asshole died a slow, agonizing death and that he would burn in the hottest part of hell.

There would be no justice for Alison Corcoran and Billy Matheson—or for Bonnie Easter. At least not in this life. But the truth had come out, if John Easter was to be believed. Now those children could sleep dreamlessly in whatever place they had gone. He hoped that those left behind would fare as well. Their pain would not end until the last day of their lives.

Theresa Madison's injuries were not as bad as had been feared, but they were bad enough and she would be recovering for quite some time. She had raised her arms at the last minute and her right forearm had taken the brunt of a savage blow. She had suffered a severe break which required several hours of surgery. She would have metal in her arm for the remainder of her life. There had been nerve damage that would take months to recover from. She might never completely recover feeling in her hand.

Theresa's upraised arms had blunted the blow from the hammer, and the side rather than the business end of the tool had struck her face. It broke her nose and her head had bounced back and struck the concrete floor. Most of the blood had been from the blow to her face. She also had a subdural hematoma, from which she was expected to recover with no lasting neurological damage.

Theresa Madison had Bill's respect. She had refused to allow herself to be a victim. Had she not fought back as hard as she did, injuring Walker seriously in the process, she might be dead. She had foiled his twisted design. And, for that, she was still alive.

She could not remember much for several days. When it all came back, she had melted into tears and could not talk for some time. When she finally did, she was very helpful in filling in the details. She was expected to recover, and would in all likelihood fulfill her dream to go to medical school.

At least one life had not been totally shattered by the madness that had transpired thirty-three years earlier at that cabin in Riverton.

Margaret met with Sister Agnes on the day following the discovery of Theresa Madison. The meeting went pretty much as Margaret had expected.

Sister Agnes listened quietly for over forty-five minutes without speaking. Margaret held nothing back.

When it was over, the older woman said nothing for a couple of minutes. She merely looked down at her hands. Finally, she looked up.

"What is it you want?"

Margaret closed her eyes for a few moments.

"I am not ready to profess. I have many things to work out in my heart. But neither am I ready to walk away—assuming, of course, you are not of the opinion that I should."

"I am not."

"I am requesting a three-year extension of my temporary vows."

"I will agree. You will return to St. Louis to complete your degree. Afterwards, I will arrange for a transfer to one of the other convents. It would be best."

Margaret nodded. It would be tempting fate to stay in Springfield where it would be so easy to find a reason to fall into Bill's arms.

"Certainly," said Margaret.

"Anything else?"

There was a cold, administrative tone to Agnes's words that seemed to communicate judgment. Margaret was beginning to wonder if this had been a good idea.

"No," said Margaret. It would, after all, be between her and God. Agnes was just a functionary. If Agnes wanted to adopt that position, Margaret could easily accept it.

Then, Agnes just kept sitting. Margaret was expecting her to make some attempt to bring the meeting to a conclusion. But she didn't move or say anything for several minutes. Finally, she looked up at Margaret again.

Margaret felt she had to break the silence.

"I am sorry I disappointed you, Sister."

Agnes recognized the statement for what it was. A lifeline rolled out in hopes of pulling in some comforting statements. Agnes wasn't there to comfort. She was there to guide the lives of the women under her charge, and sometimes that meant being very matter of fact.

Agnes had always thought that obedience, not chastity, would have presented the greatest challenge to Margaret's vocation. Her personal dislike for Margaret led her to feel somehow affirmed by this turn of events, but her struggles to emulate the Savior led her to put her feelings in check. She fought to put such thoughts aside, but her weakness was that she couldn't. Not entirely.

In spite of her feelings, however, she knew that Margaret was—and would be if she chose to remain—one of the finest sisters she had ever seen come through her doors. But the girl wasn't quite ready. Perhaps she never would be. But if she was willing to give it a go, Agnes certainly was willing to extend the period of temporary vows.

"I will arrange for you to take retreat with the sisters in Webster Groves. You may leave tomorrow, if you can arrange your schedule."

Margaret nodded.

"I know, too, how close you are to Theodora. Toward the end, I will arrange for you to return to be with her."

Thank God for small things. Margaret felt tears filling her eyes. "Thank you, Sister."

"The breach of your vow of chastity is serious, and you will have to come to grips with what it means for your life. It would be a serious breach of morality even if you were in the secular world—although, I fear, there it has become more of a badge of honor. The world has, somehow, been turned upside down these days.

"You should know, however, that it is not unheard of. There are a few sisters in the order who have done likewise, and who have still committed their lives to Christ and moved on. Others could not.

"It is what the breach represents that is most troubling. You are not a person given to licentiousness. Your breach sprang from love, and it is this love that is the greatest impediment to your vocation at the moment. Will you be like Heloise and, instead of lamenting for what you have done, be forever sighing for what you have lost?"

Her allusion was to the twelfth-century lover of the philosopher Peter Abelard, whose letters to him survived them both and made their love a legend.

"Are you certain you are ready to forsake the young man?"

Agnes was dead on, and Margaret knew it. Had this been about sex, it would have been a mere indiscretion, albeit a serious violation of her sacred vows. *But this was about love.*

"I know that I will always care very much for him. But I feel quite certain that this is where I belong, and forsaking him is the price I must pay."

"Have you told him that?"

"Not in so many words."

"Pray about it. God loves you, Margaret. Live with that knowledge. Self-flagellation is not in order here, but clear thinking is. Either embrace him, or find the strength to move on in the direction you chose five years ago. There is simply no middle ground here."

When Margaret thought about her dad, she remembered the things he said, the things he did for her, the fun times they had and the bad. Try as she might, however, she had a hard time seeing him. The face she knew so well and kissed thousands of times was somehow no longer distinct in her memory. Her dad, now that he was gone, was no longer a person but a powerful concept. She understood him, but could not see him anymore. He existed still, in her heart and mind, but he was absent from her senses. Yet, he was the source of her existence and was, in a very real way, with her yet today.

This was how she felt about God. She could not see Him. He was merely a concept. Yet, he was a concept that, as much as her father, she understood to be the source of her being. At times, when she thought she was praying to emptiness, she remembered her father's absence and how he was yet a real presence in spite of it. God was like that. There, but not there. Absent yet ever present in the stillness of her heart. She merely had to listen.

God was the greatest paradox of all.

She prayed now for all who had suffered. Johnny Easter lay in Oak Ridge next to his sister and his father. The family torn apart by such horrific evil had been reunited in death, and their rest would only be disturbed now and then by the faint footfall of the fox.

She prayed for Theodora, whose faith and strength would be tested in the months to come. She was saddened that she would not be here for her. Her sin had resulted in separation, first from God, and soon from her best friend in the world.

Theodora had set her in the right direction for her thesis. She now realized that she had only partially understood Augustine. He had really been saying something quite optimistic about life and the world in which we live. Evil is the unavoidable concomitant to a world where humans are given the choice to value themselves above God, yet it affords the chief evidence to the goodness in life. Were it not for that goodness, we would never be able to sense its lack.

She prayed as well for her young friend, Erin. Margaret had missed the prom, but Erin telephoned her when she returned from retreat and told her all about it. Erin knew nothing of how the evening had been arranged, but Margaret smiled when Erin reported that she actually found herself enjoying Cal's company—once Cal started talking to her instead of looking around to see how many of his friends were watching. How it happened didn't matter. Here the end justified the means as far as Margaret was concerned. Erin had gone to the prom, she had looked lovely, and she was happy. She was happily waiting for next fall when she would start at the University of Illinois. Her life was filled with hope, and Margaret thanked God for that.

Another small thing to be grateful for.

Now she was praying for Bill Templeton.

She heard the rear doors of the church swing open. She turned and saw Bill walking slowly down the main aisle. She rose, blessed herself, walked to the center and genuflected, and then turned and walked toward him.

As she grew nearer, it struck him once again how beautiful she was. She wore no makeup, and the beauty was not only in her face but also in her bearing and her eyes.

And in her soul.

She stopped about three yards from him and the two simply stood in the silence.

And he knew.

Their eyes met and held their connection for a minute. Neither spoke. It was that same connection that had bridged their hearts days before. It was still there.

"Why here?"

"I wanted it to be somewhere where I could trust myself with you."

"We knew each other for one week," he said. "One week, out of—what?—eighteen hundred or so weeks I have been alive. And yet, somehow that week overshadowed all the others in my life. I don't understand how that can happen."

She smiled. "And, of course, for the first half of that week you were an asshole."

Bill laughed.

"You know, driving out here I was listening to Country 104. When I pulled in, you know what was playing?"

She gently shook her head.

"Heaven's Just a Sin Away."

She laughed out loud. He loved that laugh. He loved those intelligent brown eyes that seemed to cross slightly when she looked directly at you, and her mouth that, when she smiled, seemed to light up her face. That mouth that he had kissed and could still taste. He was going to miss everything about this woman.

"You're sure about this?"

She nodded.

He ran his hand over his head and rubbed the back of his neck, something Margaret had noticed he did when he was having a hard time coming up with something to say. He took a deep breath.

"Well …"

She walked up, took his face in her hands, and kissed him gently on the lips and held her lips there for several seconds. Then she stepped back and locked eyes with him again.

"I will never forget you, Bill."

His eyes were filling up, but he didn't care. He reached up and wiped away a tear that had started to roll down his cheek.

"Yeah. Ditto."

Neither moved for several seconds. She was looking at him intently with those probing brown eyes. He read her thoughts.

"I'm fine," he said, answering her unspoken question. "Funny thing is, I feel better than I have in years."

She nodded, biting her lip.

"I must go," she said. She pulled the cell phone from her pocket, took his left hand in hers and placed it there. "County property."

He looked down at the phone. Seeing it almost caused him to break. His stomach wrenched, but he withstood the assault for the moment.

"I guess I will have to take you off speed dial," he said. He took a long breath. "Pray for me, will you?"

She placed her hand on his arm and gently rubbed it. "Always."

He nodded. "You go ahead. I may just, you know, hang around a minute or so."

"In Church?" she said. "Maybe there really are such things as miracles."

He smiled. "May be," he said. "May be."

She walked past him down the center aisle. He turned and watched as she stopped to dip her fingers in the holy water and bless herself.

Then Sister Margaret turned around to give him one last look before walking through the doors and out of his life.

LaVergne, TN USA
07 October 2009

160178LV00008B/104/P